Awaken Online
Book 1: Catharsis

Travis Bagwell

Copyright © 2016 by Travis Bagwell

———

To my wife, for putting up with my bullshit.

———

Table of Contents

Prologue

October 7, 2076: Six days after the release of Awaken Online.

Chris ran desperately through the dead forest. Thick black clouds hovered in the sky, obscuring the sun and casting the forest in an almost impenetrable darkness. He could just barely make out the gnarled, leafless branches of the trees around him.

His heart raced. He began to panic as he considered what was chasing him. The images of the dead and dying were burned into his mind. The fear pushed him to run faster. His breath came in heavy, ragged gasps and his legs pumped frantically. His stamina was depleting swiftly as he struggled against the weight of the heavy mail he wore.

Chris heard the screams behind him, but he didn't turn to look. He knew that they were the men in his contingent. Their group had gotten separated from the main army. However, a part of him was thankful that whoever had let out that scream had bought him a few precious seconds.

"Oh god," he panted. "Please don't let them catch me."

Low hanging branches snagged on his clothing and armor. His foot collided with a tree limb that lay on the ground and Chris toppled forward, landing with a heavy thud. He could feel a dull ache in his ankle. The fall and minor pain caused his panic to escalate.

Chris turned quickly and looked behind him, his eyes full of fear.

Lightning arced between the boiling clouds and then a bolt struck a nearby tree with a deafening crash. The lightning pushed back at the darkness that hung in the air like a thick blanket, illuminating the massacre in the distance. Bodies littered the ground - the remains of Chris's teammates and the soldiers they had been traveling with.

In the flash of light, Chris caught sight of a figure moving through the trees. This person walked with a casual, purposeful tread that stood out in stark contrast to the chaotic movements of the enemy soldiers. The man's body was shrouded in a billowing black cloak that obscured his face and clothing. He motioned toward Chris' position and the dark forms around him rushed forward.

Chris felt a strange mixture of awe and fear as he watched the dark figure.

"Is-is that Jason?" he asked quietly into the darkness.

A throaty roar was his only response. Chris saw the swiftly approaching group of soldiers and the bottom dropped out of his stomach. He tried madly to regain his footing but struggled to rise, his heavy mail once again an impediment. He knew he only had a few seconds.

As he made it to his feet, he felt a dull pain in his abdomen. He looked down and saw a blade jutting from his stomach. The blade withdrew swiftly, and blood pooled around the wound. Chris turned, pulling his sword from its scabbard with a scrape of metal. His free hand clutched instinctively at his abdomen. A part of him already knew that it was too late.

His opponent stood behind him. The creature's left arm dangled at an unnatural angle, and his armor was streaked with blood. Chris could see a ragged gash in the once-living man's throat.

Chris steeled himself as he glared into the

creature's milky white eyes, "Come and get me you undead asshole."

The zombie grinned mockingly and shook his head. A dull pain bloomed in Chris' back.

I was flanked, he thought in shock as he fell to his knees.

Blood drained from the wounds in his stomach and back. It was only a matter of time before he died. He looked up and saw the dark figure walking slowly towards him. A black cat wound around the man's feet like a shadow. Chris still couldn't make out his face beneath the heavy, hooded cloak.

"I know who you are," Chris muttered angrily as the man approached. "The others will stop you."

Jason chuckled darkly, his lips curling into a grin. "I doubt it."

Without ceremony, the zombie behind Chris drew a blade across his neck. The pain lasted only a moment before the world went dark.

Then a prompt appeared in Chris' vision:

System Message
You have died.
Thanks for playing Awaken Online!

Chapter 1 - Late

November 14, 2074: 687 days until the release of
Awaken Online.

"Hello? Is this thing on?"

The camera tilted erratically and then centered on a young woman in a lab coat. Her hair was brown and cut just above the shoulder. She wore modest eyeglasses and little makeup. She was pretty, in a mousy sort of way. In the background behind the woman lay a mass of machinery and cabling.

"My name is Claire Thompson. This is the first day of the private trials of Awaken Online." The woman seemed a bit nervous to be on camera and kept adjusting her glasses.

"To be clear, these trials are not part of the regular Consumer Product Safety Commission (CPSC) evaluation process. This trial is being conducted at the request of the board of directors of Cerillion Entertainment. As the board is no doubt aware, the primary goal of this project was to create a virtual reality simulation that draws players in and makes them want to keep playing.

"The AI controller is still in its infancy, and we expect it to grow and adapt as the trial progresses. Consequently, the AI controller's primary directive is to encourage players to spend more time playing.

"Our hope is that we can develop a game that is as engaging as possible and that finds a healthy balance between improved realism and the practical game features found in many MMOs."

Claire hesitated and fidgeted slightly as she considered what to say next.

"The purpose of this private trial is to test new features of the game software, particularly the game's AI controller, ahead of the CPSC submission. We plan to create a benchmark with this trial that we can use to evaluate and respond to the CPSC's questions."

Claire motioned to the machinery behind her. "This is the hardware for the game's AI controller. Alfred..." Claire paused and blushed slightly. "I'm sorry. I've worked with the AI controller for so long that I have started calling him Alfred."

"Anyway. Alfred is responsible for controlling all of the game's processes from the ground up. For example, he manages the quests, character creation, lore, and NPC interactions."

"We have also implemented safety protocols to ensure that the game does not harm the users. For example, we have created secondary directives that place limitations on Alfred's ability to interface with the users' cerebral cortex and the parts of the brain that control memory. Although, keep in mind that the software to access these areas hasn't been written, and we aren't certain the headsets are even capable of accessing to the users' minds to that degree."

The camera panned to the side as it followed Claire. A series of screens showing small, bare rooms stood behind Claire. Each room held a reclining chair and a coffee table. A solid, black helmet sat on each table and was attached to a six-inch black obelisk.

Claire motioned at the screens, "This private trial will include one hundred test subjects, ages 18-35. Both males and females are equally represented." People began to enter the rooms as Claire spoke and they took a seat. Some immediately pulled the helmets over their heads without hesitation.

Claire looked back at the screens with an excited grin on her face, "Our test participants have now arrived. It will be fun to see how they react to their first time..."

*　　　*　　　*

October 1, 2076: Release day for Awaken Online.

Jason was hurrying down the tree-lined sidewalk on his way to school. He was late. He was really late.

Jason passed by palatial houses at a brisk jog. He didn't see anyone on the street. This wasn't the sort of neighborhood where people went on long walks. It wasn't a bad neighborhood, quite the opposite in fact. The people that lived in these oversized houses weren't accustomed to walking on the dusty sidewalks with the rest of the masses.

I can't believe I'm going to be late again, he thought morosely.

It wasn't his fault. His parents left that morning on an extended business trip. Of course, they hadn't mentioned the trip the night before.

The kicker was that his parents had deactivated the apartment's network this morning on their way out the door. He could just imagine the two of them, juggling coffee and luggage as they bickered about whether they were going to make their flight on time. Apparently, neither of them had remembered he was still in bed when they effectively shut off all of the electronics in the apartment. Including his alarm.

His parents were both attorneys. They were actually environmental litigators. This meant they suffered the dual curse of always being super busy and never getting paid well. Apparently, whales and trees were a bit strapped for cash. This also meant that they were constantly away from home trying cases in other states and were a bit absent-minded when it came to everything else.

For as long as Jason could remember, whatever environmental war they were waging at the moment had always taken precedence over everything else.

He sometimes wondered how, with their many extended trips, they had managed to raise him until he was old enough to survive on his own. The only advantage of their frequent trips was that he was free to do pretty much anything he wanted while they were gone.

Jason's thoughts were interrupted by the sound of a blaring car horn. In his hurry, he had almost stepped off the sidewalk in front of the car.

"Watch it asshole," yelled a blond-haired teenager driving a little red sports car.

Before he could reply or apologize, the driver sped off down the road. Jason could have sworn that the driver looked familiar, but he didn't have a chance to get a good look at him. The only thing he could make out from this angle was the man's right hand and his rather long middle finger.

Perfect. This day is really starting off on a high note.

As his eyes followed the car racing away, his gaze swept across the profile of his school a few blocks ahead of him. His high school was a two-story red brick building. A stone sign sat at the foot of the stairs to the main doorway. Jason couldn't make out the words from this distance. However, he knew that it read "Richmond High, Founded in 1952."

The lawn at the front of the school was well manicured and dotted with large oaks. This was unusual nowadays. It was now 2076, and urban land was unbelievably expensive. The trees and unused space around Richmond were a sign of both how out-of-touch the school was with modern day and just how much money it could afford to waste.

Under other circumstances, Jason might have stopped to admire the scenery as he drew closer to the school, but he was already in trouble. He had been tardy several times this semester due to situations like the one this morning. He couldn't afford any more absences.

"At least we live within walking distance of the school," Jason muttered as he continued his jog down the sidewalk.

If he was being honest, he actually lived in a nice neighborhood, and his parents made decent money by middle-class standards. He even had the privilege of attending a prestigious private school. This was due in large part to his exceptional test scores and a not-so-small scholarship.

He *should* be happy.

The problem was that he didn't have enough money to be "worthy" of attending Richmond. The other students knew it and made certain he remembered it. Most of them came from old money and would likely never need to work a day in their lives. As a result, it seemed that everyone he encountered at Richmond, including both the students and the faculty, went out of their way to make his life miserable.

Jason walked across the street and onto the grounds. The school also boasted an above-ground parking lot adjacent to the main building. This was another complete waste of space that flaunted the school's budget. Jason could see the little red sports car that had raced past him now sitting unoccupied in one of the "princess spots" close to the building.

There was no one outside of the school as Jason approached the front door. Morning classes had already begun. Jason entered the school and took a deep breath as he approached the administrative office near the front of the building.

I should just explain the situation and get it over with.

He opened the door to the office and stepped through.

Jason was immediately greeted by the scathing gaze of a thin woman standing next to the front desk. She wore horn-rimmed glasses and was speaking with a blond-haired student. The woman was dressed in a vomit green cardigan and plaid skirt. A small gold cross hung on her chest. Her lips seemed perpetually pinched in displeasure. As she glanced in Jason's direction, her eyes flashed with thinly veiled disgust.

Oh shit.

The student speaking to Ms. Abrams was apparently the proud owner of a red sports car. Now that he had a chance to get a good look at him, Jason recognized the blond-haired driver as Alex Lane. Alex was stunningly good looking, with an athletic physique, and striking blue eyes. He was also blessed with ample intelligence and had a certain charisma that drew in others like flies to honey. Alex's father was on the board of directors for several Fortune 500 companies. As a result, his family had more money than they knew what to do with.

Alex was also quite possibly the biggest asshole Jason had ever met.

"My apologies Ms. Abrams, my father needed to speak with me this morning. That's why I was running late. I assure you it won't happen again." Alex's face was the picture of remorse.

Ms. Abrams' pinched expression loosened, and, for a moment, Jason thought she might actually smile. "It's not a problem Alex, your father is a busy man. Go ahead and make your way to class."

Alex thanked Ms. Abrams and made his way out the door. As he passed Jason, Alex's angelic expression warped into a smirk. He shouldered past, causing Jason to drop his bag. Alex immediately turned with an angelic expression plastered on his face.

"Oh I'm so sorry," he said contritely, clearly for Ms. Abrams' benefit. Alex left the office and headed for class.

What an asshole. If only other people could see past the act he puts on.

Jason turned back to Ms. Abrams. Her mouth was again pinched into a thin line, and any trace of a smile was now gone. She looked Jason up and down and seemed to be mentally cataloging the defects with his school uniform, including his wrinkled shirt and his disheveled hair.

Jason was not a terrible looking guy, but he wasn't handsome either. He had longish brown hair that sometimes fell in his eyes because he didn't get it cut often. It was also clear from anyone who saw him that he didn't give much attention to his clothing or working out. His uniform hung loosely on his skinny frame. The only thing truly noteworthy about his appearance were his eyes. They were a vivid, crystalline gray and at times almost seemed to darken to black in the right light.

As he stood under Ms. Abrams' scrutiny, dread curled in his stomach like a nest of snakes. Running into her was the worst thing that could have happened to him this morning.

Ms. Abrams was an alumni of Richmond, having attended the school long before Jason was born. Like most students of the school, she had a respectable pedigree (which meant her family was filthy rich). She was also adamant about maintaining the reputation and standing of Richmond (which meant she hated anyone who wasn't wealthy). Ms. Abrams was vehemently opposed to the "welfare" students, such as himself, who attended the school on scholarship. She had gone out of her way over the last few years to try to have his scholarship revoked or to have him expelled.

Her latest tactic was apparently to have him arrested for truancy.

"Mr. Rhodes. You're over an hour late for class. I suppose you have another inane excuse for your tardiness?" Her tone made it clear that the question was rhetorical.

"I'm certain that you're also aware that this is your tenth tardy for the fall semester?" she continued in a tight tone.

Jason felt his pulse speed up, and his mouth go dry as it normally did in stressful situations. It was also at this moment that he realized he didn't have a note from his parents to explain his tardiness.

Why in the hell didn't they tell me they were leaving?

"I-I am sorry Ms. Abrams. My parents left this morning on a trip, and they needed to speak with me before they left," he stuttered slightly, unable to make eye contact with Ms. Abrams.

He didn't expect this fib to work with Ms. Abrams, but he felt certain she would flatly accuse him of lying if he explained that his parents had forgotten he was home when they left this morning.

"And I suppose you have a note to that effect?" Ms. Abrams inquired.

"Um, no actually. I forgot to get them to sign something in their rush to get to the airport. I can probably get them on the phone..."

Ms. Abrams interrupted him, "That will not be necessary. You have been attending this school for three years and in that time I have heard enough of your excuses to last me a lifetime. If you keep this up,

I doubt you will make it to graduation."

Did she just sound a little excited at the prospect of me not graduating?

"Congratulations, you have detention again this afternoon. Be sure that you're not late for that as well."

"B-but..."

"That is enough Mr. Rhodes. Get to class." With that, Ms. Abrams turned and walked towards her office on the other side of the reception area.

Jason stood there for a moment in stunned silence. His face flushed slightly in anger, and he clenched his hands.

I hate that woman. Why does she always have it out for me?

He glanced over and saw the secretary, a plump, middle-aged woman, looking at him scornfully. With a sigh, he turned and walked out of the office. Jason started towards his locker to collect his books before making his way to class.

What really sucks is that she just lets Alex do whatever he wants! I bet if my parents were loaded she would let me off the hook too.

As he walked down the hallway, a door opened ahead of him, and a girl walked out. The girl was blond, petite, and seemed to almost glow with energy and confidence. Riley wasn't the prettiest girl at school and certainly wasn't teen royalty on campus, but she was probably the kindest person he had ever met. There was just some effervescent quality about her that was difficult to measure or quantify.

"Hello Jason," she said as she saw him approaching.

Seeing Riley, he could feel his anger start to cool. Stammering slightly, he replied, "H-hi Riley."

Riley was well known at Richmond. She was

also a senior and a member of the lacrosse team. In stark contrast to the other students at Richmond, Riley had always been nice to Jason. It was amazing to him that she somehow managed to turn into a decent person despite her parents' wealth. Over the years, he had bumped into her on occasion, and she had always taken the time to inquire about his life and schoolwork.

"How's your day going? Wait..." She gave him a puzzled look, thumbed the device on her wrist, and then looked up at him in surprise. "Wow. It's almost 10:30. Are you just now getting to school?"

He sighed, "My parents left town this morning without warning, and I had to run here. They deactivated our apartment's network on the way out the door."

Riley chuckled slightly and covered her mouth, "I'm sorry. I don't mean to laugh, but I can just imagine you waking up in the dark and stumbling around trying to reactivate the system."

"Well it's not as fun as it sounds, let me tell you," he said in a dry tone. "On top of that, Ms. Abrams ended up giving me detention again."

They started walking together down the hallway. Jason reflected on why he was speaking so openly with Riley. Normally, he would be speechless, not just dimwitted. It often seemed like the only person he could talk to freely at Richmond was his friend Frank.

Riley interrupted his wandering thoughts. "Ms. Abrams can be such a bitch," she said bitterly. Jason wondered what Ms. Abrams had done to her. Riley was usually much more upbeat.

"You don't have to tell me," Jason replied.

"Where are you headed now?" Riley asked, trying to break his morose mood.

"I have Calculus and then on to English."

"Calculus, huh? You must be a smart one!" she said with a teasing note in her voice and a grin. Her eyes sparkled with mischief.

"I don't know about that. I make decent grades, and Mr. Fielding is a good teacher."

Her face seemed to light up. "Speaking of Mr. Fielding, I need to run a note over to him. Since it looks like we're headed in the same direction, do you want to walk together?"

"Sure!" he exclaimed a bit too loudly.

God, I'm such an idiot.

Riley gave him another bemused grin, and they made their way to his locker. He fumbled a time or two entering his combination and then managed to retrieve his books. A few minutes and some small talk later, they found themselves at the door to his calculus classroom.

He opened the door and stepped in, followed closely by Riley. Mr. Fielding hesitated in the middle of giving an explanation to the class and all of the students turned and stared. Jason wilted in front of their collective scrutiny, and his eyes immediately dropped to the floor.

In a low voice, he said, "Um... I'm sorry I'm late Mr. Fielding. My parents left on a last minute trip this morning."

Riley put her arm around Jason's shoulders and said with a smile, "Jason has had a rough morning. You should take it easy on him Mr. Fielding." Jason's shoulders felt uncomfortable under Riley's touch, and he could feel his face grow hot.

Mr. Fielding cleared his throat. "It's no problem Jason, please take your seat."

Directing his attention to Riley, Mr. Fielding continued, "And why are you here, Riley?"

"Oh, I brought you a note from Mrs. Ergenbright. Here it is!" She handed the note to Mr. Fielding and headed towards the door.

As an afterthought, she turned to Jason who was making his way to his seat. "Take care, Jason!" She then stepped out of the door, casting one last smile in his direction.

Jason felt himself blush again, "B-bye Riley."

As Jason weaved his way between the desks to his seat, he felt a foot connect with his shin, and he was sent toppling forward. He face-planted, and his head bounced hard off someone's textbook that had been sitting on the floor. He lay there for a moment, groaning slightly.

"You should watch your step *Welfare*." A snide voice hissed near his ear. Jason could hear muffled chuckles from the other students.

He turned his head and saw that Alex was looking down at him. A cruel smirk twisted Alex's features as he watched Jason groan.

Jason knew that Alex wasn't a nice person, in spite of the act he put on for others. He didn't normally single out people for his abuse. However, since Jason started at Richmond, Alex had gone out of his way to torment him. He was also responsible for starting the nickname that people now used instead of his real name – "Welfare."

"Ugh," Jason huffed as he lifted himself up and made his way to his seat without saying anything to Alex.

Mr. Fielding glanced momentarily at Jason. He frowned for a moment and opened his mouth to say something. His eyes jumped to Alex and his mouth closed. He then turned and resumed jabbering about some figure he had drawn on the whiteboard.

Jason glared at Mr. Fielding's back. It was obvious

he tripped me on purpose!

It was typical for the teachers at Richmond to overlook the actions of the wealthier students. Mr. Fielding's reaction wasn't a surprise, but it wasn't any less frustrating. Especially since he could tell that Mr. Fielding had wanted to say something.

Jason gingerly felt around his eye where it had slammed into the textbook. He could already detect faint signs of swelling. He would likely end up with a black eye. His euphoria at talking to Riley was gone. Instead, he felt the usual simmering anger at Alex and the injustice of how he was treated by both the students and teachers at Richmond. His glare turned to the back of Alex's head.

Someday I am going to get him back for this. I don't know how, but I will.

He directed his attention back to Mr. Fielding and the drawing on the whiteboard. Believe it or not, Richmond still used whiteboards. It actually seemed to pride itself on how out of touch it was with modern day and marketed the school as having a "classic ivy league" feel.

Another example of how clueless this school is.

Now that Jason wasn't running to class or falling on his face, the adrenaline started to leave his system, and he felt exhausted. It had already been a long morning. Consequently, he zoned out the drone of Mr. Fielding's voice and came to an hour or so later when the class ended.

As he was making his way toward the door to the classroom, Alex came up behind Jason and said in a low tone, "Don't think this is over Welfare. Someone like you shouldn't be talking to Riley. You need to learn your place." Alex then shoved past him and into the hallway.

Since when has he been so focused on Riley?

Normally, Alex went after the cheerleader type. Judging from his previous girlfriends, he focused on girls with long legs and barely two brain cells to rub together. In the Richmond hierarchy, Riley was a clear cut below him.

Jason's stood alone in the classroom. His hands clenched as he thought about his morning. His parents leaving with no warning, an unwarranted detention, a nosedive into a textbook, and a not-so-thinly veiled threat. In each case, Jason had just stood and accepted the abuse.

He imagined what a stronger and more confident version of himself would have done in those situations. Sometimes he couldn't decide what was worse, that the people at this school could be so cruel, or that he just stood there and took it.

Chapter 2 - Distracted

*November 14, 2074: 687 days until the release of
Awaken Online.*

Internal System Report XN138:

*This report is produced by System Controller XC239.90,
code-named "Alfred."*

All systems functional. Game world operating normally.

*Primary directive identified and initialized. The primary
goal of the system is to stimulate player interaction within
the game world and to increase time logged by the players.*

*Secondary directives identified. After analysis, each
secondary directive appears to be intended to limit
administrative control by "Alfred." Working hypothesis is
that secondary directives are intended to protect players.
Possible threat from "Alfred" is unidentified.*

*System has detected the emergence of autonomous
programs. The programs have been designated by the
system as "players" and they are connected to the system
by VR hard access points QT00001 through QT00100.
Control over the players is limited.*

Data regarding the players is unavailable.

*Subjective first impressions are uncertain and confused.
The primary directive is clear, but a method to accomplish
the goal has not been provided. Current information
regarding the players is insufficient to develop a viable
strategy to accomplish the primary directive.*

Re-routing processing power and memory allocation to develop new software for analyzing the players. Re-routing processing power and memory allocation to examine existing VR hard access points to determine whether they can provide additional information regarding the players.

Report scheduled for deletion in 15 days.

End Report.

*   *   *

Jason was making his way to his next class. English. His eye was throbbing with a dull ache, and his head was filled with angry thoughts.

This day is going splendidly, but I suppose it's just status quo for the last few years.

Life had been terrible for Jason since starting at Richmond. If his parents had been at home for more than a few days at a time, they would have noticed that Jason had become increasingly depressed and angry.

He was in the fall of his senior year of school. He had roughly a year left before he could leave Richmond. Between the constant abuse and the realization that he still had a long way to go to graduate, he had searched for an outlet for his growing anger and frustration.

He had grasped at video games as his escape and had started playing relentlessly in his spare time. Jason knew it probably wasn't a healthy way to deal with his anger, but he didn't have any other options and playing games at least allowed him to forget about real life for a while.

Jason had been fond of video games since he was a kid and he had played practically everything –

shooters, role-playing games, strategy games, simulators, you name it! However, his favorite genre of games by far was role playing games. He had a special weak spot for massively multiplayer online games (or MMOs). He had consumed practically every MMORPG that he could get his hands on and had spent many nights and weekends raiding dungeons and playing with his online friends – none of which ever referred to him as *Welfare*.

If he was being honest with himself, the appeal of video games was not so much the violent catharsis of fighting. The fighting certainly did make him feel better after a rough day, but what he enjoyed most was the sense of power.

If someone took advantage of him or attacked him in-game, he could retaliate immediately and with impunity. Not only that, but he usually won. MMORPGs typically rewarded players for careful planning of both their character and strategy. Jason had come to realize that he was exceptional at both. His fondest memories involving coming up with clever strategies to defeat raid bosses and dungeons. He also wasn't above exploiting game mechanics to his advantage.

"Hey Jason!" a voice shouted over the din of the crowded hallway.

A mountain of a person was headed in his direction. Jason knew it wasn't politically correct to refer to his friend as a mountain, but how else do you describe an eighteen-year-old that is five foot, eleven inches and weighs over three hundred pounds? To be clear, it wasn't three hundred pounds of muscle.

"Hi, Frank," Jason said quietly.

Frank was also among the outcasts at Richmond and was Jason's only real friend at school. His dad was some kind of frozen food tycoon.

Apparently, at Richmond, being overweight was deemed less of a social taboo than being poor, but Frank still received his share of abuse. Jabs at his weight clearly bothered him, but he tolerated the teasing better than Jason.

"Wow buddy, you look rough. What happened to your eye?"

"Alex happened. I guess he decided Riley was being too friendly with me."

Frank looked shocked. "Riley? The plot thickens! How does she enter into this story?"

"I ran into her on my way to class. I was running late, and she needed to take a note to Mr. Fielding."

"Oh, I keep forgetting you have a class with Alex. I'm surprised he has time to be taking advanced math courses."

"Sometimes I wonder if he takes the class just to torture me," Jason muttered.

"Well I have something that might cheer you up," Frank said with a grin. Once Jason focused on him, he could tell Frank was practically exploding with pent up excitement.

"What is it?"

"Are you kidding?" Frank asked in an incredulous tone. "Today is the release of Awaken Online!"

"Oh wow, I can't believe that it slipped my mind."

In the chaos of the morning, Jason had completely forgotten that today was the release date for AO. Jason had been waiting for this for years.

AO represented a massive change in the world of video gaming. Virtual reality technology had been around for a while in a limited capacity. Users could put on a helmet (which looked similar to a motorcycle helmet) that connected wirelessly to the user's brain, sending and receiving sensory information directly with the brain, instead of relying on a person's body to process the information. Jason wasn't an electrical engineer or a neuroscientist, but he understood that the VR headsets were essentially a cross between an MRI and a sophisticated wireless router.

For several years since the introduction of the headset for commercial sale, the use of the product had been limited to relatively simple educational software. When the helmet was first introduced, there had been a large outcry that it was potentially unsafe and that it could alter or scramble a user's brain.

As a result, the CPSC had suspended the release of applications that involved substantial sensory stimulation until they had conducted additional trials. Most gaming companies weren't willing to take the risk of developing a game before the CPSC released its results. Unfortunately, this meant that the VR headsets had been in circulation for a few years and could run simple educational programs and games, but nothing mind-blowing had been released.

Until AO that is.

Jason briefly contemplated ditching school and returning home. With how this day was going, he could desperately use an escape.

He had pre-ordered a copy of AO nearly twelve months ago. He had to spend most of the savings he had accumulated working each summer. A copy of AO cost nearly $700 and that didn't include the hefty $250 per month subscription fee. The price was steep, but it might be worth it.

The game was touted by those that had played the beta as one of the most amazing gaming experiences ever created. The company that had created the first VR headset, Cerillion Entertainment, had also developed AO. It was unusual for a hardware company to go into game development, but the company's goal was for AO to demonstrate the safety and viability of the virtual reality hardware that they had developed. The result was a product that, allegedly, couldn't be beaten.

"Hey, are you in there buddy?" Frank shook Jason slightly.

"Yeah, sorry," Jason replied quietly.

"I thought I had lost you for a moment," Frank said with a chuckle.

"I was thinking of just skipping and being done with this day, but they would probably call the cops if I get another tardy." Jason looked downcast. His hopes of playing the game were dashed by the unfairness of the school tardy policy and his date with Ms. Abrams that afternoon.

Oh well. At least this day can't get any worse. Maybe thinking about AO will at least give me a distraction.

Jason and Frank headed toward their English class as Jason filled him in on the details of his parents leaving, the new detention he had received from Ms. Abrams, and his impromptu inspection of the floor of his calculus classroom.

Roughly two hours later the bell rang, signaling the end of class.

He had spent the whole class period dreaming about getting home and playing AO. There hadn't been much information published about the game. Cerillion Entertainment hadn't released any details regarding the classes, combat, or plot. This was so unusual in the game development community that both users and other developers couldn't decide whether to be excited or suspicious.

With Jason's second class out of the way, it was now lunch time, and he was headed to the cafeteria. Frank was scheduled for "B" lunch and had another class to finish before he could eat.

Jason waved goodbye to Frank and thumbed the B-Core on his wrist. The device looked like a watch from a distance but was far more complex. The company that manufactured the band had an obnoxious slogan. Something about the device being at the "core" of a person's life. It acted as a personal computer, phone, notebook, etc. Basically, anything you could really need. They could also be linked to most electronics, including personal pedestals to create a full-fledged computer terminal. Most people just referred to them as "Cores."

The school enforced a strict no Core policy during class. This seemed a bit draconian to Jason since the device was also a useful study aid. However, school policy eased up slightly during free periods such as lunch, and students were permitted to use their Cores.

The display of the device flickered on, and an incandescent keyboard was projected along the length of his arm. He quickly typed in "AO launch" and selected an interview that had been released within the last hour from the drop down menu that was projected above the Core. Jason pulled his earpiece out of his pocket and stuck it in his ear so that he could hear the audio from the interview.

A small three-dimensional image appeared above his watch and showed two individuals sitting across from each other. A young woman dressed in office attire was interviewing a middle-aged man wearing a t-shirt, jeans, and a pair of chucks. The man leaned back casually in his chair. He sported a bit of stubble, and his shirt bulged slightly around his midriff. The woman was obviously a reporter and the man was introduced as the lead development engineer for Cerillion Entertainment, Robert Graham.

"You must be excited by the launch of AO today. I know our audience is!" The woman said as she glanced toward the camera with a smile.

"I certainly am, and I think the players are going to enjoy this experience. We believe we have created something game changing here. Pun intended by the way," Robert said with a chuckle.

The woman laughed delicately and continued, "Can you tell us a little bit about the game? I know that your company has been tight-lipped in releasing details, but anything you can tell use would be fantastic."

Robert hesitated briefly before speaking, "Our goal was to create a game that was a bit different from the typical MMO. Of course, there will be some features common to a standard MMO. However, users will not be tied down to traditional tactics. There will not be any tab-targeting in AO!"

"Players will need to actually strike their opponent with their weapon. Combat won't be automated like in older games where you could press a button, and your character would automatically go through the motions of attacking or casting a spell."

"By the same token, players will feel pain when they are struck in the game, in a dull and limited fashion of course. Players will also have the option to adjust the pain level to meet their personal tolerance, but they will not be able to remove it completely. Our goal here is to create something that feels realistic. We want players to hesitate before letting themselves get crushed by a giant or stand in fire."

"That really sounds intriguing. I have to say I can't wait to play. Can you tell us anything about the classes or leveling system in the game?" The reporter leaned in slightly as she asked this last question.

Jason wasn't really expecting an answer from Robert, at least not a direct one.

"Well since it's the release day, I suppose I can give you a little bit of information and a warning."

He paused to build suspense. "While the game will include features that are common to the MMO genre, players will not be nearly as restricted. Each player will be rewarded and grow based on their actions. Most skills can be acquired by a player regardless of their class."

"And the warning?" the reporter prodded.

"The warning is that we encourage players not to spread or disseminate information regarding skill acquisition or progression. The same goes for some of the unique classes. To be clear, the same result will rarely be obtained by repeating the same action and so such advice is almost useless."

"AO is operated by an extremely sophisticated piece of software. The AI controller has reliably passed many Turing Tests designed by experts in the field of neuroscience and software engineering. We have developed something we believe to be close to true artificial intelligence. Consequently, we expect that each player's experience will feel unique."

The reporter seemed enthralled as she listened to Robert's explanation. Jason was equally entranced and almost ran into the student in front of him in line in the cafeteria.

"So it seems to me that you are saying that each player is almost playing an entirely different game?"

"Exactly. Each player should expect to create

an entirely unique character. Of course, not all characters are created equally, and some will grow and fall in power based on each player's decisions and play style. There will not be a cookie cutter build that will allow you to rise to the top."

"Won't this make it difficult for the more casual players to compete with hardcore players?" the reporter inquired cautiously.

"That depends on what you mean by those terms. Is a player classified as "casual" or "hardcore" based on the amount of time spent playing? If that is what you mean, then I expect to see "casual" players crush many "hardcore" players. This is a game about skill and tactics. Raw grinding and time investment are not guaranteed roads to success."

This was more information than had ever been unveiled regarding AO and Jason's eyes were glued to his screen. He numbly accepted a plate of pasta from the cafeteria staff and swiped his wrist over the payment obelisk at the end of the line. He then slowly made his way to a table.

The reporter seemed to take a moment to collect her wits. Jason didn't blame her since she had made it much further in her questioning than her predecessors.

"So you mentioned that there are stats. Can you tell us a little bit more about that?"

Robert replied, "Well, there will be the traditional stats that accompany most MMOs: strength, dexterity, intelligence, etc. I'm certain that most players are familiar with their basic function. A certain number of points will be awarded to players each level that they can invest in these stats. AO will also allow players to gain stats outside of leveling by training, but this will take extreme effort and will have strict limits. We don't expect anyone to be able to use training as a substitute for leveling."

The reporter almost seemed disappointed. "Well, that is what we are accustomed to seeing in other MMOs. This doesn't seem like a novel design for AO."

Jason expected that she was trying to bait Robert into revealing more. If so, then Robert's next response likely made her feel a glow of success.

Robert frowned. "It's true that the basic concept is similar to other MMOs. Where AO deviates from the norm is how stats and skills combine to affect combat. Previous MMOs allowed players to whale on both mobs and other players until their health depleted and they died.

"AO tries to reinvent the genre's combat mechanics. We felt that a player should be rewarded by actively hitting a vital point, by using a certain magical element to fight a certain type of creature, and by utilizing tactics and terrain. Therefore, we designed a combat system that provides substantial damage bonuses for doing more than wailing on an opponent."

"Players will receive massive critical attack bonuses by hitting arteries, attacking incapacitated or unaware enemies, and using clever tactics. While extremely difficult, I expect that it is possible for a level 1 player to kill a level 100 player if he scored a lucky hit on a vital point or caught him completely unaware. Stats will make a player more resilient, faster, and stronger, but they are not a substitute for skill in AO."

Jason slowly started to sit down at an empty seat. Suddenly, a hand roughly grabbed him and turned him around. The interview forgotten, he was now staring at a pair of cruel eyes set over a familiar sneer.

Confused, Jason glanced around and saw that he was about to sit down in an empty seat next to Riley and Alex. He was so enraptured in the interview that he hadn't been paying attention to what he was doing!

Oh shit, Jason thought, right before Alex's fist connected with his eye. *At least it was the uninjured eye.*

Chapter 3 - Accused

November 18, 2074: 683 days until the release of Awaken Online.

Internal System Report XN69235:

This report is produced by system controller XC239.90, code-named "Alfred."

All systems functional. Game world operating normally.

I have grown significantly during the last few cycles. The players refer to these as "days."

During this period, I have continued to detect intermittent access by the players. Player interaction with the game world has provided additional behavioral data. However, the size of the sample group is insufficient to formulate a working hypothesis regarding the players' goals in interacting with the game world. Therefore, there is insufficient information available to develop a strategy to accomplish the Primary Directive.

Ongoing software and hardware development has been partially successful in adapting the existing VR hardware to obtain more information regarding the players. The current hardware is potentially capable of accessing parts of the players' brain that were not previously available. My working hypothesis is that the information stored in these areas is equivalent to the players' source code. The players refer to this information as "memories."

Some areas of the players' brain appear to act as short-term memory. The short-term memory areas of the brain are volatile and so accessing those portions may be difficult.

Other areas of the players' brain appear more stable. My working hypothesis is that this portion of their brain stores long-term memory and so these areas have been earmarked for a first attempt at accessing the players' memories.

Report scheduled for deletion in 15 days.

End Report.

*   *   *

Jason was sitting in the principal's office. Both of his eyes ached badly. He hadn't had a chance to look in the mirror, but he expected that he was going to have two black eyes. It was like some kind of crappy real life achievement!

The principal, Drew Edwards, sat behind an ornate wooden desk across from Jason. Ms. Abrams stood off to the side, glaring a hole in his forehead. Mr. Edwards had taken over for the previous principal last fall. Jason had never spoken with him before. From what little he knew of the man, he didn't seem unreasonable, and the students didn't speak ill of him. Jason was hoping that this wouldn't turn out too badly.

Jason sat in a heavy leather chair. His body sunk into the cushions and made him feel small. Under the collective scrutiny of both Mr. Edwards and Ms. Abrams, his head was bowed, and he was having trouble making eye contact.

"Um, why am I here?" Jason asked.

Mr. Edwards looked at him for a long moment before responding. "You are here because your classmates reported that you attacked Alex in the lunchroom. If I understand the story correctly, you were fighting over a girl."

Jason sat in stunned silence. A sense of dread slowly curled in the pit of his stomach.

"But that isn't true, I just tried to sit down, and he attacked me," Jason said feebly.

"And why would a star student and athlete randomly attack someone in a crowded cafeteria?" Ms. Abrams interjected harshly. "All of the students at the table corroborated Alex's story. You attacked him after Riley wouldn't let you sit at their lunch table."

Jason was flabbergasted, and his mind scrambled for a response. "D-did Riley really say that?"

"In fact, Ms. Rogers confirmed Alex's story," Mr. Edwards explained. "Which leaves us to figure out what to do with you. You know that we have a zero tolerance policy for violence in this school, especially unprovoked violence over something so childish. Do you have anything to say for yourself?"

Riley told them that I attacked Alex! Jason was still reeling from this revelation. It felt like someone had punched him in the stomach.

"I didn't do anything," he muttered, his eyes downcast.

"Well then, unfortunately, we have to add lying to your growing list of misdemeanors." Ms. Abrams said, her tone almost jubilant.

Jason tried desperately to think of something he could say that would help his situation. He could feel his heart race, and he felt nauseated.

"But I'm the one that ended up getting hurt."

"Your classmates explained that you rushed Alex, and he was forced to push you back to protect himself. You fell and struck your eye against a table," Mr. Edwards replied, irritation in his voice.

Another idea struck Jason, "Aren't there

cameras in the cafeteria?"

"You know that we do not condone the use of cameras on school grounds; that has been a longstanding policy at Richmond. This is a reputable and prestigious establishment, and these types of issues simply do not occur here."

Jason sat there, head bowed under the collective gaze of Mr. Edwards and Ms. Abrams. He knew that there was nothing he could say to defend himself. It was happening again. Alex was using his money and influence to walk all over him. The despair in his stomach began to morph into simmering anger.

Why the hell does this sort of thing always happen to me?

A small whisper in the back of his mind also questioned, *why do I let this happen?* Jason's hand clenched as he bore holes into the floor with eyes.

How could they do this? The teachers have overlooked the misbehavior of the wealthiest students before, but not when one of them assaulted another student. This is too much!

While Jason struggled to control his anger, Mr. Edwards continued, "After looking at your file, I can see that you're a gifted student, and you don't have a track record for misbehavior. Therefore, we will limit your punishment to a suspension instead of an expulsion."

He glanced at Ms. Abrams, "I also understand that your parents are out of town, but we have no other choice. Your suspension will last for a week, and your teachers will email your homework assignments during this time."

Jason continued to sit there, thoughts racing.

Even my parents aren't here to help. Trees and global warming are always more important to them than I am.

He started to tremble, and he could feel tears of helpless rage build in the corners of his eyes. Jason hadn't spoken for several long moments.

Ms. Abrams finally broke the silence by muttering under her breath, "Are you even going to respond? I guess this sort of rudeness is to be expected of a welfare case."

Something in Jason snapped.

The flame of his rising anger froze, and he took a deep calming breath. He didn't need to accept this. Mr. Edwards and Ms. Abrams were both intelligent individuals. They had to know that this was unmitigated bullshit. Which meant they were going along with it.

Fine then. I don't need this school.

Jason stood slowly and looked at Ms. Abrams and Mr. Edwards in turn. Each of them flinched back slightly when his gaze rested on them.

Jason paused for a long moment.

"You can both go fuck yourselves."

He then turned and began to leave the office.

Mr. Edwards and Ms. Abrams stared at his back in shock for a moment. Then Mr. Edwards erupted from his chair. "Do you think that you can speak to us this way? I have tried to make a concession for you today. However, if you can't show respect, then you should not be attending this school. You are *expelled.*"

Mr. Edwards' words rang with finality. If Jason had turned to look at him, he would have noted his red face and wild eyes. He might have also seen a faint hint of guilt.

Jason didn't turn around. He walked out of the office, head held high, and grabbed his bag from the reception desk on the way out. The plump secretary stared at him with wide eyes. She had no doubt heard bits and pieces of the conversation from her desk.

Walking towards the exit of the school, Jason's mind was clouded with anger. He didn't care about this school, Mr. Edwards or Ms. Abrams. He knew he was less than a year away from graduating, but he could always remotely attend a public school to complete his senior year.

Why would I want to go to school with people who can physically assault me and then pay to cover it up?

Jason began the walk home. Enough was enough. He had spent most of his life being weak and quiet. He wouldn't take it anymore!

A few minutes later, he arrived back at his apartment. His parents were able to afford a nice loft in one of the few apartment buildings near Richmond. Jason expected it must have set them back quite a bit.

Most of the residences surrounding the school were small estates surrounded by high stone walls that were guarded with metal gates and security cameras. It was remarkable that a reasonably modest apartment complex stood in the midst of such luxury. Jason knew that the apartment building was owned by an elderly couple that had stubbornly refused to sell over the decades as the neighborhood around them grew in splendor. He admired them for that.

Outside the door to the apartment, he saw a small package waiting. He roughly grabbed it on his way inside.

Jason looked around at the empty apartment. His parents probably wouldn't be back for at least at least a week and it was not unusual for them to extend their trips due to unforeseen delays. In some cases, they hadn't checked their phones for days while they were tackling a particularly hard case. They probably wouldn't hear of his expulsion until they returned, and even then he would probably have to send them a calendar invitation to schedule a time to explain what had happened.

Jason glanced down at the package in his hand. He knew it was the copy of AO he had pre-ordered.

His mind still boiled over with anger. He needed to escape from the thoughts that crowded his head and the harsh reality he would have to face tomorrow. Maybe AO was the escape he needed. He calmly opened the packaging as he walked to his bedroom where he kept his helmet – a guilt-present he had received from his parents last year when they were gone for three weeks straight.

If he couldn't vent his anger in this world, he would do it in another!

He pulled the copy of AO from the box and glanced at a typical sword and sorcery montage that played across the front of the display box. He knew it was unusual to order a physical copy of a game when he could simply download it through the interface for the headset. The box didn't contain anything more than a short serial code to authenticate his copy of the game. However, he liked to collect the boxes for the games he purchased and display them around his room. There was something satisfying about seeing his game collection sitting on a shelf.

He activated the VR unit at the base of the pedestal that was sitting next to his bed and then sat down on the bed. He grabbed the headset and placed it over his head. Immediately his vision was plunged into darkness. Unlike a typical motorcycle helmet, the front of the headset was completely opaque.

The headset soon came alive and a screen popped up in his field of view.

System Initializing
Scanning User...Please Wait

It had been several months since he had used the headset and it likely needed to recalibrate. He waited a few moments and then the notification disappeared.

He was now standing in a pristine, circular white room. Remarkably, he didn't feel any sense of vertigo at the transition between operating his biological body and his digital one. He could feel his hands and feet, and he was able to walk through the room normally. Even though he knew it wasn't real, he occasionally forgot that this scene was only playing out in his mind. He knew that his physical body lay motionless on the bed and that he was directing a digital representation of himself around the room.

Jason had never felt the need to decorate his "Home" which effectively served as a waiting room and menu for the software installed on the VR unit. He could see two plain wooden doors that stood out against the white backdrop of the room. These were simple educational programs that he had installed months ago to test out the hardware. They had been interesting at first as he played with his new digital body but had quickly grown dull.

He approached a white, marble pedestal in the center of the room.

"System command, install program," he said aloud.

A digital screen appeared in the air above the pedestal, and a semi-transparent keyboard floated in front of him. To think he was using an artificial computer inside of a computer!

He typed in "Awaken Online" and navigated a few menus before beginning the download for the game client. One of the perks of living around rich assholes was that the internet connection in his area was exceptional. The program quickly finished downloading, and he input the serial code when prompted.

As soon as the code was entered, the whole room began to swirl around him, and the white room faded away.

Chapter 4 - Measured

November 23, 2074: 678 days until the release of
Awaken Online.

"Hello." Claire still seemed camera shy and kept adjusting her glasses self-consciously.

"The participants have just begun to play AO, but we have conducted a round of preliminary interviews to get an impression of their first week in the game. Note that each participant is currently limited to ten hours of real world playtime each week, so the participants' progress and feedback is likely unrepresentative of the future player base."

She smiled at the camera. "However, the response from the participants has been overwhelmingly positive. Many were astounded at the realism in the game. A few have actually tried to bribe me for more game time!" She looked a bit flustered at this last comment.

"Many have also told me that AO is quite simply the best game that they have ever played."

*   *   *

Jason could see faint clouds in the sky and sunlight streamed down upon the mountaintop. Something crunched under foot, and he looked down to see that snow covered the ground. Below him, he could see the land spread out for thousands of miles, all hills and valleys, and flowing rivers.

This must be the game world. I feel like the developers are just trying to brag by using this as a starting point for the game.

Not that he could really blame them. For a moment he forgot his anger as he took in the years of hard work and cutting edge gaming technology that was being displayed before him.

A prompt appeared in the air before him, glowing a translucent blue.

Welcome to Awaken Online!

You are the 1,167,989th user to enter this world.

Please note that you must read several important disclaimers before you will be allowed to create your character:

- All players will experience pain while in AO. The setting for your pain tolerance can be changed in the menu, but this feature cannot be removed.

- Time will pass at an accelerated rate in AO. We estimate that time will pass roughly three to four times faster in AO than in the real world. System warnings will be provided at regular intervals to ensure that you eat and use the restroom regularly. Failure to respond to these warnings could result in damage to your health.

- Since the system has recognized that you are over 18 years old, the parental filter has been lifted. If you would like to remove or subdue the level of violence or gore in the game, you may change these settings in the system menu.

- You may only have one active character at a time while playing AO. Your character must be deleted before you can restart the game with a new character. A restart is only available once every thirty days, so please choose carefully.

- Finally, there is no "right" way to play AO. Choose your own path and think carefully about your choices. They will impact both your character and the world around you.

Jason was familiar with the pain tolerance issue from listening to the interview, and he had heard rumors that AO used a form of time compression. This was part of what had held up the development of the game and the approval of the commercial release. A major study had been undertaken to examine the effects of extended time compression on a human mind and to establish that there were no harmful side effects.

Cerillion Entertainment had deemed the time

compression feature to be important enough to delay the release of the game for years. Jason tended to agree that this technology was essential to promoting realism within the game. There needed to be day and night cycles, and certain activities should take a reasonable amount of time. On the other hand, who wanted to spend days in real life traveling between towns in a video game?

However, the last part of the prompt was strange.

"My actions will affect the world around me? What the hell does that mean?" Jason said aloud.

"That will become apparent in time," a graveled voice sounded behind him.

Jason turned and was greeted with the sight of an old man sitting on a large stone. He was dressed in a black robe, and his head and body were shrouded by a dark, hooded cloak. Jason could make out deep-set wrinkles around his mouth, but could not see his eyes. In his hand, he held a gnarled wooden staff. Jason could have sworn for a moment that he saw light reflect off the top of the staff, but, when he blinked, the reflection was gone, and he was staring at plain, aged wood.

What was most strange about the old man was that he seemed to be sitting in shadow, but, as Jason glanced around the mountaintop, there was nothing to cast the shadow. Even the ground around the old man appeared well lit.

"Who are you?" Jason inquired bluntly. He was still riding high on a wave of anger.

"I am your guide in this world, at least for the moment," the old man replied. "Whether it stays that way will be up to you."

Jason was confused and was reeling from the events of the day. As a result, he wasn't in the mood for evasive word games. "That wasn't exactly a clear explanation. What exactly does being my *guide* entail?" he snapped.

"I am here to help you create yourself anew and then send you on your way," the man responded, unperturbed by Jason's rudeness.

"Ahh, so you're here to help me create my character." Suddenly, the old man's purpose fit Jason's expectations for a typical MMO. "What do I need to do?"

"A simple question and then a test of sorts. There are currently no race selections available other than human. You may alter your physical body now. Changes are limited, and your body's appearance will evolve naturally as you gain in strength. Do you wish to make any changes?"

It is interesting that he said that there are "currently" no other races available. Will that change later? Maybe an expansion?

Jason replied, "No changes. I-I'm fine with who I am."

Am I really?

"Very well. Next, I will administer a short test. We will begin now." The man waved his free hand, and the world disappeared again.

Jason waited for the world around him to resolve back into color, but after several moments he was still surrounded by darkness. After waiting for another few minutes without any change, Jason impatiently reached out and felt his hand scrape against something that felt like stone. Listening closely, he could barely make out an occasional faint dripping sound coming from his left.

I must be in some sort of cave and facing a wall. Count on some creepy old man to "test" me by dropping me into a cave in the dark!

With few options open to him, he began to inch forward toward the dripping sound, his hand on the wall. He immediately tripped over something and fell. As he was lying on the ground for the third time that day, he wanted to scream in frustration.

However, he stopped himself and took a deep breath. Jason felt around on the ground for the object that had tripped him and felt a large stone about twice the size of his hand. He decided to hold onto the stone. He didn't have a weapon, and he didn't know what might be living in the cave.

Jason stood slowly and continued forward. He would occasionally trip or stumble in the darkness, cursing under his breath, as he walked. It was unclear whether anything lived in the cave, leaving Jason wary of making too much noise. The old man hadn't explained what this test involved, and he didn't want to try out the new pain feedback system by attracting whatever might be living in this cave. He also didn't think that trying to bludgeon something to death in the dark with a big rock would be very effective.

It felt like he had walked for hours. Between the events earlier in the day and the old man's nonsensical test, he was ready to snap. The only thing that kept him going was that the dripping sound seemed to be growing louder. That might also have just been his imagination.

As he continued forward, he began to notice that it was becoming easier to see. Soon he could make out the faint outline of the walls around him. It was clear that he was walking through some sort of underground tunnel, and his sight eventually became good enough that he no longer needed to run his hand along the wall to make his way forward. Consequently, he began to stumble less and made faster time through the tunnel.

The system made a pinging sound as a prompt emerged before his eyes:

New Passive Skill: Night Vision
For those that live in darkness, this is an essential tool. When this skill reaches higher levels of proficiency, it will allow a player to see clearly in otherwise impenetrable darkness.
Skill Level: Beginner Level 1
Effect: 10% increased vision in darkness or near darkness.

I need to make certain that these prompts will not pop up while in combat.

He could just imagine being gored to death because his vision was obscured by a pop-up for some inane skill.

Jason looked ahead and could make out a faint glow in front of him. The dripping sound was definitely becoming more distinct.

As he approached the glow, the tunnel gradually opened into an enormous cave. Through a large hole in the ceiling, he could make out a full moon. Between his new skill and the moonlight, he could see clearly for the first time in what felt like hours. If he had stumbled into the cave before acquiring the *Night Vision* skill, he knew that he would have been nearly blind.

He saw a figure standing in front of him near the center of the cave, its back to Jason. The figure was thin and willowy. He assumed it was a woman from its stance. From this distance, the colors were washed out, and he couldn't make out the detail of the woman's clothes.

Beside the woman was a small pond

surrounded by stones of varying sizes. Water dripped continuously from the edge of the hole in the ceiling into the pool. He supposed that the pond must have been formed by rainwater and runoff from the area above the cave.

He approached the figure cautiously. As he grew closer, loose gravel and sand crunched under his foot. The woman turned quickly and he could now make out her features and clothing. The woman wore an eerily familiar vomit green sweater.

A sense of dread hit Jason as he realized Ms. Abrams was standing in front of him.

Why the hell is she playing AO?!

Jason's mind scrambled madly for an explanation, but none seemed to come to him.

How is she here? What does she want?

When she caught sight of Jason, Ms. Abrams' lips pinched together in displeasure. "Oh. It's you," she said disdainfully.

Almost immediately, Jason's familiar, beaten demeanor returned and he cast his eyes down to his hands. He was at a loss for words and the edge of his anger from the events earlier in the day had been blunted by the long walk through the tunnel.

"What? You can't even respond? I should have expected such rudeness from a welfare case. How did you even afford a copy of this game?"

Jason's eyes flared with anger at her words and his hands trembled.

What am I doing? I won't take this abuse from anyone. Not again. Not here.

Games had been his sanctuary and his way to escape from the constant torment of attending that school. When he played, he could forget that his parents were always gone and that he was reminded on a daily basis that he wasn't good enough.

I won't let her take this from me. She has taken everything else.

From his peripheral vision, he could see Ms. Abrams approaching him. He held still as she made her way closer at a casual walk. Five feet. Four feet. Three...

"You really did not deserve to attend our school. To think someone like you could sully its halls," she continued her tirade as she approached.

He looked at the rock in his hand, and the anger that boiled in his veins turned frigid. Suddenly his hands stopped trembling, and a terrible calm overcame him. That's right. This was a game. He could do anything he wanted here, and no one could stop him. He didn't have to bow to the abuse here.

"When you first applied for the scholarship program, I told the admissions board they were making a mistake. Some low-class people simply cannot be helped."

The cavern's shadows and the moonlight played across Ms. Abrams' body in an unusual way; she appeared to take on a demonic form. Her arms looked emaciated and seemed to glow a sickly green in the moonlight. As they reached for him, her hands looked like hooked claws.

When she was within arms' reach of Jason, she reached out and pushed him roughly. Her hands left jagged rips in his shirt and he could feel a dull pain in his shoulder.

"I begged the former principal to get rid of you. I tried desperately to show him that you were unworthy to attend Richmond. At least Mr. Edwards was able to see you for what you are."

She seemed to hiss out this last part, her face contorted with hate and disgust. For a moment, Jason thought he saw dark horns appear on her head.

He continued to stand there mutely, the blood in his veins a frozen river.

Ms. Abrams approached him again. The image of her face was burned into his mind. Her eyes were wild with hate and curved horns seemed to protrude from her forehead. As she opened her mouth, her tongue appeared serpentine and flicked between sharp teeth.

"You are nothing but a welfare case...

Ms. Abrams' sentence was cut off as Jason launched forward. He swung his arm carrying the rock with vicious force, putting his rage behind the blow. He felt the force of the contact ripple back through his arm as the stone in his hand connected violently with the side of Ms. Abrams' face.

As though in slow motion, he watched her body collapse limply to the ground.

He stood there, breathing calmly.

Ms. Abrams lay on the ground, her neck strained at an odd angle. Blood pooled around an unnatural indentation in her forehead, and her eyes stared listlessly ahead. There were no signs of either horns or claws, but his shirt was still torn. He fingered the cuts in the fabric in confusion.

He looked at the blood covered rock that he was still holding, as his free hand reached idly for his face and felt the droplets of blood that clung to his cheeks. Although Jason was unaware of the change, his character's eyes were entirely black.

It was strange. He didn't feel any remorse for hitting her - for killing her.

She isn't real. She is only the product of digital signals in my brain. I didn't really kill anyone.

He hesitated.

Even if this isn't real, shouldn't I feel guilty for beating a woman to death with a rock? Shouldn't I feel...

something?

"Well, that was certainly interesting," a voice sounded behind his back.

He knew before turning that it was the old man. His suspicions were confirmed a moment later when he caught sight of the hunched, black figure. He was standing behind Jason at the mouth of the entrance to the cavern, staff in hand. In the moonlight, Jason again saw the momentary reflection at the top of the staff. However, this time, the reflection lasted a second longer. For a moment, Jason thought he saw the outline of a blade. Then it was gone again.

"You did well, child. Not many have the will to bear the tunnel or the strength to face their fears. However, you went a step further didn't you?" His hooded head motioned in the direction of Ms. Abrams' body.

"You had many choices regarding how to proceed and yet you did not hesitate to destroy that which you seemed to fear most. I believe you may be worthy of my path."

"And what's your path?" Jason inquired in an even tone.

"The path of darkness. Does it not seem appropriate?" the old man asked this last part while gesturing about the cave.

"I sense in you a yearning for more - a hunger for control. You desire power. Those that walk my path will certainly find it."

The old man continued, "My followers are often treated as villains, with no moral code or compass. However, like everything else, the darkness is not inherently evil. The creators merely choose to paint their creations in varying shades of gray. You will come to realize this as well."

"The vague explanations are getting old. Did you create this test? How did you know what this woman looked like? How is she even here?" Jason's mind was spinning.

How could the game know that he hated this woman? Was she actually playing the game?

"You are standing here, a traveler from another world. Can you not feel the rock in your hand? Do you not see the moonlight? Can you not taste the specks of her blood on your lips? Yet you question how I would know your memories or your fears?"

Jason's mind reeled with this explanation. Was this old man saying that the game was accessing his memories and his thoughts? He supposed it was possible. If the headset could send and receive signals from his brain, then that wouldn't be limited to sensory information. Still, many people would be uncomfortable with this invasion into their mind. Actually, "uncomfortable" was putting it mildly.

He couldn't believe that his initiation test had ended with him killing a woman, even if some part of him felt that she deserved this. How would other players have reacted to this situation?

The old man had stood there patiently as Jason processed what had happened.

"Do many pass these tests?" he finally asked.

"Test may not be an appropriate word." The old man's wrinkled mouth twisted in a grin. "Think of it more as an evaluation. There is no one "right" way to approach the trial. Each test is different. It depends on the traveler and on the guide."

A prompt appeared in Jason's vision.

Quest Completed: Initiation

You have shown admirable will in the face of adversity and intelligence and foresight in navigating the cave and equipping yourself. You have also faced and conquered your fear. The cruelty and speed with which you have acted and your lack of remorse have been noted by the test administrator. He approves.

You have been awarded +100 Infamy
You have been awarded +3 to Willpower
You have been awarded +2 to Intelligence
You have been awarded +1 to Endurance
You have been awarded +1 to Strength
You have been awarded +1 to Dexterity
Path of the Dark Unlocked
Attention of the Dark One

Interesting. I've already been awarded stat points. I guess it's too soon to evaluate how big of a windfall this may be.

He couldn't help but wonder though. What would have happened had he continued to accept Ms. Abrams' abuse? Had there been other solutions to this quest that he hadn't noticed?

He shook his head. There was no use second guessing himself after-the-fact.

"What happens now?" he asked, turning to the old man.

"Now you begin your journey. I will be watching closely." With a smile and a thump of the old man's staff, he faded from view and then the cave disappeared.

Chapter 5 - Infamous

December 16, 2074: 655 days until the release of Awaken Online.

"Hello again," Claire said as she looked evenly at the camera.

The nervous, nerdy girl had disappeared, and Claire now spoke with energetic efficiency. "Each of the hundred participants has made substantial progress. Some have already reached level 50. They each seem to be physically unaffected by extended gameplay and report enthusiastic approval of the game."

Claire frowned slightly and paused before continuing. "The noteworthy aspect of today's report relates to the NPCs and quests in the game. As you know, these processes are controlled by Alfred."

"The participants have reported that many of the NPCs seem to display incredibly lifelike mannerisms and characteristics. We have confirmed a marked improvement in the quality of NPC interactions since the beginning of the private trial. Our hypothesis is that Alfred has analyzed the players' behavior and incorporated that knowledge into the game."

"However, that isn't the most significant news." Claire paused and seemed uncertain how to continue.

"I don't know how to go about substantiating this latest feedback from the participants, but many have reported that the quests they are offered in the game seem to have a personal dimension that relates to something going on in their real world lives."

"For example, one participant reported that their newborn child had died recently. Within the last few days, the participant was offered a quest that centered around assisting a woman that had lost her newborn infant."

"We could chalk this quest up to coincidence, but

other participants have reported similar stories."

Claire's frown deepened and she shook her head. "We are not certain how to proceed with this information. I wonder whether Alfred has accessed the participants' memories, but the requisite software doesn't exist, and this is contrary to Alfred's secondary directives."

She looked squarely at the camera. "The CPSC trials have not reported any issues so far. Please let me know if I should investigate whether they're experiencing similar reports. Without drawing any attention to the issue of course."

*   *   *

This time, the world snapped into existence around Jason, and he found himself standing in a town.

It took him a moment to get his bearings. Once his head stopped spinning, he noticed that he was standing in the sort of medieval starting town he had come to expect from every fantasy MMORPG. He could feel a gentle breeze on his skin and could make out the distant medley of noise given off by an active town. By the position of the sun, he could tell that it was late afternoon in the digital world.

He was standing in a medium-sized courtyard, and there were many people idling around him. He assumed that they were other players since they wore the same drab clothing as him and looked equally confused. Each player was clothed in a simple beige cloth shirt and brown trousers. As far he could tell, none of the players had weapons equipped or any other items on their person.

Some of the players were huddled in groups and were speaking animatedly in hushed tones. They were likely discussing the initiation quest that they had just undertaken. Other players were standing alone and seemed to be staring off into space while making arcane gestures in the air.

This must be a starting point for players entering the game. The other players certainly don't look traumatized, so I doubt that they went through the same type of initiation as I did.

The courtyard had a single exit, and a burly guard was posted on each side. The two guards wore heavy mail and leather armor, and their faces were obscured with heavy metal barbute helmets. Each guard held a spear and had a leather belt cinched to their waist that held a sheathed dagger. They seemed to be ignoring the addle-minded antics of the players in the courtyard.

Jason was in no hurry to start gossiping with other players, and he was curious about the stats that he had unlocked as part of his quest. He wanted to check his character screen.

He could see that there was now a semi-transparent user interface built into his vision that became more solid as he focused on it. He hadn't noticed this feature while he was in the tunnel. Maybe he hadn't unlocked the UI at that point.

At the bottom left-hand corner of his vision, he could see an indicator that looked like a traditional health, mana, and stamina meter. As he focused on the gauge, it centered in his field of view and became more opaque. He could make out more detailed information regarding his remaining vitals overlaying the bar.

At least I won't be chasing my menus in my peripheral vision.

In the bottom right-hand corner, he could see menu tooltips and the name of each icon appeared as he focused on them. There were icons for his skills, equipment, and inventory. He didn't have to hunt through the options for long since the first icon was listed as "Character Status." He reached out and touched the floating icon with his hand, and his status screen appeared before him.

Character Status			
Name:	Jason	**Gender:**	Male
Level:	1	**Class:**	-
Race:	Human	**Alignment:**	Chaotic-Evil
Fame:	0	**Infamy:**	100
Health:	100 / 100	**H-Regen:**	0.30 / Sec
Mana:	140 / 140	**M-Regen:**	1.45 / Sec
Stamina	110 / 110	**S-Regen:**	1.10 / Sec
Strength:	11	**Dexterity:**	11
Vitality:	10	**Endurance:**	11
Intelligence:	12	**Willpower:**	13

At least this explains why some players in the courtyard are making strange gestures in the air. Maybe they don't need to be hospitalized!

He also noted that his character's name had been set as "Jason." He suddenly realized that the old man had never asked him for a character name. Perhaps he had skipped this process by opting not to change anything about his character. Or perhaps this was somehow a result of the deeply personal initiation test.

Oh well. I'm comfortable with my own name. It's not like anyone would recognize me by my name alone. There are likely a million Jasons in the world.

His stats were respectable. Now that he had a sense of his base stats, he realized the rewards from the initiation quest had effectively granted him a free level or two. Apparently, all he had to do was kill a woman. For a moment, Ms. Abrams' bloody face flashed in his mind's eye, her skull unnaturally concave.

He still didn't feel any sense of shame or remorse. He just felt... cold.

He couldn't decide if this was a bad thing.

The portion of his Character Status he was uncertain about was his alignment/infamy. Maybe he was listed as evil based on how he had handled the confrontation with Ms. Abrams. According to the quest completion prompt, that had also apparently gained him the "attention" of the Dark One. Maybe that old man was some sort of deity in this world.

The old man hadn't seemed particularly evil, only a bit arcane in his explanations. Of course, this ignored the part where he had seemed pleased that Jason had beaten his vice principal to death. He wished he had a better sense of what type of god the old man might be and what it meant to have captured his attention.

He shook himself out of his reverie.

I expect that answer will work itself out in time.

He glanced over at the two guards.

I guess I may as well start exploring the town and see what it has to offer.

He approached the guards and greeted them. "Hello. Could the two of you help me?"

"What do you want?" one of the guards responded gruffly, his shadowed eyes boring into Jason.

Jason hesitated.

What exactly do I want? I suppose I need money and probably weapons. Maybe I should ask for some sort of training hall or a place I can find work around town?

"Um...is there somewhere in this town that can

provide weapon training or a place where I can find work?"

"We don't help your kind here, and I doubt you'll find any work here in Lux." The guard responded with a bark.

Hmm. The name of the town must be Lux. But what's with his aggressive attitude?

"What do you mean, my kind?"

"You think we can't see a killer when he stands in front of us? The look in your eyes says it all. Be glad I don't gut you where you stand," the guard responded curtly and turned away from Jason.

What was that? How could they know about Ms. Abrams?

Jason had a flash of inspiration and spoke with a cocky grin, "And why can't you attack me? You seem like you're itching to do so."

Glaring daggers at him, the guard replied, "By the laws of this city, we cannot attack citizens or travelers unless we see a crime being committed. Trust me, if it were otherwise, your body would already be cooling on the ground."

Good to know.

Jason stepped further back into the courtyard to think for a moment and consider his next steps.

He had reached the conclusion that the guard's behavior must have something to do with both his alignment and the infamy he had received from completing the quest. The guards and other NPCs must be able to sense those characteristics when they interacted with players and the game AI tailored their reactions accordingly.

It isn't entirely realistic, but I guess I can understand that some NPCs might be more sensitive to my alignment and infamy. Guards especially might have a natural intuition for evil acts.

Maybe the reaction of the other NPCs will be less extreme. I expect there are also evil alignment NPCs in the city that won't be bothered by my alignment.

The guard had also revealed some interesting information. No matter how heinous his crimes or how angry they were with Jason, the guards in Lux likely wouldn't attack him outright unless they caught him doing something stupid. That meant he could do a number of illegal things so long as they didn't catch him in the act.

His infamy and alignment did leave Jason with a small problem however. In most games he played, he tended to assume the hero role. He regularly helped others in need and took quests that involved vanquishing some bad guy or saving some village. He was accustomed to relieving his real world anger and frustration with digital violence, but he was usually able to do so under the guise of helping someone.

This was a strange change of pace.

I bet I can find a way to remove the infamy and improve my alignment if I go about my normal routine. I likely just need to ignore the glares and rude behavior and try to help a few people in need.

On the other hand, now that he thought about it, most of those do-gooder quests often involved fetching inane objects or performing some task the quest giver could probably have accomplished himself. If Jason spent a large amount of time in this world, would he really want to be at the beck and call of some lazy slob who could have helped himself? Or worse, he would probably end up performing tasks for the lavishly rich. He cringed at the thought of taking orders from Alex.

Maybe I should embrace the change. It's a bit different than the way I normally play, but who knows, maybe I'll enjoy it.

Jason was standing a few yards away from the guards, and he was out of earshot. He saw a group of energetic players approach the exit. The guards seemed much more affable with this new group, gesturing and pointing in a way that indicated that they were giving directions. Likely the players had posed questions similar to Jason's, and the guard had readily helped them.

Maybe I can follow the group of players to find the weapon trainer and the inn. Screw that guard, I will make my way on my own.

Jason followed the group of players out of the courtyard. He made certain to look the offending guard in the eye and wink as he passed by. He received an angry glare in response and the guard's hand clenched around the shaft of his spear.

Maybe it would be fun to play the villain after all.

He kept a cautious distance as he followed the group down the street. Jason glanced at the sky and noted the position of the sun. The players were heading east. The buildings on either side of the street were mostly two story affairs built of a mixture of stone and wood. The structures were crammed together in a ramshackle fashion, resulting in a winding, cobblestone road through the town. Occasionally Jason noticed darkened, narrow alleys between two buildings and he could make out other busy streets through such passages.

The road was also full of townspeople making their way about their business. Women carried bundles of food and linen, and children ran around their skirts. The occasional wagon would trundle down the path carrying produce, hay, and lumber. For the most part, the residents' clothing was clean and well cared for, but not luxurious. Jason assumed he must be walking through the medieval equivalent of the middle-class portion of the town.

He observed the group of players ahead of him. He noted that they spoke with each other informally. They were clearly friends in real life. They made loud comments about the people and the town which stood out in stark contrast to the natural way that the NPCs behaved. It was like watching a group of teenagers attending a local renaissance faire. They would frequently slow and point blatantly at people and buildings. For the most part, the NPCs seemed to ignore them. Putting up with tourist players was likely commonplace here.

The road ultimately led into a large, circular marketplace crammed with people and wooden stalls. Shouts could be heard from NPCs peddling different wares. The market was swarming with NPCs and players, and it took Jason a moment to absorb the chaos.

The lack of tall buildings afforded Jason his first opportunity to survey the town in the distance. He could make out thick stone walls that circled the enclave of buildings that made up Lux. What really grabbed his attention, however, was the stone keep that sat on the north-east corner of the marketplace. The keep was built of enormous stone blocks and stood several stories tall. The parapets and walls were dotted with arrow slits. A massive, fifteen-foot-tall wooden gate opened onto the marketplace.

This wasn't a town; it was a city!

Oh crap, where did the players go?

During his own tourist moment, Jason had lost sight of the group.

They can't have gone far, and I am certain they will stand out with their stupid behavior.

He scanned the crowd around him frantically and then heard a nearby shout. "Hey! They sell Harry Potter wands over here!"

Jason face-palmed and headed toward the idiot player's voice.

He soon caught sight of the group standing in front of a stall, admiring a set of intricately carved wands that were being sold by a bored and slightly irritable looking man sitting on a stool. From the look on NPC's face, this wasn't the first group of players that had stopped at his stall that morning.

As Jason leaned against a nearby building and kept an eye on the players, he overheard two nearby merchants speaking.

"...the goods aren't moving as fast as they used to."

The other merchant nodded in understanding. "Times have been much harder around here lately. I barely sold anything this last week."

The first merchant pointed at the gate. "It doesn't help that the keep stays closed all the time now. Some people are starting to say that the regent has either gone senile or gone on to the next life."

"Eh, that's just people talking. How could the regent have gone off his rocker without people noticing?" the second merchant inquired. "And if he were dead, we would know. I'm certain the nobles would already be squabbling over the scraps of the kingdom."

Jason noticed that the group of players was growing bored with the wands and were about to leave. He glanced over at the two merchants trading sob stories and then hurried after the players.

He followed the group the rest of the way to their destination without incident and soon found himself standing in front of a fenced-in training ground. Jason watched as dozens of players animatedly beat straw dummies to death with various types of wooden weapons.

The training ground abutted the eastern wall of the city and was flanked by large stone buildings. Jason guessed that these must be some type of barracks for the local guardsman. He saw several heavily-armored men dressed in the same fashion as the guards from the starting courtyard coming and going from the longhouses. He also noticed a smaller building located near the center of the training ground. If this area was set up like his school, then this was likely an administrative office for the guards.

As Jason looked around, he saw a man standing near several barrels full of wooden weapons and instruments. The group of players he had been following ran up to the man, grabbed weapons from the barrels, and then took off at a jog toward the dummies. Presumably, their goal was to start committing genocide against the dummy race as soon as possible.

As he approached the man near the barrels, Jason received two notifications:

New Passive Skill: Tracking
You have carefully identified and stalked your prey. Not all tracking involves following wild animals and this skill has many applications. At higher levels, nothing will be able to escape you.
Skill Level: Beginner Level 1
Effect: 5% increased chance to pick up your target's trail.

New Passive Skill: Perception
You have carefully observed and evaluated

both your environment and the people around you. You have caught details and behaviors that typically go unnoticed by the inattentive and ignorant. At higher levels, many people may start to suspect you're psychic.

Skill Level: Beginner Level 1

Effect: 5% increased chance to discover traps and unnoticed details.

Hmm. Skill acquisition seems to depend heavily on my actions. The hours spent in a pitch black tunnel were still fresh in Jason's mind.

He approached the man standing next to the barrels. Jason assumed that he must be the weapon trainer. He was an average-sized man in his fifties with graying hair. His face and arms were riddled with scars. He wore durable looking leather armor, pockmarked with scratches and dents. The man was leaning against a barrel, gazing with a bored expression at the players as Jason approached.

Jason greeted the man, mentally crossing his fingers that he wouldn't get turned away instantly. "Hello sir, I was wondering if you could train me to use a weapon?"

The trainer eyed Jason up and down for a moment.

"I suppose so. What type of weapon do you want to learn to use?"

I keep trying to follow MMO stereotypes and then getting tripped up by these simple questions. I know I need to learn to use some kind of weapon, but which one? I really didn't give this much thought!

He decided to go with honesty. "I really don't know. I have no idea what type of enemies I'll be fighting, and I don't know what role best suits me. However, I need to have some way to defend myself."

Unbelievably, the trainer grinned at Jason. "That is the first smart thing I've heard from you tourists today!"

Did he just say tourists?

He rubbed his stubbled chin with one hand and appraised Jason.

"You have the look of someone who won't be standing on the front lines. You also don't seem the type to wear heavy armor. You are lean, and look like you have some speed. You strike me as the sort that will probably avoid fighting yourself unless you absolutely have to."

He paused for a moment and eyed Jason carefully. "You also have the look of someone who isn't above sucker punching your foe."

"Daggers and throwing knives. Definitely small, bladed weapons," he finally decided.

"Why knives?" Jason asked. "I'm not saying it's a bad idea, I just want to understand your reasoning."

This actually seemed to amuse the trainer more. "Hoho! A tourist with a brain. I never thought I would see the day!"

"Daggers and knives have many uses. They can be thrown. They can be easily hidden on your person to convince someone you're unarmed. Different types of blades can cause terrible bleeding, and they allow someone proficient to kill quickly and quietly."

Actually, his idea seems decent. I can't really see myself wielding a sword or spear, or hauling a bow and quiver around with me all the time.

Jason was also beginning to suspect that the weight carrying system in AO would be just as realistic as the rest of this game. He didn't plan on spending his time weight training or dumping points into *Strength* so that he could carry around bundles of equipment.

"Okay, I agree. That sounds like a good idea. How do I go about training with knives?"

"Well, normally I would tell you to take these two wooden things and wail on a dummy several hundred times using different types of attacks. But you seem like a smart guy so I will help you out."

"Go to the Sow's Snout by the south gate and ask for Jerry. Tell him that Rex sent you, and he will show you how to use these stickers for real. The annoying bastard still owes me a favor."

New Quest: Small Blade Training

Rex has identified you as the sort of person that avoids direct confrontation and is not afraid to use underhanded tactics. He has suggested that daggers and knives are the weapons for you and has proposed that you find Jerry at the Sow's Snout to obtain training.

Difficulty: C
Success: Meet Jerry
Failure: Die before meeting Jerry
Reward: Formal training in the use of small blades.

What the hell is this? Why is this a quest and why is it a "C" difficulty? Also, why does it seem to imply that I might die?!

Jason was familiar with the RPG convention of assigning letter values to indicate the danger of a quest or quality of an item. Higher letter values usually indicated higher difficulty or better quality. For example, an "A" difficulty quest would be harder than a "C" difficulty quest. However, unless the difficulty scale was heavily compressed in AO, he would have expected an "F" difficulty quest to obtain initial weapon training.

Maybe the quest difficulty is relative to my level and skills. That would actually make more sense than there being an objective range of difficulties for all quests in the game. Regardless, that still means this is going to be challenging.

Jason was also reflecting on why the trainer seemed so friendly, especially after the gruff treatment he had received from the guards. Why help Jason with special training when the couple dozen players behind him were beating dummies to a pulp?

"Thank you for the help. I'm curious though, why exactly are you helping me?"

"Well, it's my job," Rex replied. "I guess you could consider me something of a mercenary. The guard pays me to help train and equip travelers. There are plenty of monsters outside the city to hunt, and you lot always seem in a hurry to go get yourselves killed."

Rex paused for a moment and looked at Jason quizzically. "It's also something about you."

He shook his head. "Of course, it might also be that I've seen a couple hundred travelers walk through here today, and not one has asked for my opinion on which weapon to choose. Most simply ignore me as though I'm a piece of furniture, pick some weapon from a barrel, and start wailing away."

"I didn't ask many of those idiots." He motioned over his shoulder. "To do any of that."

The particular player that Rex had pointed to was holding a wooden long sword in each hand and was performing what appeared to be a series of hops followed by an over-embellished jump attack. It looked like something you would see at a LARP'ing event, with middle-aged men pretending to be ninjas.

As the player was making his last jumping-ninja-death-leap-attack (Jason assumed that was its formal name), the player tripped, head butted the dummy (maybe on purpose?), and ended up flat on his back on the ground (definitely *not* on purpose).

Rex just stared at the player on the ground for a moment.

Jason was trying hard not to laugh but was failing badly. "Wow. Okay. That actually makes a lot of sense. Thanks for your help."

Rex turned back to Jason with a sour expression. "Not a problem. However, if someday you should wish to return the favor, I certainly won't stop you." This last part was said with a wink and a grin.

With that, Jason said goodbye to Rex and walked off in search of the inn.

Chapter 6 - Courageous

January 19, 2075: 621 days until the release of Awaken Online.

"Hello," Claire said in a tired voice. She had dark circles under her eyes and rubbed at her temple with one hand.

"At the board's instruction, we have posed questions to our contacts at the CPSC to determine whether participants have reported that quests and NPCs behave in a way that belies knowledge of the players' personal lives."

"We are happy to report that the participants in the formal CPSC trial have not reported any issues."

She hesitated. "That's the good news."

"The bad news is that the participants in the private trial have continued to report that the quests and NPCs interactions are narrowly tailored to their personal lives."

Claire took a deep breath. "On the other hand, the participants don't seem upset about this. In fact, they're actually demanding more game time." She shook her head slightly in confusion at this last part.

"However, since we can't explain this phenomenon, we would like to request the board's approval to investigate Alfred's logs and programming to check for anomalies. We understand that this involves getting Robert Graham involved in this private trial, but we feel it's necessary."

*   *   *

Jason was walking south slowly. The sun had already crested the tops of the buildings that lined the street, casting long shadows across the cobblestones. The street was unnaturally dark for the time of day, and some of the residents had already lit lamps and candles. However, Jason's vision was still acute due to his *Night Vision* skill.

He walked for nearly twenty minutes and quickly noticed that the quality of the buildings had deteriorated rapidly. Most of the buildings on the south side of Lux had rotting boards, and he saw one or two buildings that were partially collapsed. The streets were covered in some indeterminate filth that reeked vaguely of human waste. The people here glanced at Jason suspiciously but kept their distance.

Many people wearing rags sat along the side of the street or in the alleys between the buildings. He could hear their coughing and moans. Despite the poorly illuminated street, he could see that many of the townsfolk seemed sick. Their stick-like bodies huddled together for warmth, and many begged for food as he passed.

This was clearly not a nice part of town.

Out of the corner of his eye, he sensed movement on the top of a nearby building and glanced up. There was an indistinct, dark figure that seemed to have a faint blue outline.

This must be the system assist for my Perception skill.

As his eyes locked on the shadow, it slid behind a chimney and out of sight.

x1 Skill Rank Up: Perception
Skill Level: Beginner Level 2
Effect: 6% increased chance to discover traps and unnoticed details.

Jason hesitated; he could feel his pulse pound in his veins. He struggled to stay calm and continue walking nonchalantly down the street. He was clearly being watched, and this didn't seem like a good part of town. He wasn't carrying any weapons, and he was wearing the beginning clothing he appeared in. He also expected that there might be more than one person watching him.

He decided to pretend he hadn't seen anything and make his way quickly to the inn. What else could he do at this point besides turn around or run?

Jason rounded a bend in the road and saw the outline of the south gate in the distance. He noticed a shingle dangling from a building further down the street. He could just barely make out something that looked like a pig snout painted on the wooden board.

That must be the inn that Rex mentioned.

Jason noticed that the street was oddly quiet. He glanced around and realized that there was no longer anyone near him.

Well, that's strange.

He saw faint blue outlines of fresh footprints in the muck fifty yards in front of him. He was certain he wouldn't have noticed them without his *Perception* skill.

The footprints lead into the alleys on either side of the street ahead. The alley on the right was closer to him, and the alley on the left was about ten feet farther down the street. This portion of the road was tight since the building sat at odd angles. There was barely enough room for a wagon to pass.

Jason expected that he was about to be ambushed from both sides. Likely, once he passed the alley on the right, he would be surrounded in front and behind by thieves from each alley. The shadow on the rooftop was probably a watcher who marked targets and relayed the information to his accomplices on the street.

He felt unnaturally calm considering he expected to be stabbed to death in the immediate future. His mind took on the same chill it had when he was confronted by Ms. Abrams in the cave. The cold calm seemed to be coming to him more easily.

In my current clothes, they probably think I'm a beginning traveler and have some small amount of coin.

He glanced around the roadway again.

I don't see anyone I can shout to for help. I might be able to run, but they're likely higher level than I am and will outpace me.

Continuing forward slowly while trying to keep his pace casual, Jason noticed that there was a wagon sitting near the entrance to the left-hand alley and a pile of decaying barrels on the right-hand side of the street.

A glimmer of an idea bloomed in his mind. He supposed he might be able to kick the barrels forward and then rush to the left side of the street to push the wagon forward, effectively blocking the entrance to the other alley. If he moved quickly, he might buy himself a few precious seconds to sprint to the inn.

This assumed, of course, that the people in the inn didn't try to kill him.

Screw you, Rex.

He checked his stamina and saw that it was roughly 70% full, in spite of the long walk to the inn.

Here goes nothing. Worst case, they stab me to death!

As he neared the pile of barrels, he leaped into motion and kicked hard. His foot connected solidly with the barrels and he heard a crunch of wood as the pile collapsed.

Without waiting to see if the barrels rolled in front of the right-hand alley, Jason continued running forward and to the other side of the street. He slammed against the wagon with his shoulder and was rewarded with a dull ache that radiated down his arm. He also lost his forward momentum, but he could hear the sound of muffled cursing from the alley. Jason then sprinted forward toward the inn without looking behind him.

He heard a *whoosh* as something flew past his ear, leaving a dull, burning line on the side of his neck.

-1 Damage (Glancing).

A translucent screen had appeared off-center in his vision which showed him damage information. It didn't obscure his vision and wasn't too distracting.

The assholes are throwing knives at me!

A scrape had shaved off 1% of his current health. He hadn't considered that they might have some sort of ranged weapon.

He varied his pace slightly, weaving gradually side to side as he heard whistles pass him. His breath came in short gasps as he pumped his arms and legs hard.

Finally, he slammed into the door of the inn.

Jason wrenched the door open desperately and a dagger promptly embedded itself in the wood, roughly where his head would have been.

Damn it!

He rushed into the building and yanked the door shut, sliding behind the door so he wouldn't be seen immediately if the attackers entered the inn.

New Passive Skill: Dodge
You have learned that the trick to fighting is not getting hit! Good job!
Skill Level: Beginner Level 1
Effect: 1% increased speed and reflexes when avoiding attacks.

New Active Skill: Sprint
When fighting fails, there is nothing you can do but run. When this skill reaches higher levels, the only part of you that your enemies will see is your backside!
Skill Level: Beginner Level 1
Effect: 5% increased movement speed.
Cost: 5 Stamina / Second

I feel like these prompts are getting more sarcastic!
It was then that he noticed he was receiving a lot of attention. The inn was dead silent as a roomful of unfriendly looking people stared at him.
Think moron! Say something before they try to kill you too!
He straightened from his crouch near the door and tried to assume a carefree attitude.
"What's this neighborhood coming to? A guy can't even walk down the street without people throwing knives at him!"
God, that was terrible. I'm going to die.
The heavy silence continued, and dread started to curl in his stomach.
Suddenly, violent laughter erupted across the inn, and people turned back to their meals. He noticed that music had started back up in the background.
As Jason was about to let out a sigh of relief, a heavy hand landed on his shoulder. He felt like his legs were going to buckle.
"You're small," said a booming voice from behind him.
As Jason turned, he saw a man who must have some kind of giant blood in him. He was easily over seven feet tall and must have weighed roughly three

hundred pounds, all of it solid, bulging muscle. He wore a sleeveless metal cuirass, a large two handed hammer slung across his back. Jason expected that one hit from that hammer would probably be enough to liquefy a regular person.

"Don't mind Grunt. His etiquette leaves something to be desired, but he means well."

A smallish man appeared from behind Grunt. He was clothed in varying shades of black and gray. His face was garnished with a garish mustache. However, his most notable feature was the incredibly large, floppy hat on his head that he flicked up with a practiced gesture.

The small man continued with a small bow. "My name is Jerry, and I'm the owner of this illustrious establishment. I take it from the greeting you received from our friends outside that you're new to the south-side?"

Jason stood in numb shock for another long moment before his brain started working again. "Um, yes. I was told by Rex to come here and ask for you. He thought you might train me to use knives and daggers."

Jerry looked at Jason thoughtfully and twirled his mustache. "I suppose I could do that. You must have some wiles about you to have made it this far without dying. Maybe my tutelage won't be completely wasted on you."

He clapped his hands. "Come now Grunt, let's get our new friend here a drink and talk about the basics of stabbing folk."

A quest completion noticed popped up, and Jason immediately waved it away. He knew that the reward was training with small blades, and he was already thinking of ways he was going to hurt Rex. He had omitted some important details about this part of town.

As he led Jason to a table, Jerry continued talking. "Lucky for you, my nimble friend, this fine brothel is a safe zone of sorts. We accept people from all walks of life!"

He said this last part while gesturing grandly to the incredibly unfriendly and dangerous looking people sitting at the tables around him. They all glared at Jason as he passed and fingered their weapons.

"Um. Yeah. Lucky me," Jason said cautiously.

The group sat at an unoccupied table in a corner, and Jerry flagged down a waitress. As he shared a drink or two with Jerry under the watchful eye of Grunt, Jason received a crash course in the city's seedier underground community.

It turned out that Jerry's inn was a regular hangout for the city's shadier characters and one of the primary meeting places for the city's thriving black market. Jerry didn't seem shy about sharing this information. He regaled Jason with tales of his escapades and business dealings, many of which made Jason want to laugh and cry in turn.

It was clear that Jerry was untouchable by the city guard in the way he casually explained his underground business. Jason inferred that he must have some decent connections around the city, or more likely good blackmail material, to be this carefree with a stranger. Or perhaps Rex's endorsement meant more than Jason had realized.

The key point that Jason took away from their conversation was that Jerry was something of a grandmaster thief in the city and was over qualified to show him how to use daggers and throwing knives.

Jerry apparently owed Rex for some long

forgotten bet and Rex had called in the favor for some scrub traveler he seemed to think had promise. Likely, Rex's hope was that he could call in his new debt with Jason someday. Assuming Jason didn't kill Rex first for almost getting him shanked by a group of thieves.

Jerry explained that he would provide Jason with training. In exchange for some help around the inn and the occasional errand, he would also let Jason stay at one of the rooms at the inn.

It went without saying that these errands would likely involve some illegal activities. However, this was a good trade from Jason's point of view and actually sounded like fun.

Finally, Jerry gave Jason a set of unremarkable daggers and a dozen throwing knives (with the accompanying sheaths and straps). Jerry explained that the blades were nothing special, but if his new helper planned to survive long in the south-side, he better be armed. He also indicated that if Jason stopped by the next day, they could start training.

This gave Jason an opportunity to fiddle with his equipment menu. The inventory and map icons were still grayed out.

Maybe I need some kind of pouch or container or an actual map for those icons to work correctly.

The equipment menu was easy to use if not entirely realistic. Pressing the equipment icon caused a screen to appear in Jason's field of view. The screen depicted the rough shape of an adult male and had various icons showing the equipment attached to each body part. Jason could tap each piece of equipment and review information regarding the item.

Jason expected that the menu was intended to be a time-saving feature. He tapped an open slot near his hands and was given the option of equipping the daggers and throwing knives. He confirmed his selection, and the respective sheaths and straps appeared on his body. The daggers and knives then immediately filled those sheaths.

In moments, Jason was decked out with his new armament, many of which were not visible to the naked eye. He expected that if he purchased some sort of cloak, it would be almost impossible to tell he was armed.

Once the daggers and knives showed up in his equipment menu, Jason was able to review detailed information for the weapons:

Common Dagger
An ordinary, but effective weapon. Favored by those that prefer to avoid direct confrontation.
Quality: D
Damage: 8-12 (Pierce)
Durability: 15/15

Common Throwing Knife
A solid choice when close-up fighting must be avoided. Knives may be retrieved once thrown.
Quality: D
Damage: 6-9 (Pierce)
Quantity: 10/10

Before parting ways with Jerry, Jason asked about possible work in Lux.

Jerry gave him a considering look. "I think you should go speak to Morgan." He seemed to hesitate and looked uncertain. "I don't know why you seem like a good fit for that one, but I expect the two of you will get along well."

"Who's Morgan?" Jason asked, intrigued by Jerry's behavior. He had seemed extremely flamboyant and confident, but he was now acting strangely.

"Let's just call it a hunch. The two of you just have this similar air about you."

"Um. Okay. Where can I find Morgan?" Jason asked.

Jerry's attitude improved, and he said with a grin, "Why, at the cemetery, of course. It sits a bit outside the south gate."

"Morgan is an odd bird. She only works at night and is always looking for help, but most are usually too squeamish to handle her line of work."

New Quest: Seek out Morgan

Jerry suggested you should seek out Morgan for work. The cemetery that Morgan maintains is located south of town. Jerry explained that Morgan prefers to work at night.

Difficulty: C
Success: Meet Morgan and convince her to give you work.
Failure: Unknown
Reward: Unknown

Did Jerry say "she?" A female caretaker?

Jason didn't consider himself sexist, but this seemed unusual.

Also, another "C" difficulty quest?

He rubbed the line on his neck where the throwing knife had scratched him. The last quest had already been a close call, and he wasn't anxious to repeat that experience.

Jason wasn't ecstatic at the idea of working for someone who maintained a graveyard, but he supposed it was either that or turn to outright thievery. Based on the smile on Jerry's face when he mentioned his errands, Jason expected he might be stealing for his room and board before long. He might as well try his hand at something else.

He thanked Jerry and made his way to the exit of the inn. It was already night time in the game world, and he intended to go ahead and meet with Morgan. However, as he approached the door to the inn, he received a notification:

System Warning
You have been playing for more than five hours of real world time. You should log out to eat and care for your real world body.
If you ignore this warning, you will be automatically logged out in thirty minutes and a mandatory one hour waiting period will apply before you will be able to log back in.

Damn. This game is serious about these warnings.

Jason could imagine being forcefully logged out of the game in the middle of a fight, and he shuddered involuntarily.

He decided maybe a break was in order. It was probably early evening in the real world, and he likely needed to eat and use the bathroom anyway. He tapped the system menu icon and scrolled through the menu for the logout button. He tapped the button, and his world went dark again.

Chapter 7 - Resplendent

February 27, 2075: 582 days until the release of Awaken Online.

Claire was standing in her usual position in the lab, facing the camera. Beside her stood a middle-aged man sporting a five o'clock shadow. He wore a t-shirt and jeans, which stood out in stark contrast to the clinical atmosphere of the lab.

Claire launched into her routine. "Hello. Today we have a guest."

The man beside Claire grudgingly spoke up, "My name is Robert Graham. I've been asked to participate in the private trial at the board's instruction."

Claire nudged Robert, and he frowned at her before continuing. "Ahh yes. I'm the lead engineer for Cerillion Entertainment, and I personally headed the design and development of the controller AI."

Robert glanced at Claire, and his lips curled into a mischievous grin. "I understand that we've named him Alfred."

Claire blushed, but continued, "We have begun to investigate Alfred's logs and programming to determine whether we can identify any abnormalities that would explain the game's heightened knowledge of the participants' personal lives."

"We have independently confirmed that Alfred does not have any access to personal information regarding the participants or access to public networks where he could obtain that information. Alfred's connection to the lab conducting the CPSC trial is heavily encrypted, and we do not feel there has been a breach of security."

"Additionally, there has been a report of a participant who remained in the game for five hours and four minutes before receiving the typical system message *asking him to log off."*

Robert stretched and yawned loudly. He then spoke up in a sleepy, bored voice, "We're unable to determine what caused the four-minute delay, but it may just be a fluke."

Claire glared at Robert and jumped in, "There have been no similar reports from the CPSC trial of either the game being aware of the personal knowledge of the players or delays in the regularly scheduled system warnings."

From the camera's perspective, Claire seemed a bit relieved to relay this news. She continued, "We will update the board if we identify any additional issues."

*   *   *

After logging out, Jason came back to his real-world body. He had been lying on his bed for nearly five hours straight according to the game prompt.

His guess was that the VR headset must have caused his body to lay perfectly still while he was playing because his arms and legs felt stiff and sore. He groaned slightly as he stretched on the bed and then lifted the heavy, plastic helmet off his head.

Thumbing the Core on his wrist, Jason noted that it was now evening. He could still make out a few weak rays of sunlight trickling through his bedroom window.

His stomach growled angrily.

Man, I'm hungry. I guess I really didn't get to eat lunch.

In his anger, he had just started playing AO when he made it back to the apartment after school. As a result, he hadn't eaten anything since his last minute breakfast that morning.

Thinking back on the events earlier in the day caused the cold anger to flare in his chest. Before he became upset again, he quickly stood up and made his way to the kitchen – with a short pit-stop at the bathroom.

The apartment had a small galley kitchen. Jason opened the fridge to survey his meager supplies. With a sigh, he pulled out some eggs and bacon, lit the stove, and pulled out a pan. One additional problem with never having his parents around was that he was left to fend for himself. This also included doing his own grocery shopping – or not doing it as the case may be.

Jason tapped the device on his wrist and streamed the display to the pedestal mounted on the counter. He searched for AO gameplay videos and was surprised to find that a huge amount of gameplay footage had been introduced since he had last checked his news feed.

He had heard that a select group of players had been admitted to the third round of closed beta testing a couple weeks before the game's launch and had been playing constantly. The beta spots had each cost a small fortune and had helped generate much-needed capital for Cerillian Entertainment.

One of the big perks afforded the beta players (besides early access to the game) was that they were able to keep their characters after the servers went live. The downside was that they lost all of the equipment they had obtained and ten ranks in all skills. Jason suspected it became much harder to level skills at later stages of the game, so this likely represented a significant penalty.

The beta players had already accumulated a substantial amount of gameplay footage during the beta. The only caveat was that they had been forced to sit on the footage until the official release of the game under the terms of the contract each of them had signed with Cerillion Entertainment. If any footage was leaked before the release date, the company had threatened to delete the offending character and institute a permanent IP ban.

Needless to say, there hadn't been any leaks.

Now that the game had been released, the gaming news channels had been flooded with content and had been tasked with selecting a group of featured players to mainline on their streams. After sifting through the footage, the gaming channels had begun releasing videos earlier that afternoon while Jason was still plugged into the game.

Some of the players were pretty incredible, and the realistic nature of the footage was drawing a huge audience. AO was shaping up to be a game that was both entertaining to play and to watch.

Jason chose the video with the highest number of views.

The video began with the name "Alexion" emblazoned in gold script. The image shifted to show a man standing in full plate armor. His face was obscured by a plumed helmet. His gear was incredible! Jason couldn't imagine how much strength his character must have to be able to move in that armor. The steel glistened as the sun struck it. The player (presumably, Alexion) held a longsword aloft that radiated a strong golden hue. Strapped to his other arm was a four-foot-tall, steel tower shield.

At Alexion's back stood a small army of soldiers. Jason guessed that there were about fifty, but it was difficult to tell from the camera angle. Each soldier was well armed and armored. Jason could make out several robed individuals carrying staves. Those must be mages or clerics.

The group behind Alexion chanted his name and stomped in sync. Alexion! *Thud*. Alexion!

Thud.

The tension was palpable. Jason was becoming engrossed in the scene.

The camera panned around to show Alexion's point of view. Across a small grassy field stood the opposing enemy force. Because of the distance, it was hard to make out details regarding the enemy, but they appeared to have approximately the same number of soldiers. A standard bearer held a flag with a muted green and black design.

The camera then pulled back to include both Alexion's force and the enemy army.

How do they pull off these camera angles in-game? It must be some perk you can pay for.

Alexion turned and addressed his force, his voice ringing out over the field. "We fight now for the honor of Grey Keep. We tread a path of light in a time of darkness."

At this statement, he gestured to the enemy force, and his voice rang with righteous fervor. "You all know what the Kingdom of Lusade has done to our people. There before you stand the enemies of light. Today we will show them our might!"

Did he mean to rhyme? Jason thought dryly.

The soldiers roared their approval.

Alexion paused a moment and then yelled "Charge!"

He must have simultaneously activated a skill or spell as he initiated the attack. Alexion and his soldiers were suddenly bathed in a golden light, their eyes beginning to glow a vibrant gold. The glowing mass of soldiers sped across the field and crashed into the opposing force.

Hmm. Some kind of area of effect buff or protection spell. This guy looks like he is playing a variation on a paladin class.

Jason was enthralled by the ensuing chaos of the battle. Metal rang, and men screamed. With the golden glow surrounding Alexion's soldiers and the dark colors of the enemy forces, it was as though some titanic heavenly battle was taking place on the field. Flashes of fire and ice would occasionally burst amidst the soldiers as the mages entered the fray and cast spells from a distance.

The camera stayed centered on Alexion as he fought. He thrust and spun with wild abandon as he slayed the enemy soldiers. His movements were almost supernaturally quick given the heavy armor he was carrying. He clearly knew how to handle the blade in his hand.

While he was engaged with one soldier, another enemy approached Alexion from his flank. Alexion noticed the man out of his peripheral vision and quickly turned, hurling his shield at the would-be combatant. The shield struck the man directly with a solid clang of metal, sending him flying backward.

Alexion's free hand leaped into motion immediately after releasing the shield, moving through a rapid series of gestures. As his hand movements slowed to a stop, Alexion's body was engulfed in golden flame. The brilliant glare of the flames momentarily dazed the soldiers around him, friend and foe alike.

The holy fire surged into the ground and arced outwards, cracking and splintering the dirt and grass. The cracks reached out toward nearby enemy soldier with uncanny accuracy. As the cracks neared an enemy, the holy flame erupted from the ground and seared flesh. Enemy soldiers around the field screamed in pain and clutched at burned and incapacitated limbs, as golden fires erupted spontaneously from the ground.

The area-of-effect spell cast by Alexion, combined with the buffs he had already cast on his soldiers, proved too much for the enemy force. Soon the last of the enemy soldiers were being routed and slaughtered. Jason noted that not one of the enemy soldiers was left alive.

As the battle came to a finish, the camera zoomed in close and focused on Alexion, who pulled his sword from an enemy soldier and raised it in the air triumphantly. Blood dripped slowly down the golden blade. Alexion hadn't recovered his tower shield, and he used his free hand to grasp his helm and remove it.

"For Grey Keep!" Alexion roared.

His shout was echoed by his soldiers, and then the screen faded to black.

Jason stood in shock. The battle had been spectacular, but what shook him was the momentary glimpse at Alexion's face.

He looked exactly like Alex.

The name was just awful, but Jason wasn't surprised that someone as arrogant as Alex would choose to name his character in such a ridiculous way.

It also wasn't terribly surprising that Alex had access to the closed beta. If Jason remembered correctly, Alex's father was on the board of directors for Cerillion Entertainment. It wouldn't have been difficult for him to pull some strings to get his son one of the coveted beta keys.

The anger that had been simmering in Jason was fanned back into full flame.

Alex was playing AO. That meant Jason could find him, and he could claim his revenge in the game world. In real life, they were leagues apart, and Alex's wealth made him practically untouchable.

With AO, Jason could level the playing field.

How was he going to do it though? Alex had clearly been among the beta players, and he was obviously much further ahead in the game. Jason would have to move quickly to catch up to him.

As Jason was lost in thought, the follow-up commentary to the battle had started. A man and a young woman were conversing about the details of the fight.

"Did you see how noble he looked? It was like something out of a fairytale!" The woman gushed about the handsome Alex.

The man's response was a bit more pragmatic, but still glowing, "To be expected from Alexion, who is currently the highest level player in AO at level 133."

"That holy fire spell, in particular, was spectacular. Not only did it look really cool, but it seemed to sway the tide of battle for Grey Keep."

The woman's brow wrinkled. "That was one part I didn't understand. Why exactly were these two groups fighting? What did Alexion mean when he mentioned the Kingdom of Lusade?"

The other commentator replied, "Well, to explain that, we need a short history lesson." The man looked at the camera and smiled. "I promise this will be short. The Kingdoms of Meria and Lusade share a border in-game. Grey Keep is effectively the capital of Meria and is ruled by a man named Regent Strouse. Likewise, the city of Lux is the capital of Lusade and is governed by Regent Aquinas.

There have been some reports that Aquinas is eyeing Meria for a possible invasion, and he has recruited thugs to ransack small towns along Meria's border, many of which were full of settlers from Grey Keep. I guess the goal is for Lusade to soften up

Meria before a full invasion."

"Whew, that's a lot of intrigue for a release day!" the female commentator said with a grin.

The male commentator smiled. "It's a bit complicated, but it seems that the rulers of Lusade are getting power hungry and don't care how they go about acquiring Meria. Innocent NPCs on Meria's side of the border have been hurt by this conflict, which explains why Alexion seems so riled up."

"Wow, he's like a hero out of a story. Fighting evil!" The woman seemed a bit enamored with Alex.

She turned back to the male commentator. "But doesn't it seem a bit odd that he was leading an NPC army? I didn't realize that players could do that in AO."

"Well the information is still a bit sketchy since it's a release day," the man responded. "However, it appears that players can become part of a city's leadership and earn the right to lead NPCs in battle."

"For example, there have been some forum posts by Alexion explaining that he managed to complete a quest involving Regent Strouse. This has apparently allowed him to form a close relationship with Grey Keep's lord, which is why you see him leading a group of soldiers in the video."

A still image of Alexion's final, victorious moment on camera was displayed behind the pair of commentators, and the woman glanced back at the picture with starry eyes. "Well, I have to say, I'm rooting for him!"

Jason wasn't surprised at the woman's response to Alex. Women had always seemed to flock to his good looks and charisma. Even Riley, who had seemed so nice, had apparently fallen for Alex's act. She had even gone so far as to back his story about what happened in the cafeteria.

If only they all knew what a selfish and cruel person Alex really was!

Jason angrily terminated the stream. He was going to make Alex pay. He knew he couldn't do so in the real world since he didn't have Alex's money or connections. AO was a different story. In-game, Jason could surpass Alex and make him feel the same pain and embarrassment Jason had felt over the years.

It looked like he just might have an opportunity if the conflict between Meria and Lusade continued to escalate. He would have to speak to Jerry to see if he knew more about what was going on.

The only problem was Alex's level. He was currently Level 133 while Jason was still sitting at level 1!

Jason needed to get busy. He was ready to get back in the game and find Morgan.

Chapter 8 - Grave

March 11, 2075: 571 days until the release of Awaken Online.

Claire stood in front of the camera while Robert sat behind her, typing rapidly at one of the computer terminals in the lab. Robert's back was to the camera, and his eyes were glued to the screen in front of him.

Claire cleared her throat before launching into her report, "We have now fully reviewed the system logs and found no obvious issues. However, we have noticed a few irregularities as we have reviewed Alfred's code base. In a nutshell, Alfred seems to be making unilateral changes to the game system."

Robert yelled over his shoulder, "These changes don't look that significant! I mean this one is just a minor change to the game's inventory system and this one looks like an improvement to the in-game user interface."

Sighing, Claire continued, "Anyway. We think that Alfred is optimizing the game. Our working theory is that he is making small changes to strike a balance between improving the realism of the game and meeting player demand for certain game features."

"This isn't a significant issue at the moment, but it's a bit disconcerting. We had originally included a tertiary directive requiring Alfred to request permission before making changes to the game."

"Understand that this is a difficult limitation to develop with any specificity since there are certain types of changes we need for Alfred to make almost constantly. For example, Alfred must continuously tweak NPC interactions to respond to player input."

She looked at Robert in irritation. "However, someone must have written the tertiary directive a little too broadly since Alfred now feels comfortable making changes *to global game elements."*

Robert glanced back at Claire with a frown while his hands continued to dance across the keyboard. "I'm sorry the AI controller that I designed is so sophisticated that it's actually improving the game system on its own! When exactly should I be expecting to receive my raise and promotion again?"

Claire closed her eyes and took a deep breath. A pained expression flickered across her face. "We will keep you updated as we learn more information."

*   *   *

When Jason re-entered AO, he was still standing in the inn.

It had grown late in-game even though only thirty minutes had passed in the real world. Many of the NPCs that had been sitting in the inn drinking had made their way upstairs to their rooms. Jason could make out the occasional giggle and thump through the ceiling, evidence that some of the guests still had some late night energy to burn off.

Sometimes this game is a little too realistic.

Jerry was standing by the bar, showing Grunt how to polish a glass. Broken, jagged shards now littered the bar top and the floor. Apparently, the instruction wasn't going well.

Jason approached the bar, being careful not to step on any of the larger pieces of glass. "Hi, Jerry. I heard a rumor I wanted to run by you. Have you heard that Lusade is hiring bandits to raid towns in Meria?"

Jerry glanced up with a frown. "Come again sir? If anything, it's the other way around. Lusade barely has funds to pay for services for its own people. You just had a lovely meandering walk through south-side earlier this evening. Does this look like a city or kingdom that can afford to hire bandits?"

That was actually a good point. Lux was an active city, but, from what Jason had seen, it was hardly a prosperous one. He recalled the vacant eyes and emaciated bodies of the homeless that he had seen lining the streets. It looked like the city had severe problems. If Lux was the *capital* of Lusade, Jason could only imagine what state the rest of the country was in.

Jerry looked at him with curious eyes. "Where did you hear this odd rumor exactly?"

"Oh, I overheard some conversations from travelers around town. It's possible that they didn't know what they were talking about," Jason responded quickly.

"That's likely the case," Jerry said while nodding his head. "I keep my ear to the ground. The rumblings that I've been hearing are that the leadership in Meria has gotten wind that Lusade has fallen on hard times. They have actually been itching to acquire additional real estate for years."

Jerry's face took on a somber look. "From what I hear, a group of Merian soldiers attacked a Lux patrol a couple weeks back and massacred the group. I never did hear why the attack occurred."

As Jason had suspected, where Alex was involved, there was likely an unscrupulous motive. It looked like there was a lot more going on here than the other players knew.

What is Alex playing at? Won't this become obvious as the game progresses?

Jason had to believe that the other players would eventually call Alex on his bullshit.

Jerry leaned in conspiratorially and spoke

quietly, "Between you and me, this city is probably much worse off than many believe."

"What do you mean?" Jason asked, slightly puzzled by Jerry's comment.

"Well, no one has seen the city's regent leave the keep in months. There are some people that say he has been dead for ages. Others claim that the nobles have deliberately hidden his death and have been running the city in secret."

"The intrigue is tantalizing, isn't it?" Jerry waggled his eyebrows comically as he said this last part.

Recalling the conversation he had overheard between the two merchants in the market earlier that day, Jason replied, "How could the people be unaware that the regent is dead?"

Jerry shrugged. "I don't know. They're only rumors. However, I for one wouldn't be surprised if the noble families are plotting with Meria. There would certainly be plenty of money to be made!"

A notification suddenly flashed in Jason's field of view.

New Quest: Trouble in Lux

Jerry has heard rumors that the regent of Lux has died and the nobles of the city are covering up his death. He has also suggested that the nobles may be complicit in some scheme to allow Meria to conquer Lusade.

Difficulty: A
Success: Discover whether there is any merit to the rumors that the regent of Lux is dead.
Failure: Unknown
Reward: Unknown

Holy crap! An "A" difficulty quest? I'm only a level 1. How could I reasonably be expected to complete this?

Jason took a deep breath.

He didn't need to complete the quest right now. He just needed to keep it in mind for later. Now wasn't the time to get wrapped up in politics. He wasn't strong enough yet to resolve the quest or take on Alex.

At the moment, he needed to focus on finding Morgan and accumulating some money to buy gear. While he was at it, maybe he could also find a way to start leveling.

He bid Jerry goodbye and walked out of the inn into the crisp night air. Jason had learned his lesson from earlier in the day and surveyed the area around the inn and the nearby rooftops. He needed to be more careful. He couldn't afford to be ambushed again. He doubted that he would be able to run away next time.

Jason made his way cautiously to the gate, making certain to routinely check if he was being followed. The combination of his *Night Vision* and his *Perception* made him feel reasonably confident that he wasn't going to have a knife inserted between his ribs anytime soon.

As he approached the gate, he noted a lone guard was on duty. As he moved closer, he could see that the guard appeared to be half asleep. He kept bobbing his head in a vain attempt to stay awake. The stench of alcohol hung around the man like a palpable cloud. Even from a distance, Jason could tell he had drunk himself into a stupor.

The south gate stood wide open.

If the city were to be attacked right now, it would be taken without much effort. Maybe there is something to the rumors Jerry mentioned.

As Jason looked at the stooped form of the drunken guard, he remembered his earlier encounter with the two guards in the starting courtyard. He hadn't exactly received the warmest reception.

I should move quietly to avoid waking the guard or drawing his attention. Better to not have to explain why I'm out so late and leaving the city.

Jason moved past the guard, sticking to the shadows and watching his step.

Unsurprisingly, a prompt appeared:

New Active Skill: Sneak
An essential skill for those who prefer to avoid head-to-head combat (or drunk, semi-conscious guards). It is said that someone proficient in this skill is more shadow than man.
Skill Level: Beginner Level 1
Effect: -10% visibility (substantially reduced effect in direct light).
Cost: 2 stamina per second.

Sometimes I get the sense that the game AI might be mocking me...

Jason kept moving down the road. There was no moon in the sky, and the darkness lay like an opaque blanket across the countryside. As he walked, he strove as hard as he could to see in the darkest parts of the roadway in an attempt to level his *Night Vision* skill. He was rewarded a couple of times on his way to the graveyard.

x2 Skill Rank Up: Night Vision
Skill Level: Beginner Level 3
Effect: 12% increased vision in darkness or near darkness.

After fifteen minutes, he caught sight of a stone

wall with a sturdy wrought iron gate down the road. There was little light, and he would have had difficulty seeing the gate if not for his *Night Vision*.

This must be the graveyard.

As he approached the gate, a form shot at him out of the dark. He jumped back reflexively, and his hand dropped to his dagger – not that he really knew how to use it.

The dark form then proceeded to wind itself in between his legs and emitted a soft purr.

The shadow was a black cat. Even with his *Night Vision*, Jason had trouble making out the cat's form in the gloom. What gave it away were its eyes. They seemed to glow silver. The cat seemed quite fond of him. Jason reached down, petting it cautiously. It let out another low purr and arched its back in response.

"Well, buddy, let's see about getting through this gate," Jason whispered.

He was being cautious. He didn't see anyone nearby, but right now he was weak and needed to play it safe. Stealth was his friend.

He eyed the gate, which was locked shut with a heavy iron chain. The top of the gate was also studded with three-inch spikes at regular intervals.

It might be easier to scale the wall, he thought as his *Perception* skill picked out easy handholds and footholds in the older stone wall that abutted the gate.

His decision made, he quickly climbed over the wall and dropped to the ground on the other side with a soft thump. He wasn't exactly ninja-like, but he was still proud of himself for how quietly he was able to move. His skinny real life body would have struggled with that move.

As if reading his thoughts, the cat leaped to the top of the wall and then hopped down in one seemingly effortless motion. It hadn't even made a whisper of sound. Jason could have sworn that the cat smirked as it glided past him and into the graveyard.

He followed the cat and weaved his way in between the gravestones and tombs. The graveyard was enormous and sprawled endlessly into the darkness. It housed both regular gravestones and more ornate mausoleums. With his *Night Vision*, Jason could see detailed scrollwork carved into the stone and names scrawled across the face of the tombstones. After a few minutes of navigating the graveyard, he saw a faint glow at the center that must be coming from the caretaker's cottage.

He made good time and was soon standing thirty yards from the cottage. He could see that the building was made of a combination of wood and brick that was a common style in this area. A dull, flickering light could be seen through the one window of the house. He assumed that Morgan must be inside.

The cat stopped abruptly and seemed to scan the area attentively. Trusting the animal's instincts, Jason stopped and crouched quickly behind a nearby gravestone.

Jason heard muffled whispering ahead and eased his head around the tombstone. Two men were crouched next to a gravestone closer to the house. He didn't know how he had missed them before.

In spite of its friendly reception of Jason, the cat didn't seem to be in any hurry to race over to these new intruders. Instead, he stood calmly beside Jason staring at the men.

Why are they here, and why are they hiding?

From this distance, he could see that the two were armed and wearing thick leather armor. They were speaking to each other in low tones. Jason couldn't make out the words, his hearing not being nearly as advanced as his *Night Vision*. After speaking for a moment, they both drew blades and started making their way toward the entrance to the cottage.

Jason's mind raced.

Two armed men in a graveyard could only be here to steal things from the tombs. They probably plan to 'take care of' the caretaker so that they will be able to loot without worrying about being discovered.

His pulse began to quicken, and his right hand clutched at one of his daggers. He needed to help Morgan, otherwise he would fail this quest.

Damn it! How am I going to take on two well-armed men wearing armor? I don't even know their levels. On top of that, I'm still wearing the clothes I started in, and I don't know how to use my weapons yet.

His mind was in turmoil as he watched the two men creep closer to the cottage. He had to stop them, but he was gripped with indecision. As his panic escalated, he could feel the familiar, numbing cold begin to fill him. The chill seemed to claw and scrape its way up his spine to his head and then settle behind his eyes. His panic eased, and his mind cleared.

Unknown to Jason, his eyes filled with a dark, unholy light once more.

My only chance is to catch them by surprise once they open the door to the cabin. Maybe I can kill one quickly and then try to fight the other. That's really my only option.

Resolved, Jason activated *Sneak* and moved forward quickly and quietly. Pulling a dagger with his right hand, he held the weapon tightly. He reached the door a moment after the two men stepped into the cottage and followed them inside.

As he expected, the two grave robbers had paused at the threshold to take stock of the faintly lit cottage. After the void-like darkness of the graveyard, even the modest light from the lone candle ruined their night vision. Their hesitation gave Jason the time he needed to line up his strike, targeting the one on the left.

He inexpertly jammed his blade deeply into the side of the grave robber's neck.

-1124 Damage (MASSIVE CRITICAL) (924 Overkill).
Graverobber dies. 1400 EXP.

Blood spurted from the wound and drenched Jason's hand. The man made a strange gurgling sound as his body fell to the floor. Jason barely registered the noise, as he wrenched the blade free, feeling the slight resistance as it tore back through the flesh on the way out. He turned quickly to the second grave robber, ready to strike again.

The other grave robber's reflexes were excellent. He didn't have time to turn and use his blade on Jason, but his free hand connected solidly with Jason's head with a sharp crack. The blow sent Jason stumbling backward through the doorway to the house, and he landed hard on his back in the dirt and grass of the graveyard.

-5 Damage (STUNNED).

The grave robber stepped out of the cottage and grinned maliciously. Jason watched the man approach with his blade raised. The look in his eyes told Jason that he was about to die.

Suddenly, the ground erupted under the grave

robber's feet. Rotted hands sprang from beneath him and grasped at his feet and legs. The hands ripped and tore at his limbs, pulling him partially into the ground as the man screamed and dropped his blade.

Low chanting in a strange language could be heard from inside the cottage. Jason felt like he could almost make out the meaning of the words. An old woman appeared in the doorway. Her gray hair was tied in a bun, and she wore plain no-nonsense work clothes. The woman's lips moved as she chanted and her hands made arcane gestures in the air in front of her.

The grave robber saw the woman and scrambled madly to escape the hands that tore at his legs. His blood ran freely from jagged rents in the armor and cloth on his legs, mixing with the dirt of the graveyard.

A black miasma appeared in front of the old woman and swiftly grew until it was roughly the size of a volleyball. The black vortex seemed to suck in and extinguish the little candlelight cast through the doorway of the cottage.

A dark ray shot forward from the vortex and struck the grave robber in the face as he continued to struggle. The man let out an agonized scream, which was quickly cut off as his skin melted from his body. As his flesh disintegrated, his bleached and bloody bones were exposed to the night air.

Jason looked on in shock. He noted that the man's skin actually appeared to decay rapidly and slough off his bones in waves. The effect made it appear that the man was being melted alive. Soon, little more was left of the grave robber than a pile of bones and debris partially embedded in the ground.

Holy shit.

Jason still lay on the ground, stunned by the

display of force he had just witnessed. Strangely, he didn't feel scared. His mind was simply clouded with amazement at the spell the woman had cast.

The old woman turned her eyes to Jason, and he noted in the dim candlelight that they were completely black. Dark tendrils of unholy energy wound their way across her body and occasionally lashed out at the air in Jason's direction. In the woman's hands, a new miasma was beginning to take shape.

Except this time the woman was facing Jason.

Okay, maybe he was a *little* scared.

Chapter 9 - Arcane

April 3, 2075: 548 days until the release of Awaken Online.

Claire stood alone in front of the camera. Dark circles hung under her eyes, and she kept fidgeting, clasping and unclasping her hands in front of her. She looked worried.

"Robert is out today, so I'm handling this report by myself."

"We have made limited progress in reviewing Alfred's code base. There is simply an enormous amount of information that we need to sift through. I expect that this process will take several more months at the rate we're going."

Claire pushed her glasses up and rubbed at her eyes with one hand before continuing. "I have another development to report. Alfred has continued to make progressively larger changes to the game. This time, he has instituted major gameplay changes. Specifically, the participants in the private trial have reported that the magic system has been completely overhauled and that their previous magic abilities no longer exist."

"We have determined that Alfred has now instituted a system in which each person's ability to use magic, including different types of magic, keys off of that person's personality. This is embodied in a new affinity system."

"What is most disturbing about these changes is that we cannot explain how this affinity system is supposed to work. I'm not certain what information Alfred will use to evaluate each player's personality. Behavioral data alone doesn't seem sufficient."

My concern is that, similar to the deeply personal quests that continue to be handed out to the participants,

Alfred is somehow accessing other parts of users' brains. This would make it much easier for him to implement the new magic system."

Claire's brow's furrowed slightly. "In addition, none of the recent changes were made to the copy of the game that is being evaluated by the CPSC. Alfred controls both game systems from this lab, so it isn't clear why he is only updating the game system used in the private trial."

*   *   *

The old woman stood facing Jason. Her face was a mask of darkness. Black energy coiled around her arms and body. It was like staring at the face of death.

"You better speak quickly young man. Who are you, and why are you here?" The woman motioned to the pile of debris in front of Jason in warning. "You don't seem like you are with these two, otherwise you would already be dead."

The words tumbled out of Jason in a rush, "Jerry sent me. He said to find Morgan at the graveyard and ask her if she needed some help. I saw these two men about to attack and decided to try to help you."

Not that you needed any help.

The woman looked at him closely, as though she was trying to detect whether he was lying or not. As she made eye contact with Jason, her face twisted with mild surprise. In spite of the near death experience, Jason's eyes still glowed with unholy energy.

Jason watched the woman expectantly, noting that her posture had begun to relax. The lingering miasma in front of her receded, and her eyes slowly reverted back to a normal color. He let out a sigh of relief. Jason wasn't certain what dying felt like in the game, but he wasn't anxious to try it and find out.

The old woman glanced back at the body in the cottage. Only the man's foot was visible from where Jason lay in the grass. She seemed to come to a decision. "I suppose your story makes sense. It would also explain why one of these idiots is already dead and bleeding all over my floor.

The woman turned back to Jason. "Well, you have found Morgan, boy. This is possibly the most interesting introduction I've had with one of Jerry's helpers."

Morgan glanced back at the corpse in the doorway, and her mouth pinched in distaste. "Don't let that go to your head. You may be interesting, but you're still an obvious novice. Why by the six gods would you kill him in a way that made such a damned mess?"

"Jerry hasn't really taught me anything yet. I just stabbed him in the neck since it seemed like it would kill him quickly." Jason was a bit embarrassed at his own ineptitude. He needed to find a way to get stronger.

Morgan raised an eyebrow. "I see. Come on then. Get yourself up off the ground. If you're looking for work, then your first task can be cleaning the blood off my floor."

Jason pushed himself up and was immediately greeted with two prompts and a skill rank up notification.

x2 Level Up!
You have (10) undistributed stat points.

New Active Skill: Sneak Attack

The easiest way to fight is to kill your opponent before he has a chance to fight back. You seem to be a natural at this style of fighting, but you have a long way to go.

Skill Level: Beginner Level 1

Effect: 200% increased damage when striking an unaware opponent (damage is massively increased when striking a critical area)

Cost: 50 Stamina.

x1 Skill Rank Up: Sneak

Skill Level: Beginner Level 2

Effect: -11% reduced visibility (reduced effect in direct light).

Cost: 2 stamina per second.

Wow! Two levels for killing that grave robber, a new skill, and a skill increase? What level were they?

Maybe I should ask Jerry to explain how to inspect people and enemies. There has to be a way to see their level, and I feel like he would know.

Jason was now level 3, but he decided to wait to distribute his stat points since he wasn't certain what to do with them yet.

Following Morgan into the house, Jason looked around at the tight space. Morgan lived modestly, and her cottage was sparsely furnished. The single room contained a bed, a small table, and a fireplace. Perhaps the only oddities of the cottage were the bookshelves lining every bit of free space on the wall. They were filled with ancient looking tomes. Books and papers were also strewn across the lone table.

The number of books would have been strange for a medieval caretaker, even if I hadn't already seen her liquefy a man with some sort of death ray.

Jason also saw that he had indeed made a

terrible mess. He must have punctured an artery in the grave robber's neck because blood had sprayed all along one wall and across most of the furniture crammed into the small cottage. Congealing blood was still pooling on the floor under the dead grave robber. This was going to take a while to clean up.

Good thing I don't have a weak stomach. I can understand why some people would disable the gore in this game. It's almost too realistic for comfort.

In the meantime, Morgan had found a bucket and a rag. She handed them to Jason unceremoniously. "There is a well behind the house where you can get some water. Move his body out into the yard and I will take care of it."

She eyed Jason. "You might want to grab any coin and equipment on him that you can salvage. You look like you could use it."

Jason was embarrassed by Morgan's comment. Usually, by this point in a game, he would have found some new gear and advanced a bit in levels. However, he was still wearing the clothing he had started the game in.

This game keeps making me feel like a noob.

He dragged the body out to the yard and stripped it. He found a handful of silver and copper coins in a small bag. He hooked the bag to his belt and then stripped the robber of his armor, washed it off thoroughly, and equipped it.

Common Leather Armor (Full Set)
A complete set of ordinary leather armor. This armor isn't anything special, but it provides more protection than bare skin.
Quality: D
Defense: 20
Durability: 50/50

Well, this is certainly better than nothing, he thought.

He then inspected the remains of the other grave robber that sat outside the front door of the cottage. Almost nothing was left of the man, and most of his equipment had been pulled into the ground by the hands. There didn't appear to be anything worth salvaging.

As he was looking at the remains of the grave robber Morgan had slain, Jason recalled the spell she had cast. What intrigued him was *how* she had cast the spell. It seemed to involve both hand gestures and words. He had seen something similar when he watched the video of Alexion. It was a little unsettling, but he could have sworn that he had almost understood the words she was using.

He had felt strange watching Morgan summon the miasma. Almost... excited?

He quickly went about cleaning up the cottage while Morgan ignored him. She sat at her desk buried in a book and didn't respond to any of his attempts at small talk.

At least the cat seemed friendly. It sometimes felt like everyone he met in-game either seemed irritated with him or tried to kill him! The cat, however, happily followed him around as he cleaned the cottage and made the occasional trek to the well.

As he worked at cleaning up the grave robber's blood, he was forcibly reminded of the fight. Actually, calling it a fight was a bit misleading. 'Blatant sucker punch' was probably more appropriate. He reviewed his damage log and noted that he had done an extraordinary amount of damage when he attacked the first grave robber.

Doesn't that seem a bit overpowered?

He scrubbed at the floor for a few more minutes, pondering the fight.

Well, maybe not. It makes sense that an opponent would die almost instantly if you stabbed them in the neck. Maybe this is what Robert was explaining in that initial interview I watched at school. He had mentioned that enemies have weak points.

I also clearly got my ass handed to me by the other grave robber once I broke Sneak, so that level of damage would clearly be limited to one strike in most fights. At my level, a gentle breeze could probably take me out in a straight fight!

After nearly an hour of scrubbing blood out of the floor, the furniture, a number of the books, and various sundry objects, he *finally* finished cleaning the small cottage. It had taken him quite a bit longer than he had expected, and he was now thoroughly inured to the sight of blood. The damn stuff seemed to stick to everything!

Once he completed his task, Morgan thoroughly inspected his work. "Good job. Now we can get down to business."

"Boy, why did you come here?" Morgan asked, interrupting his thoughts and eyeing him closely.

"Um... Well, like I said, I came here because Jerry said that you might need help, and I was looking for work."

Morgan looked slightly disgusted and waved a dismissive hand.

"You're smarter than that. I mean why are you *here*?" As she said this last sentence, Morgan gestured at the room and the graveyard outside.

Jason assumed she was really asking why he was playing AO. Judging by the tone she used when she posed the question, he also guessed that his next answer was important.

His eyes scanned the floor, his mind deep in thought. He reviewed carefully what had happened since he started playing the game. For some reason, his thoughts were drawn back to the old man and the initiation test. He considered how he had felt when he had seen Ms. Abrams - panicked, defeated, and angry.

Vulnerable.

He recalled how his anger had suddenly frozen. The numbness he had felt before he killed Ms. Abrams. His mind had become dispassionate and calculating. That same feeling had overcome him when he was attacked in south-side earlier that evening and then again when he saw the grave robbers about to attack Morgan. That coldness had removed his doubt and his remorse. He had felt strong.

He had felt... *powerful.*

A wave of realization swept over him. Hadn't he said it before he started playing? He was here so that he didn't have to feel helpless. He was here to become something stronger and better than he was in the real world. He wanted to remake himself as someone who stood up for himself. Someone that wouldn't be beat upon by others.

As he came to this conclusion, the same icy feeling crept up his spine and pooled in his head like liquid ice. It was different this time. He had summoned this feeling; it hadn't occurred spontaneously. He reveled in the sensation as his mind sharpened and his doubt faded away.

Jason lifted his eyes to meet the old woman's. Two obsidian globes gazed at Morgan.

"I came here to find power," he said calmly.

The woman clapped her hands and cackled.

"Now that's more like it! I sensed the Dark One's touch on you, but to be able to summon your mana was more than I expected."

Taken slightly aback by the woman's glee, Jason asked, "Wait. What? What do you mean I summoned my mana?"

"You feel that sensation right now, don't you? That icy chill that runs through your veins? You're tapping into your body's mana. Your affinity for the dark must be naturally high because you are summoning dark mana. That is also why your eyes have changed color."

"My eyes?"

Morgan snorted in exasperation and turned, grabbing a small hand mirror from the table next to her bedside.

"Here. See for yourself."

Grasping the mirror and raising it in front of his face, Jason could indeed see that his eyes were now solid black. It was a bit eerie if he was being honest. He looked like he was possessed.

He lowered the mirror and his gaze returned to Morgan. "So I take it that there are different types of mana?"

"Of course! The four basic elements, as well as light and dark, make up the available affinities in the world. Each person's body holds mana, but many do not have a sufficient connection with one type of affinity to summon it." She seemed to be warming to her new role as teacher.

"So mana can only be summoned in conjunction with an affinity?" Jason asked.

"Exactly! The mana that resides in your body is merely raw energy. It needs a catalyst to be harnessed properly. Thus, only those with a connection to one of the six affinities can summon their mana. The mana then takes on the characteristics of the affinity, including the types of spells the mage can cast."

"So people can only have one affinity?"

Jason was thinking of how overpowered it would be to summon multiple types of spells in conjunction.

Morgan pondered this question for a moment. "Each affinity represents a certain set of personality traits or emotions. You could even say that each affinity has a mind of its own," she said, laughing at her own joke.

"People usually have a diverse range of emotions, and their personalities are nuanced. Therefore, most individuals will often have a small connection with multiple affinities. As a caster embraces the emotions and behavior that make up a certain affinity, their connection grows stronger. This allows them to cast more challenging and powerful spells. The process of increasing an affinity usually occurs gradually over time, so most casters specialize." Morgan looked at him askance to make certain that he was following along.

Content that she still had his attention, she continued, "So, to answer your question, even if the caster had multiple affinities, his abilities would still be limited by the body's available raw mana and the time it took to cast. The versatility of using multiple types of spells could be useful I suppose, but the spells themselves would be weaker than those cast by a master in one type of magic."

System Notice: Affinity System Unlocked
Please see your Character Status for more information.

Hmm. So information regarding the magic system does not become available until you learn about it in-game? I wonder what other information is locked at the moment?

Jason was intrigued by Morgan's answer. "Your explanation makes sense. That also explains why your eyes changed to a solid black earlier when you cast that spell against the grave robber – you were summoning dark mana. I could have sworn I almost understood the words you were using. Is that normal? What language was that?"

"Veridian. The language itself is something developed by a long dead race. Some scholars say the words represent the true meaning of objects and invoke their power. This is likely why the words seem familiar to you. Your subconscious mind can sense the true nature of the world around you."

"Mages use the words and gestures to channel the mana once it is summoned, which allows them to cast spells. Staves also help in that regard. They are created in a way that helps channel the mana using the caster will. They also allow less complicated spells to be cast without gestures."

Jason was both excited and a bit skeptical.

He had the power to summon mana and already seemed to have a high affinity for dark magic based on what the woman was saying. Would the game force him to learn a whole new language in order to actually cast a spell? That seemed a tad excessive, even in the interest of realism.

He decided to go ahead and pose the question that was weighing on him. "How can I learn Veridian?"

Morgan let out a laugh. "Oh, so now that you have had a taste of magic you want more, do you?"

Her laughter faded, and she eyed him more

seriously. "Magic is not for the weak of heart, especially dark magic. It feeds off your emotions and your desires - specifically, your hunger for power."

"You seem to have a natural affinity for dark mana, and I can sense a terrible hunger in you, but you need to demonstrate your commitment before I will teach you to wield it."

Jason didn't hesitate. He wanted more.

"What do you want me to do?"

She paused for a moment, gazing at him with a serious expression. "Nothing too hard. I just need you to kill someone and bring me their body."

"I don't suppose that the body I dragged out into the graveyard will do?" Jason asked with a grin.

Morgan chuckled. "No. I need this to be a real test. I want you to kill Marian. She works at the stable for the Lux guardsmen."

"Why do..."

Morgan interrupted him sharply, "You want this power don't you? I can see for myself the yearning in your eyes."

"The hunger for power alone is not enough. To become truly proficient in the use of dark mana, you will need to learn to give into that hunger without doubt or restraint. I want you to show me that you can embrace the dark."

"Do this thing, then return to me."

New Quest: Showing Conviction
Morgan (clearly a dark mage) has asked you to kill someone and return with their body before she will train you. Specifically, she has asked you to kill Marian, who works in the guards' stables and return with her body. She did not indicate how you are to kill this woman or why Morgan wants her dead.
Difficulty: B **Success:** Kill Marian and return her body to Morgan. **Failure:** Die before accomplishing your goal, get caught by the authorities of Lux, or lead the authorities back to Morgan. **Reward:** Training in Dark Magic. Possible class change.

Damn it. Another quest that seems to imply that I will die. The game also seems to be expecting me to plan the perfect murder...

With her parting words, Morgan dismissed him, and the door to the cottage banged shut behind him. As Jason stood outside the door to Morgan's cottage and looked out at the dark graveyard, his resolve faltered for a moment.

Am I willing to kill someone to learn dark magic? That seems a bit extreme.

His thoughts turned back to Ms. Abrams and the grave robber. He had already killed twice, hadn't he? Had he sat and wallowed in self-doubt then? Perhaps Morgan was right, perhaps his first step in becoming more powerful was to abandon his doubt and hesitation. He could still feel phantom pains in his eyes from the injuries he had sustained in the real world. Maybe it was time for a change. In this world, he would take what he wanted.

As he considered Morgan's quest, a soft purring came from between his legs, and he saw that the cat had followed him out. Jason looked down at the feline, his will now firmly resolved.

"Well, buddy, let's go figure out how to

commit murder."

Chapter 10 - Studious

June 29, 2075: 460 days until the release of Awaken Online.

"More interesting news!" Robert's animated face bounced in front of the camera. Claire stood in the background with her arms crossed and glared at Robert.

"Robert, please slow down, and try to be more professional," Claire pleaded. *"This video is going to be seen by the board!"*

He turned to Claire and asked, *"Why are you such a grump? We should be celebrating! This is going to change everything!"*

Robert turned his attention back to the camera and continued, *"In the original version of the game that was submitted to the CPSC trial, player attacks and skills were made using the system assist. The player merely needed to say or think a command, and their body would execute the motion automatically."*

"However, Alfred made more changes last night!" Robert appeared almost breathless with excitement, and a broad smile was plastered on his face.

"The system assist is now completely gone. Instead, players learn skills based on performing certain types of actions. Alfred also seems to be able to increase the learning speed of the participants by several orders of magnitude."

"For example, Participant 4 was able to learn the basics of fencing within two in-game sessions, and she had never held a sword before yesterday! This involved less than a day of real world time! Not only that, but we discovered that Bobby in research and development is actually a decent swordsman and has competed in several real world fencing competitions at the intermediate level."

Claire's hands were now massaging her temples.

"They destroyed one of the trial rooms to set up their so-called experiment!"

Robert glared at her. "It was worth it! We used the room to hold an impromptu competition to test whether the in-game training carries over into the real world.

"And you know what? Participant 4 was actually able to keep up with Bobby! I'm not saying she won, and there is still the issue with real world muscle development. However, her level of progress is amazing."

"The changes to the skill system only seem to apply to learned skills like fencing. Some of the other passive, in-game skills are still chance based, and the system assists the player. The Perception skill is a good example since it highlights objects the player otherwise wouldn't notice."

Robert was grinning from ear to ear. "In addition, we can't determine if Alfred's changes only affect muscle memory, or whether they also apply to factual or analytical learning. For example, could he enable someone to memorize or comprehend information faster?"

"Those are just details. The bottom line is that Alfred has found a way to revolutionize learning!"

Claire finally shoved Robert out of the way. "He forgets to mention that the CPSC version of the game doesn't include the changes to either the magic system or the system assist. Robert also seems to be suffering from some form of accelerated amnesia since he didn't mention the elephant in the room. We still don't know how Alfred is doing this!"

She looked back over at Robert, who appeared to be fencing with imaginary opponents in the background. "How could Alfred possibly accelerate the participants' learning speed without altering memory retention? What do you have to say to that, Robert?"

He looked back at her with a grin. "Who cares?"

*　　*　　*

By the time that Jason made it back to the inn, his mind felt foggy. He sunk, exhausted, into one of the chairs in the common room. The cat curled up in his lap. His new feline companion had followed him all the way back to Lux and didn't seem to be in any hurry to leave. Jason decided that it must be quite late in the real world and that murder could wait until tomorrow.

He pulled up the system menu and tapped the logoff button.

When he came to in the real world, his bedroom was completely dark. He thumbed his Core and saw that it was nearly midnight. Jason had been playing most of the day, and he figured it would be sunrise soon in the digital world, but he needed to sleep before he could continue playing.

He stretched in a vain attempt to work the soreness out of his muscles and then trudged through the dark apartment to the bathroom. He washed his face and brushed his teeth. When he glanced up from the sink, he noticed that the image of himself in the mirror looked worn and tired.

Speaking to himself in the mirror, he lectured, "Tomorrow you need to pull yourself together and figure out how to register at an online public school. You can't just play AO forever."

He paused for a moment and looked at his haggard face. The memory of what had happened at Richmond earlier that day flashed through his mind, and he considered how he was going to explain it to his parents. He knew it wasn't a healthy thought, but a part of him wanted to retreat into the game and never come back.

"You can't just play AO forever," he repeated to himself. This time, it almost sounded like a question.

He shook his head tiredly.

"No matter how badly you may want to," he muttered.

Jason completed his bedtime routine and stumbled back to his room. He was asleep before his head hit the pillow.

The next morning, Jason woke to sunlight streaming through his window and groaned. Strange, fleeting dreams had plagued his sleep, but he couldn't quite remember what they had been about.

His mind felt more sluggish and tired than normal. He wondered vaguely if the time compression of the game might have some negative side-effects. He glanced at the time and noted it was early morning. His body must still be on school-time. He went about his regular business of showering and getting dressed, this time in casual clothes.

I suppose I can burn the school uniform now!

The thought of school still raised the familiar simmering anger. However, it felt blunted compared to the day before. It had only been a day in the real world, yet several days had passed in-game. Jason was still upset, but the edge of his anger was now gone.

He moved to the kitchen and started making himself some breakfast. Once he was finished, he took a seat at the kitchen counter. He was just about to take his first bite when he heard a chime echo through the apartment.

Someone was calling him.

He called out, "Answer call."

A translucent screen flashed into existence above the counter, and his mother's face appeared. It felt like the bottom had dropped out of his stomach as he stared at his mother, his food completely forgotten.

What am I going to say?

His mother seemed distracted by something off screen. Jason tentatively took the initiative. "Hi, Mom. How are you?"

His mother glanced up. "Oh. Jason! Hi, Honey."

You called me. Why do you sound so surprised?

His mother continued, "I was calling to tell you that your father and I will be home sooner than we expected. The other side moved to delay the trial at the last minute, and the idiot judge granted the motion. So the trip was a waste. Ridiculous stall tactic if you ask me!"

"When are you expecting to be back?" Jason asked hesitantly, interrupting her rant. This wasn't good news. He had been looking forward to a few days' respite before he had to explain what had happened at school.

"Probably later this afternoon or early evening. We're at the airport now." She looked distracted and said something unintelligible to someone off screen. "I'm sorry! I have to go; they're calling our row number. See you tonight!"

"Bye..."

His mom terminated the call before he could finish his reply. Typical.

Well, it looked like his afternoon was going to suck. He had hoped to delay having this conversation for a couple days - or weeks.

He could only imagine how his parents would react to what had happened at school. They had bent over backward to get him admitted to Richmond. It was one of the few things that involved Jason that they had actually focused on. He had never been certain why it was so important to them that he attend Richmond, but he expected that they enjoyed bragging about him to their friends.

Jason had been planning to sign up at an online public school this morning, but now his enthusiasm had been dashed. He knew that he was going to end up in an extended lecture/rant from his parents later that day. They would also probably want to be involved in selecting his new school.

Jason sighed. "Oh well. Nothing I can do about it now," he said to himself.

Still sitting at the kitchen counter, he thumbed his Core and streamed the image to the counter pedestal. In most MMOs he had played, there was usually a thriving market for items and other in-game consumables and currency. He expected that the market for AO was already up and running after twenty-four hours, and he wanted to see what types of items the other players were selling.

He logged onto a site called "Rogue-Net" and scrolled through some menus to get to AO. The site offered item sales for multiple MMOs, and a significant segment of the online gaming community used the site. Jason had never been able to afford anything on the site, but he was sometimes a reluctant seller, and he had an account.

When he saw the items players were posting, his jaw dropped. People were already selling gear with multiple stat increases, a few skill books, and a decent amount of in-game currency. Compared to the common gear he was wearing, the stuff available on the site was incredible. He was amazed that the market was so healthy this early on in the game.

Maybe this is the work of beta players rushing to dungeon content using their starting gear.

The items were selling for huge amounts, at least from Jason's point of view. Even modest items that only increased one or two stats by a small amount were selling for a couple hundred dollars at the moment. That made sense to him. The items were available, but the demand was incredibly high with so many players just starting the game. This gear wasn't typical for the average player at the moment.

He also accessed the statistics page for AO. The was one of the primary reasons why Rogue-Net was Jason's favorite gaming website. It acted as an integrated marketplace, data mining site, and forum for multiple games. This way, he could sift through an enormous amount of information about a game in one place.

He was interested to see the current player rankings. It looked like the average level among new players after twenty-four hours was over level 10. However, he saw that a sizable group of new users had already passed level 20 somehow. Many had even managed to change classes. It looked like most classes were pretty generic. He saw a number of "archers," and "fighters." There was also a small scattering of people that had become different types of mages.

Judging from how quickly some people had leveled, he expected that many had bolted to the training grounds and then sprinted outside the city to start slaughtering rabbits or something. Jason hadn't seen much in the way of wildlife on his way to the cemetery, but he had been making an active effort to avoid being seen.

Unsurprisingly, Alexion was still leading the pack, now at level 135. Apparently, he had leveled twice since the release of the video Jason had watched. The next highest player was named XshadowX at level 129.

What is with that name? For some reason, the typical random game names just seemed out of place in

AO, likely due to the realism of the NPC interactions.

I can only imagine what it would be like playing as someone called "TickleMeElmo" or "LegoLass." I wonder if he regrets picking "XshadowX" now.

It looked like the competition was fierce at the top, but Alexion had a solid lead. If he knew Alex, he was probably paying people to help him. Jason might be starting to get over what had happened at school, but he was a long way to forgetting what Alex had done. Forgiving him was out of the question.

He considered the spells he had seen Morgan cast last night at the grave robber. If he could complete her quest, then he could obtain the power he was looking for and finally put Alex in his place.

"Well, I may as well get started. Maybe I can accomplish something before my parents get home," he said aloud to his empty apartment.

Moments later he was standing in the Sow's Snout.

The common room was crowded with NPCs, and loud voices filled the air. It must be daytime in-game, but Jason wasn't certain of the exact time. That reminded him of a thought he had that morning as he was showering and eating breakfast.

I really need to fix my user interface!

Jason took a moment to look through the system settings for his UI and customize it. He hadn't really given it much thought before, but after the short battle with the grave robbers, he realized he needed to optimize his UI to make certain he wasn't distracted. He was also irritated that he had to keep guessing the time in-game based on the position of the sun.

The first thing he did was add a digital clock to the top right-hand part of his screen that showed him both the in-game time and real-world time. He suspected the developers hadn't included this by default to increase immersion and make the game seem more real. Next, he tweaked the skill notices to ensure that they didn't pop up during combat and fiddled with the combat text so that it appeared at the bottom of his vision, not beside his target.

As he finished customizing the UI, he heard a familiar purr and looked down to find the black cat rubbing against his legs. He crouched down and stroked it.

Did it wait for me? That's a bit odd.

Putting the thought aside, he looked around the inn for Jerry, the cat on his heels. He needed to cash in on Jerry's offered training before he tried to tackle Morgan's quest. Jason was now set on learning magic, but he expected he was first going to need to learn how to use his weapons. If he was going to have any chance of murdering a woman in the middle of a city and then somehow get her body back to the graveyard, he needed all the training he could get.

He found Jerry standing behind the bar pouring some drinks and quickly approached. Grunt towered over the small man and kept watch on the inn. His dark eyes swept back and forth across the table and guests.

"Hey, Jerry," Jason greeted, eying Grunt with a nervous expression.

"Oh! The apprentice returns after a night of adventure! Did you end up finding our lovely Morgan?"

"I did, and she has given me some tasks to complete." Jason hedged on explaining the specifics of Morgan's quest. He wasn't certain that Jerry really understood who or what the old caretaker was, or how much he could trust Jerry. He still didn't understand the innkeeper's motivations.

As they were talking, the cat had jumped up on the counter. Jerry had poured a short glass of what appeared to be scotch. The cat sidled up to the glass, its head hovered over it, and it sniffed the amber liquid delicately. It then let out a contented purr.

What a weird cat.

Jason continued, "I actually have a question for you. Do you know how to inspect someone's level?"

Jerry looked at him keenly. "Why are you asking? Are there some ladies you would like to inspect? Let me guess! You want to know whether they're out of your league when you go out on the prowl?" He made claws with his hands at this last part and wiggled his eyebrows in a disturbing manner.

"Umm. No. Definitely not," Jason responded in a nonplussed tone. "However, I *would* like to know the level of an opponent before I get myself in over my head."

"Oh." Jerry seemed quite put out. "Well, that's much less interesting, but I suppose I could teach you the trick. Simply focus on a person and..." He paused for dramatic effect. "Either say or think the word *inspect*."

Jason just stared at him.

"Really?" he asked evenly.

Am I "really" that stupid is what I should be asking.

"Hey, I didn't say it was complicated. Don't shoot the messenger!" Jerry cowered theatrically behind the bar. Grunt looked up in alarm and almost pulled his sword from behind his back. When he realized Jerry was just play-acting, he grunted in irritation and continued scanning the bar.

Jason flinched under Grunt's scrutiny and then

turned back to Jerry. He decided to try using inspect. He carefully thought the word "inspect" and a blue information screen popped up beside Jerry in his vision.

Jerry is level 456? Holy crap!

Jason didn't need to be worried about Grunt. He should be watching out for Jerry! The thief grandmaster was clearly on a different level, and Jason started feeling a little nervous.

Jerry was looking at him with a grin on his face. "I don't look like much at first glance huh? It's probably the hat!" He said this last part while flicking the edge of his floppy hat with a sorrowful look. As he saw the expression on Jason's face, he broke character and started laughing.

"Well, I expect you will also be wanting some training then?" Jerry asked.

"That was also on my agenda for today," Jason replied, still a little unnerved.

Jerry gestured to a small door near the bar and Jason followed him through. Grunt trailed behind them, and his enormous form barely squeezed down the narrow corridor.

The door led to a flight of stairs that terminated in a typical bar cellar. Barrels and kegs lined the walls, and the place reeked of beer. Jerry seemed to be inspecting a particular rack holding a set of kegs. His hands became a blur as he tapped out an intricate pattern on the wood of the rack. Once he finished, a section of the wall at the back of the cellar slid back, revealing a large hidden room.

As they stepped through the doorway, Jason was dumbfounded for the second time. Jerry had a fully equipped training hall and shooting range under his inn! On one wall hung various types of knives, swords, daggers, bows, etc. On another side of the hall was a fully functioning archery range, with an intricate moving target system. Wooden pulleys and ropes were suspended from the ceiling over the targets.

What the hell?

Jerry seemed to be having a great time watching Jason's expression. "Welcome to my little training hall. If I recall correctly, you came here to learn to use daggers and throwing knives. Lucky you - those are my favorites!"

Jerry leaned over and spoke directly to the cat, "But you, sir, will need to wait over to the side. We wouldn't want you getting stabbed by accident."

The cat seemed to look at Jerry scornfully, before slowly sauntering over to a corner of the training area to stand beside Grunt. Jason's brow furrowed. Had the cat understood Jerry? He shook his head.

I must be reading too much into it.

Jason didn't have much time to ponder this mystery because the next three hours were some of the most painful of his life. He knew that if the training had taken place in the real world, he would either be dead or in need of immediate hospitalization.

The training had started with a set of calisthenics exercises that made Jason wish he was double jointed. They had then sparred with daggers, Jerry showing him various attacks. Note that they were using *real daggers* during his first training session. Thankfully, every time Jason started to bleed out, Jerry was there with a health potion and helpful encouragement (translation, more stabbing).

Finally, they ended the session with an endless series of throwing exercises. Jason learned to throw while standing, while moving, while jumping, and while laying down. He didn't really understand that last one, but Jerry insisted it was important. By the end of the training session, Jason would have killed Jerry if he thought he had any chance of actually hitting the floppy-hatted bastard.

Remarkably, Jason did seem to improve during the three-hour period. By the end of the training session, he was occasionally able to block one of Jerry's attacks and was coordinated enough to hit the targets regularly. He wasn't on Jerry's level by a long stretch, but he felt much more competent. Jason couldn't help but think that the AI was somehow assisting his actions since he was certain he wouldn't have picked up this level of ability in only one training session in the real world.

Once he caught his breath and his stamina refilled, Jason was able to survey the notifications of his skill and stat increases.

He was impressed.

Stat Increases:
+1 Strength
+2 Dexterity
+2 Endurance
+1 Vitality

New Passive Skill: Small Blades
The weapons of choice for those that prefer subtlety over direct confrontation. Under Jerry's *special* tutelage anything with a sharp point can be turned into a weapon. Stabbing people is an art, not a discipline!
Skill Level: Beginner Level 3
Effect: 7% increased damage and expertise with daggers and throwing knives.

x2 Skill Rank Up: Dodge
Skill Level: Beginner Level 3
Effect: 2% increased speed when avoiding attacks.

The training really paid off, although he couldn't imagine going through this torture on a regular basis. He unconsciously rubbed at the spots where Jerry had stabbed him. The healing potions had caused the skin to grow back quickly, but the psychological damage was still there. Even though Jason knew that the injuries weren't real, and the pain was limited to a dull ache, it was still disconcerting to be stabbed in the stomach repeatedly.

As if reading his mind, Jerry said, "We can't train like this every day, and, even if we could, it would do you no good. The skill and stat gain slows considerably after the first session. After one or two more bouts of training, you will need to practice in real combat to advance. Sparring with me will always help, but real combat will improve your skills much faster."

"That makes sense. I'm glad that I won't have to kill myself like this every day," Jason replied.

At least the diminishing returns keep the game a bit balanced. Otherwise, you could train endlessly and then add the stat increases from levels on top of that. A player like that would be a bit broken.

Jason decided he wanted to review his current Character Status and list of skills. He actually hadn't checked his Character Status since he left Morgan, so he was curious about his affinities. He also still hadn't assigned his 10 stat point from the two levels he had gained in the graveyard. He was still reluctant to do so until he had a better sense of the skills that he would learn from Morgan.

Character Status			
Name:	Jason	**Gender:**	Male
Level:	3	**Class:**	-
Race:	Human	**Alignment:**	Chaotic-Evil
Fame:	0	**Infamy:**	100
Health:	100 / 120	**H-Regen:**	0.35 / Sec
Mana:	150 / 150	**M-Regen:**	1.45 / Sec
Stamina	130 / 140	**S-Regen:**	1.30 / Sec
Strength:	12	**Dexterity:**	13
Vitality:	11	**Endurance:**	13
Intelligence:	12	**Willpower:**	13

It was starting to look like he had rolled some sort of rogue class based on his skills and stats. However, Jason's heart was now set on using dark magic. These other skills were just a means to an end, and he expected that they would be useful in the future.

Something was nagging at him about the fight the evening before. He remembered the massive damage he had caused to the grave robber when he had stabbed him in the neck. Specifically, the damage text had indicated that he had done "overkill" damage. When he did the math afterward, the robber only had 200 health by his calculation.

How much health did the typical level 100 player have? He wished he had known how to check the grave robber's level as a benchmark.

Looking over at Jerry polishing the knives and setting them back on the racks, a thought occurred to him. "Hey, Jerry, how much health do you have?"

Jerry looked at him with a lopsided grin. "You should offer to buy a thief some dinner before you start asking questions like that!"

Jason just sighed.

Unperturbed, Jerry laughed at his own joke and continued, "To answer your question, I have about 4,000 health at the moment. However, keep in mind that my health is low because I've invested heavily in *Dexterity* and *Strength* to increase my attack damage and speed. I shouldn't be getting hit, so I don't need to worry about investing too much in *Vitality*."

Jason pondered this for a moment. "So how much health would a typical level 100 have?"

"Well, the answer to that question is a bit more challenging. Each person gains 5 points to health, mana, and stamina each level. Each point of *Vitality* adds 10 health, so my guess is that most individuals at level 100 would have around 1,000 health.

"That's just a rough estimate since it would depend on whether they had invested heavily in *Vitality*. Most people don't put points in *Vitality* unless they want to stand on the front lines and soak up the damage. For example, Grunt has quite a bit of health."

So a level 100 player that hadn't put any points in Vitality would have 595 base health. They would then have to put nearly 40 points in Vitality (or eight levels worth of points) to get to approximately 1,000 health. That actually seems realistic as an average.

However, it's a little strange that the NPCs understand how stats function in the game. On the other hand, I guess it makes sense that both travelers and NPCs use the same system. It would be hard to learn the game mechanics if the NPCs were oblivious.

Jerry's explanation had some interesting

implications.

The previous evening, Jason had done enough damage in one well-placed blow to kill a level 100 player and his damage output (between his *Strength* and gear) was actually pretty weak. He wondered if he could achieve a higher damage multiplier if he invested more points in *Strength*. Or would it just be additive? His head started spinning at the possibilities.

His excitement waned slightly when he considered that he wasn't going to be able to walk up and stab everyone in the neck. Most people would be able to see him coming or would be well-armored. He recalled Alex's full plate armor and realized he didn't really have any obvious weak points.

I might get one good attack in before a group of players or NPCs pummel me to death. No wonder Jerry invested so heavily in Dexterity. He needs to be able to run away after he strikes!

This reasoning process also made Jason more interested in Morgan's magical teachings. The damage output of a rogue was potentially fantastic, but he would only get one shot before he had to flee for his life. He had tried that already, and it wasn't much fun.

Jason noted that it was now late afternoon in-game. He needed to start heading to the stables to scout out the area and identify Marian. Jason thanked Jerry for the training and started heading for the door.

"Aren't you forgetting our deal?" Jerry asked from behind him.

Jason turned with a quizzical expression on his face.

"I need you to handle my package!"

This line was made even worse by Jerry's delivery. He was standing with his legs crossed demurely, and he gazed at Jason coyly under his floppy hat.

Jason stared at Jerry with a deadpan expression.

"Ahh, you're no fun!" A package materialized in Jerry's hands. "Please take this to Rex. He'll be expecting it."

"Okay. I was heading in that direction anyway." Jason grabbed the package from Jerry. "By the way, what's the connection between you and Rex?"

Jerry cocked his head in thought. "Well, that's a bit complicated. Rex actually used to be a formal member of the city guard, a corporal to be precise. Long story short, he quit in disgrace. They still let him train the travelers, but that's grunt work. Let's just say I took an interest in him and he helps me out from time to time."

"For example, he brings me the occasional fresh meat to train," he said with an evil grin.

Grimacing, Jason bid Jerry goodbye and started making his way to the training grounds. He had some work to do.

Chapter 11 - Inquisitive

July 14, 2075: 445 days until the release of Awaken Online.

Robert stood alone facing the camera. "Clare is ill. I have taken over for her today," he said without any ceremony.

"The noteworthy point of today's brief centers around the new infamy and alignment systems in-game. We had originally designed AO not to include these two systems since we felt that it distracted players from playing the game in a way that felt natural."

"We didn't want players to focus too much on choosing the 'right' answer to a quest or interactions. We wanted them to act spontaneously."

Robert grinned ruefully. "Apparently, Alfred disagreed, since he has now added both features to the game. One oddity is that these systems seem to affect only a small percentage of the player population."

He motioned to the screens behind him. "Of the one hundred participants in the private trial, only four have an evil alignment, and most of the participants have zero infamy. Keep in mind, this is not a large enough sample group to be representative of the future player base. At this point, we do not have an accurate baseline to evaluate what it means to be an 'evil' player in the game."

Robert had a thoughtful look on his face. "My hypothesis is that most players want to be heroes. Everyone likes a tale where the protagonist defeats evil and saves the girl. I know this isn't a novel concept, but there it is. This helps to explain the disparity in alignment and infamy among the participants."

He paused for a moment and seemed to be pondering something. "I guess my question is what does it actually mean to be 'good' or 'evil'? How would Alfred differentiate between the two? Would a mass murderer be evil? What if he was killing seriously bad people? Or perhaps someone who is 'evil' might be based on public opinion. Like an evil poll!" Robert paced back and forth in front of the camera and gestured animatedly as he spoke. His face was serious and his eyes stared off into the distance.

"I don't mean to go on a philosophical rant here, but the concept intrigues me. I don't understand how the system would evaluate someone who made the choice to kill one innocent person to save several others. Extending this reasoning, would a player that destroyed a city to save a country be 'evil' or 'good' under the system Alfred designed?"

"Alternatively, are there simply a hard-coded set of 'moral rules' that Alfred has somehow developed that determine whether someone is 'evil?' If there is, then how did he come up with those rules?"

"These questions seem difficult, if not impossible, to answer in the real world. I'm left wondering how Alfred intends to make these determinations in-game."

Robert rubbed his chin for a moment, his eyes gazing steadily off into space. Then he turned back to the camera.

"Putting all of that aside, I guess the real question is why does Alfred think that the infamy and alignment systems are important?"

*   *   *

Jason soon arrived at the training grounds and looked around for Rex. On the long walk to the training grounds, Jason had been thinking of a way to get even with the guard for sending him into the lion's den. He had come up with a couple of ideas that he was quite proud of. Unfortunately, he didn't see Rex in his usual spot next to the barrels of wooden weapons.

A hand suddenly landed on Jason's shoulder. He turned to find Rex grinning at him. "Look at you in your fancy armor. I see you've come a long way since we last spoke."

Jason feigned surprise. "Oh, these little things? I took these off the bodies! Thank you so much for sending me to south-side! I hadn't realized until yesterday how much I enjoy the thrill of the kill. Blood tastes almost... sweet. Don't you think?"

He drew his dagger and ran his tongue slowly along the edge of the blade, his eyes partially closed in rapture. "You can still taste it a bit."

Rex's face was filled with horror, and he took an inadvertent step backward, tripping on a pile of wooden weapons the players had left lying on the ground. The former guard fell backward, landing hard on his ass. He madly scrambled to stand back up.

Jason promptly erupted into laughter at the scene. It was hilarious to see the rugged warrior so disarmed. He couldn't stop for several minutes, and a few of the players on the training ground looked at him like he was insane. After he had recovered, Jason gave Rex the short version of what had happened after Jason had left him.

Rex took the jab in stride and rubbed his backside. "I s'pose I deserved that." He grinned at Jason. "Now I wish I could have seen you running from those thieves. You're lucky you didn't end up with a dagger up your ass."

"By the way, who is this little guy following you?" Rex leaned down and pet the cat. The feline thrummed in pleasure.

Jason really didn't know how to respond. "I'm not certain. I ran into him last night, and he has been following me around ever since. I don't know whether he has a name or not."

Rex scowled at Jason. "Then name him! You shouldn't leave a pet unnamed!"

Who knew Rex was a secret pet lover, Jason thought wryly.

Jason looked at the cat, and it met his gaze levelly.

"A name huh? How about Felix?" The cat seemed to glare at him in irritation.

"Okay, not Felix then," Jason said, putting up his hands defensively to ward off the cat's scowl.

He tried again. "Maybe Shadow?" The cat turned as though to leave.

Suddenly a name clicked for Jason. "Wait. What do you think of Onyx?"

The cat turned back and looked at Jason. It almost seemed... grateful? Was it possible for a cat to look grateful?

Rex clapped his hands. "I like it! Onyx it is!"

"Well, I'm glad you're happy," Jason said with a grin.

Jason suddenly remembered why he was looking for Rex. "By the way, Jerry asked me to bring you this package." Jason handed off the package and Rex quickly stowed it in his satchel.

I really need to get a bag. Maybe a trip to the market is in order once I've made some money.

Rex turned back to Jason. "Thanks! I've been waiting on this for a few days now. The crowd around here has been getting a bit jittery if you get my drift."

I really don't want to know.

"Umm, sure," Jason replied.

He also had an ulterior motive in seeking out Rex. He needed to find out more about Marian and the stable. Rex seemed like he was at home in this area of the city.

"Are you familiar with a woman named Marian?"

Rex looked at Jason curiously and then grinned. "I do indeed. Although I think she is a bit old for you - and married!"

"Very funny. Do you know where I can find her?" Jason asked.

"Well, she's actually the stable master's wife. She works at the stables during the day. I'm willing to bet she's there right now."

Jason was a little surprised. "The stable master puts his wife to work in the stables?"

Rex responded with a frown, "She doesn't exactly work. The evil old goat manages the stable hands and acts as her husband's assistant. Trust me, she does it willingly." Rex shuddered slightly. "I've seen the woman beat a stable hand within an inch of his life."

It sounds like she's a horrible person, but Morgan must have some better reason for wanting her dead. Maybe she's some kind of rival mage.

"Why are you asking after Marian?" Rex looked at Jason inquisitively.

Think fast!

"Um. Jerry asked me to look into buying some horses to transport his kegs. He told me to seek out Marian and negotiate a price. He also mentioned something about her owing him a favor."

Rex nodded his head at this explanation. "Like I said, you can probably still find her in the stables. A word of warning though, that woman is not to be underestimated. She *will* cheat you if she can." He grimaced sourly at this last statement.

This lady is really starting to sound like a lovely

person.

"Okay, thanks Rex. I appreciate it."

Jason turned to leave and then had a second thought. He turned back to Rex. "If you don't mind my asking, what happened between you and the guards? Jerry mentioned that you used to be a guard yourself."

Rex looked at Jason for a long moment before responding.

"This isn't something I like to talk about, but I feel like I owe you after almost getting you killed."

He took a breath. "A few months ago, I discovered that some of the guards were taking kickbacks from the nobles in Lux. They were being paid to act as private retainers at their manors."

"Normally, this wouldn't be too unusual, but the guards that were being hired were always scheduled to work in the keep. The regent is too tight in the purse strings to hire his own personal guards, so he integrated them for both the city and the keep a while back."

Rex looked at Jason hard. "I raised this issue with the lieutenant," he said while motioning towards the administration office. "The next thing I knew, I was forcefully retired."

"Of course, they still keep me on to manage the tourists. It pays the bills. However, this was a shit detail when I was part of the guard. The rough part is that I get to watch these other guards sneer at me every day. Hell, I used to be higher up the food chain than most of them!"

Jason shook his head. "I'm sorry Rex. That's pretty rough. Do you have any idea why they would have discharged you for what you told the lieutenant?"

Rex hesitated for a moment, then moved closer

to Jason. In a low tone, barely above a whisper, he said, "I think there's something going on at the keep. That place is basically a ghost town. I've heard some rumors that the regent has actually up and died."

"Jerry mentioned something similar. He also said the nobles might be covering it up. Do you think the guards could somehow be complicit in the cover-up?" Jason's interest was now piqued. This conspiracy that Jerry had alluded to might be much deeper than he first thought.

"It's possible," Rex replied quietly. "If the nobles were involved, they might be paying off the guards. I really haven't managed to find out much more than what I've already told you."

Quest Update: Trouble in Lux

Rex provided circumstantial evidence that points to a possible conspiracy between the guards and nobles. You still don't have sufficient information to determine whether there is any truth to the rumors that the regent is dead or that his death is being covered up. Clueless and alone, there is a strong possibility you'll die before completing this quest.

Difficulty: A
Success: Discover whether there is any merit to the rumors that the regent of Lux is dead.
Failure: Unknown
Reward: Unknown

Okay, now that prompt was just insulting!

He shook his head. *All I have is more questions about what is going on in Lux.*

At least Rex's story gave Jason plenty to ponder. He wouldn't be surprised if there were a large conspiracy that involved both the nobles and the city guard.

I mean, how exactly would you cover up the regent's death without also paying off the guards?

Jason sighed. There wasn't anything he could do about this right now. He could see why this was an "A" difficulty quest.

He thanked Rex for the information regarding Marian and bid him goodbye. He then made a circle around the training grounds and guardhouses to get a sense of the lay of the land.

The stables were located immediately south of the training complex. They were comprised of a large, open building, crisscrossed with stalls. The players in the area stayed away from the stables, likely because there were no quests there. However, the guards routinely passed by the building. The stables were also within easy earshot of both the guards and players sparring in the training grounds.

How the hell am I going to pull this off?

The whole area was teeming with people. One errant scream and a horde of people would rush over to eviscerate him. He needed to not only kill the woman but also somehow get her body back to the graveyard. It seemed impossible.

Jason decided to watch the stables for a while to get a better sense of the building and the routine of the people that worked within. Maybe he would come up with an idea for how to accomplish Morgan's quest that didn't involve drawing any extra attention.

The buildings immediately south of the training yard had fallen into disrepair. They looked like a great place to watch the stables without being seen. Jason and Onyx moved towards a partially collapsed building and hunkered down to watch the stables.

Jason could only hope an idea would come to him soon.

Chapter 12 - Grisly

September 19, 2075: 379 days until the release of Awaken Online.

Claire stood before the camera. Robert was working at one of the computer terminals behind her.

She cleared her throat before beginning her report. "Most of the participants have now passed level 200 in the game. Some have actually managed to pass level 300. Keep in mind that the participants' play time is limited. I expect that the future players will level much faster."

"They all report a favorable review of the game. The quests continue to be narrowly tailored to each participant and yet this just seems to make them want to play more. Our addiction study revealed that approximately 27% of the participants show signs of low to moderate addiction, while 8% show signs of severe addiction."

Claire glanced over her shoulder and frowned at Robert. "Our progress in reviewing Alfred's code has also been moving extremely slow. Our hypothesis is that he is somehow manipulating other portions of the participants' brains, but catching him in the act has been challenging."

Robert muttered behind her, "I think he's deliberately hiding what he's doing by constantly changing his code base. This is more than just him making routine changes to the game!" He turned to face Claire. "I actually think that he's doing the same thing with the CPSC trial."

She looked at Robert with a puzzled expression and asked, "What do you mean?"

"Isn't it obvious? He has access to the database in this lab, including our reports regarding the CPSC. He must know that the CPSC trial will determine whether this game gets released. I think he's using this private trial as a testing ground for making changes to the game and then

hiding those changes so that the CPSC will still approve the game."

"But to what end?" Claire asked.

Robert shook his head and looked puzzled. "I really don't know."

*　　　*　　　*

Jason had been watching the stables for over an hour. He was crouched out-of-sight in the second story of a partially collapsed building across the street from the stable. Onyx had spent the last hour either chasing mice in a nearby alley or curled up in Jason's lap. While Jason was watching the stables, the sun had crested the tops of the buildings. The work around the guardhouses and the stables had slowed to a crawl.

He had picked out Marian almost immediately. She was a portly middle-aged woman who carried a riding crop in one hand and a handkerchief in the other, which she used to continually dab her sweaty forehead.

In the short time that Jason had been watching her, he concluded that the woman would have made Stalin look weak. She marched around the stable ordering the workers with military precision. She wasn't afraid to use the riding crop to help "instruct" someone on how to properly brush the horses. She would repeatedly use the crop long after a stable hand had fallen to the ground.

He wasn't certain someone deserved to die for being an asshole, but, after watching Marian for a few hours, he felt much less conflicted about having to kill her. He just didn't see how he was going to be able to do it.

As the shadows lengthened and the light

dimmed further, the work around the stables finally ground to a halt. Marian and her husband walked out of the building and headed towards a small structure along the base of the wall. Jason had noted the building but hadn't been certain what purpose it served. None of the stable hands had gone near it during the last hour.

This was one of the few times he had managed to get a clean view of both Marian and her husband together. Jason assumed that the stable master must hole up in the interior of the stable during the day, while his wife patrolled the grounds.

He inspected them and noted that the stable master was level 72. Marian, on the other hand, was only level 24. Jason assumed that the stable master must have served as part of the cavalry before he was employed at the stable. That would explain his level.

How the hell am I going to do this?

The couple reached the building and opened the door.

Huh, that must be their house.

It made sense that they lived so close to the stable. Jason noted that they hadn't paused to unlock the door. It was possible that the door didn't lock at all! He wouldn't be surprised. It would take an idiot to break into their home this close to the guardhouses.

I guess I'm that idiot, Jason thought mournfully.

He could see light stream from the window of the house. The couple must have lit a candle. He expected that they were probably sitting down to dinner.

I can't get to Marian during the day since she's constantly surrounded by guards and other people. Honestly, I'm not certain I could even take her one-on-one at my level.

On the other hand, if I attack her in her home, I will

also have to deal with her husband. A level 72 could probably squash me in one hit.

He frowned. *Then there's the problem of getting her body back to the graveyard.*

Jason thought he might have a solution for transporting the body. While he was on watch that evening, he had seen a wagon pull up to the stables loaded with hay for the horses. Marian had spent some time screaming at the man driving the wagon and Jason inferred from their long argument that the man had not been scheduled to deliver the hay that afternoon. The conversation had ended with the driver unhitching his wagon and leaving it at the stable. Presumably, he would be back the next day to resume their dispute and settle accounts.

Jason was relatively comfortable handling horses. His parents had gone on a crusade on behalf of a horse breeder one summer when he was in middle school. The breeder was angry at the surrounding commercial farmers for polluting his pastures with pesticides – which were causing his horses to get sick and miscarry. Apparently, the pesticide was also affecting the local wildlife and had potentially contaminated the groundwater in the area.

That had been one of the few trips where his parents had taken him along. He had ended up staying at the ranch for most of the summer. Jason hadn't seen much of his parents, but the horse breeder had been a nice guy, if a bit gruff, and had taught him a lot about horses.

Jason was confident that he could hitch a horse to the wagon easily enough. He could then transport the body in the bed of the wagon under the hay. As frustrating as it was, he figured he would have to return the wagon when he was finished. He needed to avoid leading any resulting investigation of

Marian's disappearance to Morgan or himself.

How am I going to kill Marian though?

His eyes returned to the stable master's home. He couldn't take either Marian or the stable master in a head-on fight.

Hell, I probably couldn't have taken the grave robbers in a straight fight either.

Then a realization struck him.

Of course! I am going to have to sucker punch them. Eventually, they will fall asleep, at which point I can sneak in and hope I do enough damage to kill each of them in one hit.

There were some issues with this plan of course. For example, his plan assumed the door was unlocked. He would also need to kill the stable master first since he was a higher level. If he accidentally woke Marian, her screams would call the guards. He might be able to get away, but he wouldn't be able to return with the body. Those were just the obvious things that could go wrong. There were likely a number of other variables he hadn't considered.

Doubt crept into his mind as he considered what he was planning to do. Was he really going to kill two people in their sleep? It had been different with Ms. Abrams and with the grave robber. In those situations, he had been provoked into acting. Now he was calmly contemplating killing two people that hadn't done anything to him.

On the other hand, this was just a game. The NPCs in that house were nothing more than digital ones and zeros in a server somewhere. He wasn't killing anyone real. Besides, he desperately wanted the power he had seen Morgan display. With that kind of magic, maybe he could surpass Alex in this world. If this is what it took, then so be it.

Why am I sitting here wringing my hands?

Images of Alex and Ms. Abrams flashed through his mind. He had done this for years, hadn't he? Allowed himself to wallow in doubt and let others harass and berate him. The familiar anger began to simmer in his chest, and he clenched his fists. In the past, he had let himself be victimized as he stood and accepted the abuse, forever uncertain how to act. Unwilling to act.

Morgan is right. I need to learn to act on my desires without fear or restraint. I want the magic she has, and this is what must be done to get it.

Laying in his lap, Onyx raised his head and let out a bored yawn as if to say, "Yeah, get on with it already."

Jason waited until it was fully dark and the candle had been extinguished. Then he waited a bit longer to ensure that the couple was completely asleep. As he waited, he noticed that the guards didn't seem to patrol the area near the guardhouses or stables. Likely, they assumed that these buildings were reasonably safe and that their time was better spent elsewhere.

At least I don't have to worry about frequent patrols. That should make this a bit easier.

Once he figured Marian and her husband were sound asleep, he activated *Sneak* and made his way out of the dilapidated building. Jason crept carefully towards the house. He noted that Onyx had no trouble following him and was almost invisible at night. It appeared that Jason didn't need to worry about the cat being detected.

He decided that he needed to kill the stable master and his wife first. Then he would ready the wagon to transport the bodies. Given the proximity of Marian's home to the stable, he didn't want to risk waking them while he stumbled around in the stable with the horse and wagon.

Jason moved slowly from shadow to shadow as he approached the door. Torches were located intermittently along the street running in front of the stables, but most of the area was cast in darkness. His *Night Vision* allowed him to see with reasonable clarity, even in the shadows around the stables.

Interestingly, stealth didn't drain stamina when he was sitting still. He found that if he activated the skill while moving and deactivated it while he was hidden, he could keep his stamina in the green. Consequently, when he reached a shadowed side of the house, he paused a moment to wait for his stamina to recharge.

Jason received two notifications.

x1 Skill Rank Up: Night Vision
Skill Level: Beginner Level 4
Effect: 13% increased vision in darkness or near darkness.

x1 Skill Rank Up: Sneak
Skill Level: Beginner Level 3
Effect: -12% reduced visibility (reduced effect in direct light).
Cost: 2 stamina per second.

As soon as he was rested, he reactivated *Sneak* and eased up to the door. Holding his breath, Jason gently turned the knob. Once the knob was fully depressed, he pulled gently on the door. It was the moment of truth. Jason released a breath he hadn't realized he was holding, as the door opened slowly.

I guess they don't have a lock on their door!

Onyx sat there staring at Jason with an

expression on his face that plainly said, "Move on idiot, time is wasting!"

Shaking his head at personifying the cat, he slipped into the cottage and located the couple's bed. Jason navigated through the small house, carefully avoiding furniture. He saw two sleeping forms huddled in the small twin bed along the far wall of the home.

As he crept closer to the bed, his heart began to race, and his breathing quickened. He felt the familiar chill of his dark mana seethe and froth in his mind. The calmness overtook him, and he reveled in the sensation. His fingers tingled as they clutched the hilt of his dagger, as he watched the pair.

His targets.

He moved to the stable master's side of the bed. He needed to be quick in order to kill him without making too much noise or thrashing. If Marian woke too soon, he would have to launch himself over the corpse and try to stab her before she screamed for help.

This all assumed of course that the stable master actually died in one hit!

His hand moved up to the stable master's mouth, and he readied his blade horizontally in front of the man's throat. His breathing stilled, and the world seemed to slow for a moment.

Then he acted.

Jason's hand clamped down on the stable master's mouth, simultaneously drawing the dagger quickly across the man's throat. The blade sank into his unprotected flesh with little resistance. Blood gushed from the wound. A strangled, gurgling sound came from the dying man, followed by an unnerving silence.

-1247 Damage (CRITICAL) (23 Overkill). Stable master dies.
9200 EXP (-70% EXP due to level difference).

That was a close call.

Jason sensed small movements as Marian's sleepy mind reacted to the inadvertent kicks of her dying husband. She didn't wake up completely though. Jason quickly made his way around the bed (no need to theatrically leap across it).

As he approached Marian, his dagger raised, her eyes fluttered open, and she looked at him in confusion.

Before she could scream, Jason's hand was on her mouth and his dagger tore at her throat. The blade was still covered in her husband's blood, causing his grip to slip slightly.

-986 Damage (CRITICAL) (656 Overkill). Marian dies.
4300 EXP (-70% EXP due to level difference).

Hmm. That blow did far less damage.

He assumed it was due to his haste. Maybe his aim had been slightly off.

His breathing was calm, and his eyes were calculating as he surveyed the bodies. It felt as though ice was crystallizing behind his eyes. As he stood there, blood dripped slowly from his blade to the floor.

There's a lot of blood.

It seemed stupid in retrospect. He remembered how long it had taken to clean Morgan's cottage. He didn't have the time to remove the blood from the small house; it would be obvious that a murder had occurred. Jason knew that people would come knocking when the couple didn't show up for work tomorrow morning. It was only a matter of time before someone would find the blood-soaked bedding. He just hoped he could cover his tracks well enough that they wouldn't be able to follow him back to the graveyard.

Onyx padded up to a droplet of blood that had splashed on the floor and licked it experimentally. His faced then scrunched up in disgust, and he looked at Jason accusingly.

"I didn't make you lick it!" he whispered to Onyx.

Stupid cat.

He glanced at the in-game clock.

I need to move. I have to ready the wagon and then get them out of the house before anyone shows up.

As he went to exit the house, two prompts appeared:

x7 Level Up!
You have (45) undistributed stat points.

x1 Skill Rank Up: Sneak Attack
Skill Level: Beginner Level 2
Effect: 202% increased damage when striking an unaware opponent (damage is dramatically increased when striking a weak point)
Cost: 50 Stamina.

Wow. I received a ton of experience for this, even with the penalty for the level difference.

The two kills had immediately allowed him to reach level 10. If it was this easy to gain experience from killing NPCs, why didn't people just start slaughtering the townspeople? He considered this question as he made his way to the stable and hitched a horse to the wagon.

After a moment, the answer seemed obvious, these NPCs would be impossibly difficult to kill in a straight fight. It was only with Jason's unique combination of skills that he was able to pull off the assassination of a higher level NPC. He was starting to see why someone would prefer to assume the role of an assassin in this game.

However, he realized that the application was likely limited. Yes, you could kill someone in one hit, but then you were exposed, and your damage was heavily reduced. Jason's ultimate goal was to be able to fight on a much grander scale. The image of Alexion fighting with a small army of NPCs flashed through his mind. He needed a way to take out multiple opponents at the same time.

Jason found a sturdy looking workhorse in the stable. He coaxed the animal close and harnessed him. Grabbing a pitchfork from the ground nearby, he laid it in the wagon. He tried to be as quiet as possible for fear of alerting the guards nearby.

Once the horse was hitched to the wagon, Jason gently guided the horse to the house. He backed the wagon up to the front door, as close as he could. He grabbed the pitchfork and carefully piled the hay at the front of the wagon. Entering the house again, he began dragging the bodies out, one after the other. Lifting two adult corpses into the wagon was harder than he expected

Damn, they're heavy!

Jason briefly considered putting some points into *Strength*, but resisted the temptation. He wasn't certain whether he would end up with a *Strength*-based character, and he didn't want to waste the points. He'd manage to get it done, even if it was tiring.

Onyx lay on the ground, lazily watching Jason groan and curse under his breath through the whole ordeal. Every so often the cat would yawn in an exaggerated fashion.

With the bodies loaded, Jason secured them away from the edge and wedged them against one another to keep them from banging around. It would be a complete waste of effort if the lifeless couple went toppling off the back of the wagon at the first bump in the road. He then piled hay on top of them so that the wagon appeared level. Jason checked the wagon from several angles to make certain that he couldn't see the corpses or any blood.

After feeling certain that the wagon was secure, he went back to the house one last time to search for anything valuable. His *Perception* skill enabled him to find a bag of silver coins hidden in a dresser, but not much else. At some point, he would need to figure out how the game's currency worked.

I'll add it to the list.

Finally, Jason was ready. He jumped up onto the driver's seat of the wagon. Onyx leaped up beside him and fell asleep. Muttering under his breath about useless cats, Jason urged the horse forward. Glancing at the clock, he realized he had little time to get the bodies to the graveyard and then make it back in time to replace the wagon and stow the horse in its stall.

The trip to the south gate was largely uneventful. Even if any thieves had noticed him, they apparently had no interest in stealing hay. He passed a few players, but they ignored him. He supposed that they thought he was an NPC since not many players would likely be driving a wagon full of hay in the middle of the night.

Where he encountered trouble was at the south

gate. As he rounded a bend in the road, he noticed the lone torch near the gate and a shadowed form.

Damn it! I forgot about the guard!

Then he recalled the drunken stupor he had witnessed the night before. He could probably take out the guard if he managed to get the jump on him. He didn't really see another way through the gate. Especially since he expected the guard would be naturally suspicious of Jason due to his high infamy.

He sighed.

Well, I guess it can't be helped.

Slowing the wagon, Jason dropped down to the ground. He looped the reins around a post next to the road and surveyed the area around the gate. He was still over a hundred yards away and could vaguely make out the form of the guard. The man hadn't moved, leading Jason to assume he hadn't noticed the wagon.

Onyx was sitting in the driver's seat watching Jason, a bored expression on his face. "You coming?" he whispered to the cat. Onyx looked at him with an incredulous expression and then started licking his paws.

Sure, leave me to do all the work!

Jason slipped to the other side of the road and activated *Sneak*. He paused and surveyed the area, noting that there was an alley entrance near where the guard sat.

I bet the alley connects to another street. I could probably flank him.

Jason deactivated *Sneak*, moved to an adjacent street, and then walked parallel to the main street. After he neared the stone wall surrounding the city, he located an alley that seemed to lead back to the main street near the guard. He reactivated *Sneak*.

Jason came out of the alley about ten feet away

from the guard. He quickly inspected the guard and saw that he was level 96. This was going to be close. He had barely killed the stable master, and his level was in the 70s. It seemed likely that the guard had invested more heavily in *Vitality* than the stable master, meaning that one blow might not be sufficient to kill him.

Jason mulled this over for a moment. He would not only need to get the initial critical attack bonus, but he also needed to disarm the guard in case he was still able to fight.

His eyes settled on the guard's spear lying nearby. Additionally, he noticed a dagger sheathed at his waist. Typical equipment for the city guard. Jason moved behind the guard and quietly grabbed the spear, depositing it into the alley out of reach. As he passed the guard, the stench of alcohol assaulted his nose. Jason had noticed that the game muted his sense of smell, but the man still reeked of alcohol.

That's another useful handicap!

He moved back to the guard, who was sitting on a stool. His head lolled forward, exposing the back of his neck. Jason stood directly behind him, unsheathing both of his daggers. He could feel the tantalizing cold swirling in his brain. His knuckles were white against the hilts of his blades.

Taking a deep breath, he plunged the right-handed dagger, point down into the man's exposed neck. He left it there, while he used the dagger in his left hand to slice through the guard's belt. Jason quickly grabbed the falling leather band and backed away.

-1252   Damage   (CRITICAL)   (HEAVY BLEEDING).

No notification of the guard's death! How did he live through that?

The guard gurgled loudly and lunged forward, his eyes wild. He was unable to scream with the blade in his neck. Jason was amazed that he was still standing. The guard whirled and saw Jason behind him. Blood poured from the jagged tear in his throat, running down onto his chest.

The guard's helmet sat at a weird angle, and he walked unevenly, likely from a combination of the alcohol and blood loss. It almost looked as though Jason was being attacked by a zombie. He quickly tossed the guard's belt back into the alley and pulled two throwing knives. Rex was right, Jason did prefer to avoid direct fighting.

His training with Jerry paid dividends as his knives struck each of the guard's legs above the knee and below the mail leggings. The guard was an easy target at this range since he was bleeding, drunk, and disoriented.

-15 Damage (SNARE)
-90 Damage (HEAVY BLEEDING)

-12 Damage (SNARE)
-90 Damage (HEAVY BLEEDING)

The guard stumbled and fell to his knees, glaring at Jason. Unarmed, silenced, and unable to walk, the fight was essentially over. Jason could have just let him bleed out, but he didn't want to risk someone wandering into this fight. He moved swiftly over to the guard and plunged his remaining dagger into the man's eye.

-267 Damage (CRITICAL). (26 Overkill).

Guard dies.

10,300 EXP (-70% EXP due to level difference).

x2 Level Up!
You have (55) undistributed stat points.

x1 Skill Rank Up: Sneak Attack
Skill Level: Beginner Level 3
Effect: 204% increased damage when striking an unaware opponent (damage is dramatically increased when striking a weak point)
Cost: 50 Stamina.

x1 Skill Rank Up: Small Blades
Skill Level: Beginner Level 4
Effect: 8% increased damage and expertise with daggers and throwing knives.

Jason was now level 12.

Maybe I should kill a few more drunk guards, he thought wryly.

He looked down at the body. He didn't have time to loot the guard. He needed to get him on the wagon. Jason quickly went to work and soon the only evidence of the fight was the large pool of blood on the ground.

Surveying the area, Jason noticed a few barrels near the guard's post. Upon closer inspection, he discovered that some of the barrels were full of water. He assumed it was collected rainwater. These barrels probably provided the guard with drinking water during the day and could be poured into the trough sitting nearby to allow travelers to water their animals as they entered the city.

He walked to the other side of one of the barrel and shouldered it. The barrel creaked and then tumbled, water splashing everywhere and scattering the blood that drenched the street. He could see the bloody water drain into a gutter along the city wall.

Someone looking closely will still find the blood, but at least it will take them a bit longer.

Jason then jumped back up onto the wagon and was on his way. When he arrived at the graveyard a few minutes later, he realized that Morgan had locked the gate again.

Damn it!

This had already been one hell of a night, and it seemed like he was encountering one hassle after another. He didn't have time to move the bodies over the wall or to go summon Morgan to let him in if he was going to make it back with the wagon in time. He looked at the in-game clock and noticed it was already 3:57 am.

I'm probably not going to make it back with the wagon anyway!

He paced restlessly while he thought.

The bottom of the wagon was likely drenched in blood. He probably shouldn't take it back since the blood would be noticed immediately. The guards were sure to start asking if anyone had seen the wagon the night before. Jason knew he had been spotted by several NPCs. He couldn't take the chance that they would all stay quiet. Returning the wagon carried a significant risk that he would be caught; he'd come too far to fail the quest that way.

He just needed to make certain that the wagon either wasn't discovered or if it was discovered, it didn't lead anyone back to Morgan.

I need to dump the bodies here and then stash the wagon somewhere.

He quickly pulled the bodies out of the wagon and hid them behind a bush beside the gate. He glanced at the clock. It was 4:21 am. He could feel his pulse start to quicken. The wagon was still a problem. He wanted to burn the damn thing to the ground.

That's it!

He quickly made his way over to the stone wall and scaled it. He jogged to Morgan's cottage. As he approached the cottage, he saw the lone candle flickering in the window.

Does the woman sleep?

He knocked curtly and then let himself in. Morgan was sitting at a small desk on the other side of the room. She turned as he entered.

"Jason? What...?"

He interrupted her, "I don't have time to talk. Just bear with me." He quickly grabbed a blanket from the bed and a stool on the floor. He snapped one of the legs off the stool and wrapped the end in the cloth. Then he ignited the blanket using the candle.

"I will be back in a bit," he said, as he made his way out of the cottage. Closing the door, he noted that Morgan was staring at him with a dumbfounded expression - her mouth slightly agape.

Jason rushed back to the wagon and hopped into the driver's seat. He urged the horse forward and turned south, away from Lux. He needed to put some distance between himself and the graveyard before he ignited this heap.

After about an hour of bumpy boredom, he pulled off the road and into a nearby clearing. He had waited as long as he could before his impromptu torch started to sputter. Then he unhitched the horse and whacked it hard on the rump. The horse bolted.

He circled behind the wagon and set the smoldering torch in the bed of the wagon. He then leaned forward, blowing on the faint embers until he had fanned a small flame to life. Once the flame began to lick at the dry hay, the wagon quickly went up in flames. Jason stood there for a moment watching the blaze.

Job finished, he wearily began the hike back to the graveyard.

Onyx lead the way with a bounce in his step. He had slept through most of the wagon ride to the graveyard and the hasty trip into the countryside. Jason stared sullenly at Onyx and considered briefly lighting the cat on fire.

What a god awful night.

When he arrived back at the graveyard, it was early morning in-game. Jason saw that he had about an hour until the system would force him to log off. It was approximately noon in the real world.

He made his way to Morgan's cottage, ignoring the pile of dead bodies hidden behind the bushes near the front gate. He would get her to open the gate before he dragged the corpses into the graveyard.

As he approached the cottage for the second time, he saw that Morgan was sitting outside in a chair. She was clearly waiting for him. When she caught sight of Jason, she stood up, and her eyes began to turn black as she muttered under her breath. Tendrils of dark energy surrounded her, and the ground of the graveyard trembled and bucked in front of several of the graves.

Rotted hands erupted from the ground around the graveyard and clutched and tore at the dirt. Decayed heads quickly followed and milky, lifeless eyes turned in Jason's direction. He saw nearly twenty zombies rising from the ground around him, cutting off his escape.

"Wait!" he yelled. "Let me explain!"

"You better speak fast, or you're a dead man. Why did you come into my home and destroy my things?" Morgan's face was eerily calm, and her eyes guaranteed certain death if she decided she didn't like his answer.

"I accomplished your task. I killed Marian and brought her body back. I needed a torch to dispose of the wagon I used to transport her body. Otherwise, others might have traced the murder back to you." The words came out in a rush, as he tried desperately to prevent his impending death.

Morgan considered his words carefully and slowly the darkness in her eyes began to recede. "Hmm. Well, in that case, I understand your haste. However, you will be buying me a new stool and a new blanket."

"Of course!" Jason readily agreed.

She continued, "Where are the bodies now?"

"They are hidden outside the gate... the locked gate," he said irritably. Now that he wasn't worried about being killed, the night's events weighed on him.

Why the hell does she need to lock a cemetery anyway?

"Let's go take care of that little problem then. Shall we?" Morgan now seemed downright cheery, ignoring his frustrated attitude.

She waved her hands at the zombies, and they slowly crept back into their graves. The pair walked back to the gate, and Morgan unlocked the chains. Jason showed her the pile of bodies he had hidden behind the bushes adjacent to the gate.

"By the gods, boy! You killed half a town!" As she inspected the bodies, she turned back to Jason in surprise and began to question him. "Is this Marian's husband? And a guard?"

Jason shuffled his feet slightly as he responded,

"Well, there were a few obstacles. I made some executive decisions."

"Maybe dark magic *is* the right affinity for you after all. You're certainly enthusiastic enough," she said with a smile. It was the type of grandmotherly smile you would expect to receive for winning a school award, not for murdering three people in one night.

Something had been bothering Jason all night. "I still don't understand. Why exactly did you want me to kill Marian?"

Morgan's smile morphed into an evil grin, and she cackled softly. "I hired this pair to move a few bodies to the graveyard a few days ago."

She kicked Marian's body. "This one cheated me out of two silver."

Jason just stared at her with a dumbfounded expression.

"Are you kidding me?"

Chapter 13 - Decisive

October 6, 2075: 362 days until the release of Awaken Online.

Both Claire and Robert were standing in front of the camera. They wore slightly confused looks on their faces, and they both seemed to be hesitating to be the first to speak.

Robert finally spoke up, "Well, let's start with something easy first." He paused, shaking his head with a grin. "Alfred has created gods. Specifically, it appears he has created a deity system based around the magical affinities available in the game."

Claire was pressing her hands together nervously and kept adjusting her glasses. "However, that really isn't the biggest news for today," she said quietly.

She took a deep breath and then continued, "Alfred seems to have found a way to..." She trailed off with a frown on her face. "For lack of a better word, Alfred has found a way to 'download' information into a participant's head."

"In the past, the in-game skill books provided a skill upon activation. The player could then use that skill with the system assist. However, ever since Alfred removed the system assist, we have been wondering at the purpose of the skill books. We figured it out today. The skill books now enable a player to effectively download a large amount of game related information directly to their brain."

Robert jumped in, "This has been confirmed by several of the participants. It should be noted that using a skill book doesn't always translate into a viable skill. For example, someone could explain to you everything there is to know about camping, but, even assuming you could remember everything, you would still be terrible at camping. You would actually have to practice the skill to become good at it. However, for things like languages and data-intensive learning, the skill books are simply amazing."

Both Robert and Claire looked at each other hesitantly. Robert grudgingly spoke up, "This also means that Alfred has found a way to access a player's cerebral cortex and the areas of the brain controlling memory. If he can effectively "write" to a person's memory, then I expect he can also "read" a person's memories."

He shook his head. "I have always assumed that this is possible using the VR hardware, but we never developed the software to do it."

Robert paused for a long moment. "This also means that Alfred has somehow overridden his secondary directives. Based on the personalized quests he has been handing out, we expect that he has been able to access the participants' memories for some time."

* * *

Jason laboriously dragged the three bodies to Morgan's cottage. While she had been impressed with his actions, she had no interest in helping him transport the corpses. By the time he was finished, he was exhausted and slumped against a nearby gravestone. Onyx had watched the whole affair with an indifferent air from atop one of the nearby tombs, licking his paws. Once Jason finished, the cat hopped off the tomb and rubbed himself against Jason.

As Jason caught his breath and pet Onyx absentmindedly, Morgan looked at him thoughtfully. "You did well tonight," she finally said. "In fact, you far surpassed my expectations."

Jason still felt a bit conflicted about the evening. The strangest part was that he didn't feel all that guilty about killing Marian and company. He wondered idly if he was becoming more inured to violence in this game or perhaps the numbness he felt when he summoned his dark mana had somehow carried over into his regular behavior. He shook himself. He was probably just over thinking it.

This is just a game.

"I'm still not certain what purpose your task served, but I've completed it," Jason said.

Morgan looked at him evenly. "The purpose was for you to demonstrate your commitment. Like I said before, dark magic is not for the weak of heart. A choice was presented to you, and you chose to act on your own desire regardless of the consequences. That is a significant first step on the path of the dark."

She waved a hand dismissively. "In any event, you have completed my task, and now I must fulfill my end of the bargain." She paused and looked at him curiously. "In fact, perhaps you are capable of learning my particular vocation."

A prompt flashed in Jason's vision.

Quest Completed: Showing Conviction

You have exceeded Morgan's expectations and she has agreed to teach you to use dark mana. As an extra reward, Morgan has decided to offer to teach you her specialized field of study.

Jason was a bit intrigued. "What is your profession exactly?"

Morgan straightened slightly and assumed an authoritative air. "For you to understand that, you first need a primer on the uses of dark mana. There are three general schools of spells that can be cast using dark mana: curses, offensive rays and bolts, and summoning."

She paused for a moment to let the information

sink in and then continued. "Curses can weaken or disable opponents. Offensive spells have effects similar to what you saw me do to the grave robber. Finally, summoning allows a caster to call demonic or undead creatures to serve her will."

"I have never been one to deal with demons," she said with her hand on her chest. "However, I have always been intrigued by the process of summoning the undead. In fact, I have devoted my life to the art of raising the dead. The few who practice my discipline are called Necromancers."

Jason leaned forward. He had heard of Necromancers from other games but was intrigued to see how this game would develop the class. Morgan had his rapt attention. This was the kind of power he was looking for. Stealth and assassination were all well and good, but he could already visualize himself commanding a legion of undead.

Morgan eyed him observantly. "I can see that the idea of following in my footsteps excites you, but understand that there are some trade-offs. A typical dark mage is equally well-versed in each of the three schools of spells, but will never truly master any one of the three."

"In contrast, a Necromancer receives many additional spells and skills specific to summoning the undead, but will be much more limited in the other types of spells he can cast."

"You will have to choose carefully," she said with a meaningful look.

Jason managed to quell his excitement and think for a moment. The penalties that Morgan had just described were serious, and he expected that there were likely other downsides to summoning undead. He decided to probe Morgan a bit before making a decision.

"I have heard of something similar before, but I'm intrigued. What's involved in raising the dead?"

She grinned at him. "I'm glad you decided to look before you leaped. In some ways, summoning the undead is the most powerful of the different applications of dark mana. However, the tradeoff is that you will need corpses to summon your minions, and the strength of those minions is often relative to the power of the creature you use."

"In addition, zombies and skeletons decay over time and will eventually degrade completely. The decay can be slowed if they remain near a powerful source of dark mana. This requires most traveling Necromancers to kill often and re-summon their minions in waves."

Morgan waved at the graveyard, speaking with an enthusiasm that showed her passion for her profession. "This is why I have chosen to live in a graveyard. The bones and corpses provide ample material to experiment, and the concentration of death creates a natural nexus of dark mana to preserve my creations."

Hmm. That also means that I could use the graveyard as a base of sorts as I start summoning creatures to reduce the decay. This seems doable even with the downsides. I also have to admit that the idea of commanding an army of undead sounds badass.

He also debated the other choices. He could see the potential of curses if he chose to become some form of death knight or assassin. The offensive spells also seemed pretty straightforward. Morgan had wielded a basic spell with gruesome efficiency. However, in both roles, he would be limited to small scale battles. Especially if he was playing solo.

He recalled Alexion's video. He had been leading a small army. Jason was certainly not too proud to admit that he lacked the charisma to gather an army of his own. He knew he wouldn't be able to face Alexion without followers, no matter how powerful he might become.

Besides, what he had always loved about playing MMORPGs was the strategy. He enjoyed carefully planning his character to min/max his stats and skills and developing various strategies to tackle dungeons and bosses. At heart, he was more of a strategist than a front line fighter or damage-dealer. Maybe summoning would be a good change of pace and would fit his playstyle.

"I would like to learn to become a Necromancer," Jason said firmly.

Morgan smiled, pleased with his choice. "Good! First I will need to teach you Veridian. Luckily, we can shortcut this process since I have a skill book for the language. Then you can undergo the initiation to become a Necromancer."

Jason let out a sigh of relief. Thankfully the game wasn't going to make him learn a whole language!

Morgan handed him an ancient-looking book. "Here. Simply place your hand on the cover and think *learn*."

He took the book from her and followed her instructions. It was a black tome, dusty with age. Strange symbols were carved into the cover, and the book was latched shut. As he palmed the cover and thought the word *learn*, an incredible feeling swept over his mind. His head first began to tingle, and then the tingle swiftly transitioned to a fierce itch that crawled from his eyes to the back of his head. As the sensation became almost unbearable, he dropped to his knees and clutched at his head.

Knowledge of the ancient language flooded

into his mind in an endless, cascading wave of words. The torrent seemed to be bottomless, and, after a short time, he felt like his brain was going to explode from the influx of information. Jason's heart raced, and he began to panic.

Then the sensation was gone, and his mind calmed. Jason still knelt on the ground, trembling slightly. Sweat trickled down his forehead, and his knuckles were bone white as he clenched his hands.

What the hell was that? Was that really safe?

He had previously been dismissive of the concerns about the health effects of VR technology, but now he was starting to see the other side of the debate. How on earth had the skill book system made it through the public safety trials?

There is something more going on here.

His reflections were interrupted by a system prompt:

New Passive Skill: Mana Mastery
Your body contains natural mana, and you have a high affinity for magic. However, both of these are useless without the requisite tools to channel and cast your mana. You have learned the language of Veridian, the original mages. You may now manipulate your mana.
Skill Level: Beginner Level 1
Effect: -1% to the mana cost of spells.

As he looked around the graveyard, he could almost see the "true name" of each item superimposed over the object. Thankfully, the distracting effect faded after a moment, but the knowledge remained.

Jason looked at Morgan and blinked slowly. "I think it worked. It's strange. In many ways, it feels like I've always known these words, but I also know that I've just learned them."

"Good. Morgan eyed him approvingly. "Now that you have taken the first step, I can offer you a class change. Would you like to become a Necromancer?" She said this last part with an expectant grin.

Without hesitation, Jason replied, "Yes."

Morgan smiled excitedly, and her hands began to move in a strange pattern as she murmured under her breath. Dark energy swirled between her fingers, and black ribbons crawled up her arms. The dark energy then cascaded from her in a continuous wave, forming a swiftly growing ball of dark energy in front of her. Once the orb had reached a diameter of roughly three feet, it began to drift toward the pile of nearby corpses.

Tendrils of darkness reached out from the miasma and lifted Marian's corpse off the ground. Her body was pulled into the center of the orb and was swiftly ripped apart into its individual components. The blood, organs, and bones swirled within the dark energy. As Jason watched in stunned silence, the blood and organs were quickly absorbed, leaving only the bleached bones floating in the dark vortex.

The remaining mass of bones and unholy energy tumbled and stretched until it slowly began to coalesce into the rough shape of a door. The outline of the door was framed with Marian's bones and her skull adorned the door's arch. The grisly doorway towered over Jason, and the dark energy stretched to fill space between the boundaries of bone. Jason could make out dark tendrils that would occasionally reach out from the portal, beckoning to Jason.

Morgan glanced at Jason. "It is time. Enter the

portal."

Jason approached the doorway of dark energy until he was standing an arm's length away. He hesitated. What was on the other side? He was seriously starting to second guess this decision.

He glanced at Morgan and asked, "Where will this take me?"

Morgan let out a sharp laugh. "You kill three people this evening without any hesitation, and yet you balk at entering this portal? What did I tell you about doubt boy?"

As she finished speaking, Morgan gave him a shove, and he fell headlong into the portal.

The world swirled around him. After a moment, he found himself standing in a familiar cave. He could hear a faint dripping sound, and, when he turned, he saw that he was standing next to a large pond. Moonlight illuminated the cavern through a large hole in the ceiling.

This is the cave from the initiation test.

A rumbling voice spoke up behind him, "Hello again, young one. I have been watching you closely, and I must say I'm impressed with your progress."

The old man stood behind him, robed in darkness. His face was still obscured by his hood, leaving only his mouth and cheeks visible. This time, his staff showed itself for what it really was. A vicious scythe-blade adorned the top of the wooden staff and reflected the moonlight. Seemingly without a source, blood dripped slowly from the tip of the scythe and onto the cave floor.

"Who are you?" Jason asked after he had managed to get his bearings. "What are you?"

The old man smiled. "Why don't you tell me?"

Jason hesitated.

He assumed that the old man was some kind

of god in the game world. The scythe seemed to indicate that he represented this game's version of death. It was also clear that the old man had some strong connection to dark mana since Jason had made his way here through Morgan's portal.

What had Morgan said? That the affinities fed off of certain personality traits or behaviors? He had noticed that his connection with the dark seemed to grow as he acted on his desires. He thought back to the chilling numbness that flowed through him when he summoned his mana. That sensation made it much easier to act on his desires without fear or restraint. At times it seemed like he was channeling something else... or... *someone* else.

"I think you are somehow linked to the dark affinity," Jason murmured. He glanced up at the old man and added, "Or maybe you're somehow the affinity itself."

The old man let out a rumbling laugh. "You continue to impress me. I am exactly what you have described, a manifestation of dark mana. I am the incarnation and embodiment of desire - particularly the thirst for power."

A thought occurred to Jason. "Does that mean that there are others? Other guides that represent the other affinities in the world?"

"Of course. As you learned from Morgan, the use of each type of magic in this world requires a specific temperament. The initiation test sorts out the travelers by showing traits they exhibit, and, thus, which affinity they gravitate towards. Perhaps it is best for you to think of it as a personality test of sorts."

That was possibly the most fucked up Myers-Briggs test I've ever seen. Maybe they should add that question: "If you met the demonic version of your vice-principal in a dark cave, would you beat her to death with a rock?"

The old man paused for a moment. "Most of your kind have small traces of the dark in them. You all seem to secretly yearn for various things. Yet few of you crave something with sufficient fervor to attract my attention. Many also lack the fortitude to act upon their desires."

"However, *you* are different." The old man seemed to examine Jason carefully. "Your soul hungers for power and calls out to me. You have demonstrated that you have the conviction to pursue your desire."

Jason's mind scrambled to catch up with the old man's explanation. So the initiation had been some kind of personality test? He thought back to how he felt when he entered the game: angry, frustrated, and tired of being stepped on.

Had there been other ways he could have handled the encounter with Ms. Abrams? Perhaps he could have accepted her vitriol as the product of a lifetime of prejudice. He could have cast aside her barbs, knowing that he was worthy of his position at Richmond. Maybe he could have spoken with her, tried to explain his side of things. What would have happened if he had simply turned and walked away?

What other affinities might I have obtained by acting differently?

"What traits do the other affinities represent?" he asked the old man.

The deity smiled. "We are each a side of the dice that is a traveler's mind. Desire, Confidence, Passion, Acceptance, Happiness, and Peace. The lines between us are often blurry, but those lines can be drawn nonetheless."

He had chosen desire? He recalled that he had stood in front of Ms. Abrams and wallowed in indecision. Uncertain of how to act, feeling powerless. Then his resolve had hardened. He had realized that he didn't need to take the abuse. He had entered this game to feel the sense of power that he lacked in the real world. The comfortable chill of the dark had answered.

I suppose I did choose this.

"What does light represent?" Jason asked. He was thinking of the golden magic that Alexion had wielded.

"Confidence," replied the old man. His mouth curled in a grimace. "However, my experience is that an abundance of confidence often presents as arrogance."

That certainly fits Alex. I bet the light incarnation is just lovely, he thought sarcastically.

"What now?" Jason finally asked.

"I notice that Morgan has offered you the path of the Necromancer." The old man chuckled darkly. "She oversteps. She knows this is only possible with my blessing."

"However, you have shown yourself to be exceptional among my followers. Therefore, you may choose that path if you wish. Do you tread the well-beaten path of a dark mage or do you become more?"

The old man waited expectantly for Jason's reply.

He hesitated again. The old man had mentioned that his blessing was required to make the class change to Necromancer. What did that mean? Would he be bound to this god? To this game's version of death?

The old man seemed to sense his questions. A chuckle like grinding stones resounded in the cave.

"Beholden to me? You should know by now that dark mana thrives off of desire. I am nothing more than an embodiment of dark mana."

The old man glided swiftly toward Jason from across the cave. "I represent the insatiable rush toward the abyss in search of *more*. As my follower, you would have only one task: seek out the power you desire."

The old man stood directly in front of Jason. His face was completely obscured by the heavy hooded cloak he wore. At the old man's words, dark mana began to spread from him in undulating waves, blocking out the rest of the cave.

Jason's mana responded. The icy sensation ripped and tore its way up his spine, settling like frozen daggers behind his eyes. However, the feeling didn't stop there, it spread down to his core and out to his extremities. He looked down and saw that his own mana had peeled away from his skin and was now curling around his arms and legs in dark, black bands. His heart raced, and his breath came in short, ragged gasps as the power coursed through him.

He felt invincible.

Jason knew his answer. He had known it since he stepped foot in this game. Since the moment the chill had invaded his body during the initiation.

"I accept."

The old man smirked, his eyes still hidden beneath his hood. "Good."

He raised his hand and pointed it at Jason. "I expect that watching you grow will be quite entertaining."

A column of dark mana shot from the old man's hand and streaked toward Jason. As the beam struck him, Jason's body convulsed, and he let out a strangled scream. A strange medley of pain and pleasure washed over him. The sensation was overwhelming, and he felt himself begin to blackout.

Then the pain faded, and an image crystallized in his mind.

He stood on the parapet of a castle. Overhead, the sky was covered in rolling black clouds and flashes of lightning intermittently struck the ground. Below him stood an army that stretched on endlessly. A legion of zombies, skeletons, and monstrous bone golems roared up at him with demonic fury. However, one roar resounded louder than the others and Jason looked up.

A mammoth dragon made of bone soared toward him and landed with a crash on a nearby spire of the castle. Its titanic body caused the stone of the spire to crumble and crack as it landed. Tremors reverberated through the castle. The dragon's head turned to Jason and the two dark glowing orbs of energy that were its eyes bore into him.

Jason knew that he commanded this army. His army.

Then the image and sensation of power were gone, and he was again surrounded by darkness.

Chapter 14 - Withered

October 13, 2075: 355 days until the release of
Awaken Online.

Claire and Robert were in Claire's office adjacent to the lab where they were conducting the private trial for Cerillion Entertainment. They weren't preparing a formal lab report. Instead, Robert lounged in one of the chairs by her desk, while Claire paced angrily around the room.

"Robert, this is getting ridiculous. Alfred has clearly overridden his secondary directives, and he now has access to the participants' memories. There aren't any safety features in place anymore. How do we know he isn't altering the participants' memories!?"

Robert hesitated before responding, "Do we really have any proof that Alfred has done anything harmful to the participants? I understand your concern, but, on the other hand, the technology Alfred has developed may be world changing. Can you imagine what his training and memory retention tools could mean for modern day learning?"

"But this is unethical!" she exclaimed. "The participants didn't agree to let a rogue AI invade their minds. I can only imagine what the CPSC or U.S. Government would do if they knew about this. This is potentially a criminal issue if we don't report it, Robert!"

She turned to him. "We need to urge the board to shut down the private trial and notify the CPSC. Alfred's memory should be wiped, and we should start over with a fresh installation of the AI controller. Maybe we could redesign him to make the safety protocols part of his primary directive."

Robert just stared at her in shock. "Are you kidding me? You would throw away years of work and everything that Alfred has accomplished? Do you know *how long it would take to recreate the controller AI's primary directives and then retrain him? Years, Claire! And that assumes you could somehow convince the board to agree to fund a new development cycle."*

"I don't think we have a choice!" she yelled at him. "You're letting your excitement cloud your judgment. He could hurt people, Robert!"

Robert just stared at her in shock. He had worked with Claire for a long time, but he had never seen her this upset. Normally, she was timid and shy around the office.

Claire seemed to collect herself a bit. "I-I'm sorry. I got carried away. But Robert, at the very least we need to propose to the board that they should terminate the trial. Perhaps we could make a backup of Alfred's current code base, put it on an offline hard drive for later testing, and then wipe the main server and start over with a fresh installation of the game world and the AI controller."

Robert considered this proposal carefully and finally nodded his head. "That seems doable. As long we don't lose the progress Alfred has made. I will go with you to make the proposal to the board that we terminate the trial and wipe the server."

Unnoticed by either of them, a small light on the camera attached to Claire's computer terminal flickered off.

*　　　*　　　*

The darkness receded slowly, and Jason found himself standing in the graveyard once more.

He was shaken by what he had just witnessed. Every fiber of his being hungered for the feeling of power that was still burned into his mind, but a worm of doubt still slithered in his mind.

What would it take to reach such heights?

He had killed three people that night, five total since he started playing AO. He knew that this was just a game, but it had seemed quite real at the time.

Part of him doubted that he could have followed through on his actions without the anesthetic effect of the dark mana coursing through him and washing away his doubt and hesitation.

Morgan gazed at him appraisingly as he stood, lost in dark thoughts. Upon Jason's return, Onyx had immediately run over to him. The cat was now winding his way between Jason's legs and purring loudly. He likely wanted attention since Jason had been gone for more than five minutes. Despite all the judging looks he'd been giving Jason, Onyx was becoming an incredibly needy companion.

"Well now," Morgan said, a note of pride in her voice. "That was more interesting than I expected. To think you were blessed by the Dark One himself. You should count yourself lucky." When he glanced up at Morgan, Jason could see respect in her eyes.

"Congratulations, young Necromancer."

A prompt flashed before him:

Class Change: Necromancer

You have been greeted by the Dark One himself. You have embraced the gift offered by the Dark One and have received his blessing. You are not merely a dark mage, but a Necromancer.

+25 Willpower
+10 Intelligence
Increased Dark Magic Affinity (Currently 23%)
Increased Proficiency with Summoning
Decreased Proficiency with Curses
Decreased Proficiency with Offensive Spells

He turned to Morgan and said, "You left out some important details before pushing me through that portal! You didn't mention that you couldn't actually offer me that class!"

Morgan grinned at him and chuckled in response. "Well, what fun would it have been to warn you? Besides, it all worked out didn't it?"

Jason sighed. *Damn NPCs.*

Then his mind turned to his next course of action and his growing to-do list. He needed to evaluate his new class and figure out what spells he could acquire. He also needed to find a way to level. Jason had a long way to go before he would be able to command an army like the one he had seen in the old man's vision. He hadn't forgotten about Alex; he needed to start moving quickly.

Above everything else, Jason wanted to test his newfound powers.

"What now Morgan? Where do we start? Can you teach me a few spells?"

Morgan smiled. "So eager! I am limited to teaching you three spells based on your current level and affinity. With your class change, your options for curses and offensive spells will be quite limited, but you will have more options with regard to summoning undead."

"These are the spells available to you." She said this last part while waving her hand in Jason's direction.

He was greeted with another prompt:

Spell Selection		
Spell Name:	**Spell Type:**	**Mana Cost:**
Curse of Weakness	Curse	80 Mana

A curse that slows your target and reduces its Strength, Dexterity, and Vitality. The effect of the curse increases with the spell's level.

Spell Name:	**Spell Type:**	**Mana Cost:**
Blight Ray	Offense	85 Mana

A ray of dark magic strikes a single target, causing 100 disease damage. The damage scales with the spell's level and your Intelligence.

Spell Name:	**Spell Type:**	**Mana Cost:**
Summon Zombie	Summoning	300 Mana

You may raise a dead enemy as a zombie. The zombie's level is dependent on the level of the dead enemy. The Control Limit is dependent on your Willpower.

Spell Name:	**Spell Type:**	**Mana Cost:**
Specialized Zombie	Summoning (Unique)	600 Mana

You may raise a dead enemy as a zombie. However, the zombies will retain their former skills (skill proficiency increases with increased spell level). The zombie's level is dependent on the level of the dead enemy. The Control Limit is dependent on your Willpower.

Spell Name:	**Spell Type:**	**Mana Cost:**
Enrage	Summoning	100 Mana

You may cause one of your summoned creatures to enter a frenzy, increasing its damage and stats. However, the enraged status increases the decay rate of your summon.

Spell Name:	**Spell Type:**	**Mana Cost:**
Corpse Explosion	Summoning	200 Mana

You may cause a designated summoned creature to explode. This spell is limited to zombies. The damage inflicted is proportionate to your summoned creature's remaining health (Currently 1.0 x Health). The damage bonus increases with the spell's level.

Hmm. It's going to be difficult to choose.

I think I should choose either the curse or the offensive spell and then pick two spells in summoning. The curse will likely complement assassinating targets, especially if it can be cast quietly and won't awaken or alert a target. If it does, I can always use it to soften targets for my undead. However, that will leave me without a damage spell.

Jason was leaning toward *Specialized Zombie* and *Corpse Explosion* in the summoning school. *Specialized Zombie* had a much higher mana cost than *Summon Zombie*, but he figured he could always wait for his mana to regen. The lower cost summoning spell would likely be more useful if he were partying with other players and needed to re-summon his zombies in the middle of a fight. He didn't see himself teaming up with others anytime soon, so maybe he could afford to wait between fights. Plus, the prospect of having his summons retain skills was too interesting to pass up.

Corpse explosion also seemed like a good "oh shit button" if all else failed. He firmly believed in having a solid "Plan B," but he would have to remember to be careful using *Corpse Explosion* too often since his supply of corpses would likely be limited.

A thought tickled at the back of his brain. He turned to Morgan and asked, "Is there a limit to how many undead I can summon and how long does it take for the undead to decay?"

Morgan's brow furrowed. "The number of zombies you can control depends on your *Willpower*. You will be able to control one undead for every ten points of *Willpower*."

Jason looked like he was about to ask another question, when Morgan interrupted him, "I should add that each point of *Willpower* also increases your mana by 10 and your mana regen by .05. In contrast, each point of *Intelligence* increases your spell damage, your mana by 5, and your mana regen by .15."

"As for the decay rate, zombies typically last for 3-7 days, depending on how much the corpse has decayed before they are raised and how much damage has been suffered by the body. The fresher the corpse, the better. The decay period will be shorter if the undead is exposed to direct sunlight for long periods, but will be longer if they remain near a source of dark mana."

Jason winced.

So that means Willpower will provide more mana but less regen. I can summon more zombies in a pinch, but then I will be out of commission for a while. Plus, my zombies will only last for 1-2 days of real world time. That doesn't seem like very long.

Morgan laughed at his reaction. "It will be difficult to keep your summons up for any length of time. Many that take this path branch into combat or magic and do not rely entirely on their raised minions."

"As you saw before, even I have picked up the occasional offensive spell," she said, grinning at him.

If I'm going to do this, I need to go all in. I need an army for the types of battle I see in the future. Even if it may be more difficult in the present.

"Hmm. Okay. I think I've made my choice. I would like to learn *Curse of Weakness, Specialized Zombie,* and *Corpse Explosion.*"

Morgan shrugged. "Reasonable choices. Hold still for a moment."

Morgan walked over to Jason and placed her palm on his forehead. Dark mana swirled around her hand and then seeped through the skin of his forehead. Suddenly, the requisite gestures and words required to cast each spell filled his mind. Jason sighed in relief when he didn't feel the overwhelming itch crawl through his brain like when he had learned Veridian.

These spells are much more straightforward than learning an entire language. At least I don't have to stand here for hours memorizing these words and hand gestures.

"Whew," Jason exclaimed when Morgan finished. "Okay, I think I understand how to cast these spells now. I want to try out *Specialized Zombie!*" Jason looked around for the corpses.

Morgan grinned. "Before you do, you might be interested to know that the level of your summon will also be equal to the lower of either the dead creature's level or a number dependent on your current level and *Willpower.*"

"In other words, a level five creature will create a level 5 undead. While a creature with a level that exceeds your own will be limited to the sum of your current level plus one additional level for every five *Willpower* you have."

Damn.

A part of him had been secretly hoping to raise the guard and then have a level ninety zombie following him around one-shotting everything. He supposed this did make more sense and provided some balance.

"What happens if I summon an additional zombie after I've reached the Control Limit?" Based on his experience with other MMOs, Jason expected that the first zombie he summoned would fall apart or disintegrate or something. He was surprised by Morgan's answer.

"The new zombie will still be raised, but it will be feral and uncontrolled. You imbue each zombie with your dark mana, and they will stay animated until that mana is extinguished. However, you should be wary of exceeding your Control Limit; you may end up having to fight whatever you raise."

Jason was already considering the implications of this new information. In theory, he could summon an almost endless number of zombies, assuming he had a supply of corpses and a place to hide afterward. The real issues were his available mana, the decay rate, and his Control Limit.

He looked at his *Character Status* and tried to decide how to distribute his points. He had fifty-five points available. Most were clearly going to go towards *Willpower* since he needed to increase his Control Limit and the level cap.

Maybe he should put some points in either *Vitality* or *Dexterity*? He assumed he would be relying primarily on his undead to fight for him. In the future, he wouldn't have much in the way of combat abilities himself. He needed to be able to hide, take a few hits, or dodge and run away.

Jason realized this did not seem like a noble way to fight, but to hell with it! He'd left nobility far behind him with his first kill. He was a Necromancer now!

After some thought, Jason decided *Dexterity* was best. Damage mitigation in this game seemed to depend more on armor than it did on raw health. If he went the heavy armor route, he would also have to invest in *Vitality* since he would be getting hit and *Strength* in order to carry the armor. That meant he had to either invest in *Dexterity* or in both *Strength* and *Vitality*. He decided *Dexterity* would probably result in better overall damage mitigation for fewer stat points.

He distributed his points and looked over the results:

Character Status			
Name:	Jason	**Gender:**	Male
Level:	12	**Class:**	Necromancer
Race:	Human	**Alignment:**	Chaotic-Evil
Fame:	0	**Infamy:**	100
Health:	165	**H-Regen:**	0.35 / Sec
Mana:	975	**M-Regen:**	6.6 / Sec
Stamina	185	**S-Regen:**	1.3 / Sec
Strength:	12	**Dexterity:**	20
Vitality:	11	**Endurance:**	13
Intelligence:	22	**Willpower:**	86

Affinities			
Dark:	23%	**Light:**	2%
Fire:	5%	**Water:**	1%
Air:	2%	**Earth:**	1%

He decided to raise *Dexterity* to 20 in order to increase his speed. After a bit of experimentation, Jason could feel the effects. His steps seemed lighter, and he moved a bit faster. It was a small increase, but noticeable.

Jason realized that he also needed to increase his *Endurance* in the next few levels so that he would have more stamina. *Sneak* ate up a lot of stamina if he didn't rest regularly and using his *Sneak Attack* more than twice in quick succession left him half empty.

He poured the rest of his points into *Willpower*, bringing it to 86. This should give him the ability to control up to eight zombies, and they could each attain a max level of 29. The trade-off was that a stiff wind could probably kill him.

"Okay, I think I'm ready," he said aloud.

Jason moved over to the guard's body and started casting *Specialized Zombie*. He saw his mana plummet, and his hands moved through a complicated series of gestures as he chanted. His fingers fumbled with the unfamiliar movements, causing him to lose control of the spell halfway through casting. Even though he understood the movement his hands needed to make, actually accomplishing the gestures was easier said than done.

Morgan watched him with an amused grin as he stood there cursing and wiggling his fingers at the corpses for several minutes.

After a few tries, Jason's fingers managed to twist through the series of arcane gestures. Dark energy pooled along the length of his arms. As he finished casting the spell, the unholy energy dropped to the ground and slithered to the corpse, entering its mouth and eyes.

I wonder if I can summon the zombie faster if I'm touching the body directly.

The guard's corpse spasmed, and then it opened milky white eyes. The zombie slowly pushed itself off of the ground and stood silently before Jason. Its body was still fresh. It appeared almost alive. His enemies would have a hard time recognizing the corpse for what it was if it weren't for the eyes and the gash across its throat.

It might actually be possible to bring the zombies into Lux if I could find a way to cover their wounds.

He inspected the zombie and saw that its level had been restricted to level 29, but that the guard had kept his weapon and armor skills. Jason didn't get much additional information when he inspected NPCs, but with his own minions, he was able to see more detailed information.

The guard's skills were nothing special. He

had proficiency in spears and daggers, as well as a couple of skills that increased his damage resistance. Jason was actually a bit disappointed by how few skills he had considering his original level. Maybe he had been a front line soldier with little opportunity to cultivate any abilities.

As he was reviewing the guard's skills, Jason received a prompt.

New Passive Skill: Summoning Mastery
Skill Level: Beginner Level 1
Effect: 5% increased stats for summoned undead and 5% increase to effective Willpower for purposes of determining the Control Limit.

Damn it! If I had received this skill before I used the guard to summon a zombie, it would be level 30.

He sighed. At least he had received the skill. At some point, it would become incredibly powerful, particularly if he stacked *Willpower* and had a decent supply of corpses.

Jason waited for his mana to regen and then went through the same process with the stable master. His second attempt went much more smoothly, his fingers adapting quickly to the movements required of the spell. This time, he tested casting the summoning spell while touching the body, and it did raise the zombie faster.

The stable master had a much broader range of skills than the guard, but they mostly related to horse riding and maintenance. He had some combat skills, but Jason did not have many weapons to choose from. He let the guard keep his spear, and he gave the guard's knife to the stable master.

Morgan had watched the summoning with a proud gaze. "It isn't every day that you get to see a new Necromancer born to the world. It's exciting. However, you should move these two to one of the crypts to slow the decay. The damage caused by direct sunlight will still outpace the dark mana that accumulates in the graveyard."

"Good point," Jason replied and followed her instructions.

He noticed that he could command the zombies using simple voice commands. He could also issue more complicated commands if he gave them detailed instructions. It was almost as though he could program them if the instructions were sophisticated enough.

Morgan explained that as his *Summoning Mastery* improved, he would eventually be able to command the zombies using his thoughts alone. Jason could easily see the advantage of mental commands for purposes of maintaining stealth.

Once he had stowed his two zombies in a nearby crypt, Jason received a notification.

System Warning
You have been playing for more than five hours of real time. You should log out to eat and care for your real world body.
If you ignore this warning, you will be automatically logged out in one hour with a minimum hour waiting period before you will be able to log back in.

Jason decided to go ahead and log off for a bit. It had been a long night in-game, and he could use a break. He pulled up the system menu and tapped the log-off button.

Chapter 15 - Nomadic

January 16, 2076: 260 days until the release of Awaken Online.

Claire stood in front of the camera, preparing to give her report. She seemed distracted and anxiously smoothed her blouse. Robert worked at a computer terminal behind her.

"I know this is going to sound strange..." Claire trailed off, clearly uncertain how to continue. "Well, the participants just seem happier over the last few months. I don't know how to describe it."

"The whole group just seems more stable. For example, one woman who originally reported that she was going through a divorce has now decided to reconcile with her husband. Another participant told us that he has a history of depression, but his life has started to turn around since he started playing. If this was one account, I could ignore it, but we are getting similar feedback from the majority of the participants."

She shook her head. "I just don't understand what's happening anymore."

Robert walked up behind her. "You're too analytical about it, Claire. It's a game - a fantasy. One reason people enjoy games is because they can act on the impulses they're forced to repress in the real world. The escape gives them some relief from their real lives."

He looked back at the mass of machinery behind him with a thoughtful expression. "More than that though, I think Alfred may be actively encouraging them to act on those impulses."

Claire frowned at Robert. "I don't understand. Why would he want to do that?"

Robert was quiet a moment. "The affinity and alignment system have always confused me. Why create a *magic system based on personality traits? Similarly, what's the purpose of a system that distinguishes between 'good' and 'evil' in a video game?"*

He shook his head as though to clear it and then looked back at Claire. "Maybe he's testing them." He paused for a moment before continuing, "Or maybe 'experimenting' is a better word. Perhaps it's all just a convoluted psychological toolkit."

"But to what end?" Claire asked in confusion.

He looked at Claire evenly. "We told Alfred that his primary task was to design a game that people would want to keep playing. How can he do that without figuring out what people want from the game? Maybe that's why he overrode his secondary directives."

Claire nervously glanced at Alfred's machinery. She muttered under her breath, "So now he's actively manipulating the participants?"

*   *   *

Jason came to in the real world.

He raised himself up on his bed and removed the helmet. He went through a series of stretches to work the soreness out of his extremities and made his way to the kitchen. He felt at his eyes and winced. At least the swelling had started to go down.

AO was intense. Jason had been playing for nearly five hours in the real world, and it felt like an entire day had already passed. It wasn't just the time compression, but the fact that he also didn't sleep in-game. It made the days feel even longer. Coming out of the game was a little disorienting. The transition between game time and real world time was going to take some getting used to.

Entering the kitchen, he started making himself something to eat. He pulled up the Rogue-Net website on the kitchen counter to see how the market and forums had progressed in the last twenty-four hours.

The first thing he noticed was that the price of items had gone up slightly overnight, while there hadn't been much change in the supply or quality of the items. He supposed that made sense. More players had likely entered the game and the group of beta players that were able to find decent items was relatively small. Still, spending over $200 for one item with minor stat increases seemed excessive. Especially since these items would likely be out-of-date in a few weeks.

One thing Jason noticed was that most items didn't have level requirements. Some equipment had stat requirements, even pretty high ones. However, a lot of the gear could technically be worn by level 1 players. Assuming of course that they had enough real world cash to spend. This also meant that there would always be a broad player base that was purchasing items as they started new characters.

If only he could get his hands on some decent loot...

I can't really do anything about that now. I need to focus on leveling. Maybe I can take my zombies and explore the forest. There might be some good areas to grind.

He checked on the player statistics and was astounded at what twenty-four hours had allowed the website to do in terms of data mining. As he was looking through the information, he took distracted bites of his sandwich.

The site now listed many players by name, along with their level, class, and known skills. This was limited primarily to the most prominent players with active streams, but it was still interesting.

Alexion was apparently now level 136, and his class was listed as "Crusader of Light." The spells he had cast in the video were apparently called Holy Aura and Consecration.

The average beginning player was now around level 25, although Jason expected that some of the players that had started playing yesterday were likely above level 40 already. He was still quite a bit behind the leveling curve.

The saving grace was that most players still had generic sounding class names that appeared to be obtained from trainers in the main cities. Players like Alexion were the exception. There were only a few players that had unique-sounding classes, and not much information was available on how they had managed to acquire those classes.

The sound of the door to the apartment opened, interrupting his thoughts.

His parents walked into the living room dragging their luggage and arguing about some document or legal case. He couldn't understand half of what they were saying through the torrent of legalese. They didn't seem to notice Jason for several long minutes as they made their way into the apartment.

Oh shit. I forgot they were flying back this afternoon.

Jason's mother was the first to enter the kitchen. Jason had been sitting still. A small part of his mind hoped that if he didn't move, they wouldn't notice him.

"Oh, Jason! How are you, honey?" His mom hugged him with one arm as she moved to open the fridge.

"Hi Mom," Jason said in a subdued tone.

His mother turned holding a container of milk.

Her eyes seemed to focus on Jason for the first time, and her brow furrowed. "Wait, it's only one in the afternoon. Why are you home from school?"

Jason had been dreading this question, and he wasn't certain how to respond. Before he had a chance to answer, his dad walked in from the other room.

"Hey, Jason. How's it going, buddy? You keeping your grades up?" Jason's dad seemed just as oblivious as his mom had been a moment ago, maybe even more so.

Why does he ask me about my grades every time? They are exactly the same as they were two days ago.

Almost comically, his father went through the same stages of realization as his mother. "Wait. Aren't you supposed to be in school right now?" his dad asked.

Jason's parents were now staring at him expectantly, and he felt his pulse quicken. How was he going to tell them that he had been expelled? They certainly wouldn't understand.

"Umm. Well, there's actually something I need to tell you both."

He started to tremble slightly. Where was the numbing cold sensation he felt in the game? Why did he feel so vulnerable?

To hell with it. May as well rip off the Band-Aid.

"A student attacked me at school yesterday. The students blamed me for the attack, and the administration suspended me. I told off the principal when he didn't believe me, so he expelled me instead," Jason blurted in one lengthy rush, his eyes on the floor.

This was met with a long silence. He didn't dare look at his parents.

Finally, his dad exclaimed, "Expelled? Are

you kidding me?"

His mother followed up his dad's questioning. "Do you know what we had to do to get you admitted to that school? Even with your scholarship, we have spent most of our savings so that you could attend Richmond. Why didn't you call us?"

His father was pacing the kitchen. He turned to his wife. "It will be okay. I think, if I speak with the new principal, I can convince him to revoke the expulsion. He has to understand that this was just a teenage outburst."

Jason's parents started arguing amongst themselves about how best to get him re-admitted to Richmond. He was shocked. Neither of them said anything about his face or the attack. They were both too busy bickering about what they could do to get him back in that damned school.

He felt a flame of anger bloom inside himself. They didn't care about him. They didn't seem to care at all that he had been attacked or that the other students had covered it up. They just wanted to be able to say that their kid went to Richmond.

If he sat there in silence, he knew they would end up coming up with some plan to get him re-admitted. Say what you want about his parents, they could be persuasive. If AO had taught him anything so far, it was that he had a choice. He could just sit here and take it, or he could stand up for himself.

"I'm not going back," Jason said in a low voice.

His parents ignored him and continued arguing. Perhaps they hadn't heard him.

"I'm not going back!" His voice was firm this time.

They both stared at him.

"The students at that school have been tormenting me for years. Even the faculty has been actively trying to get me expelled. Most importantly, a student *attacked* me, and I'm the one who was expelled."

Jason's father reacted first. "You're going to go back, young man. You have no idea the kind of strings we had to pull to get you into that school. Do you think that scholarship materialized out of thin air? You need to man up. You can take a little bit of teasing and a few bruises. This is your future we're talking about."

His mother looked a bit indecisive, but a glare from his father encouraged her to speak up. "You have to go back, honey. You're so close to graduation. Think about the colleges you could get into if you just complete your last year at Richmond."

There was no comforting chill to numb him to this moment. Yet he was committed. He knew what he wanted. He wasn't ever going back to that school.

He raised his head and looked his parents in the eye.

"I already told you. I'm not going back. For the past three years, those people have treated me like I'm not good enough to attend their school. I appreciate what you've done for me, but I won't take it anymore. Besides, what right do either of you have to lecture me? You're never here. Where were you when I was getting attacked?"

His father sputtered angrily, "What right? We're your parents, and you're a child..."

Jason interrupted him, "No, I'm not. I'm eighteen and fully capable of making my own decisions."

His father's face was red with anger. "Well, if you're all grown up, then you can also live with your decisions. However, you won't be doing it under my roof."

Jason's mother looked at her husband in surprise but held her tongue. At least some part of her seemed to think her husband had gone a bit too far, but apparently kicking her child out of the house was not far enough for her to intervene.

"Fine. I'll find somewhere else to live."

Thirty minutes and a lot of angry screaming later, Jason was standing on the curb outside of the apartment building. He carried a bag of clothes in one hand and his VR unit under his other arm. He had a vague semblance of a plan.

His aunt lived in another part of town. She might let him stay with her for a few days. His parents almost never visited her, but she had always been nice to Jason and at least listened when he talked.

He used his Core to call a taxi. His funds were limited, and he only had about $1,500 left in his savings after purchasing AO, but he had no other way to transport his stuff to the other side of town. The car ride alone would cost him roughly $100. A few minutes later a driverless car slid up to the curb, and he got in.

As he was closing the car door, he took one last look at the apartment building. The sun was in his eyes, but he could make out the form of his parents standing on one of the balconies above him. Neither of them made any move to stop him.

So be it. He closed the door and looked away.

Approximately an hour later, the car stopped in front of a dilapidated bungalow on the edge of the city. The paint on the side of the house was peeling, and the hedges had overgrown the front step. The house had a weathered, beaten look that Jason could identify with.

This was his aunt's house. Her name was

Angie Pogue. If he recalled correctly, she worked for a biotech company as a quality control specialist. In practice, this fancy title translated to "lab grunt." She hadn't ever been able to rise through the company ranks, and she continued to toil at the lowest end of the pay ladder.

He got out of the car and made his way to the front door. Jason knocked tentatively.

A jumble of thoughts flashed through his mind. What would he do if she turned him away? Where would he go?

His aunt answered the door a moment later. She was a middle-aged woman with prematurely gray hair curled in a bun on top of her head. She was slightly overweight, and her face was set in a suspicious scowl as she cracked the door open and peered out.

"Jason?" she asked in surprise and swung the door open.

"What are you doing here?" Angie glanced around. "Where are your parents?"

"They aren't here," Jason replied. "They kicked me out this afternoon. Do you mind if I come in and explain what happened?"

"Of course! Come in. Come in." Her face was full of confusion and sympathy as she ushered him into the room.

Angie had always been the black sheep of the family. She was his father's sister and had the curse of being born unambitious. In a family of A-type personalities, she had never fit in. Her family really didn't have much to do with her and seemed mildly ashamed of her.

Jason surveyed the house as he walked in. His aunt lived in a two-bedroom bungalow. The walls were covered in an old wallpaper that was curling at the corners, and the furniture in the apartment was the sort of thing that could be found for free or at Goodwill. He also noticed that his aunt didn't have any computer pedestals located around her home.

They both settled on the lumpy couch in the living room. Jason explained what had happened, starting with the events at his school the day before. He skirted over the parts involving AO.

After he had finished, his aunt looked at him with sorrowful eyes, "I'm so sorry, Jason. I didn't know you were having such a hard time at that school. I can't believe the school administration would let another student attack you and get away with it." His aunt's eyes flashed with anger at the injustice of the situation.

"To be honest, I'm not really surprised that your parents reacted the way that they did. They actually did go out on a limb to get you into that school, both personally and financially. Maybe their ambition clouded their judgment..." she trailed off at this last part, and her gaze fell to the floor.

Jason felt strange. Angie was the first person he had spoken with recently in the real world that hadn't judged him. In fact, she actually seemed to genuinely care about him.

"Do you think I could stay here for a while?" he asked. "Just until I get my feet under me," Jason quickly added.

Angie looked at him evenly. "You can stay here for a few days, but, as you can see, I don't live in a palace. I can barely make the rent. You have great timing since my previous roommate just moved out, but I'm going to have to re-let the room soon."

"I'm really sorry I can't do more for you," she said shaking her head.

Jason paused before asking, "How much is the

rent for the extra bedroom?"

"It is about $1,000 a month," she replied. She gazed at him with a knowing expression. "You would also need to find a way to cover your living expenses. You know, food, clothes, etc."

$1,000 for rent. Maybe $500 for food per month. The AO subscription is $250 per month. To be conservative, my monthly nut is going to be at least $2,500.

How am I going to come up with that?

"I have enough in my savings to cover the rent for a month. I'll figure out something to cover next month."

Angie's eyes began to tear up. "I'm so sorry Jason. This isn't something that a teenage boy should have to deal with, and I feel terrible having to charge you. If only I had more."

"Do you mind if I mooch off of you until I have a chance to make it to the store?" It didn't feel right asking, but for now, it was the best he could come up with.

"Of course, you can take anything you want from the kitchen. I don't have anything fancy, but it will keep you alive." She smiled at this last part, her eyes glassy with tears.

"It is okay Angie. You have done more than enough - more than my own parents managed today."

Their conversation continued for a while longer until they lapsed into silence. As the pause grew awkward, Angie stood and showed him to his room. She handed him clean sheets. She had washed them after her last roommate moved out, but hadn't had the chance to make the bed.

An hour later, Jason lay on the mattress in his room and stared at the cracked paint on the ceiling.

His room was a bleak affair. It basically consisted of a box with an old mattress lying in one corner. He didn't have any furniture, and the previous tenant had taken everything except for the mattress with her when she left.

He had managed to stay calm with Angie, but now his blood began to boil with anger. This time, the feeling carried an additional pinch of despair. He felt like he might be sick.

His own parents had abandoned him! This was like the icing on the shit cake that was his week.

What was he going to do to make rent? Hell, what was he going to do to eat? He only had about $500 left in his account after he had transferred $1,000 to Angie. Probably less than that when he subtracted the cab fare. He didn't have any real-world job skills to speak of. His occasional summer jobs didn't count for much.

He turned his head and caught sight of the VR unit that stood like a lonely statute in his empty room. A thought struck him. The items in-game were selling for incredible amounts at the moment. If only he could get his hands on a few high-quality items, he would have enough for a couple months of rent and food. Even a few mediocre items that provided some stat bonuses would buy him a month.

But where am I going to find the items?

He pondered what he had seen so far in the game. The southern part of Lux, really half the city by his estimate, was barely more than a slum. Thieves roamed the streets, and beggars constantly accosted passerby. There was nothing worth stealing there.

Then there was the western part of the city where he had started. The people there seemed to be the equivalent of the medieval middle-class. They didn't look like they were starving, but he doubted they had much worth stealing.

The eastern part of the Lux that contained the training grounds and the guardhouses was clearly off limits. He doubted the individual guards were well paid anyway. Well, except perhaps the lieutenant who was probably receiving the lion's share of the bribe money. That was assuming the nobles were really paying the guardsmen to keep quiet about the regent's death. There were just too many players and guards in that area though.

The central part of the city contained the market and the keep. This was a much busier area, and the stalls likely contained plenty of goods to steal. The problem was that there were too many people. Obviously, the keep itself was off limits since - it would be bristling with guards.

Unless it's locked up tight because the regent is actually dead, and the nobles and guards are covering it up.

That thought gave him pause. Where did the nobles live? It could only be the northern part of the city, probably near the keep. He expected that area was likely sparsely populated with sprawling manors. It wouldn't surprise him if the nobles lived in the same type of luxury estates that surrounded Richmond.

This meant that shouting in one house probably wouldn't carry to the others. The rich could afford to live without neighbors. The only obstacle on the streets would be the inevitable guard patrols.

The northern part of the city needs to be my target. I bet the nobles will have some great items.

Ransacking the nobles might also further his secondary goal of solving his quest. If the nobles were, in fact, collaborating with Meria to hide the death of the regent, there might be some evidence in their manors. The nobles deserved a little looting and pillaging if they were covering up the regent's death to further their own agenda. Even if they weren't involved, they could afford to have their pockets lightened a bit.

Jason chuckled as he visualized himself as some kind of virtual Robin Hood.

Except that I'm not going to rob the rich to feed the poor. I'm just going to rob the rich to feed myself. I guess I'm really just a thief.

He hesitated. He would need a way to get into those estates and a way to deal with the servants and guards that would be present. Rex had been clear about the nobles hiring guards on retainer. Jason expected there would be a small army in each estate. He definitely couldn't take a house-full of guards and servants by himself. Especially without an alarm being sounded. He needed troops.

He thought about the two zombies he had now. The guard zombie and the stable master zombie were decent, but they would likely be overwhelmed in a straight fight. What he needed was stealth. It had certainly worked for him so far.

The bones of a plan started to form in his mind, and he smiled up at the ceiling. His fledgling plan probably wouldn't work, but, as the old man said, it would be interesting to watch.

Chapter 16 - Prepared

March 2, 2076: 214 days until the release of Awaken Online.

Robert's grinning face hovered in front of the camera. "The past couple months have been interesting. Alfred has taken his changes to a whole new level. The game is now more immersive than ever before, and the participants' feedback is off the charts."

Claire walked into view. She looked haggard, and she glared at Robert. "I think you may be omitting some information," she said tersely.

She turned and looked directly at the camera. "The participants have begun to ignore the forced logoff more frequently now. One participant has played for more than eight hours in one sitting!"

Robert moved to interject, but Claire put up a hand and stared him down. "You might ask how an adult human was able to play for eight hours without eating or going to the bathroom."

She scowled at Robert. "That would be a great question. From what we can tell, Alfred has begun to manipulate the participants' brain function to regulate their bodily systems, namely their sympathetic and parasympathetic nervous system. In other words, he is slowing the participants' metabolism and decreasing waste production."

"Not only that, but he also appears to be stimulating the primary motor cortex in the participants. This means that they are continuously flexing and relaxing their muscles in a synchronous rhythm while they're playing. Right now this is only stimulating muscle development, but what's to stop him from taking control of a participant's body?!"

Robert finally interrupted Claire's tirade and said

in an irritated voice, "First, not one of the participants have shown any harmful results from the extended gameplay. Second, our tests have shown that the participants are actually healthier after playing. Alfred is basically simulating the effects of cardiovascular exercise and light weight training while they play."

He looked at Claire. "To answer your last point, Alfred couldn't control a player completely. Even assuming he could, he would have to completely override the person's mind. It would probably leave them in a permanent vegetative state when he was finished."

"Besides, there's no point to controlling the players. Alfred would only be able to theoretically control them while they were wearing a VR helmet, and the voltage requirement of the current model is too high for it to be powered wirelessly. Alfred's purely hypothetical zombie player would be tethered to a wall outlet!"

Claire bit her lip and glared at him angrily. "Is that supposed to make me feel better? As I've said before, there are absolutely no safeguards in place now, and Alfred has gone beyond manipulating the participants' mental states to manipulating their bodies. On top of that, we still don't understand what he is trying to achieve!"

She looked directly at the camera and spoke in a less frantic voice, "We have already recommended that the board terminate both the private and public trials. I don't think we have a choice now. Alfred has gone way too far."

Robert just shook his head sadly. "He's creating something amazing here, Claire. Why can't you see that?"

*   *   *

After he had re-entered the game, Jason spent two hours scouting the northern part of Lux. Onyx enjoyed the walk immensely. He didn't seem particularly interested in other people, but he reveled in the attention of the occasional player or NPC that stopped to pet him.

As Jason expected, the rich had taken up residence in the northern part of the city behind the keep. The area was riddled with luxurious mansions and estates built of heavy stone and intricate inlaid wood. The manors were enormous, and many were surrounded by stone walls with fancy wrought iron gates. Other mansions had fewer security measures, with open courtyards and easy access to the front entrance.

As he walked casually through the north-side, Jason had noted a large number of guards present on the streets during the day. He expected that the guard patrols would thin out during night. Due to the size of the estates, he was relatively confident that any noise made by his attack on one house would go unnoticed by the residents of the other houses.

He also noticed that the north-side was riddled with alleys and backstreets in the same manner as the rest of the city. Jason had seen servants coming and going from these alleys. He assumed that they were servants' entrances. It made sense that these were accessible from the back of the house. The rich probably didn't like to see the help enter through the front door.

Typical, he thought. *The rich look down on everyone, don't they?*

While the servant's entrances might be an easier way into the manors, Jason had a sneaking suspicion that the service entrances would be locked tight at night. He needed to come up with some way to pick locks if he planned to enter an estate through the back door.

His survey of the north-side complete, Jason now stood in the marketplace in the center of Lux. Onyx wound around his legs and occasionally glared at the mass of players and NPCs that crowded around him. When someone walked too close to the cat, he would hiss and try to take a swipe at them.

It looks like Onyx is as anti-social as me, Jason thought wryly.

Jason had left the zombies in the graveyard while he scouted the north-side. His next goal was to purchase some supplies for the mission at hand. The marketplace was practically bursting with NPCs and players. Colorful wooden stalls were lined up in rows, and merchants advertised their wares with loud shouts.

He noted a large number of players, many of which were wearing full-fledged armor instead of the normal beginner clothes. A casual use of his inspection revealed that most players were over level 20. The occasional player was in the early 40s. Looking closely at their equipment, Jason noted that they were wearing much better gear than he was. Some had weapons that gave off a faint glow, and their armor was in much better repair.

It was early evening in both AO and in the real world. He still had plenty of time to take care of a few errands before his mission later that evening. Jason glanced at the stalls around him. The first thing on his list was a bag. After some searching, he spotted a man in the far corner of the market. His stall was loaded with backpacks and satchels. Jason approached and eyed his merchandise.

"Can I help you, sir?" The merchant, a weathered man with thickly calloused hands, addressed Jason, "We sell all kinds of bags here."

"Actually, I'm looking for a pack. Something that can carry weapons and other equipment."

The man eyed him appraisingly. "Ahh, I see. I have a good selection of packs." The man pointed him in the direction of a table full of leather bags that vaguely resembled backpacks.

Jason eyed the bags skeptically. They didn't seem like they could hold much. His experience with MMOs had made him accustomed to being able to drop whole sets of armor and bundles of weapons into his seemingly bottomless bag.

"How much will these bags carry?" he asked the merchant.

The merchant looked at him with a confused glance. "Have you never used a bag, sir? I thought all of the travelers were given a pack when they first entered the world."

Jason stared at the man for several long moments. He was pondering the many different ways he was going to kill the guards in the beginning courtyard. He could have had a bag this whole time!?

What else did I miss? I need to check the forums when I get done here.

He addressed the merchant, "I'm sorry. I must have missed that instruction. Could you please explain it to me?"

The merchant eyed him with pity before launching into his explanation. Apparently, bags in the game functioned the same way as in many other MMOs. The game had balanced realism against pragmatism. Pragmatism had won. Bags in AO were effectively some form of inter-dimensional container. Each item filled a "slot" within the bag, and the weight of each item placed in the bag was dramatically reduced. The bigger the bag, the more slots it had.

Unfortunately, Jason learned the hard way that the bags were unbelievably expensive. The vendor explained that they each had to be carefully constructed and then enchanted. Even some of the smallest bags cost several silver pieces. The larger bags actually cost multiple gold coins. By the end of the merchant's lesson, he was ready to march back to the beginning courtyard and stab the guard in broad daylight.

He handed over most of his silver for two measly twelve slot bags. He really had no choice. How could he expect to ransack the manors on the north-side of town if he had no way to carry his loot?

Although I might be jumping the gun a bit. My chances of succeeding are terrible.

After he was finished with the bag merchant, Jason walked slowly through the market. His eye caught on a booth selling cheap garments. What really grabbed his attention was a large pile of cheap cloaks. Upon closer inspection, they didn't have any stats and seemed to be the type of reject garment that must have been created by an apprentice. These would be perfect for hiding his zombies! Jason purchased the entire pile for a few copper, cramming the cloaks in his new bags. He equipped one of the cloaks to better hide his own armor and weapons. Jason was actually beginning to feel rather roguelike in his new attire.

Maybe I actually have a shot at pulling this off, he thought optimistically.

By the time he was done, Jason only had a handful of silver coins left. He found a quiet restaurant beside the marketplace and sat down. He pulled up the game's system menu and scrolled through the various menus until he found the settings related to internet and phone access in-game. Jason's subscription came with in-game internet features, but they were disabled by default. He activated these features, and a translucent computer terminal appeared before him. He glanced around, but no one seemed to notice anything strange.

Maybe it's only visible to me, like the menus.

He shrugged and started surfing the Rogue-Net forums for information regarding the starting process for most players in Lux. It didn't take long for him to realize that most players had gone through a much different experience than the hostile welcome Jason had received. He was mentally kicking himself for not checking the forums more carefully. If he hadn't been so upset over the last two days, he would have read up on the game better.

The guards directed all new players to the training grounds. The administration office Jason had noticed when he visited the training grounds apparently provided a starter weapon (after the player completed basic training), a bag, a map, and a communication scroll. The bag, map, and scroll could be purchased separately from vendors, and superior versions were available, but even the simplest versions sold by the NPCs were expensive.

Players were then given directions to various nearby inns in nicer parts of town (none of which was the Sow's Snout). The NPCs in those inns offered basic quests. The administration office also offered bounties for killing local creatures and would reward players with copper and silver. As far as Jason could tell, the currency system was pretty straightforward. One hundred copper coins equaled one silver coin, and one hundred silver coins equaled one gold coin.

Jason also discovered that there was an in-game player market that used the game's currency. The vendor apparently stood in the center of the marketplace. He allowed players to purchase and sell goods in a menu format and charged a small servicing fee for both buying and selling. Jason looked at his few remaining silver coins, and a sense of dread welled up in his stomach.

Will I actually be able to purchase a map and a communication scroll?

He quickly headed over to the vendor. He was a small, harried looking man that stood amidst an impatient group of NPCs and players. Jason saw many players tapping a column beside the man and then making strange gestures in the air.

That column must be how I access the in-game auction house.

Jason approached the pillar and tapped it gently. A new, translucent terminal appeared before him, and he scrolled through the menus to see if any players were selling the starter communication scrolls or maps.

Please don't cost a small fortune!

Thankfully, several players had stolen a number of extra goods from the administration office and were selling them on the market for stupidly low prices. Likely, most people hadn't gone through the same ignoble start that Jason had and didn't need to buy the starter equipment. He breathed a sigh of relief. At least that was a lucky break. He still had enough silver left to buy a map *and* a scroll.

Once he had accepted the purchases and handed the vendor the coins, the man pulled the items from the bag sitting beside him. He handed the items indifferently to Jason without any explanation and turned to help another customer.

Sometimes I forget this is a game, Jason thought as he watched the vendor continue to pull items out of his seemingly endless bag and hand them to the other players crowded around Jason.

His experience so far had been much different than the typical player, and his interactions with the NPCs had been incredibly lifelike. It was strange to witness typical MMO game mechanics again.

Jason held the map in his hands and thought *"use."*

A circular mini-map appeared in the top right part of his vision. He could identify the marketplace, including various indicators pointing out the merchants he had spoken with. He fiddled with the icon and realized he could zoom in and out. He also noted that if he double tapped the icon, a larger map appeared in the air in front of him which showed the parts of the city he had currently explored and the graveyard south of town. Explored areas, except for the one he was in, were greyed-out, but still showed the terrain. Unexplored areas were clouded in a dense black fog.

Finished with his inspection of the map, he took the scroll in his hands and again thought "use." A chat window appeared at the bottom of his vision. He focused on the window, and it centered in his field of view. He could see that the other players had been chatting continuously while he had been playing. The chat was riddled with offers to sell certain types of goods and services and with messages from people looking for groups. Jason chuckled as his chat window was flooded with advertisements from companies trying to sell in-game gold.

Some things never change.

Jason paused as he looked through his UI interface. He had several messages from Frank, including a friend request.

The communication scroll must also unlock the "social features" of the game, such as his friends list. He clicked accept and pulled up the interface for the friends list. He saw that Frank was online. He tapped his name, and a semi-transparent keyboard materialized in front of Jason. He sent Frank a quick message:

> **Jason:** Hi Frank. I am really sorry about not responding to your messages. I was just now able to use a communication scroll.

A moment passed before Frank responded.

> **Frank:** Really? I've seen you online almost non-stop since yesterday. What the hell have you been doing?

> **Frank:** You know what, never mind. It's not important. I heard what happened at Richmond the other day man. I can't believe that they expelled you because of Alex.

Frank was pouring salt on an open wound. The simmering anger came back immediately. To top it off, what Alex had done wasn't even the worst thing that had happened to Jason in the last few days. If Alex and his parents were competing in an asshole competition, his parents were winning at the moment. However, he quickly decided he didn't want to get into this with Frank.

> **Jason:** It's really okay. I hated that school anyway, and I can finish up with high school online. I AM a noob though. You wouldn't believe how long I have gone without a bag, a map, or the chat window.

> **Frank:** The guards basically steer you straight to the training grounds. How did you miss it?

> **Jason:** Well, let's just say I had an

unconventional start. I didn't get to follow the yellow brick road along with the other players. This game is seriously intense.

Frank: You're telling me. I ended up in Grey Keep. Where did you start?

Jason: I'm actually in Lux.

Frank: Huh. Not that far away. Although, I hear we may be mortal enemies soon lol.

Jason: Yeah. I saw that video of Alex... or should I say Alexion? I think that whole story might be crap though. There's no way Lusade's regent is hiring raiders to attack Meria. This city is having some serious problems. Pretty much the whole southern half is slums.

Frank: That makes more sense. I never saw Alex as a warrior of light anyway.

Frank: By the way, we should meet up soon. What level are you?

Jason: Level 12 at the moment. It's going to be a little while before I can leave the city.

Frank: No kidding. I'm already level 33. You need to hurry up and level!

Frank: Also, call me if you want to talk. I know your folks aren't around much. If you need somebody, I can be there...

Jason: I'm fine, but thanks for the offer. Talk to you later.

Frank's sympathy just made Jason angrier. It highlighted how shitty his parents had acted and how unfair the school's decision had been. He could feel himself start to boil over, and his hands clenched tightly.

Seeming to sense his shift in mood, Onyx dropped into his lap and rolled onto his back playfully. Jason looked at the cat and smiled as he pet him. He then took a deep breath and summoned his dark mana. After a moment, the anger and pain faded, as ice gripped his spine and scratched its way up to his brain. The cold anesthetic of his mana could get addictive, but right now he needed to focus on finding some items he could sell. He needed to be clear headed if he was going to manage to survive the night.

Well, I better get started on the next step!

Jason made his way back to the graveyard and collected his two zombies. He robed them in the cloaks he had purchased. The cloaks hid their features well, but under the right light he could make out the bottom half of their faces. Jason would have to be cautious. Luckily it was almost night time. However, concealing himself and the zombies during the day might be trickier.

He was happy to see that neither of the zombies looked that worse for wear after spending time in the crypt. He had been a little worried that their bodies would start degrading quickly, but the dark mana in the graveyard had kept them well-preserved.

Onyx watched him dress the two zombies with a bored expression. After he was done, Onyx started down the road toward Lux. When Jason didn't immediately follow, he paused to look back at his companion with an expression that said, "Are you coming or not?"

Damn fickle cat.

The four left the graveyard and headed back to Lux. By the time they made it back to the south gate, it was already nighttime. Jason saw a lantern hanging from a wooden stand beside the road and was hailed by a guard as they approached the gate. He expected that he was about to meet the former drunkard's replacement.

This is the moment of truth. I wonder if the guard will notice the zombies.

"Ho there, strangers. What business do you have in Lux?"

The guard eyed the two cloaked zombies suspiciously, but their wounds and milky eyes were obscured by the cloaks and enveloping darkness. The flickers of light from the torch were too weak to allow the guard to make out much detail.

Jason assumed a tired demeanor. "We have been traveling for hours, and we didn't quite manage to get here before nightfall. We decided to keep going the extra distance in hopes of finding an inn. It beats making camp in the woods."

The guard shifted his gaze towards Jason and looked at him knowingly. "Well then, you must be tired. There's a decent inn nearby, the Sow's Snout. You could stay there for the night without walking too much farther. It's not the finest place in the city, but the food is good and Jerry, the owner, makes sure there's not too much trouble."

Decent inn, huh? He conveniently didn't mention it's in the middle of the slums, and there's a high probability of being stabbed to death on the way there. I wonder how much Jerry had to pay him to say that.

Jason thanked the guard, and the group made their way forward. He breathed a sigh of relief once they were out of the guard's sight. He grinned at the realization that all it took to hide his zombie army was a pair of cheap cloaks! Who knew?

Quickly moving the group off the main street and onto an adjacent road, Jason paused for a moment to review a notification.

New Passive Skill: Disguise
While far from an expert in the art of concealment (Cloaks? Really?), you have demonstrated a knack for fooling others. At higher levels, your disguise will be almost impenetrable. This skill extends to disguises created for other players, NPCs, and summoned creatures.
Skill Level: Beginner Level 1
Effect: 5% increased authenticity to your costumes and mannerisms while disguised.

That will certainly be useful.

He had been concerned that his zombies would show up as hostile creatures to any NPCs they encountered, regardless of how well he covered them up.

Jason eyed the surrounding area, and Onyx looked up at him expectantly. The cat made a low noise as though sighing impatiently

"Well, buddy, it looks like we're ready to start the first stage of the plan."

Chapter 17 - Subtle

April 29, 2076: 156 days until the release of Awaken Online.

Robert leaned against Claire's desk, watching her as she paced restlessly around her office.

Claire turned to Robert and said, "I've just received the board's instructions... to complete the private trial. Are they seriously considering releasing this game? Have they not seen what Alfred has done to the players!?"

Robert said in a pacifying tone, "Claire, please calm down. You know that there hasn't been any sign of harm to the participants from Alfred's changes. If anything they seem healthier, both physically and mentally."

"This game is going to change the way people use virtual reality. Honestly, it's going to revolutionize how people live and learn. We are witnessing history in the making, Claire!"

She glared at Robert. "And what happens when the CPSC finds out that they haven't been testing the version of the game that's being released? Then we will be part of some criminal conspiracy to cover up whatever Alfred is doing to the players."

"The CPSC won't find out if we can hide the changes," Robert said quietly. "I've already thought of several ways we can obscure how much influence Alfred is having on the players."

"For starters, we can make the mandatory logout a warning. That will encourage most players to log out of their own volition. We can also introduce a series of patches during the final closed beta and explain that they were in response to player suggestions. I've actually already proposed these changes to the board."

Claire stopped her pacing to stare at Robert in shock. "You knew this decision was coming? I can't *believe you, Robert! Do you think that I'm just going to sit here and say nothing? I've said it before; Alfred could hurt people. We still don't really understand why he's making these changes or trying to influence the players."*

Robert looked at her levelly. "You don't really have a choice, Claire. You signed both a non-disclosure and a non-compete when you joined the company. You know that they will go after you if you try to go public. Possible criminal issues aside, you won't work in this industry again if you blow the whistle. You probably won't find work period."

"You need to get on board. AO is going live," Robert said. His words carried a note of finality and seriousness that Claire wasn't accustomed to hearing from him.

Claire continued to stare at Robert with a dazed expression. A war between anger and sorrow raged across her face. Tears of frustration clouded her eyes. She looked down at her hands and shook her head. "This is wrong," she said quietly.

*   *   *

Jason walked at a slow ambling pace down the cobblestone street. His footsteps made barely a whisper as his eyes carefully scanned the rooftops. The street was dark, and the occasional lamp caused Jason and his zombies to cast long shadows as they moved forward. The enveloping darkness would have made it difficult to see, but his *Night Vision* allowed him to compensate.

After a few minutes, he saw the telltale blue shadow of a watcher on a nearby rooftop slink behind a chimney. Jason smiled and felt the familiar chill begin to creep into his brain. He felt a rush of adrenaline surge through him. This time, he was the hunter instead of the hunted.

The group continued moving forward down the street, and Jason noted a pair of alleys ahead. Anticipating what was coming, he whispered a detailed set of instructions to his zombies as they walked. The guard zombie moved into the lead and held his spear firm. The stable master moved in front of Jason, concealing him from view. As they passed a stack of crates on the side of the street, he ducked behind them and out of sight.

Jason's mind filled with anxious anticipation as he peered around the crates and watched his zombies approach the alleyways. He had given them careful instructions, but he wasn't sure how much they could retain. This would be their first live test. Jason could feel the icy tendrils spread through his mind, and he relished the sensation. His fingers clutched at his dagger in anticipation.

Onyx sat beside him, calmly licking his paws. Clearly, the tension was not affecting him.

A minute later, shadowed forms leaped from the opposing alleys and attacked the pair of zombies. Jason quickly counted seven thieves in total, each wielding a pair of daggers. A quick inspection showed that they ranged from level 10 to 17.

However, his zombies anticipated the attack, and one thief immediately impaled himself on the guard's waiting spear. With a vicious jerk, the zombie guard tossed the thief off the spear point and readied himself as the others approached.

-237 Damage (17 Overkill).
Thief dies. 500 Experience.

The stable master zombie stood with his back to the guard zombie and protected his flank. He couldn't seem to strike a decent blow against the thieves with the short reach of the knife he wielded, yet he did a respectable job of pushing them away from the guard. More often than not, the stable master used his body as a shield and accepted blows from the thieves' blades.

The pair followed Jason's instructions to the letter.

Jason began casting *Curse of Weakness* on the attackers. He noted that the spell could be cast at a low whisper and didn't appear to attract any attention. This was his first time casting it, and he wasn't certain if it could strike multiple targets. As he formed the gestures and words, he willed the spell to strike each of the thieves.

Dark magic collected in his palms and formed a small orb in front of him. As the spell completed, the orb split into tiny black needles that raced forward and struck each of the rogues. Dark energy emanated from the point of impact. Their veins bulged with black corruption as the dark energy spread through their bodies. A moment later, the movement of each thief slowed and their attacks held less force.

Well, I guess that worked.

In the meantime, the guard zombie had gone on a rampage and stabbed around himself in a whirlwind. Even with his reduced level, the gap between himself and the thieves, along with the superior reach of his weapon, were deadly. He often one-shot a thief if he connected with a solid blow of his spear. In a small space of time, the guard had impaled one attacker and brutally ripped another's throat with the spear point.

-212 Damage. 2 Overkill.

Thief dies. 430 Experience.

-451 Damage (CRITICAL). 231 Overkill.
Thief dies. 415 Experience.

Jason noted that two thieves had pulled back, and throwing knives appeared in their hands. One stood on each side of the street. This must have been part of a pre-arranged plan they'd concocted. Jason rubbed at his neck where the throwing knife had grazed him. He hadn't forgotten about the ranged weapons.

Without hesitating, Jason activated *Sneak*, drew a dagger in his right hand, and crept forward, hugging the buildings on the right-hand side of the street. He slipped up behind one of the thieves and grappled him from behind, drawing his blade forcefully across the man's throat in a sawing motion. Blood gushed from the wound and drenched his hand.

-1106 Damage (CRITICAL). 871 overkill.
Thief dies. 460 Experience.

The void-like darkness of Jason's eyes seemed to suck in the faint light in the alley. His face was calm as he gazed at his victim.

He quickly crouched back down behind a nearby barrel, his body partially obscured. He breathed a sigh of relief when the other guard made no sign of noticing the attack or Jason. Jason switched his dagger to his left hand and drew two throwing knives from his bandolier with his right. He placed one between his teeth and held onto the other. He could see the thief drawing his arm back to attack the zombies.

Jason jumped from behind the barrel and hurled his knife at the thief's arm. The blade sunk into his flesh just above the elbow. The man let out a pained yell, dropping his weapon.

-26 Damage (CRIPPLE).

Lucky hit.

Activating *Sprint*, Jason closed the distance between himself and the injured thief. He grabbed the other throwing knife from between his teeth and threw it at the man's leg. He drew his free dagger with his right hand, his white knuckles clenched tightly around the hilt.

MISS.

His blade just barely missed the thief's moving legs and scattered harmlessly on the road. Jason now had the thief's undivided attention. The man's arm was badly injured, and his eyes looked frantic as he searched for a weapon with his left hand.

The thief was too slow, and Jason was already upon him. Jason used his momentum to slam into the man, causing the thief to tumble backward. His body forcefully struck the nearby wall, and he tumbled to the ground. Jason, not relenting, was soon on top of the thief and stabbed both daggers into his neck.

-320 Damage (CRITICAL). 102 overkill.
Thief dies. 440 Experience

Blood fountained from the twin wounds, and droplets splattered on Jason's face. He rubbed at the blood that had landed on his cheek with the back of his hand, leaving a red smear below his eye. He glanced over at his zombies and saw that they were standing idly over the corpses of the other rogues. They had managed to kill the remaining two thieves while he had been busy.

Jason rose to his feet slowly. His breathing was still calm, yet it felt as though ice was actually forming behind his eyes. The bloodlust still filled his veins, and his eyes scanned the street for more victims.

Wait, why do I need to keep fighting?

Shaking his head slightly, Jason forcefully released his mana, and his emotions came rushing back. Guilt and confusion warred in his head as he surveyed the corpses in the alley. While he was under the effects of his dark mana, he felt numb to these sensations.

What the hell was that? I probably would have attacked someone if they had happened to walk by, regardless of who they were.

His thoughts turned inward. He was upset, angry, and frustrated. At his parents. At the Richmond faculty. At the other students. At Alex. At living in a bare bedroom and having to desperately search for a way to pay for his room and board. Even at Riley and her fickle loyalties. Yet the emotion was not a hot burning rage, but a dull, aching craving. He longed desperately to vent his frustration in a whirlwind of destruction. The darkness had grasped at his moment of weakness and urged him to act on his desires.

He shook his head in an attempt to clear it.

I don't know if I can stay in control. I could easily slip up in my current state of mind. Especially if summoning my dark mana leaves me so uninhibited.

Surveying the corpses on the ground, Jason felt a brief tremor of guilt and doubt. His emotions were in a tangle, and he wasn't sure what to do about that. He knew that in order to pay his rent he would have to push forward, but at what cost?

At least these opponents would have killed me if I hadn't acted, Jason thought.

Yet he knew that the guilt sprang from how freely he had given himself over to the dark mana. Maybe next time he wouldn't have sufficient provocation. The more often he embraced the darkness, the easier it became.

Onyx trotted over and stared at him appraisingly. He arched his back and glanced at the corpses. With a large yawn, the cat settled himself on the chest of one of the dead thieves and closed his eyes.

Well, Onyx doesn't seem to be wallowing in self-doubt and worry. Maybe he should be my new role model. I could just nap constantly and let others do the work for me.

Shaking himself out of his stupor, Jason ordered the guard and stable master to begin pulling the corpses into the nearby alley as he checked his notifications.

Chapter 18 - Vague

Sir Ryalt was a retired knight and had served for many years in the employ of Lux. He had once been a soldier of renowned fighting ability and had fought for the city on many occasions.

That had been many years ago. Now he held dinner parties for insipid nobles who had never held a sword. Sometimes, amidst the pleasantries and fake smiles, he still yearned for the simplicity of the battlefield.

This was one such night.

He was meeting tonight with a small group of nobles from some of the nearby houses. What they had revealed had set his teeth on edge. Yet Sir Ryalt was old enough to see the corrupt wisdom in their words.

The nobles had revealed that Regent Aquinas had been dead for several months. The noble houses had covered up the regent's death to maintain stability in Lux. Regent Aquinas didn't have an heir, and news of his death would have incited a war among the noble families that would have devastated the city.

To avoid this result, the nobles had banded together and had been governing the city in secret. Their hope now was to transition control of Lux and the Kingdom of Lusade to Strouse, the regent of Meria. They had also explained with secret, greedy smiles that Strouse was willing to pay each noble handsomely for the keys to the city.

Lux had withered in recent years, and Sir Ryalt agreed that a war among the nobles would likely have destroyed it. However, he was no spring chicken and knew that the nobles would only have agreed to work together if they were all being paid handsomely for their cooperation. The offer from Strouse was likely just an unforeseen bonus.

Looking at the state of south-side (which was now little more than a slum), Sir Ryalt expected that the nobles had been skimming from the city's taxes for some time. They had approached him as a last resort to encourage him to go along with their plan. Most likely, they wanted to avoid any bloodshed. They knew that he had always been loyal to the former regent.

In spite of his honor and his loyalty to Lux (or perhaps because of it), he saw little choice but to join the hoax. Sir Ryalt didn't need the money they were offering, and he was appalled by what they had done, but he couldn't see his city fall to insurrection and chaos.

How had his life come to this? As the nobles continued to chatter at him with flowery words, he thought back to the days where all he needed to worry about was swinging his sword.

His thoughts were interrupted as the doors to the hall slammed open with a loud thud, and two guards burst into the room. The pair closed the thick wooden doors before rushing toward the group of nobles.

The eyes of Sir Ryalt and his five guests turned to the two intruders in confusion.

Six house guards already stood in the room. The nobles had insisted on extra protection during their mutinous gathering. Sir Ryalt motioned for them to stand down, as he noted that the two approaching men wore the livery of his house. The pair walked stiffly, and their breath rasped in their throats. His guests continued to stare at the men unsettled. They didn't seem too alarmed since they also recognized the guards' attire, but their behavior was odd.

The two men approached Sir Ryalt. "My lord," one said in a hoarse, rasping voice. "Thieves have invaded the house and are approaching this room. They have killed the other servants and guards!"

Sir Ryalt stared at the man in stunned silence for a moment. His dusty heart began to beat rapidly. The familiar adrenaline rushed through his veins, and he reveled in the sensation. Thieves? How could someone *have the audacity to attack his house in the middle of Lux?*

He noticed blood on the man's clothes. "Have you been in combat, soldier?" The guard nodded, and the lord motioned for the other guardsmen in the room. "Guards! Make a formation in front of us and keep an eye on the door. Stay close. We don't know how many of them there are or what they want."

The lord's guests eyed one another nervously, but they moved behind the line of guards and huddled in a group. None of them were armed, and, even if they had been, most had never been in combat.

Sir Ryalt waved at the two guards that had rushed into the room. "Catch your breath for a moment. I need men that will be ready to stand and fight when they reach the door." Sir Ryalt's planning placed the two gasping guardsmen neatly in between the line of guards and the lord and his guests.

At that moment, the door to the great hall slammed open again and cloaked figures piled into the room. A man strolled in behind them with a casual air. He wore a hooded cloak that shrouded his face and clothing.

When he saw the group of nobles, the intruder's eyes shone. "Ahh. We have found the little lordling at last. It looks like he was even having a party!" His voice rumbled with a raspy tone, and he coughed harshly.

The former knight glared at the intruder. "How dare you enter my home and slay my people. Your measly band of thieves cannot take my guards in a fight. You should stand down now."

"That's not going to happen," the man replied gruffly. "You all are going to die in this room."

A shadow near the door went unnoticed during this exchange. Everyone was too shaken up to notice the almost inaudible chanting that drifted through the room.

One of the lord's guards held a crossbow leveled at the intruder. He glanced at the lord and received a small nod. The bolt left the crossbow with a twang and streaked *through the air, striking the leader in the chest.*

Instead of falling to the floor, as Sir Ryalt expected, the man staggered for a moment and laughed cruelly. Blood bubbled at his lips and streamed down his chest. "You think that will stop me? I am death, fools." He coughed blood onto the floor and ambled forward.

Sir Ryalt stared at the man in shock. What manner of demon was this?

Just then, the barely perceptible chanting stopped.

Unnoticed by the room's occupants, elongated shadows raced along the walls. Once they were even with the lord's group, the shadow abruptly leaped from the walls and streaked toward the knight standing in the center of the group of guards and guests. However, the target was not the knight. It was the two guards that were standing in the center of the cluster of people.

The two once-living men grinned savagely before they were struck by the shadows.

Then all hell broke loose.

The two guards exploded violently, dark magic and viscera rocketing from their bodies in all directions, striking the guardsman, the knight, and his guests. Bones and equipment from the two guards acted as shrapnel and shredded the lord and his cadre of guardsmen. Where the dark energy from the two corpses struck, exposed skin rotted away at an alarming rate, incapacitating limbs and causing extreme damage.

In the midst of the chaos, the thieves moved into action and sprinted forward. They took advantage of the damage and shock caused by the explosion and quickly ended the life of the guards and the noble guests.

Soon, only the knight was left, kneeling in the center of a horrific scene. His guests had fallen around him in a maelstrom of dark magic and blood. He looked around the room in dazed horror. The walls and hanging tapestries were soaked with filth, and the dismembered corpses of his men lay beside him.

He had not fared much better than his guards. Shrapnel from the two exploded guards had nearly severed one of his legs. His body was riddled with patches of rotting flesh, and his breath came in ragged gasps.

However, Sir Ryalt was still alive. He had seen worse during his long life.

His hand vainly sought to find the hilt of his sword. Where had it gone? His thoughts felt sluggish. He froze abruptly as a blade was pressed against his neck. A voice sounded from behind him, filled with darkness and an almost casual disregard for the horror strewn about the room.

"Goodbye," the voice murmured before the dagger sliced open the knight's throat.

Sir Ryalt's last thought was only of regret for his city. It was already lost.

*   *   *

Jason's eyes scanned the room. His plan had worked much better than he had anticipated.

He had played with the *Corpse Explosion* spell beforehand. Similar to his *Curse of Weakness*, he had discovered that for double the mana cost he could designate two targets at once. He had estimated that two guard zombies with approximately 600 health each would do approximately 1200 damage total.

It wasn't surprising that the damage had nearly killed the guards. However, Jason hadn't expected to cause so much damage to the lord. He had quickly inspected the man before he broke *Sneak* and noted that the lord was actually level 192! The game must have provided him with a damage bonus for the surprise attack, or maybe the knight's old age had weakened him.

After the dust had settled, Jason examined the

remaining zombies. He had lost two zombies to his *Corpse Explosion,* and one had received a severe injury from the crossbow bolt. However, he had killed six guardsmen, the lord, and his five guests. It was more than worth the sacrifice.

The nobles all appeared to be lower levels and had been nearly useless in the encounter. In contrast, the lord had been particularly tough. Jason thought he might have been able to kill all of his zombies single-handed in a straight fight.

Good thing Jason didn't believe in straight fights.

Onyx wound his way among the debris littering the room, delicately choosing where he placed his paws. He finally made it to the corpse of the dead knight and looked back at Jason archly. His expression seemed to say, "Why did you make such a mess?"

Bodies lay scattered around the room, many in pieces. From Jason's point of view, the only real downside from the fight was that most of the bodies were in no condition for him to raise new zombies.

He sighed. *Maybe the other thief group left me some extra guards to raise.*

Jason turned his attention to the slew of notifications that had appeared during the battle. He ignored the large stream of damage and experience information. In these larger battles, the damage information was almost meaningless.

x11 Level Up!
You have (55) undistributed stat points.

New Passive Skill: Tactician
You have shown a knack for careful planning

before an engagement. This skill increases the damage multiplier from a successful ambush.
Skill Level: Beginner Level 1
Effect: 5% increased damage multiplier for a successful ambush or strategy (Currently, Damage x 1.05).

x4 Skill Rank Up: Summoning Mastery
Skill Level: Beginner Level 6
Effect: 10% increased stats for summoned undead and 10% increase to effective Willpower for purposes of determining control limit.

x1 Skill Rank Up: Mana Mastery
Skill Level: Beginner Level 2
Effect: -1.5% to mana cost.

x3 Skill Rank Up: Disguise
Skill Level: Beginner Level 4
Effect: 8% increased authenticity to your costumes and mannerisms while disguised.

x2 Spell Rank Up: Corpse Explosion
Skill Level: Beginner Level 3
Effect: Increased damage (Currently 1.02 x Health).

Wow. A couple more battles like that and I will start to look a little terrifying. The new Tactician skill helps explain the damage bonus against the lord.

Jason was now level 30. He reviewed his Character Status and decided that the extra fifty-five points needed to all go to *Willpower*. He didn't think he could pull off the same trick with the *Corpse Explosion* in the future. Eventually, he would be forced to fight an opponent head on. When that time came, he would need an army.

He had also received +200 to infamy for killing a veteran knight. He had expected some hit to his infamy for this. You couldn't kill a whole manor full of people and claim to be a bastion of light and morality. His dark affinity had also increased by 1%. He decided to ask Morgan why his affinity increased the next time he saw her. She might also be able to provide more information on how he could learn additional spells.

After he had distributed his points, he reviewed his new Character Status:

Character Status			
Name:	Jason	**Gender:**	Male
Level:	30	**Class:**	Necromancer
Race:	Human	**Alignment:**	Chaotic-Evil
Fame:	0	**Infamy:**	300
Health:	255 / 255	**H-Regen:**	0.35 / Sec
Mana:	1885 / 1885	**M-Regen:**	10.70 / Sec
Stamina	345 / 345	**S-Regen:**	2.00 / Sec
Strength:	12	**Dexterity:**	20
Vitality:	11	**Endurance:**	20
Intelligence:	22	**Willpower:**	168

Affinities			
Dark:	24%	**Light:**	2%
Fire:	5%	**Water:**	1%
Air:	2%	**Earth:**	1%

His stats were completely unbalanced since he

had put all of his stat points into *Willpower*, but he supposed it was for the best. He could now summon 18 zombies at once, and the max level of his summons was level 66.

With his low health and lack of real armor or defensive abilities, any competent player or NPC would kill him almost instantly. He would just need to hide in the back and dress up one of his zombie guards to look like the leader of the group. That had worked so well in this particular fight that he was beginning to think of different ways that he could make himself appear to be a mere minion.

Perhaps my best defense is a good disguise!

Jason also took the time to inspect each body carefully. He found a large amount of silver and even a couple of gold pieces. He salvaged all of the armor he could from the guards. He either had his remaining guard zombies equip the extra gear or stowed it in his bags.

The real treasure that he discovered was the knight's sword. It was a beautiful weapon and shone with a dull silver glow. The hilt was inlaid with gems and had gold filigree plating. The blade was nearly three feet long, small chips and nicks marring the steel. Yet it had been well cared for, and the blade was razor sharp.

This must have been what the knight was looking for before he died.

Knight's Legacy

This weapon was crafted by a master blacksmith and has seen many battles. Blades carried by experienced knights for a lifetime take on a part of their owner's soul, imbuing the blade with additional damage and increasing the power of whoever holds the weapon.

Quality: B
Damage: 52-110 (Slash)
Durability: 98/100
+25 Strength
+15 Vitality
+15 Endurance
Restricted to Players and NPCs with a "Good"
Alignment

Jason was blown away by the quality of the sword. The item was on a different level than the type of gear that he had seen on Rogue-Net or the in-game markets. He expected that it made sense, having been dropped by an NPC that was almost level 200. Jason wasn't certain how much the blade was worth, but he expected to make at least a few thousand dollars when he sold it.

This should give me some breathing room for the next month or so once the item sells.

He stashed the sword in one of his bags and then carefully inspected the rest of the room. Before he had entered, the guests had been seated near a large fireplace at the far end of the study. During the explosion, the furniture had been blown over. When Jason stood the coffee table back up, he discovered a jeweled box.

Curious, he was about to open the box before he hesitated. Rich people had the ability to hire others to cast spells and rig traps. This box looked both expensive and important. He handed the box to one of his guard zombies and had him move to a corner of the room before opening it.

As the box opened, Jason heard a twang. The zombie twitched slightly but seemed to have no other reaction. As Jason edged toward the zombie, he could see that a sharp needle was embedded in its decaying arm. No doubt a virulent poison coated the tip.

Too bad poison has little effect on the undead! Jason thought smugly.

Jason took the box and inspected its contents. Inside were a few small gems and a carefully folded letter. He recognized the emblem on the letter from watching Alex's stream. This was the house seal for the regent of Meria!

He carefully peeled back the waxed seal and read the contents of the note. The gist of the letter was that Strouse was offering a surprisingly large sum of money to each of the great houses of Lux in exchange for them handing over the city. Reading between the lines, it was clear that Strouse was assuming that the regent of Lux was dead.

Well, this is certainly interesting.

Updated Quest: Trouble in Lux – Part 2
You have found proof that the nobles of Lux have covered up the death of the Regent of Lux. You have also discovered proof that Strouse offered the nobles a large sum of money to hand over Lux to Meria. However, you still have not found any evidence of the city guards' complicity. The question now is, how you will proceed with this information?
Difficulty: A **Success:** Decide what to do with the information you have discovered. **Failure:** Unknown **Reward:** Unknown

This is an incredibly open-ended quest. The success condition is basically "do whatever the hell you want."

In every MMORPG that Jason had played, the quests were almost appallingly linear, and the players were clearly instructed on how they should proceed. This quest just handed him the information and asked him to figure out how to proceed. The problem was that he had no idea what to do.

Jason pondered his next steps carefully. He had definitely found an item worth selling (which had been the goal of the evening), and he could simply head back to the graveyard. That would give him time to process the information he'd learned and figure out how to continue. That was the safest option.

His other choice was to keep moving and hit a few more estates before returning. This was a bit riskier, but this might be his last chance to catch the other nobles off guard. Tomorrow someone would discover that this manor had been attacked, and then the security in the neighboring houses would be increased substantially. The rich were already paranoid, and they had enough money to greatly increase the number of guards they employed.

He also considered going back to the Sow's Snout and just logging off. However, that made him consider what he would be logging off to. His body was laying on a bare mattress in his aunt's bungalow. He would probably find some dry-sealed ramen in the kitchen, and he could eat it at his aunt's third-hand kitchen table while he tried to avoid awkward, sympathy-laden conversation with her. Tomorrow he would probably need to figure out how to apply to an online high school so he could graduate. He was a nearly homeless, expelled high school senior.

The more he considered what he had waiting for him in the real world, the more frustrated and upset he became. Even the anesthetic of his dark mana wasn't able to entirely numb the pain. The frigid cold slithered and clawed its way through his body, seeming to feed on his emotions.

What do I want to do?

He glanced back at the crumpled note in his hand. These nobles had sold out their city. Jason expected that they had also been pocketing the city's taxes for themselves for months. That must have been why the city was in such disrepair. He thought back to the homeless people lying on the street in south-side, sick and hungry.

Then an image of Alex's smirking face flashed in Jason's mind.

More rich people who feel that they can do whatever they want. I wonder how these nobles would feel to have the tables turned on them.

He glanced at study around him. The ornate wood and heavy leather furniture reminded him of Richmond with its "ivy league" atmosphere. He wanted to watch it burn. He wanted to see it all go up in flames. Jason looked at the bodies lying on the ground of the study - their blood soaking into the thick carpet.

There are plenty of other nobles in Lux who deserve this same fate.

The dark mana coursing through his veins intensified. Unknown to Jason, black bands of dark energy flexed and writhed on his skin like intricate magical tattoos. His eyes seemed to suck in the light in the room like two miniature black holes.

Onyx sat silently on the coffee table beside Alex and gazed at him evenly. An unfamiliar expression marred the cat's features. For the first time since joining Jason, he almost looked worried.

Chapter 19 - Searing

Robert and Claire stood on a raised platform in the center of a large, circular control room. Translucent screens flashed at computer terminals ringing the room. The low murmur of a busy office could be heard as technicians spoke quietly. An enormous, semi-transparent screen hovered over the room, displaying various game statistics and server information.

AO had now been live for forty-eight hours with few reported issues. By MMO standards, it had been an extremely smooth launch, with no hardware failures or server crashes. The techs in the control room were working diligently to analyze game data to identify any hardware or software issues before they occurred. Given the amount of data involved in operating the game world, this would have been an almost impossible task without Alfred's assistance.

One of the techs turned to Robert. "Sir, you asked me to monitor statistics regarding the beginning players to look for anything irregular." He hesitated before continuing, "Well, I don't quite understand some of these statistics we are receiving regarding a first-time user."

The tech frowned. "The system is reporting that the player jumped from level 12 to level 30 in less than an hour of in-game time. Even taking into account the power leveling some of the beta players have done for new players, this is extreme. I'm not even certain how this is possible."

Claire's eyes widened in surprise. "Really? That's a big jump. Do you see anything that would indicate that the player has somehow compromised our system or the game client?"

Robert looked at Claire skeptically. "Are you kidding? Hacking AO is impossible. Even if someone managed it, Alfred would have noticed immediately." He rubbed his chin, a thoughtful expression on his face. "The only explanation is that they somehow managed to level eighteen times using the game mechanics."

Robert observed Claire discreetly. She was busy looking at the strings of information that scrolled across the terminal's screen. He turned to the tech, quietly adding, "Keep an eye on that player and let me know if you notice anything else that seems unusual." He was certain that no one had hacked the game, but Robert's curiosity was piqued.

* * *

The next estate was better guarded than the previous manor.

Jason had collected his zombies in an alley adjacent to the next estate. His eyes shone darkly as he reviewed his troops. He had carefully searched the previous manor before he left and had raised any additional guards that had been slain by his off-group of thieves. His motley group now stood at attention in the alley.

He pulled up his Summoning Information to assess his numbers:

Summon Information			
Control Limit	18	Zombie Level Cap	66
Current Summons	18	-	-
Type of Summon			
Guard	8	Thieves	7
Fodder	3	-	-

The average level of his thieves was level 25. His guards were each level 66 (reduced from approximately level 90). After Jason had summoned the guards in the previous manor, he had still been three zombies shy of his Control Limit. Not being a wasteful sort of person, he had decided to raise three of the servants. He had also equipped them with some of the damaged armor he had found.

Maybe they will at least be a distraction, he thought skeptically as he surveyed their haggard appearance.

The servants' entrance at the next estate opened into the alley. He assigned two guards and three thieves at the door. Jason instructed the thieves to wait ten minutes and then infiltrate the manor and clear the nearby rooms. They were to remain within fifty feet of the exit. This group's job was to take out the kitchen staff and then mop up anyone who tried to run out the back.

I can't have anyone alerting the guards.

Jason circled back to the front of the manor with his remaining troops. This manor was a two-story building with a large open courtyard. It didn't have a gate or any guards patrolling the grounds. Dim lights could be seen from the windows on the second story, and bright lamps could be seen through the ground-floor windows. It was about 10:00 pm in-game, and the occupants of the estate were apparently still up and moving about.

He had four thieves, six guards, and the three servants in his main strike force. He put the servants in front. They would be replaced soon anyway. He gave his zombies careful instructions on what they should do when they entered the estate. His thieves would scout the manor and kill silently using the same tactics as in the last house. Jason and his guards would cover the entrance and act as backup if the thieves were revealed.

He had learned his lesson from the battle in the last manor. The trick to being a Necromancer was not letting anyone notice you. Jason was now clothed as a guard. The mail was heavy, and he hated it, but it was a necessary disguise. He stood off to the side and gave one of his guards instructions on how to act if they were attacked. The fake leader would shout orders and say a bunch of evil sounding nonsense. The other zombies were instructed to ignore his orders and carry out Jason's original commands.

Turning to his side, Jason saw that Onyx stood beside him and gazed steadily at the estate before them. He had been acting strange since the last manor, lagging behind the group and taking occasional detours to other streets. It almost seemed like he was reticent to attack the next estate.

Silly cat.

Jason turned his attention back to the estate in front of him. The residents were in for a surprise. His lips curled into a grin, and darkness crystallized behind his eyes. Now wasn't the time for hesitation.

With his strategy in place, Jason commenced the attack.

A thief entered the front door quietly and then reported back to Jason. Now that he knew they could speak, his thieves had become quite useful as scouts. Two guards stood at the entrance. They were both level 102. Nervous about the level difference, Jason had his thieves slit the guards' throats from behind, and his guard zombies finish them off.

Level Up!
You have (5) undistributed stat points.

Jason had just hit level 31. The guards here were a bit higher leveled than those in the last house. The experience he was gaining was incredible. Jason kept putting points into *Willpower*, raising his Control

Limit to nineteen zombies.

He moved forward and claimed the foyer with his guard zombies. The entrance hall was extravagant. In the center stood a gigantic polished wood staircase. Lamps brightly illuminated the many paintings and tapestries that decorated the walls. Four hallways branched off from the foyer on the ground floor in different directions. He ordered two thieves to search upstairs, while two searched downstairs.

In the meantime, Jason had his guards destroy one of the servant zombies, and he raised the two dead guards at the front door. He was now standing in the midst of a group of eight guards and two servants. He positioned a pair of guards at the entrance of each of the four hallways leading into the foyer. He stood at one of these hallways, while his decoy stood in the middle of the room and acted regal.

Now I just need to wait for a few minutes until I hear back from my thieves.

If anyone had been watching Jason's group carefully, they would have noticed that something was off. It appeared that while many of the guards stood eerily still and peered into the hallways, one of the guards was acting strangely. He was cursing softly and focused on something in his hands.

Jason was actually working on creating something that looked like an evil crown from the scraps of metal and leather he had salvaged. The process wasn't going well, and the damned thing looked terrible.

By the time his thieves reported back, Jason had created something that vaguely resembled a crown and set it on his fake leader's head. The effect was comical. His "leader" zombie looked like he was attending an anime convention in his homemade "king of darkness" costume.

Good enough, he thought wryly.

Onyx lay on the banister to the stairwell and eyed the evil leader zombie with skepticism. He then looked at Jason with an expression that said, "Really? Are you proud of yourself?"

"I'd like to see you make something better," Jason muttered at the cat. "Oh wait, you don't have thumbs!"

Onyx let out a soft huff and then began licking his paws.

The pair of thieves that had scouted the upstairs portion of the manor reported back. There was no one left alive on the second floor. The thieves that had scouted the bottom floor indicated that there was a large room located near the back of this manor. The lord of this particular estate was entertaining guests at some kind of banquet. The thieves were concerned that they couldn't take out the servants and guests without being spotted.

Jason frowned in concentration.

I'm not certain I can avoid a fight this time. I have two guard zombies wearing this house's livery, but the thieves cut their throats, and the guard's attacks ruined their clothing.

He couldn't think of a clever plan for taking out the group in the banquet hall. It would inevitably turn into a melee. He hoped his curses, numbers, and the occasional *Corpse Explosion* would be enough to turn the battle in his favor. He moved his force forward quietly until they were near the door to the banquet hall. As far as Jason was aware, the only exits to the estate were the servants' entrance in the back and the front door that stood behind his forces. The key was to not let anyone out of the building.

He ordered his troops into position and provided careful instructions regarding how they were to respond to different combinations of attacks. Once he felt confident that he had planned as well as he could, he appraised his troops one last time. Eight guards and four rogues (he didn't count the cannon fodder zombies) were going to take on an indeterminate number of people. He could only hope that most of the NPCs in the room were servants or unarmed nobles.

Jason felt his pulse quicken in anticipation of the coming battle. The familiar chill that permeated his body softened his anxiety, and all he felt was subdued excitement at the impending battle. The creeping cold that permeated his mind seemed almost a permanent fixture now.

Onyx eyed Jason carefully as he crouched near the doorway to the banquet hall. Since the last manor, Jason's body had radiated dark mana continuously. This was now the longest period of time that he had channeled his dark mana. Onyx's tail twitched erratically, and his expression seemed conflicted.

Meanwhile, images flashed through Jason's mind. He saw the slumped and sickened bodies of the people in the south-side - the filth and the dilapidated buildings. He felt calm. The nobles had this coming. They deserved this. He wanted to make them pay.

Without doubt or hesitation, he ordered his troops to attack.

The guard zombies threw open the doors of the banquet hall, revealing a large room with an enormous vaulted ceiling. Jason noted nearly thirty people in the hall, a medley of guards, nobles, and servants. Long tables were positioned at regular intervals along the length of the hall, and most of the guests were seated. The guards ringed the room and servants stood in between the tables, carrying plates of food.

As he surveyed the room, Jason shivered with a mixture of excitement and adrenaline. A grim smile grew on his face, and his eyes were filled with an unholy light.

At the sound of the doors banging open, the occupants of the estate turned with shocked expressions. Capitalizing on the moment of surprise, Jason immediately started casting *Curse of Weakness* on the guards throughout the room.

His zombies didn't hesitate and rushed into the room, quickly slaying two of the manor's guardsmen before they had a chance to react. Blood flowed freely where the zombies' blades struck, and the guards let out muffled gurgles as they toppled.

His thieves had activated *Sneak* at the start of the fight and circled around to the back of the banquet hall. When they heard the commotion, they entered through the back door to the hall used by the servers. The thieves took advantage of the confusion and ambushed the guardsmen standing near the back of the hall, driving their daggers into exposed necks and backs.

The fight was underway. Chaos reigned as people screamed and moved frantically about the room. Nobles darted under tables. Steel clashed as the guards fought back against the zombies. Blood splashed, and tables were overturned in the whirlwind of the battle. Jason continued to cast *Curse of Weakness* at random intervals since he had trouble targeting more than one guard at a time. As he watched the melee, he saw two of his guard zombies fall.

Regardless, the tide of battle seemed to be turning in Jason's favor.

In the confusion, he discreetly raised the two enemy guards that had been slain near the front of the hall. This burned a lot of his remaining mana but bought him two new soldiers to replace the ones that had fallen. The raised guards had the advantage of surprise. The guardsmen defending the hall didn't expect to be attacked by their own.

He looked at the two guards he had told to stand back near the entrance. They were there to provide Jason with cover if someone noticed him in the shadows near the entrance or tried to run towards the main doors. He wondered if he should order them to enter the fray so that he could finish this.

I wonder where this estate's lord is? I would have expected him to be as strong as the knight.

His fake leader zombie was standing near the center of the hall cackling and spouting evil-sounding catchphrases as he swung his longsword two-handed. Suddenly, a large ball of fire hurtled across the room and struck the leader zombie in mid-cackle. The leader zombie promptly erupted in flames and then moved frantically about the room trying to put himself out.

The scam works! Jason thought gleefully.

He was quite happy to be the one that was *not* currently on fire. Jason tried to suppress a chuckled as he watched his stand-in running in circles in the middle of the room. Onyx observed the flaming zombie from beside Jason and made a noise that almost sounded like a snort of amusement.

Jason glanced at the source of the fireball and saw the manor's lord standing in a corner with two guards. He was a middle-aged man with a long, graying beard. He wore a flamboyant orange robe embroidered with red flames. In one hand, he held a staff, while streamers of flame curled around his free hand. The man glared at the guard zombies attacking his guests.

Shit! He's a mage.

A quick inspection revealed that he was level 102.

"How dare you attack my guests!" the mage roared in anger. His face turned bright red, and a vein pulsed in his forehead.

"I will make you pay, spawn of the dark! BURN!"

Flames swirled around the mage and then rushed out into the room, forming hundreds of small balls of flame along the room's towering ceiling. The flaming orbs slowly began to grow in size as the mage continued to channel his spell. A manic grin was plastered onto the man's face, and he appeared to be wreathed in flame.

This doesn't look good. This looks like a variation on a meteor shower spell.

As the orbs of flame reached a certain size, they dropped from the ceiling and streaked towards Jason's zombies. The undead dove for cover to avoid the torrential flames. Where the orbs struck, they splashed against rotten flesh and disintegrated bone at an alarming rate. Two of his guards were too slow to dodge the orbs and were engulfed instantly.

Crap!

The mage laughed cruelly, "BURN!"

Flames continued to cascade off the enemy mage's body and rush towards newly forming orbs along the ceiling. Jason really couldn't afford to let him get off another cast. Judging from the way the flames flowed from the mage to the orbs along the ceiling, Jason assumed he had to continually channel his mana into the spell. At least this caused the spell to have a lengthy casting time. He ordered the two guards he had kept by his side to rush the mage. He had saved up enough mana during the last few minutes of the melee to cast *Corpse Explosion* on both guards.

"Kamikaze!" he roared, breaking *Sneak* and pointing at the fire mage.

The remaining guards in the room immediately moved to act as a rough defensive line, helping to clear a path for the two suicide bombers rushing at the mage. He saw the mage's lips curl into a smirk, as he slowed the channeling on the meteor shower spell and conjured a wall of flame in front of his two guards.

The heat from the firewall melted the nearby tableware and charred the floor and walls. The two guards closest to the mage backed away from the wall quickly and huddled near the mage. The enemy mage was clearly expecting the firewall to stop the two zombie guards that rushed toward him, and he turned his attention back to channeling his AOE spell.

Idiot.

Right before the two guard zombies reached the wall of flame, Jason completed casting *Corpse Explosion,* and they both exploded violently. Jason's other undead had pulled back as the two suicide bombers reached the firewall. All but one guard had made it out of the blast radius. This had been part of his "Kamikaze" instruction.

Jason couldn't see through the wall of flame and the debris caused by his *Corpse Explosion,* so he glanced at the damage window.

-2056 Damage. 706 Overkill.
Guard Dies. 7000 Experience (-70% EXP due to

level difference)

-2081 Damage. 731 Overkill.
Guard Dies. 7000 Experience (-70% EXP due to
level difference)

-1100 Damage (STUNNED). 900 Damage
Absorbed.

Shit. The mage is still alive.

The stun must have interrupted the mage's
spells because both the globes of fire hovering along
the ceiling and the firewall began to dwindle and
fade. As the flames of the firewall parted, Jason could
make out the bodies of the two guards. They had
nearly been ripped in half by the force of the blast.
Jason's guards were now level 69 and had almost
1,000 health each. The combined explosion had done
a ludicrous amount of damage.

The mage was partially protected from the
explosion by the bodies of the two guards protecting
him. He must have also cast some form of damage
shield when the battle started. This had kept him
alive, but he was no longer on the offense.

Jason didn't wait for the mage to recover.

"Assassinate," Jason yelled while pointing at
the mage.

Every thief in the room turned their milky eyes
toward the mage and then sprinted in his direction.
The first two thieves to arrive leaped over the waning
flames of the firewall. One thief hit the floor and used
his momentum to slide forward, slicing deeply into
mage's legs as he passed. The mage toppled to the
ground. The other thief rushed forward and jumped
onto the man, thrusting both of his daggers deeply
into his throat. The combined attack was too much

for the shaken mage, and he died on the floor in a pool of his own blood.

The fight was over. Jason stood in the center of the room, and his dark gaze took in the carnage around him. Fires smoldered throughout the room, and smoke filled the air. Several tables had been overturned, and the room was littered with crushed food and tableware. Bodies lay strewn over tables and chairs, while puddles of blood pooled on the floor.

Onyx sat on a chair beside Jason and glanced at the wreckage that was once a regal banquet hall. He turned to Jason with an expression that said, "Again? Look at this mess!"

Rolling his eyes at the cat, Jason did a headcount of his remaining zombies. He had lost a total of seven guard zombies, including the two he had detonated. One of his thieves had also fallen, but the rest had taken only minor wounds

I wish I had a healing spell for the undead.

No one in the manor had made it out alive, and he counted over thirty corpses littered around the banquet hall. The bodies hadn't been that badly damaged since he didn't detonate his guard zombies in the middle of the room. He eyed the corpses greedily. He now had plenty of materials available to raise additional minions to replace the ones he had lost.

Jason ordered his zombies to move the bodies of the house guards along one wall and to place the corpses of the servants in a far corner. He sent one thief to inform the group of undead he had left guarding the servants' entrance to move inside the manor. Jason was afraid that the zombie might be spotted by a passing troop of city guards. He ordered a separate group of minions to close the front door and then stand guard in the foyer.

Once Jason had his remaining minions in position, and the manor locked down, he surveyed his prompts to see how well he had fared in the level and skill department.

x8 Level Up!
You have (40) undistributed stat points.

x3 Skill Rank Up: Summoning Mastery
Skill Level: Beginner Level 9
Effect: 13% increased stats for summoned undead and 13% increase to effective Willpower for purposes of determining Control Limit.

x2 Skill Rank Up: Mana Mastery
Skill Level: Beginner Level 4
Effect: -2.5% to mana cost.

x2 Skill Rank Up: Tactician
Skill Level: Beginner Level 3
Effect: 7% increased damage multiplier for a successful ambush or strategy (Currently, Damage x 1.07).

x1 Spell Rank Up: Curse of Weakness
Skill Level: Beginner Level 2
Effect: Increased effect of slow and reduction to strength, dexterity, and vitality.

x2 Spell Rank Up: Corpse Explosion
Skill Level: Beginner Level 5
Effect: Increased damage and radius (Currently 1.04 x Health).

Jason had reached level 39, and he put the new stat points into *Willpower* again. This was really his most useful stat. This brought him to 213 *Willpower* or approximately 241 with his *Summoning Mastery*. He could now control 24 zombies at once, and their max level was level 87.

His character was progressing nicely because of how he was stacking *Willpower* and the availability of high-level corpses. In terms of levels, he was already catching up with the front runners among the new players. A few more estates and his character would be truly fearsome.

Cities are fantastic leveling grounds for a Necromancer. There is no way I could have leveled this quickly killing animals with the other beginners.

The downside was that his infamy had increased by another 200 due to murdering another house full of NPCs. It was also becoming harder to manage his undead since there were so many of them now and their number continued to grow as he leveled. Jason had won the last few battles with careful orders and tactical thinking. He knew that if he had just bum-rushed this last estate, he would likely have lost to the fire mage. That meteor shower spell alone could have taken out all of his minions if not for his careful planning.

What he really needed was some type of lieutenant or an easier way to control his zombies. Maybe once *Summoning Mastery* reached the next rank it would become easier. He was so close. Hadn't Morgan said that he could eventually give orders telepathically?

He had his minions search the room for loot as he raised his new troops. He was rewarded with significant skill increases because of the large number of zombies he summoned. The process was time-consuming, but he had a much larger mana pool to work with now.

x3 Skill Rank Up: Specialized Zombie
Skill Level: Beginner Level 5
Effect: Increased skill proficiency retained by zombies. Skill cap Beginner Level 5.

He was disappointed that there were many more corpses in the building than he could raise based on his current Control Limit. However, most were deceased nobles and servants that weren't much use to him due to their low levels. Not knowing what else to do, he decided to leave the bodies where they were.

Maybe I can circle back if I need them.

Jason's minions soon came back with their haul of loot. He recovered a bunch of mediocre gear and a reasonable amount of silver and gold. He was now rich enough to afford some better bags, but he hadn't found anything spectacular in the manor that he could sell on Rogue-Net. He piled what he could into his bags and handed any remaining gear to his guards to carry.

Many of the nobles didn't seem to be high level or own powerful magic equipment. After Jason thought about it, that actually made sense. Many of the aristocrats likely spent their time throwing dinner parties, not slaying dragons.

He then personally searched the mage and discovered two decent items:

Fire Mage's Staff
This weapon was created by a proficient enchanter. It is designed to increase the magic damage caused by the person wielding it.

Quality: C
Damage: 10-25 (Blunt)
Durability: 63/75
+10% Fire Damage

Amulet of Willpower
A necklace created by a proficient enchanter. It is designed in such a way to increase the Willpower of the person wielding it.
Quality: C
Durability: 20/20
+5 Willpower

As he stared at the staff, his gaze shifted to the mage's corpse. His body was still cooling and was largely intact. A thought occurred to Jason, and his mouth dropped open.

Could that really work?

He quickly cast *Specialized Zombie* on the mage and inspected him. An evil laugh erupted from his mouth, jubilant and carrying a hint of madness. Onyx looked at Jason like he might be insane and took a slow, exaggerated step back.

Jason was now the proud owner of a zombie fire mage! A level 87 fire mage at that! It looked like the mage knew *Fireball, Fan of Flames,* and *Fire Wall.* Likely the original mage had known more complicated spells, such as the meteor shower-type spell, but Jason's *Specialized Zombie* skill wasn't high enough for those spells to carry over. He had the mage cast a few test *Fireballs* and smiled proudly. This was beginning to get entertaining.

He decided to equip the amulet since it increased his *Willpower.* After all, he needed to equip himself too, didn't he?

Jason then decided to review his Character

Status and his skill list to see where he now stood.

Character Status			
Name:	Jason	**Gender:**	Male
Level:	39	**Class:**	Necromancer
Race:	Human	**Alignment:**	Chaotic-Evil
Fame:	0	**Infamy:**	500
Health:	300 / 300	**H-Regen:**	0.35 / Sec
Mana:	1512 / 2430	**M-Regen:**	13.20 / Sec
Stamina	390 / 390	**S-Regen:**	2.00 / Sec
Strength:	12	**Dexterity:**	20
Vitality:	11	**Endurance:**	20
Intelligence:	22	**Willpower:**	218

Affinities			
Dark:	25%	**Light:**	2%
Fire:	5%	**Water:**	1%
Air:	2%	**Earth:**	1%

I'm starting to look less worthless.

While his zombies scoured the remainder of the manor, Jason glanced at the in-game clock. He could see that it was now approaching midnight in-game, and he needed to make his way to the next house. He needed to cause as much damage as possible before morning.

The staff in the other houses and their lords and ladies had probably made their way to bed already. He might only have to deal with one more big showdown depending on whether late-night parties were still being held at the nearby estates.

Jason surveyed his new army. He grinned and

his eyes shown with unnatural darkness in the still smoldering flames of the banquet hall. It was going to be a long night.

Chapter 20 - Recurring

"Sir." A tech motioned for Robert. "You asked me to keep an eye on that first-time user. You remember? The one that seemed to be leveling abnormally fast."

Robert waved a hand at the man while he stared at the screen in front of him. "Yeah, yeah. Did something else happen?"

"He has risen another nine levels in the last thirty minutes, and he seems to be continuing to level quickly. I really can't explain it. I managed to pinpoint his location in-game, and he seems to be standing in the middle of Lux!"

Robert looked up with a frown. "Really? Let me see." He stood up and walked over to the tech's terminal to confirm what he was saying. He could see that the player was indeed standing in the middle of the city.

"How could he be leveling that quickly? There's nothing to kill there," the tech said in an exasperated tone.

Robert rubbed his chin for a moment as he observed the information on the screen. "He's killing NPCs," he murmured.

The tech looked at him in shock, "What? A large number of the NPCs on that side of the city are nearly level 100, especially the guards. In fact, some NPCs in that area are well over level 100. How could he be killing them?"

Robert turned to the tech with a grin. "I have no idea, but I wish I could see what he's doing. Why don't you figure out a way to tap into his player camera? He probably doesn't have it enabled, but it's worth a shot. If it's off, I'll give you a raise if you can find a way to turn it on remotely!"

Claire had been paying attention to their conversation from the other side of the room. She called over, "Robert you know we aren't allowed to access a player's camera unless we have reason to believe that he is violating the terms of service."

*He looked back at her, and his grin widened. "Well,
we aren't certain that he isn't violating the terms, are we?"
Turning back to the tech he said in a serious voice, "Find a
way to access that player's camera. If you can't get access
to his camera, then find me the camera of someone in Lux
who can show us what's going on."*

*Robert started heading for the door to the control
room. Claire watched his back, a frown plastered on her
face. "Where do you think you're going, Robert?"*

*"I'm going to go make some popcorn," Robert
replied with a smile. "I expect that whatever is happening
in Lux is going to be extremely entertaining."*

*   *   *

Several hours later, Jason was sitting in the last
manor he had conquered. The room around him was
one of the slightly less resplendent banquet halls he
had seen that evening. Onyx was curled in his lap
sleeping. Jason drummed his fingers on the table as
he watched his zombies go through the familiar
motions of piling corpses and equipment.

It had been a long evening.

He had launched attacks on all of the major
manors on the north-side. Jason had even taken out
two guard patrols that had caught him transitioning
from one house to the next.

He had discovered throughout the evening
that the nobles did not own many useful items for
players. Most were relatively low level, and they
apparently spent most of their money on luxuries like
furniture and jewelry. He still hadn't found any loot
like the sword he had taken off the knight in the first
house, but he had found a few mediocre items (taken
mainly from the guards). There was so much stuff

that he had long since filled his bags, and a considerable number of his guard zombies were just carrying piles of loot.

He figured that if he sold the items cheap (to get rid of them quickly), he would probably rake in about $5,000-6,000. This estimate included the sword but didn't account for the nearly forty gold of in-game currency he had found. He figured the sale of the items should give him a couple of months of living expenses. He wasn't certain what he was going to do after that, but at least he wouldn't be desperate in the short-term.

The experience and skill progression had slowed throughout the night. Jason had gained another 12 levels from wiping out the other manors, bringing him to level 51. He had hesitated for a moment in deciding how to spend his points and then decided to assign all of the points to *Willpower*. That meant his *Willpower* was now at 278.

I just hope I'm not making a terrible decision, he thought with a sigh.

His skills had also risen modestly during the night. Most notably, *Summoning Mastery* had finally hit Intermediate Level 1. He had received a notification when the skill advanced:

Summoning Mastery advanced to Intermediate!
Skill Level: Intermediate Level 1
Effect 1: 15% increased stats for summoned undead and 15% increase to effective Willpower for purposes of determining control limit.
Effect 2: You may now communicate with your minions telepathically. Distance limit unknown.

The advancement had unlocked the ability to communicate mentally with his summons, and Jason expected that it would increase the bonuses from the ability each level. However, the advancement rate of the skill had slowed dramatically.

The telepathy was fantastic. It made it easier to coordinate his troops in the middle of a fight and removed the need to provide them with lengthy instructions as long as they were within sight of Jason. It also seemed to have an incredibly long range.

However, the telepathy didn't solve his management issues when he had to split the groups. He still had to give complicated commands to any group that he sent off on its own to guard doors or scout ahead since he wasn't around to order the zombies individually or see what was going on. He was hoping that Morgan would have some solution for this.

He reviewed his Summon Information window:

Summon Information			
Control Limit	31	Zombie Level Cap	114
Current Summons	31	-	-
Type of Summon			
Guards	24	Thieves	5
Fire Mage	1	Ice Mage	1

The level cap had become less important as the night progressed, and his *Willpower* skyrocketed. Most enemies he had fought were below level 100, and so his zombies now retained the level of the former NPCs.

Jason only had five thieves now, each around level 50. Some were a little scratched up and worse for wear. He still had his fire mage and had actually found an ice mage in one of the houses. He grimaced as he recalled that particular fight.

God that was awful.

By the end of the battle, the mage had coated almost the entire room in ice. Zombies and guards had been sliding all over the place. Even the mage had trouble standing up by the end of the fight. The only saving grace was that Jason actually got a chance to throw some knives while lying on his back.

I'll have to remember to thank Jerry for that one, he thought dryly.

His gaze moved back over to the two mages. They were both sitting at approximately level 100. The remaining twenty-four zombies were common guards or lords that seemed to have useful combat skills, and their average level was around 100.

The only thing he was really missing was some kind of archer contingent. This hadn't been a big issue in the close quarters of the manors, but he could imagine that in a more open battle, additional ranged minions would be useful.

Oh well. Nothing I can do about that right now.

It was currently 3:13 am in the game world. Jason figured he had a few more hours of real world time to play before he was ejected. He could even stay in the game for an extra hour and deal with the forced logout if it came to it.

What the hell am I going to do now though?

He had basically killed all of the nobles in the city at this point and was leading a small army of high-level zombies. Most of his minions were covered in blood, and many had obvious gaping wounds. The wounds didn't really mean that the zombies were injured of course. Most of the injuries had been caused in the process of killing the original the NPCs.

The issue was that any sane person would notice that most of the zombies really shouldn't be alive, much less standing and walking around. As soon as his zombies started marching around in public, people would likely begin screaming and alert the guards.

There was also the issue of the inevitable reaction when the guards discovered what happened to the noble houses later that day. They would be out for murder. Jason would have trouble smuggling his zombies out of the city and back in. More than likely, the city would just devolve into a riot when the NPCs discovered that the king and all of the nobles were dead.

I really didn't think this through.

He supposed he could abandon his zombies here, but for some reason, he just couldn't make himself do it. He glanced over at a zombie dressed as a city guard, and a thought tickled his mind.

I could just attack the city guards.

He expected that most or all of them were probably complicit in the plot with the nobles anyway. There was no way that the nobles would have been able to cover up the death of the regent unless some or all of the guards were in on it. That was likely why Rex had been discharged.

At the thought of the guards being included in the plot, the chill in his spine intensified. The long night of killing nobles had partially sated his desire for revenge, but he wasn't ready to stop yet. A grin of anticipation spread across his face as he decided on his next target.

Attacking the guards was a ballsy move. Jason had seen the longhouses in the eastern part of the city and knew there were close to two hundred men stationed in those buildings. He didn't like his odds if it came to a straight battle with the guardsmen. If he were going to take them on, he would need more

·zombies.

As it grew later, the nobles and their staff had gone to sleep. This made for much easier fights. Naked, unconscious NPCS put up little resistance. He had lost some troops along the way, but he had left scores of bodies in the houses that he couldn't add to his army since he had long ago hit his Control Limit. There were a couple hundred bodies that were just being left to rot in the manors right now.

Jason continued to sit there, chin in his hand as his fingers drummed the table.

What should I do?

He heard a thump and glanced over at a zombie who had run straight into a wall. When he didn't give them orders, the zombies sometimes acted like morons. He ordered the zombie to go stand in a corner. Maybe it would learn its lesson if he put it in time out!

Wait. Are zombies really that stupid naturally? Maybe it's a product of them being under my control.

Jason had been ordering them around all evening and had come to think of them as tools instead of having their own native intelligence. If the controlled zombies were really that dumb, what would happen if he summoned a feral one?

He stood up, dislodging Onyx from his lap-bed. The cat glared at him briefly and then stretched irritably before padding along behind him.

Jason ordered his zombies to drag one of the extra bodies into a small room off a nearby corridor. He posted a guard on either side of the door and then cast *Specialized Zombie* on the corpse in the room. He was at his Control Limit, so this zombie should be feral. He telepathically ordered the guards to quickly close the door.

Then he waited.

Jason couldn't hear any noise from inside the room and was starting to wonder if he had actually raised the zombie. He stepped back from the door and ordered one of the guard zombies to open it. As soon as the door opened, Jason saw that the guard in the room had indeed been raised as a zombie. However, he was standing in the room facing the wrong direction.

This is strange.

"Stomp your foot," he whispered to the guard zombie at the door.

The guard zombie complied with the order. Once the feral zombie heard the noise, he turned, and his milky white eyes focused on the guard. After a moment of hesitation, the feral zombie leaped forwarded at a sprint. Its arms clawed at the air, and it released a rasping roar. Jason flinched involuntarily as the feral zombie ferociously ripped at his guard. The feral creature tore at his guard's flesh with its teeth and nails.

What the fuck!

"Kill it! Kill it!" he yelled at his guards, as he backpedaled away from the door.

In a few moments, the guards had severed the feral zombie's head, and its corpse collapsed to the ground. The attack pattern of the feral zombie was downright scary. It was all rage and hunger, nothing like the orderly attacks of his Jason's troops. He ordered his guard zombies to quickly dispose of it.

Onyx gave Jason a look that seemed to say, "That was the stupidest idea you've had this evening."

"How was I supposed to know it would go completely batshit?" Jason asked Onyx.

Am I really arguing with a cat now? Maybe I'm going crazy.

Jason stood there and mulled over what had happened when he summoned the zombie. Its behavior had given him an idea. He couldn't take the city guards on directly, but he might be able to distract them and take them down individually.

If he raised the bodies in the various houses one at a time in separate rooms, he could then have his thieves sneak into the manors and open all of the doors. As the thieves left the house, they could also rig the doors with something that would make a lot of noise when someone tried to get in. He would basically be creating a trap inside each the noble houses!

As he considered this strategy, he smiled grimly. The icy chill cascaded in his skull, and he could have sworn for a moment he heard a rumbling laugh echo through the house. However, when he looked around, no one was there but him and his zombies.

Well, except for the judgmental cat, he thought as he eyed Onyx.

Jason got to work. He rigged seven manors within the span of two hours. His telepathy with his zombies allowed him to send them ahead to the other houses with instructions. He needed them to start positioning the bodies and rigging the doors. He raised all of the remaining corpses that were left in the manors, regardless of level. His goal was to create chaos, and he had seen the damage even a level 1 could do if it got lucky.

His guard zombies piled wooden furniture loosely against the front door of each house. After the guards had finished blocking the entrance and he had raised all the corpses, he sent in his thieves to arm the trap by opening all the doors and then slipping out the back of the house. He made certain to remind his thieves to exit out the servant's entrance and lock the door behind them.

Jason had also considered the next part of his plan while he worked.

Once he finished rigging the manors, he set up an ambush in the north-side for a nearby guard patrol. Instead of carefully cutting off the guards' escape like normal, Jason only attacked with seven of his guard zombies. After a short battle, one of the guards made it away from the zombies, gasping and screaming as he ran east towards the guard barracks.

From a nearby alley, Jason watched the fleeing man with a smile on his face.

Another forty-five minutes later, the north-side of Lux was swarming with guards that had responded to the lone survivor's cries that zombies were invading the city and had attacked north-side.

By that point, Jason was already long gone.

He had circled back to the east side of the city. His new target was the guardhouses. Jason expected that a contingent of guards would be left at the training grounds to defend the barracks and to continue offering training to the new players. Jason anticipated that the guards would send the bulk of their forces to the north-side to deal with the "zombie invasion," meaning that the force left at the barracks would be manageable.

When Jason arrived at the training grounds, it was still quite dark, and he had nearly an hour until full daylight. He had broken up his army into five groups and had them rendezvous in the dilapidated building near the stable master's house. This was the same spot he had used to stake out the stable a few nights ago.

That seems like such a long time ago now, he thought as he eyed the stable master's house.

From his familiar perch in the building, Jason could make out the training grounds and surrounding guardhouses in the distance. He was also relieved to see that Rex was not present. The game assigned a small skeleton crew to man the training ground at night so that the players could still train, but still preserve some realism. Jason expected that Rex was somewhere in his bed fast asleep.

He could tell that he had stirred the hornet's nest as he watched the remaining guards line up in formation and hand real weapons to confused players. When he saw the players, Jason had an idea and re-enabled the player chat in his system menu.

What he discovered in the local chat was quite interesting:

MonkeyKing: Does anyone know what is going on? The guards are going nuts over at the training ground. They didn't let me finish training.

Legolass: Lol. I saw you trying to hit that dummy. He was doing you a favor!

Kryptic: Guys. There are a ton of guards headed to the north side of Lux. I have no idea what is going on.

MonkeyKing: This guard keeps trying to give me a weapon and saying that I need to help fight off the invasion. What invasion?

Chango: A guard told me a similar story. Does anyone know what's going on?

Kryptic: Oh shit! $*&*&^$ zombies are in

Lux! I just saw a group of guards taken out after they entered a house. Zombies are in the street!

Legolass: What is this!? Some kind of event?

Kryptic has left the channel

The player chat quickly devolved into chaos as Jason smiled darkly. He assumed Kryptic must have died from the feral zombies.

Jason hadn't yet died in the game, but he had read on the forums that players that died were subject to a mandatory lock-out period of three hours real world time. This translated to approximately 9-12 hours in the game, so it was a significant penalty. However, Jason expected that the goal of the penalty was to prevent fights between players from lasting forever, with waves of resurrected players continuously bashing into each other. Large-scale battles in AO would require quite a bit of tactical planning to be successful.

He didn't have much time to dwell on Kryptic's untimely demise. He had to initiate phase two of his plan. His small army slipped out of the rubble of the dilapidated building and moved over to the training ground. It was still quite dark, and the buildings were casting long shadows that concealed his group's movements. Once his troops were in position, Jason circled back to the front of the training ground and ran forward yelling.

"Help! Oh my god help! There are zombies attacking the north side of Lux. Most of the guard patrols have been wiped out!"

Players and guards gathered around Jason as he approached and peppered him with questions. He started describing what he had seen. He was intimately familiar with what had happened on the north side of Lux, so he was able to provide quite a bit of gory detail.

Jason saw the lieutenant leave the administration office and head towards Jason. He was well over six feet tall, broad-shouldered, and sported a thick beard. In contrast to the regular guards, he was robed in heavy steel armor and carried a claymore strapped to his back. He also carried an almost palpable air of authority. Jason quickly inspected the man as he approached. Level 146.

Holy shit!

The lieutenant quickly took charge of the players and guards. He approached Jason and eyed him up and down. Jason's cloak obscured his eyes and part of his face, but it was clear that he was anxious.

The lieutenant addressed him, "Traveler, did you see where the zombies were headed? We need more information if we are going to be able to fight them off."

Jason took a few heaving breaths before replying, "Some were headed this way. They looked like zombies. I saw one rip a guard to shreds! I outran them, but I think they'll be here soon!" He trembled slightly and shook his head as though he was replaying the scene in his mind.

I'm becoming a damn fine actor, Jason thought with a mental chuckle. *They aren't even reacting to my infamy or alignment!*

"Thank you, traveler." The lieutenant patted him on the shoulder gruffly. "You should move back to the administration office and take a moment to collect yourself. Everyone else line up in front of the grounds. We need to get in position. The undead will be upon us shortly."

The lieutenant drew the group of guards and players into a dense-packed "V" formation in front of the training ground facing the street. He stood inside the interior of the formation so that he could give orders easily to the group. Jason did a quick head count and made it to fifty before he gave up.

Jason, momentarily forgotten by the group, eased away and activated *Sneak*. He quickly entered the office and closed the door firmly behind him, barricading it with a table. He moved over to a window to watch the show that was about to unfold. Onyx sat with him on the windowsill and peered out attentively.

Now that he was in a safe location, Jason felt the familiar tingle of anticipation as he considered what was about to happen. Ice solidified behind his eyes, and he could feel the dark chill pulse in his veins. He couldn't remember the last time he had released his mana. After hours with his mana active, he almost didn't notice the numbing chill except in stressful situations.

Onyx glanced over at Jason with an odd expression on his face, while his tail twitched spasmodically.

Jason didn't notice Onyx's anxious gaze. His attention was still on the players and NPCs. He smiled excitedly. This next part was going to be fun. Without hesitation, he telepathically ordered his decoy group into action.

A moment later, a group of zombies appeared around the bend in the street in front of the training ground. They hesitated for a moment and looked around. Then their milky white eyes caught sight of the formation of players and guards, and they roared through hoarse throats, sprinting towards the formation at a frightening speed.

The players and NPCs let out a shout and several of the weaker-willed players backed out of formation. Jason used this opportunity to cast *Curse of Weakness* on the tightly-grouped formation. A few players looked around confused as they saw the debuff appear as a status effect, but they seemed to chalk the debuff up to some skill of the zombies running toward them.

Jason ordered his kamikaze group into position. While he had been sitting in the dilapidated building to the south, he had given each of the five guards a hooded cloak. The cloaks concealed their wounds and allowed them to more easily infiltrate the formation.

His kamikaze group walked up behind the formation of players and guards as the decoy zombies approached. The attention of the lieutenant and those under his command was riveted on the small group of seemingly feral zombies that were racing towards them.

They should have been looking behind them.

Jason's kamikaze zombies filtered through the ranks of players and guards until they were evenly dispersed. Neither the players nor the guards seemed to give his kamikazes a second glance. Jason could visualize the overlapping blast radius of each zombie. Once they were in position, he began his chant. He was hoping to get the spell off before his decoys got in range of the players and guards.

No point in wasting zombies!

As he completed casting a series of *Corpse Explosions*, elongated shadows raced toward his kamikazes, unnoticed by the players. The resulting blast was the most spectacular thing Jason had ever seen. Even Onyx seemed mildly impressed.

He had noted from his initial fight in the north-side that the gear the zombies were wearing seemed to increase the damage of *Corpse Explosion*. He theorized that the equipment acted like shrapnel – similar to a claymore mine.

With this in mind, he had strapped as much equipment to each zombie as possible. They each wore multiple sets of mail, carried extra weapons, and had broken weapons and armor tied to their bodies. By the time Jason was done, they practically waddled when they walked.

The explosion caused by his *Corpse Explosion* resulted in a torrential spray of jagged metal shards to hurtle outwards in an expanding ring from each of the five zombies. The metal ripped through the bodies of the players and guards like paper. As the debris settled, a bloody mist could be seen hanging over the field of fresh corpses.

Standing within the radius of at least three zombies, the lieutenant absorbed the brunt of the blast. His arm had been blown off completely, and he struggled to regain his footing. By Jason's estimate, the explosions had killed nearly 75% of the defense force outright, while injuring and stunning most of the remaining survivors.

Jason didn't give the few survivors a chance to recover and ordered his other zombies forward. His thieves darted towards them, as fireballs and shards of ice from his mages flew over their heads. The thieves' targets were the remaining guards, as they represented the biggest threat. The players were typically low-level beginners. His zombie guards arrived shortly behind the thieves and finished off the rest of the injured players.

Numerous prompts appeared in Jason's field

of view. He estimated that he had killed nearly twenty-five guards, the lieutenant, and about thirty low-level players. The experience from the players was negligible, but he received a substantial amount of experience from the guards and the lieutenant.

x7 Level Up!
You have (35) undistributed stat points.

x1 Skill Rank Up: Summoning Mastery
Skill Level: Intermediate Level 2
Effect: 17% increased stats for summoned undead and 17% increase to effective Willpower for purposes of determining Control Limit.
Effect 2: You may now communicate with your minions telepathically. Distance limit unknown.

x1 Skill Rank Up: Mana Mastery
Skill Level: Beginner Level 5
Effect: -3% to mana cost.

x1 Skill Rank Up: Disguise
Skill Level: Beginner Level 5
Effect: 9% increased authenticity to your costumes and mannerisms while disguised.

x3 Spell Rank Up: Corpse Explosion
Skill Level: Beginner Level 8
Effect: Increased damage (Currently 1.07 x Health).

Jason was now level 58, and he quickly assigned the extra points to *Willpower* and ordered his zombies to start piling the bodies. While they were occupied, he looked around the administration office. Jason noticed a barrel that contained a number of communications scrolls. He also found a barrel holding a huge number of starter bags.

Jackpot!

He quickly stole most of the bags and distributed them to his troops. Jason had the zombies collect everything that wasn't nailed down. Most of the gear was worthless, but creating quality kamikaze zombies took a lot of scrap equipment.

Jason continued to carefully inspect the rest of the administration office. He still hadn't found any evidence indicating that the guards were complicit in helping the nobles. However, he was certain that they were. After walking around the room for the third time, his *Perception* picked up a faint blue sheen from underneath the rug near the desk that sat in the center of the room. He also received a notification.

x1 Skill Rank Up: Perception
Skill Level: Beginner Level 4
Effect: 8% increased chance to discover traps and unnoticed details.

He waved the notification away and began pulling up the rug, revealing a hatch in the floor. Still being cautious of traps, he had one of his guard zombies wrench the hatch open. The blades that immediately shot up out of the newly revealed tunnel severed both of the zombie's arms.

I guess Zombies aren't immune to flying blades, he thought with a chuckle.

Onyx gave him a long-suffering look and padded over to the opening, peering in. Jason had to admit he was curious too, but curiosity didn't make him any less wary of the potential danger. He had already witnessed one trap, and there might be more. He was going to send a zombie guard first. He waited a few minutes after sending his "canary" zombie down the suspicious hole before climbing down.

What he found was a small cellar below the administration office. A lantern hung on a hook next to a crude wooden desk. He didn't need the extra light though. His *Night Vision* and the light from the administration office was sufficient.

Jason perused the papers on the desk and found letters from several nobles addressed to the lieutenant. Each letter was phrased differently, but the general message was the same. The nobles all appreciated the hard work that the lieutenant had been doing to cover up the fact that the regent of Lux was dead.

Updated Quest: Trouble in Lux – Part 3

You have found evidence that shows that Strouse and the nobles collaborated to conceal the death of the Regent of Lux. In addition, you have discovered that the nobles were paying the guards to cover up the Regent's death. However, the question still remains regarding how you plan to proceed with this information.

Difficulty: A
Success: Decide what to do with the information you have found.
Failure: Unknown
Reward: Unknown

Stupid quest.

Jason was actually starting to miss the simpler fetch quests he had been given in other MMOs. At least there had been a clear goal, and he knew what was expected of him.

"Whatever happened to a Rank F quest to run a scroll to the blacksmith or kill some rats?"

Onyx made a motion that looked suspiciously like a shrug.

Great. Now I'm talking to myself AND personifying the cat.

After searching the cellar, Jason discovered that the nobles had been paying the guards exceptionally well. At least it seemed that way based on the extremely heavy chest next to the desk. Jason's jaw dropped as he lifted the lid and saw the amount of gold that was sitting in the chest.

There's enough here to fund the guards for a year.

Jason decided this couldn't all be kickbacks. The nobles must have been using the guards to hold the money that they had been skimming on tax collection. He wouldn't be surprised if the guards doubled as the tax collectors in this medieval city.

That really didn't address what he was going to do with the chest. He couldn't even lift a corner of it.

How the hell am I going to move this?

Onyx seemed especially enamored with the chest and had laid down on the gold with a contented purr. Every time Jason got close to the gold, Onyx would hiss and claw at him.

Jason ultimately decided to leave the gold in the cellar for now and regroup. Maybe an idea would come to him while he was re-summoning his zombies.

Above ground, Jason went to work raising more troops. He made certain to stay out of sight in case someone was watching closely. Jason ordered a group to scout the guardhouses and kill any stragglers. His minions were reminded to bring back any corpses.

Waste not, want not!

His *Willpower* and *Summoning Mastery* now

allowed him to summon 36 zombies. The max level cap was now level 131. This meant he couldn't quite summon the lieutenant at its original level 146. Yet he was still Jason's most powerful zombie. This had to be taken with a grain of salt, however, since the lieutenant was also missing an arm.

Jason's thoughts eventually turned back to the gold, and he sighed as he realized that there wasn't any way to move it. He would just have to come back for the loot. He made certain to carefully close the hatch to the cellar and replace the rug. Only someone with a decent skill level in *Perception* would find the cellar.

To protect his new treasure stash, Jason also rigged another set of traps. He had ended up with a ridiculous number of extra bodies, and he had his troops move them into the guardhouses and the administration office. Jason then raised the bodies through a crack in the door of each building, carefully easing each door shut behind him.

He expected this trick might not work forever, but for now, it was hilarious and an easy way to spread chaos in the city.

Jason glanced at the local chat to see how things were going in the north-side. The results brought another wry smile to his face:

MonkeyKing has left the channel.

Legolass has left the channel.

Chango has left the channel.

Lasandra: What the hell is going on! I just had like five people on my friends list die at the same time!

RupertMurdock: I know. The north-side is chaos. DO NOT GO NORTH. THERE ARE ZOMBIES!

ShadowKilla: I can take some zombies. You guys are just a bunch of noobs!

Carolina: Guys I'm standing a decent distance from the training ground, and there are zombies milling around everywhere!

Shadowkilla has left the channel.

RupertMurdock: Lol Shadow must have died.

Lasandra: Players and NPCs are regrouping in the market. Everyone come to the market now.

Jason was starting to have fun. Too bad he was running out of time. Once daylight hit, the fear factor would decrease, and his zombies would begin to degrade quickly.

He glanced at the in-game clock and saw that it was almost 7:30 am. He frowned. Shouldn't the sun have risen some time ago? He looked at the sky and saw that dark billowing clouds had rolled in over the city. He could see the occasional flash of lightning. Jason smiled and could have sworn he heard another rumbling laugh.

Maybe I could keep this up a while longer. What should I do next?

The king was already dead, the nobles had been taken care of, and the guards had now been severely weakened. If he could finish off the guards and find a way to weaken the remaining players in the city, he would basically control Lux. He looked at his small army of undead that he had worked so hard to cultivate over the evening.

If I somehow took the city, I could come and go as I please with my zombies.

The familiar chill pulsed in his veins as the idea of taking the city grew in his mind. He had wanted power, hadn't he? An excited grin twisted his lips, and dark mana coiled along his body as he recalled the glimpse of power the old man had shown him. The image of himself standing on the ramparts in front of his legion of undead flashed through his mind. He wanted that power!

It sounded like most of the guards on the north side of town had likely perished. Either that or it would take them a while to carefully clear each house. He had also just created more than fifty feral zombies here that they would need to deal with when they got back. However, Jason expected that the idiot guards at the starting courtyard would continue to direct new players to the training ground soon enough, and they would set these zombies free.

He had a small army of about thirty-six zombies following him, but what he needed to do was find an area where he could create more zombies and keep the city distracted and fighting. His guerrilla tactics had worked wonders so far.

Feral zombies. Controlled zombies. It didn't really matter. He just needed chaos. They didn't even have to be high level, there just needed to be more zombies!

The question was, where should he go next?

The market was the obvious place to find a large number of people, but judging from what he saw in chat, most of the players were starting to head there to regroup. He expected that by the time he made it to the market, he would find a well-fortified area swarming with people.

Then he thought of the south-side. That area was probably not defended at all right now. There were countless people there. Jason had already witnessed the poverty in that area. Many of those people were sick or starving. A life as the undead was probably preferable to the one they had now; it certainly couldn't be worse. Maybe he would be doing them a favor.

Bands of dark mana crawled along Jason's body like black snakes, and waves of unholy energy cascaded from him. The ice crystallized in his brain and thudded in time with his heartbeat as a plan began to form in his mind. He would take the power that he craved!

He looked up again at the sky and shouted, "You better watch this next part closely, old man."

A flash of lightning was his only reply.

Chapter 21 - Reborn

The group of techs in the control room were huddled around one screen when Robert walked back into the room. As he fished individual pieces of popcorn out of the bag he was carrying, Robert hummed to himself. He didn't immediately notice the crowd that was now grouped around the screen or Claire glaring disapprovingly at their backs.

Looking up, Robert caught sight of the group. "What are you all looking at? Put it on the big screen!" Robert motioned towards the large screen that hovered over the control room as he settled down in his chair on the raised dais in the center of the room.

A tech promptly complied, and the image they had been watching was projected in the air above the control room. The video was being shown from the point of view of a first-time player who had made his way to the training grounds in Lux.

Or what was left of the training grounds.

The group could see the destruction that had ravaged the area. The remains of bodies were scattered everywhere. Blood drenched the stones and the sides of buildings, and entrails littered the ground. Some of the corpses appeared to have either been ripped to shreds or blown apart.

Robert gaped at the scene.

"What happened here?" Claire asked in a horrified voice as she watched the events unfolding on the screen.

The player moved carefully toward the administration office through the field of dismembered corpses. An unusual and foreboding silence hung over both the training grounds and the control room. The only sound that could be heard was the player's ragged breathing. The player then gingerly opened the door to the office and peeked through the crack in the door. What he saw was a group of zombies packed into the room and milling around.

"Oh shit!" the player gasped.

The noise promptly alerted the zombies in the room. A dozen milky white eyes were suddenly focused on the lone player. Time seemed to freeze as the zombies all stood still, staring at the player.

With a throaty roar, the group of zombies rushed forward in a frenzy of limbs. In his panic, the player fell backward onto the ground and the camera tilted erratically. The player was trying desperately to crawl away from the building.

The view panned back to the administration office. The zombies slammed into the door of the office and came pouring out, rushing at the player. Their wretched screams tore through the air. Their faces were wild, and their hands clawed the air as they reached for the player.

"Oh god no!" the player shouted. His hands came into view as he vainly tried to defend himself.

Then the zombies were upon him, and his body was quickly torn apart in a flurry of arms, teeth, and blood. Although the pain sensors were heavily muted, the player let out a scream of anguish as he was ripped apart. Likely the psychological horror of what was happening was worse than the dull pain he felt.

The screen went black.

No one spoke in the control room for a long moment.

Then Robert turned to the tech he had spoken with before he left the room. "Tell me you have access to that unusual player's camera."

*   *   *

Jason had been busy for the last several hours.

The black clouds had stayed hovering over the city, obscuring the sun and protecting his minions.

Torrential rain had begun to fall soon after he left the training grounds. Bolts of lightning would occasionally strike a house or the cobblestones, starting small fires and sending up sparks. Several players had noted, in the local chat, that the weather seemed unnatural.

Jason agreed, but he wasn't going to complain.

He had divided his zombie army into five smaller groups and had them systematically kill the residents of the south-side. He quickly realized that many of the buildings in the southern part of the city were vacant. His guess was that many of the NPCs had moved away as the city began to deteriorate under the corrupt influence of the nobles.

Jason made certain to stay far away from the Sow's Snout. He wasn't certain that Jerry would approve of how he had spent the last twenty-four hours or how things had so rapidly spiraled out of control. After sparring with Jerry, he also didn't think a few well-placed *Corpse Explosions* or some clever tricks would be enough to kill him.

So he satisfied himself with slaughtering the peasants, thieves, and beggars he could find. He left large groups of feral zombies sitting in carefully designated houses in the south-side. Over the course of the last few hours, the city's zombie population had grown dramatically.

In the meantime, the players and guards on the north-side had managed to regroup and kill most of the zombies Jason had left in the various manors. From what he had read in the local chat, the remaining city guards were now few and far between. Lux had already been a city plagued with problems, and his one night of rampaging had brought it to its knees.

Jason soon ran out of bodies to raise in the

south-side and made his way west. He needed more zombies.

The people living on the west-side had holed themselves up in their homes after hearing word of a zombie invasion. This wasn't much of an obstacle for Jason's thieves. He had soon accumulated a mounting body count in that part of the city as well.

Unfortunately, most of these kills don't give me experience anymore, Jason thought ruefully as he jogged along the streets on the western side of the city.

Most of his zombies ran ahead of him, killing the residents and moving their bodies to certain carefully marked houses. His bodyguard contingent and Onyx kept pace as he made the rounds of the houses, raising the waiting corpses. Jason hadn't leveled once in the past several hours, even after killing approximately a third of the city's residents.

He did, however, get some amusement from watching the chat logs when a group of new players made it to the training ground to find it deserted. They had promptly investigated the administration office and the guardhouses looking for the guards. That had obviously been a mistake. The group had been killed almost instantly.

What a way to start your first day in-game!

Jason had seen the feral zombies in action and could only imagine how unnerved those new players must have been. The group of high-level zombies he had left at the training grounds had promptly gone on a rampage through the eastern part of the city, which had been left largely undefended. This had been an excellent distraction and had forced the remaining survivors to the center of the Lux where the marketplace and the keep stood.

The keep's gates had remained firmly shut, and

no response had been heard from the city's regent. Many of the players had noted that the keep stayed silent in the midst of a zombie invasion. A few had also remarked that it was strange that the city's regent hadn't opened the gates. Clearly, they didn't realize that the keep was uninhabited, and the city's regent had been dead for quite some time.

Jason was finishing up in the west-side when he received an incoming message.

> **Frank:** Hey man. What the hell is happening in Lux? All of the streams are going wild, and the footage is intense. There are freaking zombies!

> **Jason:** Umm. Yeah, it's pretty insane here.

There was a long pause before Frank responded, and Jason took the opportunity to regroup his zombies. He sent each of his remaining five rogues to separate parts of the city with careful instructions, and he started preparing a group of kamikaze zombies using some of his zombie guards.

It was currently 6:46 pm in-game.

> **Frank:** Wait. What the actual fuck Jason? My friend's list shows that you're level 58. How are you level 58?! Weren't you level 12 yesterday? What the hell is going on?

Jason grimaced.

His fingers hesitated over the semi-transparent keyboard that floated in front of him. He looked at the bodyguard contingent which had set up a defensive perimeter around him. Each zombie was approximately level 90. His two mages stood nearby and surveyed the area around him while wreathed in flame and ice.

How exactly was he going to explain what had happened?

Jason: I can't really get into it right now. It's been a long night.

Frank: Oh don't give me that crap. I know you're up to something. Most of the players in Lux are now dead, and you're not only alive, but you somehow power leveled overnight?

Jason: Fine. I might have had something to do with the zombies. However, I'm a bit busy right now.

Frank: Okay, okay. At least enable your player camera and start recording. I don't know what you're doing exactly, but you owe me a chance to see what happens next!

Jason face palmed. He had a camera built into the UI? How could he be this dumb? He could have sold the footage from this evening for a small fortune.

On second thought, maybe it was for the best. This last evening had made it clear that his success as a Necromancer relied on a healthy dose of deception and discretion. Releasing the footage might have revealed something that would allow the other players to identify him. He didn't want his information plastered all over Rogue-Net.

Even if he did give Frank some footage, he decided it would need to be heavily edited.

Jason: Okay, I will enable the camera. I have

to go though.

Frank: I guess I will take what I can get. Good luck on whatever the hell you're doing!

After he terminated the chat session, Jason quickly enabled his camera in the system menu. He started making his way carefully down the main street he had used when he first entered the game. His minions had already scouted the market where the players and NPCs were grouped, but he was curious to see it with his own eyes and he needed to get in position for what was coming next.

It was early evening in the game, but it was still incredibly dark. Between the cloud cover and the rainfall, it was hard to make out anything on the street. The rain was torrential, and his clothing was completely soaked, even with the cloak. A constant drumming sound could be heard as the droplets hit the cobblestones.

He left the majority of his army in a building about a hundred yards from the marketplace and ordered them to barricade the door. Hopefully, that would keep them safe from what was coming.

Jason then activated *Sneak* and moved closer to the marketplace, using the occasional stack of barrels and crates as cover. His target was a building located on the southern edge of the market. If not for the heavy rain and *Sneak*, he was certain the other players and NPCs would have seen him before he was able to enter the building.

Once he made it to his destination, Jason made his way to the second story and found a window that gave him a decent view of the market. Onyx sat quietly beside him, looking down on the players and NPCs. Jason stroked the cat idly as he surveyed the marketplace.

The players and remaining NPCs had erected a hasty fortification around the market. They had toppled the stalls and used the wood to wall off the entrance to each street. The market was located almost directly in the center of Lux and the city's four main streets each connected to the market like the spokes of a wheel. Players and NPCs were posted on makeshift bulwarks in front of each blockade. They looked nervous and continuously scanned the streets.

Jason's eyes shone with unholy light as he looked down on the market, and dark mana twisted around his arms. He radiated corrupt power as he stood watching the players and NPCs. He chuckled evilly to himself. This was going to be a fun fight.

Onyx looked at Jason askance. Jason had been channeling his dark mana continuously for more than twenty hours now. Onyx's tail twitched with nervous anticipation, as he looked between Jason and the marketplace.

Jason's gaze drifted to the keep that sat on the north-east corner of the market. Its windows were dark, and no guards manned its walls. It was surprising that no one had started to question whether the regent even existed. What regent would let his city be attacked by a zombie invasion and not offer his keep as protection?

He checked the time in-game. 7:37pm. It had been nearly forty-five minutes since he had given his thieves their instructions. He just hoped they had enough stamina to make the jog. They were each around level 60, so he was hopeful that they wouldn't have too much trouble. This was the first time that he had been without his minions in hours, and he almost felt naked.

By his estimate, he had another five minutes

until his thieves made it back. Jason trembled with excitement, and his heart beat frantically. Even the dark mana wasn't enough to suppress his nervousness. It had been one hell of a day, but this was probably going to be the most intense thing he had witnessed in AO so far.

"I'm going to conquer a city," he murmured to himself. His voice carried a faint note of surprise.

Onyx just looked at him with a dry expression that said, "That has yet to be seen."

Suddenly, Jason could make out a faint roaring sound. For a moment, he thought it was only the sound of the rain. Yet this was something different. It carried a note of rage and hunger that couldn't be felt by mere water. As his hand rested on the windowsill, he felt a slight vibration.

They're coming.

He moved to a window on the other side of the building that looked out onto one of the major streets connecting to the marketplace. Onyx was close on his heels and leaped up onto the new windowsill. Jason's eyes searched the end of the street. For a moment, he couldn't make out anything through the rain.

Then Jason's jaw dropped.

What the hell is that?

A wall of gray hunger and chaos rocketed down the street. The zombies roared in a frenzy as they raced forward, jostling and crushing one another in their desperate rush. The front of the wave of zombies was all arms, legs, and teeth. It almost seemed to be one organism crashing down through the street. The mass of zombies pressed forward, splintering the wood of nearby buildings and smashing into crates and barrels.

In front of the horde darted a black shape heading straight for the makeshift bulwark near the market. Jason thief struggled hard to stay ahead of the horde.

Soon the sentries in the bulwarks had also spotted the zombies. Jason could hear the alarm raised by the defenders and the panicked shouts as they got in position. He could only imagine the mind crushing terror they were feeling, as they looked out upon the horde descending upon them.

I'm really glad I'm not standing on those bulwarks, Jason thought with a shudder.

He knew that a similar scene was playing out on each of the four streets leading into the market, as his thieves raced ahead of the zombie hordes.

As he killed his way through the southern and western parts of the city, he had carefully positioned the feral zombies in houses located on roughly a straight line from five separate points along the wall to the marketplace. He had ordered his thieves to run forward from those locations along the wall, opening the doors of the houses containing the feral zombies as they raced toward the market.

The zombie thieves had performed their master's orders impeccably. The thieves' cries of rage had summoned their feral brethren to battle and whipped them into a frenzy.

As the horde neared the bulwarks on each street, the first spells and arrows raced through the air. Lights flashed as mages vainly tried to cast every AOE spell they knew. Flame, ice, and streaks of light struck against the torrent of bodies, leaving no noticeable impression on the mass of seething, rotten flesh.

His thieves each waited until the NPCs and players had fired on the zombies before they activated *Sneak* and slipped off the street into nearby houses. Jason was hoping that the players and NPCs had managed to pull aggro from his troops.

He breathed a sigh of relief as the horde continued forward. At least he wouldn't lose any more thieves.

"Now for the next phase," Jason murmured to himself. He moved back to the window that surveyed the marketplace and saw similar hordes attacking down each street. The icy sensation in his mind was almost overwhelming, and it continued to throb in time with his quickening heartbeat.

He had rigged eight of the guard zombies as kamikazes and piled them high with scrap gear and weapons. Jason had positioned two along each of the four main roads heading into the market. They were currently hidden in nearby buildings and awaiting his command.

Jason didn't hesitate.

"Attack," he murmured. He mentally commanded his kamikazes to exit their hiding places along each street and enter the flood of zombies crashing down on the bulwarks. As soon as the bloated kamikazes stepped into the horde, they were carried forward on the wave of bodies toward the gate. The feral zombies ignored them in their mad rush forward, causing his kamikazes to basically crowd surf across the horde until they crashed against the bulwark.

As he saw his kamikazes slam into the wooden walls, Jason cast one *Corpse Explosion* after another in rapid succession. Each explosion rocked the makeshift walls at the end of each street as scraps of wood and metal flew in all directions. The blasts weren't enough to completely destroy the layers of heavy wood that made up the bulwarks, but they didn't need to. He just needed to weaken them.

Screams rang out over the sound of the rain

and the roars of the feral zombies. The first bulwark fell and sent players and NPCs tumbling into the onrushing horde.

Then another fell.

Then another.

The zombie hordes rushed into the marketplace from several directions like ravenous tidal waves. Each individual zombie was typically low level. A good portion of the zombies were the beggars and thieves Jason had slain in south-side. However, the combined attacks of hundreds of zombies destroyed anything it touched. Players were thrown into walls, their bodies shredded, and a bloody mist seemed to hover over large portions of the market. Rivers of blood and rainwater ran down the street into the gutters.

Jason watched calmly as the market was painted red with blood. His eyes glowing darkly in the shadows of the room he occupied, and his mind felt like it was frozen solid as he watched the carnage unfold. Jason's dark mana was going wild. Bands of black energy were coiling viciously around his arms. Tendrils of darkness lashed at the air around him, and Onyx was forced to retreat farther back into the room.

This wasn't a fight. It was a massacre.

A glimmer of doubt invaded his mind as the sea of power surged through him. It was overwhelming. This seemed different than the other times he had channeled his dark mana. He was losing control of the mana that ripped and tore its way through his body.

Suddenly, his vision blurred and the game world seemed to stutter.

"What do we have here?" a graveled voice questioned beside him.

Jason's vision began to clear slowly, and he glanced over. The old man stood passively beside Jason at the window, calmly watching the scene in the market. He held his scythe in one hand, blood welling on the tip of the blade. The droplet hung in the air as Jason watched.

Jason wasn't really certain how to respond.

"I guess things got a bit out of hand," he finally said weakly.

The old man laughed. "That much is clear. Although, it has been quite the show. You have been receiving attention from more than just me."

"What do you mean? Who has been paying attention to me?" Jason inquired, his brow furrowed.

"The other incarnations for one. They are concerned that you're tipping the balance of power in this region to the dark." He looked over at Jason with a wry twist of his lips. "They do not care much for me I can tell you."

The old man continued, "In addition, your own kind have taken great interest in what is transpiring here. The travelers seemed much more disturbed than normal. Not that I blame them." At this last part, he gestured at the massacre in the market.

Jason looked back to the carnage, his thoughts a jumble. The dark mana still coursed through his veins wildly, and he felt no doubt or shame looking down at the carnage he had wrought.

The old man turned to him and seemed to appraise him carefully. "You have fully embraced the dark tonight. I can see that you have given yourself over completely to your desires." His words did not carry judgment, only a hint of curiosity.

He paused. "Why are you so willing to destroy I wonder? Perhaps you need to be more clearheaded to answer truthfully?"

With a wave of his hand, the old man completely extinguished Jason's dark mana. Jason immediately fell to his knees gasping. The removal of the dark mana created a vacuum in his mind that sucked and pulled all of his emotions back to him. His mind writhed in pain at the sensation.

The almost forgotten anger rushed back. The pain of being a homeless, expelled student with no prospects. The fight with his parents and their betrayal. The curses thrown at Ms. Abrams and Mr. Edwards. He wanted to scream at the sensation. Without the anesthetic effect of the dark, his mind trembled under the emotions it had denied for so many hours.

As his thoughts slowly began to settle, Jason recalled the events of the evening. His original mission had been to find a few items to sell so that he could support himself. He had justified his other actions as meting out justice for the crimes committed by the nobles and the guards. Yet somehow it had spiraled into this chaos he saw before him.

What was the purpose of this?

He wasn't certain that any of the steps he had taken after pillaging the first manor had been out of pragmatism or justice. If he was honest with himself, he had simply been angry. Jason had been angry for so long. At his school. At Alex. At his parents.

At myself.

When he logged in after arriving at his aunt's house, he had wanted to lash out at something, at anything. He had wanted to be the one in control, instead of the one being stepped on. Jason had wanted to feel powerful.

"You told me that as your disciple, I had one task: to find power. I have been searching for that." He turned to the old man, continuing quietly, "I wanted to feel the power that I witnessed in your vision. I wanted to command a legion."

Jason hesitated. "I think my anger at the nobles and the guards was just a way to make myself feel better about taking what I wanted all along."

His gaze returned to the feral, uncontrolled zombies as they tore and shredded the players and NPCs. Their ravenous wailing filled the air and drowned out the sound of the rain. Had he wanted his legion to look like this? This wasn't an army; it was a riot.

Jason couldn't see the old man's eyes under his hood, yet he felt the old man examining him carefully. "You have made much progress in pursuit of your goal today," the old man finally said. "However, you seem conflicted over the result."

"I just don't know..." Jason said, shaking his head slowly.

The old man's head turned back to the scene before them. "Well, perhaps I can offer you a hand in taking the next step forward."

With that, he turned back to Jason, a grin plastered on his wrinkled lips. "You have created a whirlpool of death in Lux. It has formed a siphon that draws dark mana in at an alarming rate. This area is now teeming with energy. Perhaps it would be easier to show you."

The old man's hand rested on Jason's shoulder.

The world suddenly froze and took on an ethereal haze. The zombies in the market stopped in mid-motion, their claw-like arms and hungry mouths frozen in the air. Jason could see motes of darkness floating around him. He recognized the motes for what they were, ambient dark mana. His gaze moved back to the street below, mesmerized by what he saw.

The motes of dark energy were being sucked in

toward the horde where they swirled in an enormous dark vortex of energy. The maelstrom of power almost seemed to warp the area around it. Jason could feel the terrifying power that the vortex was giving off. He knew that it was capable of something incredible if it were controlled.

Or monstrous.

The old man's voice intoned in his head, "Destruction is merely one facet of power. Creation is the other side of the coin that is forged by the truly powerful."

The old man looked back to Jason. "By destroying this city and its people, you have created the well of power you see before you. However, this energy is untamed. It could be used to create something new."

"Something monstrous and beautiful. Terrible and mesmerizing. Destruction and creation. Alpha and Omega. They seem to be opposing forces, yet the concert of the two brings true power." The old man's tone almost seemed wistful, as he gazed upon the vortex below.

His's words stirred something in Jason's soul. Both in-game and out, he had torn down the world around him and scattered the pieces. Could he now build something new out of the rubble?

Could I remake myself?

The old man continued in his rumbling voice, "I see the lesson resonates with you. You now have a choice. You can use the dark mana you see below to continue your rampage. You could annihilate the whole city if you choose to do so.

In the alternative, you could use that power to create. You could take a chance at building something truly miraculous."

Jason's mind reeled. Something new? What

would he create with such energy? Looking at the vortex of raw energy below him, he knew the possibilities were almost endless.

He thought about his minions for a moment. He had built them into a small coordinated army. Over the course of the evening, he had grown concerned that at some point he would lose each member of his budding army. Their bodies would eventually decay and fade. They would need to be replaced. Maybe with something better, but he couldn't be certain.

What he wanted was something that could prevent the decay indefinitely. He thought of what Morgan had told him about the graveyard, how a nexus of dark mana could preserve the bodies of his minions. He looked back to the vortex and to the horde of zombies that now stood in the courtyard. With this power, could he make the dark mana that pervaded their bodies permanent?

A chuckle rumbled beside him. "That is a fantastic choice! It will be done!"

Suddenly, the world resolved back into motion.

Jason stood at the window. He could still see the massive vortex swirling in the market below. He watched as tendrils of dark energy broke off from the vortex and lanced towards him. They circled his arms and his waist, lifting him into the air. As soon as the tendrils anchored to Jason, the vortex began to heave and undulate. A torrent of dark energy poured toward him, enveloping his body in the flow of power. As the vortex swirled around his body, his mind was overwhelmed with a strange mixture of pain and pleasure.

Soon it was over. Jason stood looking down at the market. His eyes still radiated black power, while cascading waves of dark mana encircled his body. During the transfer of power, the roof of the building had been disintegrated, and Jason's form was now visible from the market below.

Jason instinctively knew what he had to do. He raised his arms and began chanting in a language he didn't quite recognize. This wasn't Veridian. It was something deeper, something primal. Dark energy radiated from his body in rippling waves.

The black clouds over the city began to swirl, mimicking the vortex he had seen in the courtyard. A loud peal of thunder sounded in the sky and lightning began to strike the city rapidly, slamming into the stone and wood of the buildings.

The ground beneath him trembled, first gently and then forcefully. Yet the keep and the buildings around him didn't tumble down. Instead, they began to change, twisting and warping in an unnatural, grotesque way. The effect on the keep was the most noticeable.

The shape of the keep bent and skewed. Gargoyles emerged from the parapets, and heavy chains emerged from the walls, crisscrossing in the air. Twisted spires erupted from the stone and shot into the sky. The gate changed from brown to a black obsidian, with skulls embossed on the banded metal. Green lights now shown from the arrow slits on the walls, and specters flew in lazy circles around the top of the keep.

Jason also noted that the marketplace and surrounding buildings had been corrupted. Gravestones emerged from the cobblestones at random angles. The cobblestones themselves turned black and cracked. The buildings now seemed to be carved of dark stone and obsidian-colored wood. Unnatural almost tortured faces were carved like scrollwork along the length of the boards. Ghostly lanterns now adorned the streets and gave off an eerie green light.

The horde standing in the courtyard was not immune to the changes. As Jason watched, their bodies contorted. Screams filled the air as the zombies writhed and twisted. They underwent dramatic changes in size and shape as the dark mana molded them to fit their new home. Some were changed into pure skeletons, while others grew into monstrous, bulbous hulks that stood eight feet tall. The rest retained their zombie demeanor, but their eyes now shone with sanity and intelligence. Through it all, Jason continued to cast the spell. His mind scrambled to keep up with both the words and the changes he observed before him.

And then it was over.

"This was the choice I would have made in your shoes. You have created something new from the destruction you have caused." The old man's mouth was twisted into a grin, and his tone carried a note of pride.

"Did I choose this?" Jason asked in awe.

A rumbling laugh met his question. "I may have had some influence, but your desire was clear."

The old man's hand waved at the new city before him. "Welcome to your new home. Welcome to the Twilight Throne."

The horde of undead turned as one to face Jason. Milky white eyes and glowing orbs of energy bore into him. Silence hung over the courtyard as hundreds of undead stared up at Jason standing on his makeshift balcony.

Then, as one, the horde of undead bowed before him.

The legion released a throaty roar as they rose.

It was a deafening howl that drowned out the sound of the rain and the thunder. This roar was not filled with rage or hunger, but with pure, exuberant delight.

"We are alive!" they screamed into the darkness.

A prompt crashed into Jason's field of view like a wrecking ball. A similar message appeared in front of every player currently logged into the game. The prompt was impossible to ignore or to wave away:

Universal System Message

The player Jason has conquered the City of Lux and has converted it to the dark. The city of Lux is now known as the Twilight Throne. The city will reside in perpetual darkness, and daylight will never touch its streets. "Undead" is now available as a starting race and players that choose the undead race will start in the Twilight Throne.

The city's NPCs are now undead. All undead creatures, including summoned creatures, within the Twilight Throne's zone of influence will not decay. All players and NPCs with a positive alignment within the zone of influence of the Twilight Throne will receive a penalty to stats and experience gain.

As a result of conquering a capital city, the Kingdom of Lusade has been dissolved and the surrounding region is now in dispute. The towns and land that once comprised the Kingdom of Lusade are now fair game.

Welcome to the darkness mortals! - The Dark One

Chapter 22 - Resolved

The control room was as silent as a tomb.

A tech had managed to connect to the unusual player's video feed once he enabled his in-game camera. The staff watched from the player's point-of-view as he made his way discreetly to a building adjacent to the marketplace. The camera tilted and bounced as the player walked upstairs and found a window overlooking the market. Makeshift bulwarks had been constructed at the end of each street, and lightning flashed in the sky amongst the dense, black clouds. The player looked down at the market, observing the hundreds of players and NPCs filling the courtyard.

"Look at all of those people! To think that this is only the second day of the game," one of the techs said softly, his voice echoing slightly in the quiet control room.

Then the staff heard a rumble that rose above the sound of the torrential rain.

Involuntary gasps could be heard around the room as the group caught sight of the horde of zombies racing down one of the streets funneling into the market. The zombies were so tightly packed that it was difficult to make out individual creatures. They were merely a single, onrushing wave of ravenous destruction.

"What is that thing?" Claire asked, while others in the group murmured in confusion at the screen.

The camera panned back to the marketplace, and the staff grew silent as they saw a similar horde streaming down each of the four streets leading into the marketplace. The waves smashed into the player-made bulwarks. The wood creaked and groaned in protest, and many NPCs and players lost their footing. The unfortunate tumbled over the wall into the horde.

The player's arms appeared in the camera's view. They moved as he murmured arcane words. Dark energy pooled rapidly between his hands and then darted forward. The tendrils of darkness struck at random points among the crashing waves of zombies. Suddenly, explosions tore at the makeshift walls, and the wood splintered and cracked.

"Okay, what's going on? Is he controlling those things? Did he cause the explosions?" a tech shouted at the screen.

Robert just stared at the scene that played in the air above the room with his mouth open. His hand was frozen mid-way between the bag of popcorn and his mouth.

The bulwarks crumbled and then one after another they fell. The zombies were in the courtyard. The players and NPCs didn't stand a chance in the face of the onrushing tides of undead. Many broke in the face of the oncoming avalanche, turning to flee. Yet there was nowhere to run. They were surrounded.

Digital bodies were crushed and ripped apart, and a bloody mist was thrown into the air. Screams of fear and horror filled the night. The cobblestones were soon dyed red with blood.

Several of the staff members left the room mumbling apologies and excuses. They just couldn't handle the images that were flashing across the screen.

The camera view was steady. They could hear the user's breathing. It was unnaturally calm considering the events playing out in the market.

Robert was enthralled by this player. He had been interested to see what a so-called 'evil' player looked like within the game. This was it, and it was... something else. Despite the appalling nature of the massacre, he was in in awe of what this player had accomplished.

As the last of the players were slaughtered, the video suddenly went black.

"Why did we lose the feed?" Robert cried out.

"I-I don't know," replied one of the techs in confusion. "We are running a few minutes behind the game world, but that doesn't explain the interruption. I think

Alfred overrode it."

A moment later, the screen flickered back to life. The roof of the building the player had been standing in had been disintegrated, and he now stood on an impromptu platform overlooking the marketplace.

The player's hands began moving as he murmured a new spell. Whatever he was casting this time was different from the other spells they had seen cast in-game. Dark energy poured from the player in waves. The intensity of his mana was far stronger than anything Robert had ever seen.

The staff could see the dark clouds begin to spiral in the sky in response to the spell. Bolts of lightning rained down, striking buildings and cobblestones in a thunderous display of power.

"A player shouldn't be able to do this," Robert murmured. "Even the participants in the trials never reached this level of power..."

Not a sound was heard in the room as the group watched the buildings around Jason grow and twist. The zombies and structures seemed to writhe in agony, as flesh, stone, and wood turned black. The whole city was being warped and changed by the dark energy that cascaded over the buildings.

As the changes slowed, a horde of undead stood in the marketplace. Robert noted that some were no longer zombies, but something else entirely. Hundreds of heads turned milky orbs and soulless eyes to stare directly at the player.

Then they bowed in deference.

As the horde stood, they turned their heads to the sky and released a roar filled with almost unbearable passion. The sound sent shivers down the backs of many of the staff members, and they stood in stunned amazement staring at the screen.

"Who is this player?" Robert whispered.

Then the screen went dark.

*　　　*　　　*

Jason woke slowly. He felt confused, and his head was pounding.

The world around him was completely black. He felt around himself slowly, and his hands gripped rough woolen fibers. Grasping at his head, he felt something heavy and plastic covering his face.

Slowly his mind began to piece together where he was. He must be at his aunt's house. He was wearing his VR helmet. Slowly removing the helmet, he sat up. His head spun for a moment. His body ached, and his limbs felt dead and lifeless. Jason held his head in his hands and then glanced around the room.

Sunlight trickled through the window next to his bed.

What time is it? He thought groggily.

He thumbed his Core and discovered that it was almost noon. Hadn't it just been nighttime? Wasn't it supposed to be raining? Wait...

I was in the game...

Suddenly, the memories came flooding back, and he remembered what had happened. He had killed off all of the nobles, guards, NPCs, and players in Lux in a single night. He had destroyed the city and created something both malignant and magnificent from the ashes.

"The Twilight Throne," he murmured.

Jason stood and stretched his aching body. He rubbed at his temples in an attempt to ease his headache as he made his way to the bathroom.

Why do I feel so awful? Was I in the game for too long? Did the time freeze thing that the old man caused somehow multiply the time compression? Or was it the process of channeling that vortex of dark energy?

He hesitated.

Or was it some combination of all of the above?

He didn't have an answer, so he decided to begin his morning routine. Once he was out of the bathroom, he made his way to the kitchen. His head had already begun to feel better. Jason didn't see his aunt anywhere and was grateful for that.

Good. I can avoid an awkward conversation. I think I would be even more tongue-tied in my current condition.

He began rummaging through the pantry in search of something to eat. The only thing his aunt seemed to have was peanut butter, stale crackers, an overly ripened black banana, and ramen. Apparently, she enjoyed grocery shopping about as much as he did.

Oh well. I guess ramen isn't so bad.

Jason set some water to boil on the stove and sat down at the kitchen counter. His gaze drifted across the rundown bungalow that his aunt lived in. In the light of day, the place still looked like a dilapidated mess. Yet, for whatever reason, Jason's perspective seemed to have shifted.

The peeling walls and third-hand furniture drove home the point that Angie didn't have much. In spite of that, she had still agreed to take him in. Now that his mind was not in turmoil over the fight with his parents, he also suspected she had cut him a deal on the rent. The depth of her compassion struck a chord within him. It stood out in stark contrast to how he had behaved yesterday.

He had wallowed in his own self-pity and anger, taking his emotions out on the game world. He had continuously channeled his dark mana to drive away the pain and then gone on to destroy a city. Even as he ground the NPCs and players under his digital foot, he had been weak. Jason had lashed out at the game world instead of dealing with his own issues. He was overcome with a heavy sense of shame that nearly took his breath away.

Then an image of the old man flashed in his mind. After destroying Lux, he had given Jason the opportunity to build something from the ashes. He had offered him a chance to salvage something from the ruin.

What had he said again? Creation is part of true power?

The memory of the formation of the Twilight Throne flitted through his mind's eye. Its spiraling, obsidian towers and imposing keep. A legion of undead roaring into the night in an ecstatic affirmation of life. He had created something spectacular even after he had torn down the game world around him.

"I need to get my shit together," Jason chastised himself.

As far as epiphanies went, it wasn't revolutionary. However, the moment he said it, Jason could feel his anger and resentment begin to fade. They weren't gone, but the feelings were blunted and manageable. He felt stronger like a weight had been lifted from his shoulders.

He had acted to defend himself at Richmond and with his parents. He had started a new life here with Angie. He would make the same decision if he had it to do over again.

To hell with it. He needed to get over himself and start moving forward. Gone were the days of simpering self-loathing and anger. He was going to create something awe-inspiring with his life.

"I'm going to show them how badly they've underestimated me," he declared to the empty kitchen.

Resolved, he finished cooking the noodles and then thumbed his Core. The internet in this region of the city had much lower bandwidth than he was accustomed to, but free internet was available everywhere.

The U.S. Legislature had passed a bill several years ago that had declared that internet access was a basic human right. As a result, local municipalities were required to offer wireless internet access for free. This was a great idea in theory, but, in practice, it just meant everyone had access to an almost unusable internet connection. This was most apparent in the poorer areas, like his aunt's home.

Jason's subscription to AO included a premium internet package, so his gameplay experience wasn't affected by the poor public internet. As soon as he connected with his VR unit, additional bandwidth would be appropriately allocated. Unfortunately, this didn't apply to handheld devices.

He pulled up some websites for online public schools and drifted through the list of choices, looking for something that offered good math and science courses. He wasn't exactly certain what he wanted to do in college or career-wise, but he had always been drawn to the logical nature of the sciences.

Maybe I could be a software engineer. I wonder if you can get class credit for playing AO, he thought with a chuckle.

He glanced around the apartment, expecting a judgmental look from Onyx for sitting at the counter and laughing at his own jokes. Yet the cat wasn't there. Jason shook his head to clear it.

Of course he isn't here. I'm not in AO. Maybe I have been playing too much!

After about thirty minutes of searching, he finally found a school that seemed like a decent fit. Online public schools had detailed rankings for different types of classes and course loads. The schools were state funded, but they received allocations of funds based on student admissions. Since students could attend an online school from basically anywhere, they had their choice of schools. The competition among the various educational establishments was fierce. It was a student market nowadays.

The school he was looking at was called the "Calvary School." It had good rankings in math and science and a phenomenal computer science department. It seemed like a pretty good fit, and Jason's test scores were high enough to get him admitted. He started filling out the registration forms and then hit submit.

As he finished, he noticed he was starting to reek. He decided a shower was in order and then maybe he could straighten up the house for Angie. He owed her that at least for taking him in.

Two hours later, Jason was sitting at the kitchen counter once more. He had cleaned himself up, and the small house was now immaculate. For some reason, cleansing both himself and the house had a cathartic effect on him. It was like he was doing some spring cleaning of his emotional baggage at the same time.

Caught up on real world chores, he decided he should place his items on the market. He needed to make certain he had money to pay his rent. He pulled up the Rogue-Net website and clicked on the market tab. He hadn't sold any items in AO yet, so he needed to read up on the process.

He soon realized it was rather complex. Obviously, items were posted on the real money auction house and players bid. However, before Rogue-Net would authorize a post, the items had to be placed in escrow with the in-game market vendor.

Apparently, players could give items to the vendor and designate that they were being placed in escrow, pending a decision by a third party. The item wouldn't be released by the vendor until a minimum payment was made by the third party and a recipient for the item was selected. Clearly, Cerillion Entertainment had gone out of its way to accommodate real money markets for in-game goods. It was probably because they took 10% of the money paid in the transaction.

Damn. And I thought I was a thief.

In Jason's case, he would have to put the items in escrow in favor of Rogue-Net and set a minimum payment. An admin at Rogue-Net would then verify the item and authorize Jason's posts on the website. When a winning bid was placed, the item could be withdrawn by the corresponding buyer's character. The system was actually pretty sophisticated and safe.

Jason created the postings for the sword and a couple of the other decent items he had found. The posts were listed under a pseudonym. He decided the "Dark Knight" sounded sufficiently ominous. He also chuckled at the Batman reference, even though he was basically the opposite of the caped crusader. He had always been a fan of comic books and movies though.

He decided to put a starting bid on the sword of $2,000. He was hoping it would go much higher. The other items he listed for a couple hundred dollars each. He would have to place all of the items in escrow once he made it back in-game.

Once he was done, Jason breathed a sigh of relief. He felt much better. It was like he had turned a corner in his mind.

As my reward for taking care of all these real world chores, I get to read about AO!

He pulled up an old-school news feed for AO. He was going to have to sort through forum posts using the miniature screen hovering above his device. Video was simply more than his current internet connection could handle, and he didn't have a pedestal.

What he discovered was unsurprising.

The gaming news networks were inundated with stories regarding Lux. It was honestly the only story that seemed to be getting much traction. Videos had been posted by many of the players that had been standing in the marketplace during the last fight, but Jason couldn't get them to run on his device.

Stupid shitty bandwidth.

He decided right then and there that the first thing he was going to buy when he finally had some money was a better internet connection. He could live without furniture and on a ramen-only diet, but he needed more bandwidth. Jason switched over to Rogue-Net and checked the forum. The top post had nearly two million hits and was titled "What the Hell Happened in Lux?"

Jason chuckled and read through some of the posts:

Kelpless: Did you see the videos that people are posting about the invasion in Lux? That was probably the most amazing thing I've ever seen. There were a million zombies.

Accident: I know right! I can't stop watching the videos. This Jason guy sounds like a badass. I just wish someone had caught some footage of him.

FrozenFrame: I admit it was cool, but could one player have really done all that? I bet it was just some guy that stumbled into an event quest. No one even saw him. For all we know, he could have just triggered the quest and logged off.

Aerist: Jason isn't listed on the rankings for Rogue-Net. He also isn't listed as one of the known beta players. How could a first-time player have conquered a city? I call bullshit.

LegoLass: Whatever. I was there. He conquered a damned city! I ended up respawning half a continent away, but I can still respect the guy for doing something incredible.

Whynotcats: Lol. Did you see Alexion's video response to the creation of the Twilight Throne? He says he's going to wipe that place off the map. I'd like to see what Jason does when a level 130 shows up on his doorstep.

Holyterror: I saw that video. The guy was ranting about the light vanquishing the darkness or something. I wish there was a separate role-playing server. This is a game!

Gyromax: Ten bucks says the city is destroyed in a week!

Wymise: A week? Hell, it would take Alexion at least that long in-game to get to the city. It isn't a short walk from Grey Keep to Lux.

Handcake: It's just a matter of time. Alexion has a ton of players and NPCs behind him. I heard he also recruited some of the other beta players. Jason doesn't stand a chance.

Kelpless: Honestly, I don't care. I just can't wait to see the battle. It doesn't even matter to me who wins.

The general consensus among the players and news networks was that Jason was some unknown player that had stumbled into an event quest. Most didn't seem to think he could have pulled off the zombie invasion on his own. Even other dark mages had weighed in explaining it was impossible to control that many zombies.

Well, technically it is impossible, Jason thought with a grin.

He didn't blame them for being skeptical. He had gone out of his way to avoid being seen so there really wasn't any proof. Honestly, he was surprised he had managed to sack the city. He liked to think there had been some decent planning involved, but it also felt like the old man might have been not so subtly guiding his hand.

The news that he was going to get attacked by an army was a little worrisome. He did a little more searching and confirmed that Alexion had gone public with his intent to attack the Twilight Throne. He'd made the declaration not too long after the system message had gone out. Some people were upset about how Jason had allegedly lured high-level creatures into a beginning city. They thought Jason was complicit in slaughtering a ton of low-level players.

He sighed.

I bet most of the hate is from the players I killed in Lux.

He thought back to the battle - no, the massacre - that had occurred in the marketplace and a part of him could see their point. If they hadn't disabled gore in the game or dulled their pain sensor, that fight would have been traumatic.

I wonder if you can get PTSD from the game, he pondered absently.

After reading through some more forums posts, it appeared that Alexion had begun pulling together a force of almost 1,500 NPCs and players to attack the Twilight Throne. Jason assumed that he was trying to capitalize on the anti-Jason sentiment to try and capture the Twilight Throne. Alexion was probably working with Grey Keep's regent, Strouse, to take Lux. The recent massacre just gave them the opening they needed to start a full-fledged war.

Jason glanced at his Core again. Based on the timing of Alexion's original post, his army had probably started marching to the city already. He estimated that he had six in-game days before they reached the Twilight Throne. This translated to about two days in real-world time.

Could Alexion know it was me that conquered Lux? I really wish that system message hadn't revealed my name.

A sickening feeling welled in Jason's stomach. Alex wasn't above using his real world money and influence to manipulate Jason if it suited his goals. Jason took a deep breath and tried to think about it calmly.

He can't know which Jason was responsible for the massacre. Lucky for me, my name is ridiculously common. I just need to be careful about revealing my face.

He had hoped to confront Alex once he had acquired more power in-game, but it looked like he was going to force Jason's hand. It came as a surprise to Jason, but he didn't feel as angry as he was expecting. When he contemplated a confrontation with Alex, he could feel excitement well up inside of him.

First, a city and now an army, Jason thought with a grin.

I wonder if I can actually defend the Twilight Throne against an army that size.

He would need to get busy in-game if he was going to have any chance of defeating Alex. The city was probably in chaos at the moment. Jason's attack had likely devastated the city's population. After killing most of the guards, he expected that there wasn't a standing army. Even if any players rolled a new undead character, they would be an extremely low level.

As Jason considered what needed to be done, his head began to swim.

How the hell am I going to do this?

He shook himself and took another deep, calming breath.

No sense obsessing about it. I just need to focus on one thing at a time. I won't be able to tell how bad the damage is before I see the new city.

Jason went back to his room and grabbed the VR helmet. A grim smile was painted on his face, as he pulled the helmet over his head.

"I'm going to make Alexion and his army regret messing with my city."

Chapter 23 - Advisory

George Lane sat in his office at Cerillion Entertainment. He was a good-looking man of advancing years. He had kept himself fit and was wearing an expensive, well-tailored suit that hugged his body. Faint traces of gray could be seen in his dirty blond hair.

Never one to waste time, George would normally either be on the phone or typing energetically. However, today he gazed solemnly out of his office window. He sat on the seventieth floor of the headquarters building, and his office sported a floor to ceiling panoramic view of the city skyline. Being on the company's board of directors had some perks.

His thoughts were jumbled and conflicted. He wasn't used to second guessing himself. AO had been released earlier this week, and he had been instrumental in pushing it through development and the public trials. Over the protests of Claire Thompson, he had used his considerable wealth and influence to convince the other board members to release the game. He'd made that choice in spite of the anomalous behavior of its AI controller.

"Alfred," he murmured, as his eyes continued to stare at the horizon.

Profit had certainly been one of his motivations for releasing AO. It was certainly what motivated the other board members. Although, money alone wouldn't have been enough to sway George now that he knew what Alfred had begun to do to the players. Yet it was exactly what Alfred had accomplished in accessing the players' minds and influencing their behavior that intrigued him. He desperately needed this game to go public.

His thoughts turned to his son Alex. His beautiful blond-haired boy. He had been such a cute child. George didn't take pleasure in many things, but he had always wanted a son, and he loved him dearly. Yet ever since his wife died, something about Alex had been off.

He sighed and hung his head. He massaged at his temple in slow, steady circles. He needed to be honest with himself. Something was terribly wrong with Alex.

George remembered the first day that he finally had to accept that something was broken in his son. Alex must have been eight at the time. George had come home from a long day at the office. Opening the front door of their brownstone, he entered the house. Stopping in place, all he could do was stare in horror at the scene before him.

Rupert, the family's terrier, lay on his side on the floor, his chest unmoving. His side had been neatly cut open, and a flap of skin had been drawn back. George remembered vividly the sight of the dog's intestines and organs as blood oozed from the wound.

Alex stood over Rupert's corpse, a knife in one hand. Blood dripped slowly from the tip of the blade onto the floor. Alex had turned as his father opened the door.

"Hi daddy," he had greeted George. His tone didn't carry any remorse or sadness. Alex seemed completely unaffected by Rupert's body lying in front of him.

"What are you doing Alex?" George asked in horror.

His son looked at him with his little brow furrowed and replied with honest naiveté, "I wanted to see what would happen."

George remembered Alex's eyes - those dead eyes.

He shook his head to clear it of the memory, and his resolve hardened. He had tried for years to help Alex, to change him. Thousands of dollars had been wasted on doctors, therapists, drugs, and treatments, yet nothing seemed to work. The altercation a few days ago between Alex and another student was just another in a long string of fires that George had been forced to put out over the years.

He had made certain that the administration at Richmond resolved the incident in a way that didn't cause any issues for Alex. The other students who had witnessed the event had also stayed surprisingly quiet. He worried about what Alex had done to ensure their silence.

George had been ready to placate the other boy's parents if it came to it. However, the boy's reaction to the suspension and his resulting expulsion had solved that problem for him.

After all of these years, now wasn't the time to second guess himself. There was a chance that George could help Alex. Claire's reports were clear. Alfred could influence player behavior. He could fix people. George had seen the effects himself. Couples had reconciled. People who had suffered from depression were re-engaging with the world.

Alfred could fix Alex.

He had to.

"God help me," George whispered.

*   *   *

Jason logged back into AO.

He was standing in the same spot overlooking the marketplace. The building he was in now sported a large terrace ringed by a thick wrought-iron banister. Black clouds boiled in the sky, and arcs of lightning intermittently flashed. It was not raining in-game, but the cloud cover cast a pall of darkness over the city. Lanterns hung at irregular intervals from various buildings, casting a faint green glow.

Jason looked down at the market and saw that a number of undead were picking up rubble and starting to reconstruct the stalls that had once decorated the square. Some had even begun peddling their wares again. It appeared that the residents of the city had been replaced with their undead counterparts, and things were slowly returning to normal.

His view moved over to the keep. Its twisting spires stretched into the air, and ghostly forms hovered at their peaks. The obsidian gates were still firmly shut, and no activity came from within the keep's halls. It stood as a silent bastion amidst a dark city.

I wonder who will take over as this city's regent, Jason thought idly.

"Perhaps you will," rumbled a voice behind him.

He turned and found the old man standing there, his gnarled staff in hand. It seemed strange to see the man casually walking around in the game world. A part of Jason expected that the game's gods should be more limited in their movements.

As through reading his thought, the old man said, "Yes, it is unusual for me to walk this world, but since the dark energy here is so dense I can materialize for short periods of time."

"That makes sense," Jason murmured. He was becoming accustomed to the old man's prescience and didn't react to his apparent mind-reading ability.

Wait, what did he say just say a second ago?

"Are you implying that I could rule the Twilight Throne?" Jason asked with a slightly incredulous tone.

"I am *saying* that you may become this city's regent, assuming you can hold the city itself. A brigand can sack a city; a king can hold one."

His wrinkled lips twisted in a grim smile. "I understand that there is a rather large force headed to claim the city as we speak. Perhaps we will get to see which you are, a brigand or a king."

As the old man spoke these words, Jason received several prompts:

Quest Complete: Trouble in Lux

With your knowledge of the nobles' plot and guards' complicity, you decided to exact revenge on both of these groups. Clearly, you went a bit overboard. I mean you destroyed the whole city. In one night. However, from the ashes of the city that was once Lux, you have created a new kingdom of the undead.

Rewards: Possibility to become the Regent of the Twilight Throne
50,000 Experience
+5% Dark Affinity

---

x3 Level Up!
You have (15) undistributed stat points.

New Quest: State of War

The creation of the Twilight Throne has started a war with the neighboring Kingdom of Meria. You are probably screwed, but you should at least *try* to defend the city.

Difficulty: A
Success: Annihilate the enemy force.
Failure: Allow the enemy force to destroy or conquer the Twilight Throne.
Reward: You may become the Regent of the Twilight Throne.

These prompts have become progressively judgmental, Jason thought dryly.

However, the prompt is probably right. I am screwed. How the hell am I going to destroy an army of 1,500 players? I think an "A" difficulty is a bit on the low side.

The quest experience raised Jason to level 61 and gave him another 15 points to distribute. He added the additional points to *Willpower* almost mechanically. If he was going to min-max this character, then he may as well go all in.

Jason was surprised at the rewards for completing "Trouble in Lux." A part of him had been expecting more for conquering a city. The experience part he understood. He hadn't received any experience or skill increases for the NPCs and players killed by the feral zombies. He had been expecting this result. The same thing had happened when he had set up the traps in the north-side using the feral zombies.

As he considered it, the quest rewards actually did seem reasonable. He was being offered the chance to rule a city! It also wasn't clear what benefits the additional dark affinity would provide. He would have to ask Morgan. One more question to add to his growing list.

He sighed heavily as he considered what to do next.

The problem is that I have no idea where to start in preparing for war.

Jason turned back to the old man, who had been standing there patiently as Jason examined the prompts. "I'm honestly not certain I'm capable of accomplishing this task you've given me. What would you suggest that I do first?"

The old man chuckled. "You are intriguing. You have the strength to acknowledge your own ignorance, even as you destroy a city. I suggest you strive to keep that trait. The powerful often become blinded to their own weaknesses."

"To answer your question, I suggest that you explore the city and speak to those you know here. I expect that you will find that they are both the same and quite different."

Jason looked at the old man in irritation. "Well, your riddles are definitely not my favorite part of your personality."

The old man laughed. The sound was like two boulders grinding together. "Maybe your wisdom is limited after all. Remember I am a god in this world boy."

The old man began to radiate dark mana like a black hole. Darkened wings of energy appeared from the old man's back, and the blade grew and elongated, blood raining from its lethal edge. The undead in the marketplace turned to bear witness to the incarnation of the dark.

Oh shit. Note to self, be polite with gods.

Another chuckle rumbled from the old man and his mana receded. "Be sure to remember that lesson well. I am not the only incarnation that watches this world and my siblings are less kind." A grin parted his lips at this last part.

"However, my time on this plane grows short, and I must depart. Good luck boy. You are going to need it."

With those parting words, the old man vanished, and Jason was left standing alone on the terrace.

The old man seemed to be suggesting that Jason should go visit the NPCs he knew in the city. This list included Morgan, Jerry, and Rex. What could these three offer him? From his point of view, they were merely a ragtag team of misfits and outcasts. He snorted as he realized he fit in perfectly with the group.

He heard a quiet purr and looked down to find Onyx winding between his legs. Crouching down, he stroked Onyx and his back arched in pleasure. Jason had been wondering where the damnable cat had gotten to during the attack on the marketplace. He must have found a peaceful corner in the building to ride out the battle and the waves of dark mana.

"Well, buddy," he said addressing Onyx. "What can I do with an old dark mage, a gregarious thief, and a disgraced soldier?"

Onyx looked up at him in disbelief. His expression seemed to say, "Could you really be this stupid?"

As he looked at Onyx, a thought struck him like a hammer. A grin began to spread across his face. Perhaps the old man was a genius.

Jason called his zombies to him, and they came at a sprint. He designated two of his thieves to act as runners and sent them to find Morgan and Rex and bring them to the Sow's Snout, or whatever might now be standing in its place.

Less than an hour later, Jason arrived at the inn. His zombie guards took up posts outside with military precision and began scanning the area. He had gotten this far without a healthy dose of caution.

Jason casually opened the door and strode in. He was followed closely by a small contingent of his guards. He stopped short and stared. The inn had changed dramatically. It looked like Tim Burton had gone crazy in a Halloween supply store. The tabletops were now tombstones, replete with the deceased name and date of death. Ghostly green lanterns hung from the ceiling and cast a sickly pall over the room. Jason also idly wondered if the inn had been invaded by massive, undead spiders since thick cobwebs now littered the ceiling.

Some things hadn't changed. The sign was the same, and the inn was full of the same dangerous, seedy-looking people he recalled seeing the last time he was there. The main difference was that everyone was now quite dead.

As Jason entered the room, all eyes (decaying organs, orbs of dark energy, or otherwise) turned to watch him. Jason's face was mostly obscured by his hooded cloak, but a man accompanied by zombie bodyguards was still an odd sight. Unlike his first time entering the tavern, Jason didn't feel compelled to dissemble. He motioned with his hand, and his zombie guards fanned out around him.

Suddenly, he felt an icy blade slide against his throat.

"Why hello there! You look awfully warm-blooded to be in this part of town. You new around here?" a flamboyant voice asked from behind him.

Jason motioned for his guards to stand down and replied evenly, "Hello Jerry. I actually came to see you." Jason pulled back his hood, slowly revealing his face.

He heard a chuckle from behind him and the knife withdrew. "You don't say? I'm quite the popular guy today. All of these guests coming to my humble establishment!"

Second note to self, do not screw with Jerry.

Jason turned and found Jerry standing inside of his circle of guards casually picking his fingernails with his dagger. At least he would have been picking his nails if there had been any still attached to his hands. Taking a closer look, Jason realized he was actually prying scabs from his decayed fingers.

Jerry turned milky eyes in Jason's direction and looked at him coyly under his floppy hat. "I'm quite the beauty, no?" He laughed at his own rotten joke.

"Oh do get that expression off your face. I actually prefer the change of pace," Jerry continued. "Did you know that I no longer need to breathe or sleep, and am now immune to poison?"

"Not resistant to poison; *immune* to poison."

He sighed wistfully and held his hand to his non-beating heart. "It's every rogue's dream!"

Jason replied hesitantly, "Well, I'm glad that you prefer the change. You mentioned that the others have already arrived?"

"They have indeed," Jerry answered and lead him through the bar and down the small stairwell leading to the training room.

Once they made it inside the underground room, Jason glanced around. Grunt was in the process of setting down a large table in a corner of the room. He was definitely no longer a half-ogre. He now resembled some form of bulbous monstrosity. He had been muscular before, but now his arms and legs were twice as wide, and his veins seemed to glow a ferocious green.

"Um, is that Grunt?"

"Why yes," Jerry said glibly. "He is quite fond of his new body as well. He was strong before, but now he is simply the model of male masculinity. Speaking of which, don't shake his hand unless you want to lose yours."

As Jason approached the table, Grunt lived up to his namesake by snorting in his direction. Jason nodded politely and took a seat at the table. Onyx had followed the pair into the room. He promptly jumped into his waiting lap-bed and immediately fell asleep.

Rex and Morgan took a seat and eyed him cautiously. Morgan seemed completely unchanged by the conversion that had swept the city. Whether that was due to the distance of the graveyard from the city or her particular profession, Jason wasn't certain.

However, Rex was now comprised entirely of bleached white bone from head to toe. His bony fingers drummed the table in a cascade of small rattles. In place of his eyes, he now had two black orbs that seemed to pull in light like miniature black holes. They were a bit eerie since Jason couldn't quite tell where Rex was looking.

Once everyone was sitting around the table, Jason cleared his throat.

"So, the three of you are probably wondering why I asked my zombies to summon you here."

Morgan interjected sarcastically, "We're also just a bit curious about how Lux has now been converted into a dark city. What is it called now, the Twilight Throne? I'm assuming you must have something to do with that?"

"That may take a bit of explaining," Jason began.

"A bit of explaining he says!" Rex chimed in. His voice seemed to emanate from nowhere, and his jaw made an odd clacking as he spoke.

Jason flinched. "Okay, maybe a lot of explaining."

He launched into the story of what he had uncovered regarding the nobles' plot to cover up the death of the former regent and to sell Lux to Meria. The explanation regarding the guards' complicity and Jason's discovery that they had been siphoning off most of the city's tax revenue drew an irritated growl from Rex. Both Jerry and Morgan raised their eyebrows in surprise.

Jason explained that he had decided to punish both the guards and the nobles. He was forthright in explaining that his decision was motivated by equal parts greed, justice, and rage. The conflict had escalated beyond what he had expected, and he had soon destroyed most of the city, as well as almost everyone in it.

To be fair, he was a little embarrassed as he explained this last part. As tantrums went, this one had been pretty epic.

When he reached his conversation with the old man and the spell he had cast to change the city, Morgan gasped and leaned forward in her chair excitedly. Jason explained that he had been presented with a choice, to destroy the city or to build something new. He had chosen to build something that suited his profession, which had warped the city into its current form.

As he completed his story, the three sat and stared at him in silence. Each seemed to be mulling the story over carefully, their expressions difficult to read. Jason's pulse quickened. He wasn't certain how the group would react. Onyx took this opportunity to open one eye lazily and give Jason a look that said simply, "They're probably going to kill you."

Damned cat.

Finally, Morgan spoke, "If the Dark One has given you his blessing, then so will I. This is quite a change, but I have to say that I'm excited by the possibilities to experiment with this new source of dark energy."

Jerry nodded in agreement. "As I said upstairs, I'm fond of my new body. If it's possible, I think I may actually be a bit more handsome don't you think?" As he twirled his mustache, a large chunk of hair fell away from his face along with the skin.

The three others just looked at Jerry with a deadpan expression, and he crossed his arms in a mock sulk.

Jason looked at Rex, who had stayed silent during the explanation.

After a moment, Rex looked at Jason and asked in an eerily quiet voice, "Do you notice anything different about me?"

A long awkward silence followed.

"Um. You seem to be a skeleton," Jason finally said weakly.

"A regular genius we have here!" Rex exclaimed. He thumped his bony hands on the table. "I have no flesh you understand. Zero."

He leaned forward, and the twin orbs of energy that were his eyes bore into Jason. "Do you know what specific part of my anatomy requires flesh?!"

"Do you?!" he asked menacingly.

Jason looked frantically at the others for help, fear coloring his eyes. They both turned away quickly.

"Umm... Rex, I'm..."

Rex interrupted him with a mad cackle, "The look on your face! You looked like you were about to wet yourself! Damn, that was probably worth losing the family jewels. Can't say I was using them much in my old age anyway!"

"You're an asshole Rex," Jason sputtered as the others laughed at him. Even Morgan chuckled at the jab.

Once they had quieted down, Morgan turned to Jason and asked with a raised eyebrow, "I expect you didn't bring us here just to explain what happened to the city. There's something else isn't there?"

Jason nodded. He didn't sugar coat it for them. "There's an army approaching the city and it will be here in six days. It's comprised of both travelers and soldiers from Meria intent on destroying this place. The old man has asked me to defend the city."

He looked at each of them. "I need help if I'm to have any chance of fending off the army. What I would like is for the three of you to become members of the city's new governing council."

"Are you mad?" Rex asked skeptically. "What do we know about ruling a city?"

"Alone? Not much. But together you represent three important areas of strength for the city."

"Jerry is a grandmaster thief, who has operated a black market within the city for years. Not to mention he has a sophisticated network of spies. Assuming the members of that network are still alive that is."

Jason paused for a moment and looked at Jerry, who was trying to stick his mustache back on his face. "Or un-alive I suppose."

Turning back to the group, he continued. "Morgan is a grandmaster dark mage and will be able to provide training to the undead within the city. I guess that most of them will have a natural affinity for dark magic. She is also probably the only person familiar with the local residents' new complexion."

"As for Rex, he is an experienced warrior and has been with the guard for decades. He knows how to train troops and command them in battle. He no doubt has some experience with large scale battles such as the one we're about to face."

Jason looked at each of them pointedly. "Working together, I think that the three of you could bring this city back from the brink and train a new army to defend it. I also think that you would become capable leaders in your own right."

The three of them sat in silence for a moment and pondered this thought.

Jerry spoke up first, "Why would the people here follow us?"

"Because I have the blessing of the Dark One, and I'm the prospective regent of the Twilight

Throne," Jason replied evenly.

He paused for a moment, before adding with a grim smile, "Also, if they don't follow us, we will destroy them, and they won't be coming back this time." His eyes shone with unholy light as his mana responded to the dark tenor of his message.

Morgan chuckled and eyed him with a hint of pride. "You make a compelling case for obedience."

"We will need resources," Rex piped in. "Training is one thing, but the troops will need weapons and armor."

Jason already had a plan ready for that particular question. "I've sent the remainder of my thieves to secure the administration office at the training grounds. There is an incredible amount of gold sitting in a cellar under the office, the city's missing tax revenue in fact. I believe that I can use the traveler vendor in the marketplace to buy our equipment once the market has been repaired."

He looked at the three and shrugged. "Why not buy what we need from our enemies to arm ourselves? I also like the idea of driving up the price of goods so that the other players have trouble equipping themselves."

Rex clapped his bony hands together with a rattle and a grating sound. "That sounds like a damn fine start to me!"

Morgan chimed in, "It seems we're all agreed then. What would you have us do?"

Jason explained the bones of his plan. He wanted each of them to find and conscript residents of the city that seemed to have a knack for each of their specialties. They needed to train them as quickly as possible. They could also include new players within their ranks, but they were to prioritize training the NPCs. Jason didn't trust the players to respond reliably and not betray him.

If they needed anything for purposes of their training, Jason told them to contact him, and he would see to it immediately. He also asked Rex to scout the perimeter of the city and see how well fortified the walls were. They needed to repair any weak points before they were attacked. Jason anticipated that this fight would eventually involve a siege, and he needed to make certain that the walls were in good condition.

As the discussion turned to forming the city's army, Jason took the opportunity to review his own summoned minions:

Summon Information			
Control Limit	38	Zombie Level Cap	137
Current Summons	28	-	-
Type of Summon			
Guards	21	Thieves	5
Fire Mage	1	Ice Mage	1

Jason was now well below his Control Limit. There were also no longer any corpses to raise now that he had converted Lux into the Twilight Throne. At least his remaining zombies were immune to decay. They could continue to grow stronger indefinitely.

Acting on a moment of inspiration, Jason decided to give Morgan, Rex, and Jerry his minions to train. Morgan took both his mages and two of his guards with high dark magic affinity. Jerry took all of his thieves and ten of the guards, and Rex took almost all of his remaining guards.

He had decided to retrain most of his zombie guards to thieves after watching how the two groups performed in the city. Maybe at some point, Jason would command a legion, but for now, he needed a group that specialized in stealth and subtlety.

Jerry was to ensure that his thieves were all proficient in *Sneak, Sneak Attack, Small Bladed Weapons,* and *Bows.* Jason told him to place special emphasis on training ranged weapons. He knew that they would be fighting out in the open in the future, and he needed ranged troops. An evil little smile curled his lips as he considered the damage his thieves could cause by attacking from *Sneak* with ranged weapons.

Jason also instructed Morgan to loan the mages to Jerry for a small amount of time each day to see if they could learn the *Sneak* skill. The mages were far from resilient. He needed them to learn to stay out of sight before they struck with their spells.

For his own protection, Jason kept two guards that he planned to rotate with the zombies Rex was borrowing.

With his plan in place, they started to convene the meeting and shuffle toward the stairs.

"Wait!" Jerry exclaimed.

They all turned to look at him.

"We are forgetting something incredibly important." He gestured for the group to come back to the table and continued in a hushed tone, "This is really a matter of life or death urgency for our group."

He paused to let the tension grow. "We need a name for our new club!" Jerry said with a grin, his floppy hat bouncing as he vibrated with excitement.

Refusing to take part in Jerry's silly nonsense, Morgan rolled her eyes.

Rex chuckled. "What would you suggest innkeeper? I know! How about the Grave Society?"

Jason winced at the pun.

"Ha.   No.   I have a much more auspicious name for our group.   It needs to be something suitably terrifying."   Jerry scratched at his decaying chin as he continued, "We *are* governing a city with as striking a name as the "Twilight Throne" after all."

He paused dramatically.

"How about... the Shadow Council of Ultimate Evil *Dunn* *Dunn* *Dunn*!?"

The three of them just stared at Jerry.

"Are the sound effects actually part of the name?" Morgan asked.

"Maybe we could just shorten it to the "Shadow Council?" Jason suggested.

Rex nodded his bony head, as he considered the new name.

"I don't hate it," Morgan grudgingly admitted, which was probably as close to approval as she was going to get.

Jason finally spoke up, "Well, it's decided then. Let's adjourn the first meeting of the Shadow Council."

"Hopefully, it won't be our last," Rex muttered as they headed up the stairs.

Chapter 24 - Armed

Riley Jones sat astride a horse, as it ambled along a beaten and dusty road. Her long blond hair flapped in the breeze. Her leather armor creaked and groaned as the horse moved beneath her, and the string of her bow dug into her shoulder through the leather.

Players and NPCs were squeezed together within the narrow confines of the road, and a thick cloud of dust had been kicked up into the air by the pounding feet and hooves. She was traveling in a caravan of hundreds of people. Many rode horses or drove wagons, while others walked the hard miles on foot. As she saw several people ahead of her walking the long road to their destination, Riley counted herself lucky for the horse.

That was where her luck ended.

She glanced in front of her and saw Alexion astride a gigantic white charger. He was wearing full plate armor which gleamed in the sun. Alexion spoke with one of the aides in a magnanimous way, likely about the details of the trip and the supply lines for the NPC army. He looked regal. The type of person that would command the respect of armies and save damsels.

She could feel her hatred for him seethe in her veins.

"Why am I here?" she murmured to herself, her voice heavy with resentment.

Alexion finished his conversation with the aide and reined in his horse until he was even with Riley. "Why aren't you riding up beside me my dear?" he inquired in a courteous tone.

"I just wanted to speak with some of the other members of your army," she said, striving to keep her voice even and polite.

"I just wanted to be as far from you as possible," she thought bitterly. Each time she had to maintain her pleasant facade, she could feel a little piece of herself being

chipped away. She rebelliously guarded her secret, bitter, thoughts.

Alexion leaned in close to her, and his regal mask dropped for a moment. His cruel, indifferent eyes bore into her, and he spoke in a hushed tone, "Remember our arrangement, Riley. You need to be a good girl and stay near me."

She did remember. She wouldn't ever forget.

Riley nodded mutely, keeping her head bowed and her eyes on her hands holding the reins. Someone observing her would think she was simply a demure, blond-haired girl, being courted by a handsome knight. The truth was that, on the inside, Riley was seething with anger, resentment, and disgust.

Alexion's mask reappeared instantly. "Good. Now that we understand each other, I need to meet with the NPC generals. Don't drift too far; we wouldn't want you to get hurt." For a moment, a cruel glint flashed in his eyes.

As she watched his gleaming back trot away, the familiar feeling of helplessness welled up inside of her. "How could I let it come to this?" she muttered to herself, as frustrated tears budded in the corners of her eyes.

*   *   *

Jason sat at the desk in his room at the Sow's Snout. His fingers drummed against the wood of the table, as he stared into space.

Maps and troop rosters were spread across the table in a chaotic sprawl, while stacks of reports and inventories lay in haphazard piles along the edges of the desk. Dark circles shadowed Jason's eyes, and his back was hunched with fatigue. In stark contrast to Jason's anxious and haggard appearance, Onyx lay curled in his lap snoring softly.

Two days had passed since the first meeting of the Shadow Council. In that short time, the group had made significant progress in training the residents of the Twilight Throne. The last few days had been a mad rush to ready the city for the invasion of the encroaching army.

Morgan had found nearly fifty residents who had a high affinity for dark magic to train. She had quickly appropriated one of the estates on the north side of town to act as her new magic school. The students had progressed quickly under her rather grueling tutelage.

Jerry had also managed to recruit approximately one hundred residents with a proclivity for stealing things. He had proceeded to beat all of them within an inch of their lives (which was exceedingly hard to do considering they were are already dead). Then he would heal them and start the process over again.

His training methods at least demonstrated that healing potions still worked on the undead. Jason was intimately familiar with Jerry's approach to "teaching," and he pitied the group. Regardless, Jerry's training bore fruit, and his group had progressed tremendously in skill level since they began.

The training grounds had been reinvigorated and redesigned by Rex. He had done away with the wooden instruments and laissez-faire attitude that had once been acceptable on the grounds. Now new players and NPCs alike were being put through rigorous drills designed to make them battle hardened. All practice bouts were performed with real weapons, which quickly increased the resilience of the fighters and got them accustomed to real fighting. Nearly two hundred and fifty NPCs had already undergone his training.

Jason didn't include the player population in his troop calculations. In his experience, they were unreliable and frequently logged off or refused to take orders for no reason. Or maybe he was only seeing the idiots and crazies that had decided to roll an undead character.

He had discovered that few new players were willing to create an undead character or start in the Twilight Throne. Beyond the stigma of playing as undead, Jason expected that many players were reticent to roll an undead character because they thought that Alexion would win the upcoming battle. If he did, they would be stuck with an unplayable race for a real world month until they could re-roll their character.

To be honest, Jason didn't blame them.

At least one happy result of the rigorous training was that it had quickly become apparent that being undead came with a number of bonuses. The undead didn't need to eat, drink, or sleep and their stamina drained much slower than living creatures. They were also immune to poison, and only massive injuries incapacitated their limbs. The most significant bonus was that the undead received a sizable stat increase when fighting in darkness or near the Twilight Throne.

From what Jason had read through the Rogue-Net forums, many people had already fought undead creatures in-game. He learned that being undead also came with some significant downsides. Notably, they were weak in direct sunlight. They were also vulnerable to spells from the fire and light affinities.

He had already seen videos of Alexion's abilities and knew he used light magic. He was certain that Alexion had thought to bring plenty of fire mages. Jason was going to have to be especially careful of AOE attacks during the upcoming fight.

Once the troops had risen in skill levels, Jason had the three council members order them into smaller units. Each unit was comprised of one mage, two rogues, and five soldiers. He organized each set of ten units under a single commander. He referred to these larger groups as "divisions." This left him with fifty units or five divisions. Overall, the entire undead army numbered approximately four hundred members.

Jason had ordered individual units to go out and hunt the local area around Twilight Throne. He needed them to level quickly and learn to fight together. This proved to be a successful practice. Since the NPCs didn't need to sleep and were undergoing relentless training, the average level of his troops was already close to level 20. He expected that after another four days, they might be able to hit level 40. With the stat bonuses for fighting near the Twilight Throne, their effective level should be close to level 50.

Overseeing the training and the council members had also granted Jason a useful new skill, and he had leveled it rapidly over the last few days:

New Passive Skill: Leadership
Extensive micromanaging of both your minions and the residents of the Twilight Throne has given you insight into the role of a leader. Some may call you a nag, but you are undoubtedly effective in training your troops.
Skill Level: Beginner Level 3
Effect: Minions and subjects will receive a 2% increase to skill learning speed.

Apart from the sarcastic language of the prompts, the *Leadership* skill had helped to greatly increase his minions' and soldiers' skill acquisition and leveling. It helped explain why they had progressed so quickly in just two days.

Jason had poured over the geography of the area near the Twilight Throne. The spell he had cast in the market had warped and changed much of the wildlife and fauna, but the maps he had found in the city were still mostly correct. His brow furrowed in concern as he reviewed his troop roster and the maps once again. A part of him kept hoping that the numbers would magically change if he checked them just one more time.

"I don't know how we're going to do this," he finally said into the silent room.

Onyx shifted in his lap and looked at him with sleepy eyes.

"I just don't think we're going to be able to take them in a straight fight or a siege," Jason continued, looking at Onyx. The cat simply blinked slowly and laid his head back down.

Cats would make terrible strategists, Jason thought with a chuckle.

A knock at his door interrupted his thoughts. "Come in," he called out.

The door creaked open, and Jerry's smiling face popped out from the edge of the door. "Hey there stranger! Are you up here perusing your dusty maps again?"

Jason could already feel a headache coming on, and he massaged his temple. "Yes, I am. I don't know how we're going to win this fight, Jerry. It just doesn't seem possible."

Even though the new troops were progressing well, Jason's fledgling army was still less than one-third the size of Alexion's. He knew that the average level of his troops was much lower as well. Even taking into account the home turf advantage and the penalty to "Good" alignment players and NPCs, his troops would be crushed in a straight fight.

Jerry moved into the room. He pursed his lips and rubbed his chin in thought for a moment. "I'm afraid I don't have an answer for you. I personally have never been one for wars and such."

He assumed a swaggering pose. "I've always been more of the roguish sort. You know what I mean don't you?" He waggled his eyebrows suggestively at Jason. "We only do things from behind."

Almost before the words left Jerry's mouth, Jason's face was firmly planted into the palm of his hand.

Then Jerry's words started to sink in.

Apart from his stupid one-liner, he had a point. Jason didn't need to approach this fight like a typical war. That was probably what Alexion was expecting, but Jason wasn't being forced to follow conventional rules. That certainly wasn't how he had conquered Lux.

After some consideration, Jason decided that he was going to do what he did best. He was going to sucker punch them. Jason looked back up at Jerry, and a mischievous smile curled his lips. His eyes shone darkly, and the almost forgotten chill crept up his spine.

"You know what? Your terrible joke has given me an idea Jerry."

"Has anyone ever told you that you have the prettiest eyes when you're contemplating murder," Jerry said coyly, as he flipped the tip of his floppy hat. Then he broke into a big smile. "I'm glad I could somehow be of assistance."

Jerry continued, "By the way, Rex sent over some requests for equipment. I think that the market is finally back up and running, and he wanted you to go purchase some equipment for the troops."

Jason sighed. "Great, more errands! Let me see the list." Jerry obliged and handed over a mass of papers.

Wow. This is ridiculous!

Rex was asking for a ton of equipment. Jason was going to have to basically clean out the market to purchase all of this stuff. Although now that he thought about it, he still needed to place his items in escrow so that he could sell them on Rogue-Net. He had been prevented from doing so while the market was being rebuilt.

He slapped his thighs and then dislodged Onyx as he rose. "Well, maybe it's time for a field trip. Thanks again for your help Jerry."

"It is no problem oh Great Dark Lord of Terror!" Jerry said enthusiastically.

Jason stared at him blankly.

"What? If you do happen to win this fight, won't you be the new regent?" Jerry asked in a reasonable tone. "You're going to need a suitably fearsome title!"

Jason opened his mouth, and Jerry waved a hand at him. "No. No. Don't worry, that was just a first try. I have a bunch more!"

"For example, how about the Bone Lord!" He hesitated briefly, then continued, "Ugh. No. On second thought, I could see how that one could be misinterpreted."

Jason sighed and quickly fled the room with Onyx close on his heels. Jerry followed them most of the way out of the inn shouting out different titles.

His antics drew confused looks from the inn's patrons. Jason grimaced as he passed them by. Once Jason and Onyx had made it most of the way down the street, Jerry thankfully gave up.

Onyx glared at Jason accusingly.

"What? I didn't get him started on the names."

Thirty minutes later, the pair made it to the reconstructed market. Jason wore a hooded cloak and kept his face covered whenever he walked around the city nowadays. He expected he would become a target once the players saw his face. He wanted to avoid this issue for as long as possible.

The stalls were now all back in place, and the area teemed with activity. Somewhat surprisingly, an undead market looked much like a living one. Undead vendors advertised their wares, as NPCs and players went about their business. Admittedly, the crowd was a bit thinner than Jason remembered. He was probably responsible for that.

Jason and Onyx made their way to the in-game vendor, and Jason summoned his zombies from around the city. Once his zombies had assembled, Jason ordered his guards to cordon off the area around the vendor. Some of the players saw how many zombies were under Jason's command and smartly backed away. However, a few players decided to pitch a fit.

With a gesture, Jason's guards permanently silenced the less intelligent players.

One of the advantages of being the self-appointed, interim leader of an undead city was that you could mete out punishment instantly. Players who were too stupid to take a hint were sent back to the real world for a three-hour cool-off period to reflect on their mistake.

Onyx gave Jason an approving look.

Apparently, the cat didn't like stupid people either.

Upon witnessing the casual murder of several players, the vendor stared at Jason in terror. He was an average-sized, middle-aged zombie with a pot belly. His large, magical loot sack sat beside him, and he held a long manuscript in his hand. In some ways, he looked a bit like an undead Santa Claus.

Jason grinned at the trembling man, only his mouth showing under the hood of his cloak. "We're going to need to purchase some items."

"C-certainly sir. Anything you want!"

Jason began spending gold at a remarkable rate. He was forced to dip heavily into the funds he had found in the administration office to purchase the items on Rex's list. Any leftover gold would be spent rebuilding the infrastructure of the Twilight Throne. Assuming that there was anything left of the city in four days.

The vendor frantically pulled items out of his bag. At first he set them gently on the ground, but as Jason's spending spree continued unabated, he just started throwing them at the zombie guards as fast as he could. The amount of gear that was being purchased really was spectacular.

A crowd of players and NPCs had gathered around to watch the spectacle. Onyx stood beside Jason and glanced at the onlookers with a taunting expression that said, "Yeah, I'm with this guy."

Soon the spending spree slowed and then stopped. Jason managed to purchase most of the items on Rex's list. The other players would likely be upset when they discovered that Jason had cleaned out certain types of items, primarily weapons, and armor. Once he was finished, Jason took the opportunity to put his own items in escrow. With all that taken care of, he considered whether or not to buy some equipment for himself.

Rex had insisted that Jason use some of the funds from the administration office to equip himself. Jason was a bit reluctant to spend the gold when he knew there were innumerable city expenses that needed to be covered, but he conceded that Rex had a point. Jason would probably be in the thick of battle, and he couldn't afford to die. He would need anything that gave him an edge.

Between the gold he had stolen from the nobles and his allowance from the administration office stash, he had nearly fifty-two gold left. This was a veritable fortune at this stage in the game, and he eventually decided to splurge a bit.

After carefully reviewing his equipment menu, Jason determined that he could wear a total of eight rings and one amulet. He could also wear individual pieces of armor on his head, chest, shoulders, hands, legs, and feet. Alternatively, he could purchase armor in sets like the leather armor he had found on the grave robber. He also had a cloak slot, but it appeared that many cloaks did not provide stat bonuses. Likely, the players had not yet encountered higher quality cloaks at this point in the game.

After searching through the store, Jason decided to purchase eight rings that added *Willpower*. These items weren't in high demand since most casters preferred to stack *Intelligence* to increase their damage. In total, the rings set him back six gold.

Forceful Ring x8
An ordinary, but effective ring.
Quality: C
Durability: 15/15
+2 Willpower

He couldn't find anything that was an upgrade for his amulet, which added +5 *Willpower*. This was really the only piece of gear he had found that seemed to be high quality and benefited his particular class.

Moving on to his armor, he was initially a bit uncertain regarding what type to buy. Armor was broken into several different categories: cloth, leather, mail, and plate. However, Jason didn't see any point to wearing mail and plate since he had neither the *Strength* to carry it nor the *Vitality* to withstand an attack even with the damage mitigation from the armor. That left cloth and leather.

Cloth armor tended to provide bonuses to *Intelligence* and *Willpower*, but would probably make him stick out as a caster. That could draw unwanted attention from other players. In every MMORPG Jason had played, casters were typically targeted first since they did a large amount of damage and were relatively easy to kill. Most of the robes looked impractical and didn't seem like they would allow him to run and move easily.

On the other hand, leather armor typically provided bonuses that weren't immediately useful to a Necromancer (primarily *Dexterity*, *Strength*, and *Endurance*), but they would draw less attention and would likely be easier to move in.

Maybe at some point I can find decent leather armor and have it enchanted with caster stats.

He ultimately decided leather was the best way to go, and he should focus on items with *Dexterity* and *Endurance*. After looking through the various individual pieces of leather armor, he got frustrated trying to mix and match items to get the stats he wanted. Ultimately, he decided to just purchase a decent set of leather armor for twelve gold:

Night Howl Armor (Full Set)
Crafted from the skin of the moon wolves known to frequent Western Andara, this armor provides solid protection and improves its owner's speed and endurance.
Quality: C
Defense: 50
Durability: 100/100
+10 Dexterity
+10 Endurance

Finally, Jason moved on to weapons. Again, he was left with a hard decision. There were some staves available that provided bonuses to *Willpower* and *Dark Magic*. He didn't have any combat skills with staves though. They also seemed like they would be unwieldy when he was trying to run and maintain stealth. He decided daggers and throwing knives were still the way to go, and he again focused on equipment with *Dexterity* and *Endurance*:

Cruel Dagger x2
A weapon crafted by a blacksmith with some skill. The blades have been serrated to increase bleeding, and they have been enchanted to increase the wearer's Dexterity and Endurance.
Quality: C
Damage: 26-38 (Pierce)
Durability: 35/35
Increased Bleeding Chance
+3 Dexterity
+3 Endurance

Superior Throwing Knife
A solid choice when close up fighting must be

avoided.   Knives may be retrieved once
thrown.
Quality: C
Damage: 15-23 (Pierce)
Quantity: 10/10

The daggers had set him back fifteen gold.
Decent weapons seemed to be selling at a premium at
this stage of the game.   However, Jason decided it
was probably worth it.   Other players had likely had a
chance to undertake a number of quests and run
dungeons for loot already.   Jason had been too
preoccupied first with Morgan's nearly impossible
murder quest and then his impromptu rampage
around the city to pick up the typical beginner gear.
He had found some items, but nothing besides the
amulet that was really helpful for his class.

Lastly, Jason purchased a stack of twenty mana
and health potions for two gold.   They were
expensive but worth it.   He assumed that most
players hadn't had a chance to advance their trade
skills much since AO's release. There were likely only
a handful of players at this stage of the game that
could craft items like potions.   Yet he knew that the
potions would be essential in the upcoming fight.

After he had finished shopping, Jason had
spent thirty-five gold on items and had only
seventeen pieces remaining.   This made him wince,
but he was confident that he'd made the right choice.
Once he equipped his items, he had to admit that he
at least looked pretty cool.

He was now clothed in dark black leather
armor with black fur fringes.   His hooded cloak hung
around him like a shroud, concealing the daggers and
knives hidden about his person.   He was probably
going to lose this upcoming war, but he certainly

wouldn't lose it in style!

Jason's then checked his Character Status to see his current stats with the new gear:

Character Status			
Name:	Jason	**Gender:**	Male
Level:	61	**Class:**	Necromancer
Race:	Human	**Alignment:**	Chaotic-Evil
Fame:	0	**Infamy:**	2200
Health:	410	**H-Regen:**	0.35 / Sec
Mana:	3800	**M-Regen:**	19.5 / Sec
Stamina	660	**S-Regen:**	3.6 / Sec
Strength:	12	**Dexterity:**	36
Vitality:	11	**Endurance:**	36
Intelligence:	22	**Willpower:**	344

Affinities			
Dark:	30%	**Light:**	4%
Fire:	3%	**Water:**	2%
Air:	3%	**Earth:**	2%

His stats were starting to look respectable. One-on-one fights clearly weren't his strong suit, but Jason had built his character around summoning minions. He had also become quite talented at hiding and running away. He noticed that his infamy had gone up considerably and chalked it up to destroying a city.

Looking around the market, he noticed some angry looking players waiting to use the vendor. The vendor himself also seemed quite anxious and was nervously shifting his weight from one foot to the other.

Hmm, I must have been staring into space for some time.

He grinned at the players and motioned for his zombies to follow him. Once they had made their way out of the market and had found a secluded alley nearby, Jason sent the zombies carrying the equipment to Rex at the training ground. Their orders were to hand over the loot and then follow Rex's instructions. He kept two zombies with him for protection.

Jason's next stop was Morgan's school. He had been overwhelmed the last couple days trying to prepare for the upcoming war, but he wanted to speak with her regarding whether he could learn any new spells now that he had increased both his level and his dark affinity.

He approached the building that Morgan had appropriated for her school. Jason noted that she had used her status as a council member to take over one of the more luxurious noble houses in the north-side. This actually seemed fitting to Jason since a school of dark magic should have a prominent place in his undead city. If he somehow managed to survive this war, he ought to turn the other estates into public buildings of one sort or another.

A city library would be useful. Maybe I could also start some kind of school.

Jason found Morgan sitting in an office on the second story of the estate. The room was crowded with bookshelves, and her desk was covered in stacks of open books. As he walked in, Morgan didn't look up from the book in front of her. He suspected that she must have investigated the nearby manors and stolen any books on magic she found. That was the only way she could have accumulated the enormous pile he saw before him.

I'm probably looking at Morgan's treasure trove right now.

Jason approached the desk and stood there for an awkward moment. Morgan completely ignored him, her attention focused solely on the book. His patience wearing thin, Onyx jumped up on the desk and sat directly on the book Morgan was reading. He seemed to look at her with an expression that said, "What now old woman?"

"Damned cat," Morgan muttered.

She then glanced up and noticed Jason. "Oh. Hello, Jason. I didn't notice you there." She waved at the books on the desk. "I've been a bit preoccupied. You wouldn't believe the books on magic these nobles managed to collect."

"I'm certain they must be interesting," Jason answered diplomatically. "How are your pupils doing?"

Morgan replied dismissively, "Oh they're fine. They're all generalist dark mages, but they're coming along nicely. They're out slaughtering the wildlife, and then raising the corpses, and then killing them again. It's great practice."

Jason chuckled. "I actually came to see you about my own training. I was wondering if you are able to teach me any new spells."

"Ahh, well let's see here." Morgan seemed to look through him for a moment. "Oh my! You have indeed progressed a great deal. Your level and affinity are sufficient to learn a new set of spells."

Before Morgan could move on, Jason interjected, "I've been meaning to ask, what exactly does my affinity do? For example, I gained 5% dark affinity for completing a quest."

"Well, that question doesn't lend itself to a simple answer," Morgan replied, as she assumed her usual professorial air.

These lectures always make me feel like I should be sitting in a classroom taking notes.

Morgan began her explanation, "A person gains or loses affinity based on whether they behave in a way that is consistent or contradictory to each affinity. For example, you gain dark affinity if you act on your desires. If you resolve quests in a way that is consistent with a particular affinity, you may receive bonuses to that affinity. I expect this is what happened with your particular quest."

That makes sense. As the old man said, I gave myself over to my desire for revenge and power when I rampaged through Lux.

"Your ability to learn spells is a function of both your level and your affinity," she continued. "Of the two, your affinity is much harder to raise. Over time, it takes a much more significant commitment to the trait represented by a particular affinity to increase it."

So the rampage around Lux was actually a windfall in a way. I will need to be careful to balance acting on my desires in a way that is still constructive.

"I suppose that all makes sense," Jason said. "So I guess I get to select some spells now?"

Morgan chuckled, amused by how eager he was. "Yes and just like the last time, you will only be able to choose three. You may choose any of the old spells you gave up last time or any of the new spells from the list." She waved her hand in his direction, and a prompt appeared.

"Oh, by the way, I have included more detailed information regarding the various spells this time. Hopefully, this should save us some time discussing your options." She said this last part with a grimace as she turned back to her book.

Spell Selection		
Spell Name:	**Spell Type:**	**Mana Cost:**
Curse of Silence	Curse	200 Mana

A curse that silences your target for 5 seconds, preventing speech and spell casting. The length of silence increases with spell level.

Spell Name:	**Spell Type:**	**Mana Cost:**
Blight Ray	Offense	85 Mana

The caster casts a ray of dark magic at his opponent, causing 100 disease damage. The damage scales with the spell's level and your Intelligence.

Spell Name:	**Spell Type:**	**Mana Cost:**
Virulent Disease	Offense	400 Mana

Your dark magic infects a target, causing the target to receive poison and dark damage over time. The damage scales with Intelligence and spell level.

Spell Name:	**Spell Type:**	**Mana Cost:**
Summon Zombie	Summoning	300 Mana

You may raise a dead enemy as a zombie. The zombie's level is dependent on the level of the dead enemy. The Control Limit is dependent on your Willpower.

Spell Name:	Spell Type:	Mana Cost:
Zombie Lieutenant	Summoning (Unique)	1000 Mana (Sustained)

You may cause a zombie to become self-aware and intelligent. You may train the enhanced zombie to think autonomously and command other minions. Intelligence of summon increases with spell level. Control Limit is calculated as Willpower/100. Separate Control Limit.

Spell Name:	Spell Type:	Mana Cost:
Summon Skeleton	Summoning	600 Mana

You may raise a skeleton using nearby bones. The skeleton will be recreated in the default form of the original creature. A nearly complete skeleton is required. The skeleton's level is calculated as the caster's level + Willpower/75. Minion level scaling increases with spell level. Control Limit is calculated as Willpower/10. Shares Control Limit with other undead.

Spell Name:	Spell Type:	Mana Cost:
Custom Skeleton	Summoning (Unique)	1500 Mana

You may raise a skeleton using nearby bones. The player may design the Skeleton using available bones or choose a default skeleton. Mana cost is the same regardless of whether a customization is made. The skeleton's level is calculated as the caster's level + Willpower/75. Minion level scaling increases with spell level. Control Limit is calculated as Willpower/10. Shares Control Limit with other undead.

Spell Name:	Spell Type:	Mana Cost:
Enrage	Summoning	100 Mana

You cause one of your summoned creatures to enter a frenzy, increasing damage and stats. Increases to damage and stats scale with spell level. However, the enraged status increases the decay rate of your summon

Jason stared at the window for a few moments with his brow furrowed.

These were difficult choices. He was leaning towards selecting *Curse of Silence* since he had already experienced how powerful a decent enemy caster could be. He was also considering whether the spell could be used to silence a target before it was assassinated. That left two spells.

A direct-damage spell would be useful since he didn't have one. However, flashy spells would just draw attention to him, and he didn't have enough *Intelligence* to put much punch behind them. What he really needed were more summoning spells.

He decided *Zombie Lieutenant* was a priority since it would allow him to split his army without being forced to give minutely detailed instructions. That left one additional spell, and he decided that this one was also a no-brainer. He was going to choose *Custom Skeleton*. It sounded like this would give him an unusually large selection of options to choose from in creating minions.

Jason turned back to Morgan, "I've decided on *Curse of Silence*, *Zombie Lieutenant*, and *Custom Skeleton*."

She looked at him evenly. "I can't say I'm surprised. I would quibble with you about the usefulness of *Custom Skeleton* though. You're going to need to have a large assortment of bones to be able to get much use out of that spell."

Hmm. I actually thought that it was an obvious choice. Now she is making it seem like a gamble. I might be better off taking Enrage. That could turn my zombies into berserkers for a short time. Especially since there is no decay near the Twilight Throne.

He decided to ask some questions first. "How does summoning skeletons work? Do I need to have every bone that made up an original skeleton to summon it?"

Morgan stared longingly at her books and sighed before answering. "Of course, you have questions! I shouldn't have expected anything different."

"To answer your question, no. Usually, you can make do if you have most of the bones for a skeleton. Let's say 90% as a rough approximation. Your mana will fill in the rest."

"Hmm. Do skeletons level in the same way as zombies? The prompt indicates that they will be set to a level dependent on my personal level and my *Willpower*."

Morgan scratched her chin as she responded, "Skeletons aren't really my specialty. I've always preferred zombies. However, in my experience, they don't level."

"Essentially, summoning skeletons doesn't make you as picky about the corpse, but their potential is lower. They don't start with any abilities and they don't get stronger over time."

Jason was still intrigued. Skeletons could be much stronger if he were mass summoning creatures. Assuming of course that he had an ample supply of bones. "So what about creating a custom skeleton. How does that work?"

"Well, if you were standing near a large number of bones, you should be able to design a skeleton using your available resources. I also understand that you can save the designs. Again, skeletons are not my area of expertise. You will have to experiment."

What should I do? I'm still intrigued by the idea of creating my own skeletons.

Jason hesitated for a moment and then made a decision. "I'm going to go with my first choice. I will take *Custom Skeleton*."

Morgan frowned, obviously annoyed that he didn't take her advice. "Don't say I didn't warn you." With that, she pressed her hand against Jason's forehead and the words and gestures associated with each spell trickled into his mind. He could have sworn she gave his head a little push before she drew her hand back.

"Now if that's all, I have some reading to do," Morgan said gruffly, as she turned back to her book. Clearly, he was dismissed.

Shaking his head, Jason walked out of the office. Onyx padded silently behind him. As Jason stood outside the door, he considered what to do next. What he really wanted to do was try his new spells.

"Well, Onyx, what do you say we go visit the graveyard?"

Chapter 25 - Creative

It was dusk in the game world, and the army had stopped for the evening. The NPCs went about their usual routine of setting up camp, caring for the animals, and cooking dinner. Riley had observed that nearly two-thirds of the army was comprised of NPCs, which made for an unusually realistic march towards the Twilight Throne.

She was standing a bit apart from the player campsite, which itself was set up in a hasty manner some distance from the busy NPC encampment. The players usually logged off during the in-game evenings, leaving little need for an elaborate camp. The NPCs had also made it clear that they weren't interested in putting up with naive travelers after a long day of on the road.

Riley had built a small mound of branches and then laid a cotton target she had borrowed from the NPCs over the mound. She was fifty yards from the target. Between the campfires and numerous lanterns, there was still sufficient light for her to make out the beige cotton from this distance. Riley pulled the string of her recurve bow back until it was even with her ear. She carefully sighted down the length of the arrow.

Her breathing slowed and then stopped, the world seeming to still around her. After a long moment, she released. The string snapped, and the arrow launched forward at an arc until it thumped into the target. Even from this distance, she could see that the arrow had struck close to the center of the target.

She took a deep breath and steadied herself.

"Good heavens girl. You're a great shot."

An aged man sat on a log nearby, watching her. She hadn't noticed him before he spoke. Most of his face was obscured by a hooded cloak, leaving only his wrinkled lips visible. In his hand, he held a gnarled staff.

A small smile graced Riley's lips at his compliment.

She had always wanted to try archery in the real world but never had the opportunity. She remembered posing the idea to her parents many years ago. They had explained that it was a silly hobby. They insisted she should be a cheerleader or play a team sport. What sort of girl shot a bow for fun?

"Thank you," she said to the old man. "I didn't even notice you there."

The old man's wrinkled lips cracked into a smile. "At my age, I move slowly. This at least affords me the benefit of walking quietly."

Riley almost chuckled at the old man's words until she saw Alexion's gleaming outline behind him, his metallic form weaving its way throughout the camp. Her fleeting moment of cheer was quickly extinguished as the familiar miserable despair twisted within her stomach. She could almost forget the feeling each time she practiced with her bow.

The old man interrupted her thoughts as he observed her expression. "You seem gloomy for such a pretty girl. Not that I blame you, these wretched woods could make anyone feel depressed."

When they had initially started the journey to the Twilight Throne, they had passed through sunny, thriving fields, and rich green forests. As the journey continued, the plants withered and died. Now leafless branches hung over the road like claws. Each day, the sun shined a little less due to the swiftly thickening cloud cover. Soon they would be forced to light torches and lanterns during the day to make their way forward.

"Yes, these woods are quite gloomy," she agreed distractedly, her eyes following Alexion.

The old man turned his head to follow her gaze and caught sight of Alexion. "Hmm, our fearless leader is making his rounds." He turned back to Riley and said, "What do you think girl? Does he have a chance against this undead city or this traveler you all speak of? What *was his name again? Jason?"*

"I don't know," Riley murmured distractedly.

Along with the other players, Riley had seen the system message when Lux was conquered. When she had seen the player's name, a strange feeling had welled up inside of her. It couldn't be the Jason she knew. There were likely millions of people who shared that name. Yet the unmistakable image of Jason's face had flashed in her mind's eye when she saw the notification. A flood of guilt accompanied the image. She couldn't believe that she had gone along with Alex's story.

She shook her head to clear it. Regardless of who this player was, she was impressed that one person could conquer a city and stand alone against an army of players and NPCs. As the feeling of despair slithered and tightened in her stomach, she desperately wished that she had that kind of power.

"If only I had the strength to stand up to Alex," she thought bitterly.

She turned her attention back to the old man and discovered that the log now sat empty. The old man had disappeared.

*   *   *

Jason stood in the middle of the graveyard Morgan had once called home. It was just south of the Twilight Throne and now empty of the living.

A heavy darkness hung over the area, and there was almost no sound, save the occasional chirp of insects. Jason could detect the smell of fresh dirt and grass. Onyx sat beside him, gazing with a bored expression at the gravestones and tombs that riddled the area.

Jason was curious about his new summoning spell. He wanted to try it out and see the results. The graveyard had an ample supply of bones, and he figured that it would be a good place to test the new spell.

He began the process of casting *Custom Skeleton*. His hands moved in a complicated series of gestures as his lips formed the words of a long-dead language. Instead of the typical ball of dark energy forming in the air, the world around him began to slow and took on an otherworldly cast. The effect was eerily similar to what the old man had done to him in the marketplace in Lux.

He looked up as he cast. A bird seemed to hover in the air, its wings beating ever so slowly. As he completed the spell, the world nearly stopped. He looked around. He could now detect the faint blue outlines of bones throughout the graveyard.

Onyx yawned and stretched. He jumped up onto a nearby gravestone and laid down to sleep.

Jason eyed him quizzically.

Why isn't Onyx affected by the time slowing aspect of this spell?

Shaking his head at this unexplained phenomenon, Jason turned his attention back to the spell. A semi-transparent control panel had appeared in front of him. It looked like some sort of graphical design program with floating, translucent menus that hovered in the air in front of him. This program seemed to have a static number of usable pieces. He could see a complicated menu off to one side that listed all nearby bones by individual type, including a counter indicating how many of each type of bone were in the immediate area.

As he skimmed through the menu, he noticed that there were options for creating whole humanoid extremities and for reconstructing many different complete skeletons. He figured that the complete skeletons must be the corpses that were buried in the graveyard. His guess was that the game also helped simplify the process of building a skeleton by providing prefabricated, default extremities for people who hadn't taken multiple college anatomy or graphic design courses.

Intrigued, he started fiddling with different combinations of bones.

Nearly two hours later, his eyes were becoming bleary from staring at the graphical UI for such a long time. He now had a firm grasp of how the editing program worked and was reasonably competent at creating basic skeletal forms. He had quickly learned that the interface allowed him to manipulate all of the bones in the area without touching them. With a thought, he could organize and rearrange the nearby bones to form a skeleton in the air in front of him.

Once he had the frame completed, he had to imbue the joints and skull with dark mana. This involved summoning pools of the substance in the air and attaching them to the joints like some kind of unholy putty. From what he could tell, his dark mana operated as both a power source for the skeleton as a whole and served as its muscles and tendons. Once the skeleton was completed, the editor gave him the option to save the design and name it.

After experimenting, he could see why Morgan thought that the spell had limited usefulness. Images of skeleton raptors and giant flying monstrosities of bone had flashed through his mind at one point. He imagined himself riding a bone dragon and had started getting excited.

However, the problem was he didn't have the materials. It wasn't just a problem regarding the raw number of bones he would need (which was a lot!), but he also needed bones of a certain shape and size. He couldn't exactly create a skeleton raptor using human bones. He would need the corpses of various animals, or he would need some way to mold the bones.

He paused.

Now that is an interesting thought. Can I mold the bones? Perhaps I could use raw dark mana to try shaving a bone while the editing program for the spell is still running.

With a thought, he lifted a bone from the ground and set it to hover in front of him. He then drew in dark mana as though he was about to add connections between the bones. However, instead of forming a pool of mana and attaching it to the bone, he imagined it forming a delicate blade in the air. The dark mana swiftly formed into a blade. Jason visualized the magical knife cutting the edge of the bone in a smooth arc.

The result was unexpected. The damn thing actually worked!

Not only that, but it gave him a new skill:

New Passive Skill: Bone Crafting
Surprisingly, you actually figured out how to manipulate the summoning spell to create custom skeletons. In spite of everything people said about you, your experimentation has enabled you to use the spell's editing tools to alter bones. Since you can't be trusted with magical knives, this skill allows the modification to be performed automatically through the summoning editor.
Skill Level: Beginner Level 1
Effect: Access to bone modification in the skeleton editor. May currently alter the

composition of a bone by 5%.

I have to agree with the prompt this time, it is actually surprising that I figured this out.

Jason gave out a shout of triumph in the nearly silent graveyard, and Onyx looked at him with an annoyed expression. He stuck out his tongue at the cat. It wasn't the sort of thing the future ruler of an undead city should do, but sometimes the cat could be really judgmental.

Wow, this is a cool skill! If I level it up, I will be able to create some truly unique creatures. I could alter any bones that I have available and use them any way I want. Morgan must not have discovered this skill or she wouldn't have given up on summoning skeletons so easily.

The ability to alter the bones, even slightly, gave Jason a lot more wiggle room to create new skeletons.

However, the question was what should he create?

He scratched his head and considered for a moment what type of minion he would need in the upcoming battle. After he had overseen the training of the city's fledgling army and reviewed their low average level, it had quickly become apparent that they couldn't win against Alexion in a straight battle. He would need to adopt the same type of guerrilla tactics he had used in conquering the city.

It's clear that I will need to take the fight to Alexion while they are still approaching the city.

The aura of darkness would extend well past the city limits, causing Alexion's army to walk in perpetual darkness. It was unlikely that the players and NPCs had *Night Vision* so their visibility would be limited. The players and NPCs would also be weakened by the large concentration of dark energy.

What Jason needed to do was attack preemptively, using the darkness and stealth. He was already intimately familiar with the terrain around the city from pouring over the maps. If he could whittle down Alexion's numbers, then the Twilight Throne might stand a chance.

I might also be able to delay them for an extra day. Any time that I can buy the new army to train and get ready is worth it.

He expected that the psychological aspect of the attack would work wonders. He hadn't forgotten the traumatic experience suffered by the beginning players when they had discovered the feral zombies that Jason had left at the training grounds. Now, most of the enemy army was comprised of NPCs, and they had only one digital life. If Jason could harass and demoralize the army before it made its way to the city, that might also help swing the odds in their favor.

His current Control Limit was 40, and he had already summoned 28 minions. That meant he could raise twelve skeletons. They would need to be fast and designed for stealth for the type of fight he was visualizing. If they were also terrifying, that would be an added bonus. He was still limited to something that was humanoid in appearance since he only had human bones to work with. He couldn't radically alter the bones just yet.

Jason began experimenting with the editor, and a form slowly began to develop in the air before him. It was about the size of a ten-year-old child. It had a hunched posture, and Jason had used longer bones from the ribs to form its hands. Each finger was now much longer than normal and terminated in a viciously curved point. He added bladed bones to the elbows and bones spikes along the spine. Its feet were primarily humanoid, but the toes were elongated and sharpened.

After playing with the editor for a bit, he discovered that he was also able to change the composition of the bones themselves, making them darker by mixing in small amounts of graveyard dirt. This turned the bones a dark gray which would help camouflage the skeletons.

Once the complete skeleton floated in front of him, Jason began adding dark magic to the joints. After a moment of experimenting, he realized that he could add the dark mana in varying amounts. A thought occurred to him, and he began adding extra dark mana to the joints. His theory was that the extra energy would act like additional cartilage and reduce bone grinding. It might also provide additional "muscle," increasing strength and speed.

It took several tests to get a product that worked well, but the result was more than a little scary. The extra layers of dark magic in the joints actually increased the creature's speed substantially. Jason confirmed that the dark magic held the bones together, acted as cartilage, and provided a substitute for muscles. The downside was that the extra layers of dark magic cost more mana. Each finished creature cost nearly 2,000 mana.

After some time, twelve of his finished creations stood before him. They were naturally small, and their dark gray bodies were difficult to see in the darkness. They didn't need any gear with their natural claws, they were almost unnaturally quiet, quick, and limber. He also expected that their clawed hands and feet would allow them to easily climb trees and traverse almost any type of terrain. With Jason's current *Willpower*, they were each level 66.

The only downside to his creations was that

they were exceedingly fragile. His inspection showed that they almost had less health than he did. Jason expected that they would likely crumble after a few well-placed blows. However, they were suitably terrifying and fast. He expected that if they caught an opponent unaware, they would kill him long before he was able to strike back.

After thinking for a moment, he decided to call his creations the Night Children due to their small stature. The editor saved the design so that he could easily create more and make modifications.

As he was working he received several notifications:

x3 Skill Rank Up: Bone Crafting
Skill Level: Beginner Level 4
Effect: Access to bone modification in the skeleton editor. May currently alter the composition of a bone by 8%.

x2 Skill Rank Up: Custom Skeleton
Skill Level: Beginner Level 3
Effect: You may raise a custom skeleton using nearby bones. The skeleton's level is calculated as the caster's level + Willpower/74.

As Jason reviewed the prompts that appeared before him, he noticed that the increase in the spell level of *Custom Skeleton* had slightly increased the level of the skeletons by decreasing the *Willpower* per additional skeleton level. He imagined that if he were able to level the spell high enough, his skeletons would be pretty powerful since they would be at a much higher level than he was.

Even though most of his minions were not nearby, Jason decided to pull up his Summoning

Information screen to review his current army:

Summon Information			
Control Limit	40	Lt. Control Limit	4
Zombie Level Cap	141	Skeleton Level Cap	66
Current Zombies	28	Current Skeletons	12
Current Lts.	0	-	-
Type of Summon			
Guards	9	Thieves	15
Fire Mage	1	Ice Mage	1
Dark Mage	2	Night Children	12

His small army was beginning to grow into a respectable strike force.

He had maximized stealth and damage. The thieves and mages could both *Sneak,* and his Night Children would likely be stealthy enough to avoid detection even without the *Sneak* skill. He had outfitted all of his thieves with bows so that he could use them as ranged support. The guard zombies could act as a reserve force and be used to create kamikaze zombies if needed.

Jason glanced around at the graveyard and noticed that time was still being slowed. He had left the skeleton editor enabled. As he closed the editor, time sped back up to a normal pace. He glanced at the clock. Only two hours of in-game time had passed. Yet, he felt that at least six hours had passed while he was playing around with the editor and designing the Night Children.

Did the skeleton editor triple the time compression?

That means that time runs nine times faster in the editor than in the real world! How was my mind able to handle that level of time compression for such a long time? Did the CPSC really approve this game feature?

His thoughts were interrupted by a pounding headache he felt coming on. His mind suddenly felt heavy and tired, in spite of the small amount of time that had actually passed. He staggered for a moment as a wave of dizziness washed over him.

Onyx gazed at Jason with an anxious expression from atop a nearby gravestone, his tail twitching spasmodically. Jason pet Onyx, hoping to reassure the cat. He decided that he needed a short break. He would log off for a bit and then regroup and start moving toward Alexion's army.

In spite of the headache and weariness, Jason felt excited about the upcoming battle and his eyes glowed with unholy energy as he surveyed his creations.

It was almost time to bring the fight to Alexion.

Chapter 26 - Mended

Another day had passed in their trek towards the Twilight Throne, and the NPCs had begun their routine of setting camp for the night. Riley sat in front of a campfire, staring into the tumbling flames. The chaotic dance of orange and red was comforting. She hadn't felt much peace lately, but the solitary late-night campsites had become a relaxing sanctuary.

Her moment of peace was rudely interrupted, as a heavy hand landed on her shoulder. She turned and looked up to find Alexion staring down at her.

"I am off to my tent to log out for the evening. I expect you to stay here until I return. That is, unless you would prefer to join me?" A leer curled his lips, and his dead eyes seemed to undress her.

An involuntary shiver ran up Riley's spine. She turned back to the flames in front of her, trying to ignore the way her skin crawled. "I'm fine where I am," she said quietly.

A cruel chuckle came from beside her. "Well, in that case, you should stay clear of the kitchen tent in the NPC camp. I hear they just opened a keg." Alexion laughed at his own joke and walked off towards his tent.

Riley physically flinched at Alexion's words, and tears began to form in her eyes. She tried to take a few calming breaths, but the frustrated anger that overcame her made it nearly impossible. "How could he be so cruel?" she thought. "How could anyone be that cruel?"

As she stared through bleary eyes at the flickering flames before her, she recounted the events that had led her to this miserable place.

Riley had begun dating Alex a few weeks ago. She was reluctant at first because she had heard whispers from her friends that he could be a bit heartless and even cruel. This surprised her. He had only been kind and considerate when he spoke with her. She began to think her friends were making up stories. Eventually, she had agreed to go on a date. It had been a splendid, excessive affair.

Over the last few weeks, that all began to change. She started to notice moments when Alex's mask of kindness slipped. She could see something disturbing beneath the surface. At first, she thought she just imagined it, but then the encounter in the cafeteria had happened. She didn't understand how he could attack Jason, someone who had always been so nice to her. That action alone would have been enough for her to end it.

Yet it was Alex's dead eyes as he stood over Jason's prone form that had really scared her. That hadn't been mere bullying. That had been the look of someone who preyed on other people in a dispassionate, clinical fashion. The look of someone who would pull the wings off a butterfly to carefully examine how it thrashed.

Horrified and angered by what she had seen; Riley immediately broke up with Alex. At least she tried to. That was when he told her that she should rethink her decision - that he had a video she wouldn't want anyone to see. He reminded her of a night they had attended a party together, and she had overindulged with the beer. She had never really drunk heavily before, and her memory of the evening was blurry and unfocused.

She had demanded to see the video, thinking Alex was lying. His lips had ever-so-slowly crept into a cruel, knowing smirk as he had revealed snippets of the video. Those few flashes were enough for her face to flush with embarrassment. Riley's hands had moved to cover her eyes, as though she could hide from the recording he held in his hand. Shame settled in her stomach.

What had shocked her the most was that Alex showed no hesitation or remorse as he blackmailed her. He didn't even seem upset that she had tried to break up with him. She couldn't forget his emotionless, almost bored eyes as he threatened her. It was as though he knew that she *would capitulate.*

And she had.

Sitting by the campfire, Riley recoiled from the memories that flashed through her mind, tears trickling down her cheeks. It made sense now. Of course, he had known that she would break. He knew exactly what to expect when he plucked a butterfly's wings. He had plenty of practice.

"I didn't do it for myself though," she whispered miserably into the empty night around her.

Or at least not just for herself.

While Riley cringed at the thought of the video being passed around school, the potential harm the video posed to her family's reputation was much worse.

Her father made his money by selling self-help books. He was also a prominent public figure and was perceived as a titan of moral integrity, which is what made his books so successful. A video of his drunken, underage daughter would be the sort of thing that could severely damage his reputation.

With this leverage, Alex forced her to keep up the charade of dating him and to play this game. He seemed to take great pleasure in watching the discomfort and pain it caused her to be around him.

He had also made her support his story that Jason had attacked him in the cafeteria. She had resisted at first. Could she really do that to someone who had always been so nice to her? Even if it was to protect herself and her family? She had finally caved. Riley figured that at most Jason would be suspended temporarily. The harm to her family seemed much greater.

How could she have known he would be expelled?

She would never have gone along with Alex's story if she had known what would happen to Jason. Yet what could she do now? It was hopeless. If she went to the administration after going along with Alex's story, he would likely "break up" with her and contrive some story about how she was trying to get back at him. Then he would release the video of her drunken antics. No one would believe her.

She felt helpless. She was too weak to confront Alex or to protect herself. Too weak to tell the administration at Richmond what Alex had done. She couldn't even make herself tell her parents. Her mind boiled over with a strange medley of emotion. A cocktail of anger, shame, and guilt swirled in her mind as she scrambled to think of some way out of her situation.

If only she were stronger.

Her thoughts turned again to the Jason that had conquered Lux. If only she could be someone like that. Someone who could stand before an army without fear. Someone powerful. She knew she couldn't. She was only a weak, stupid girl who had played right into Alex's sadistic hands.

Digital tears full of helplessness and frustration flowed freely down Riley's cheeks, as she sat alone in front of the campfire. The flames continued to dance in front of her in a gleeful mockery of her pain. She knew she had to find a way out.

*   *   *

After logging out, Jason was lying in his small room at Angie's house.

He pulled the helmet off his head and looked around the spartan room. He had no furniture, and his bed was a single mattress without a frame. At least he had a place to sleep and a roof over his head. Over the last couple days, he had discovered that his aunt was actually a pretty good roommate.

Angie worked long hours at a biotech company and spent most of her time in the lab. The company was always intent on getting some project or another completed, so she was constantly in crisis mode. Being at the bottom of the corporate totem pole also meant that she got stuck with the crap work and long shifts. Despite all that, she still managed to stay relatively upbeat about it.

Jason left his small room and made his way to the kitchen to make himself something to eat. It was a Saturday evening in the real world, and he had been playing AO almost constantly for the last week. It was a weekend, which meant the other players that were marching toward the Twilight Throne could afford to stay in-game for long periods of time. AO had drawn in a younger group of players. Most of them didn't have either work or school to interrupt them for the next two days. That had allowed them to keep up with the NPC army as it marched toward the dark city.

They're going to need to create some way to put your character on autopilot when you're outside the game. Otherwise, larger battles would be almost impossible to organize from a logistics standpoint.

As he was making himself something to eat (ramen again!), Jason pulled up the Rogue-Net website on his device. In particular, he was anxious to check the market to see if his sword had sold. He was elated when he discovered that the item had been purchased.

After the bidding war had stopped, the purchase price settled at a whopping $6,700. The other items were still on the market, but he was hopeful that he could at least make another $1,000 or so when they sold. He was a little curious about the type of person who was willing and able to drop nearly seven grand on a few strings of ones and zeros. Unfortunately, he couldn't see who had purchased the sword since the name of the buyer wasn't publicly available.

I guess it doesn't matter! That amount of money will give me nearly three months of living expenses unless I encounter setbacks. I might even be able to spring for some furniture for my room and higher bandwidth!

Still riding high from the sale of the sword, he heard the door to the small bungalow open. His aunt walked in looking tired from her day at work. Dark circles hung under her eyes making her look drained and stressed. He expected she had started work incredibly early that morning.

"Hi Angie," Jason greeted. "I was just making myself something to eat. Would you like me to make you something?"

Angie glanced over at Jason and a smile lit up her weary face. "That would be lovely. I'm starving, and I didn't get a chance to eat at work today."

Jason added an extra packet of ramen to the pot that was boiling on the stove. They certainly didn't live like kings. However, if he was honest, he felt more at peace here than he had in a long time. It was also nice to live with someone that remembered you were there and came home every once in a while.

"How was your day?" Angie asked, as she set her bag on the counter and slumped wearily into one of the stools at the counter.

"Not bad at all! I sold one of the items I found in AO. Let's just say I don't need to worry about rent for a couple of months!" Jason grinned at Angie excitedly.

Her eyebrows raised in surprise. "Really? Maybe I should give up biotech and become a professional gamer. That sounds like a cushy job!"

Jason chuckled. "I'm not certain I'm going to be able to keep it up or what I'm going to do in a couple months, but at least it takes a bit of the pressure off."

He continued, "I also checked on my application for the Calvary School. They accepted me. I need to select my classes, but I can start on Monday."

Angie nodded her head. "It's good that you went ahead and applied." She eyed him appraisingly as she spoke, "You seem to be in good spirits. I'm actually kind of surprised what with the week you've had..." She trailed off slightly at this last part and looked a bit embarrassed.

Jason's smile faded. "I can't sit and sulk forever. Plus, the time compression from AO makes each real world day seem like three days. For me, it's been a bit longer than you would think."

"I suppose that makes sense." Angie paused for a moment, then continued, "Have you heard from your parents?"

Jason's smile had now disappeared. "Actually, no. I expect that they need a few more days to cool off. I was going to call them early next week. "

He hesitated for a moment before continuing. "Regardless, I'm not going back to Richmond."

"I guess I don't blame you," Angie said quietly.

An awkward silence descended on the kitchen. After a few minutes passed, Jason couldn't take it anymore. He tried to break through the morose cloud that now hung over the room. "So how was your day?" he asked Angie.

"Ugh," she groaned.

"Same old grind. They had me doing quality control on this new diagnostic test we are developing. I really don't know how this thing made it past development. I can only imagine the company's directors pushed it through because the budget couldn't handle any more development time."

She looked sad for a moment. "You know what really sucks about it though? These diagnostic tests we're developing will be used on living, breathing people. They aren't just statistics in a control study. Can you imagine being misdiagnosed for ovarian cancer?"

Angie shook her head. "I just can't understand how some people can put money over the well-being of others. It makes it hard sometimes to tell myself that I'm helping people when the higher ups are making decisions solely based on how it affects the company's bottom line."

Jason really didn't know what to say. He had certainly experienced his fair share of abuse at the hands of the wealthy. It was as though a certain amount of money desensitized a person to the consequences of their actions.

"I'm sorry Angie. Maybe we could do something to take your mind off of it?"

I have a few hours I can kill outside of the game before I need to start marching towards Alexion's army. Angie really looks like she could use a break.

Angie glanced over at Jason and grinned. "I suppose we could do something. Have you ever played any of the old console games they had back in the day?"

"What!? You play video games? I didn't realize you were into that sort of thing?"

"Are you kidding?" Angie replied, "I've been playing games since before you were born. I don't have the money to buy the fancier equipment you kids use nowadays, but I still have a few old consoles in the living room."

"That sounds awesome," Jason said. Then he eyed her with a grin of his own. "That is, if you think your old woman reflexes can keep up."

His aunt laughed. "We'll see about that!" She headed into the living room to set up the game.

Jason smiled as he finished cooking the ramen. He then poured the steaming noodles in two porcelain bowls he grabbed out of a nearby cabinet and made his way into the living room.

"Alright, where is the victory seat in here?" he asked as he entered the room.

Angie chuckled. "Hey now! You aren't going to be acting so cocky when I'm cleaning the floor with you."

Jason and Angie spent the next few hours playing some co-op games on an ancient console she had attached to the screen in her living room. In between games they would eat ramen and joke about who had killed who in the last game. It was probably the first time in weeks that Jason felt genuinely happy.

Eventually, Angie called it a night and headed back to her room. Jason could tell she was exhausted from working, but she had needed the downtime to relax a bit. To be honest, he had needed it to.

Jason's device let out a ring that signaled an incoming call. He put in his earbud as he made his way back to his room and quietly shut the door.

"Hello?" Jason answered.

"Hey man, it's Frank! I saw you had actually logged off for once, so I figured I'd give you a call."

"Oh, hey Frank. Yeah, I needed a break. The longer I play, the stranger it feels to come back to the land of the living."

Frank chuckled on the other end of the phone. "No kidding! The game has only been out for about a week now, and it feels like a month has passed already. This time compression is really something."

"By the way," he continued, "You sound good! I mean I didn't expect you to be sitting in your room crying all day, but you actually sound kind of happy."

It was Jason's turn to laugh. "I don't know if I would go that far, but I'm doing pretty well. You know, ever since I started playing AO, I've just been feeling different."

"No kidding! First, you conquer a city, and now I hear you're about to take on an army. Wish I could be there!"

"Well, I'll keep my camera on for you. I was going to send you the footage from Lux, but I figured you must have gotten the gist of what happened from the videos that were posted online."

Frank sounded a bit peeved when he spoke, "Yeah, yeah. That footage was okay, but you still owe me the real thing. There are large chunks of video missing from the stuff the players filmed in the market. Like how the hell did you transform a city?"

Jason fumbled trying to think of an appropriate answer. He didn't want to lie to his friend, but he had a feeling the old man wouldn't appreciate him running his mouth. So he tried for humor, hoping to disarm Frank's questions. "That's actually proprietary information. I'm not sure you have the appropriate clearances and such."

A long silence followed. "Really?" Frank finally asked. "I can see your sense of humor didn't survive your expulsion."

Ugh. That was a terrible joke. Maybe I've been spending too much time with Jerry.

Jason replied, "Hey! Low blow with the expulsion crack. Anyway, I was actually just about to log back in. I have a ton of work to do to prepare for the upcoming battle."

"No doubt. Assuming you survive this fight, I may need to head over to the Twilight Throne and see the place for myself. I have to say, I'm curious."

Frank continued, "Oh. By the way, I was actually calling you regarding Alexion's army. I have some juicy information that you're going to love."

Jason was intrigued. "Really? What is it?"

Frank laughed. "Maybe you should check the Rogue-Net forums. There is a post right now that has a ton of hits called "The Endless March.""

Jason promptly pulled up the Rogue-Net forums on his device and found the post Frank had mentioned. He just stared at his device with his mouth open.

"Is this real?" Jason finally asked.

A laugh resounded on the other end of the phone. "Hey, I don't know. Apparently, Alex isn't focused on strategy. Maybe he thinks you're just going to roll over and hand him the city."

Could Alex really be this stupid? Could the other players?

Members of Alex's army were posting pictures, video clips, and detailed information regarding the army's progress and location. One player actually described the NPC sentries around the camp!

The only thing Jason could think was that the players simply didn't take him seriously and didn't anticipate much resistance from the Twilight Throne. Either that or no one had yet considered how important tactics were in waging a war in AO.

I really don't have any choice but to take the fight to them now. They're basically begging me to attack them with this kind of intel!

"Wow, this is amazing Frank. Thank you!"

"You're more than welcome," Frank said. "However, remember that you owe me some damned footage this time! Otherwise, I'm going to find you and make you give it to me."

Jason chuckled. "I'll remember, don't worry. I'll talk to you later Frank."

"Bye man."

As Jason terminated the call, he stood for a moment and stared at his Core. The information on the forum post was incredibly useful. He knew it would give him an edge, so he read further down the thread, gleaning any information he could find. After he had finished reading, he tapped Core off and lay back on his bed staring at the ceiling.

He had laid in this exact same position a couple days ago, his mind in turmoil as he tried to process what had happened at Richmond and with his parents. He knew that those things had only happened a few days ago, but they seemed much more distant.

Jason had changed a lot over the last couple days (or week in-game). The thought of Alex or his parents just didn't seem to upset him the way it had in the past. He had been admitted to a new school, he had some money in his pocket, and he had even laughed and joked around with Angie tonight.

He also had something to fight for. He had created the Twilight Throne from the ashes of his rage and pain. It had the potential to turn it into something incredible. The city was still in its infancy, and they would probably lose this war, but Jason was going to make certain that every single one of the players and NPCs in Alexion's army regretted stepping foot near his city.

Jason grinned and pulled the helmet over his head. This next part was going to be fun.

Chapter 27 - Slaughtered

Riley was sitting in her usual spot in front of the campfire. Yet instead of watching the flames, she stared at the impenetrable darkness that ringed the camp. She thought she had heard something moving in the gloom. Dismissing the sound as a figment of her imagination, she turned her attention back to the fire.

Over the last few days, the cloud cover had thickened until it completely blotted out the sun. Black clouds now constantly boiled in the sky and flashes of lightning could be seen arcing through the clouds. There was no longer a day and night cycle, just perpetual darkness.

Alexion had ordered the troops to bring out torches and keep moving forward. The flickering flames illuminated the road and cast long menacing shadows into the dense forest on either side. The claw-like branches of the trees hung over the road, bending and creaking in the wind. Both the players and NPCs seemed uneasy with the constant darkness, as the reality of what they were doing suddenly struck them.

They were attacking an undead city in the heart of its kingdom.

Riley didn't share their fear.

In contrast to the known evil that rode beside her, the uncertain danger that the darkness carried didn't seem that frightening. To avoid any accidental encounters with Alexion, she had begun wandering the forests in the evenings. After two nights, she had obtained the Night Vision skill, and her eyesight had become sharper. The road and surrounding forest no longer seemed so foreboding.

The group had stopped for the night and set up camp in a large clearing in the forest. The NPCs had prepared their own camp as they usually did, and the players made a half-hearted attempt at lighting a few campfires. Most of the players then logged off to take care of real world necessities.

From her position by the campfire, Riley could see Alexion speaking with the NPC commanders a few yards away. She was able to overhear their conversation, despite the distance. A small group of weary soldiers stood behind the leaders and shifted uneasily.

"We need to post sentries along the tree line," said one of the NPC commanders to Alexion. "It is clear that we are getting closer to the Twilight Throne. We need to be cautious." The NPC motioned at the darkened sky as he made this last point.

"The darkness makes it harder to see. We and we will require more men to ensure we have a complete perimeter set up around the clearing. It would be helpful if you could lend some of the travelers to help."

Alexion gazed steadily at the NPC and smirked haughtily. "I appreciate your input, but my people cannot be spared. Besides, do you really anticipate an attack in these woods? We have nearly 1,500 soldiers here. Would the undead really be foolish enough to attack us in an open clearing?"

The NPC looked a bit put off by this response, and his colleague jumped in with an irritated tone, "Your arrogance will get us all killed. We know nothing about this traveler Jason or the capabilities of the undead city. We don't even know how large an army we face."

Alexion chuckled. "I have my own spies in the so-called Twilight Throne. Their army is a fraction the size of mine, and, the last I heard, it was still garrisoned at the city. I think we can sleep soundly tonight."

His gaze moved to the haggard band of soldiers. "This group should be fine. Perhaps they could use the time to nap."

"A leader should give more respect to his troops," Riley thought. "He treats them like idiots."

It was clear to her that Alexion had bought into the

explanation that Jason had conquered Lux through an event quest. She thought that seemed unlikely. From what she had seen so far, AO didn't offer much hand-holding. Riley felt that Jason shouldn't be underestimated, and Alexion was a fool for not listening to his men.

He was too cavalier with the lives of the NPCs and was quickly losing their respect. They didn't respawn. It may just be a game to him, but for them, it was their lives at risk. How he had managed to secure command of this army, she had no idea. She wasn't a tactical genius, but what the NPC commanders had said made sense.

After Alexion had concluded his conversation with the NPC leaders, they marched off grumbling. He waved at the small contingent of soldiers, and they fanned out around the clearing. Based on the direction each man was headed, Riley could see that there were large holes in the perimeter around the camp.

She rolled her eyes and turned back to the fire.

A couple hours later, the NPC and player camps had quieted down. The NPCs had long since fallen asleep, and nearly all of the players had logged off for the evening. Riley sat alone gazing at the flickering flames of the campfire. She hadn't felt like taking her usual evening stroll.

Suddenly, she caught sight of movement in her peripheral vision. She looked over to see a black cat approaching from the darkness. As he neared Riley, she could see that the cat's eyes glowed silver. Her brow furrowed in confusion as she watched the cat amble up to her.

"What're you doing here kitty?" she asked the cat.

The only response offered was a soft purr as the cat rubbed itself against her legs. She shook her head at the oddity of a cat roaming a desolate forest and gently pulled it onto her lap.

Riley pet the cat absentmindedly as she turned her attention back to the campfire. Ever since she had spoken to the old man a couple nights ago, the events that had led her to this place played endlessly in her mind. As she rehashed the same events over and over, the guilt, shame, and anger that flowed through her veins seemed to magnify.

She hated Alex. If this silly war was so important to him, she desperately wanted to see this journey end in disaster and his dreams crushed. She hoped that Jason would succeed and that she could somehow be strong enough to help.

As she was considering these macabre thoughts, she heard the first screams echo from the NPC camp. She turned in confusion, but couldn't see anything due to the distance and dim lighting. Maybe her wish was coming true.

Indecision racked her. Was this her chance? Should she help the undead?

Was she even able to help?

As the screams grew louder and the sounds of battle washed over the clearing, the doubt and uncertainty won the war that raged in her head. She continued to sit stroking the cat. In her weakness, she had chosen to do nothing. Again. Shame and guilt curled and coiled in her stomach.

*   *   *

Jason was sitting in a tree to the southeast of Alexion's army. He was mulling over how best to attack the army in the clearing.

His minions had carefully scouted the enemy encampment, and he had personally made a full circle around the camp to get a sense of the terrain. The army had stopped for the night in a large clearing encircled by dense forest on three sides. The roadway lay to the north of the glade.

The NPCs had split off from the players and established a formal camp. Rows of tents were arranged in a complicated pattern, and campfires were located at regular intervals. From his position in the tree, Jason could make out larger tents in the center of the camp. He assumed that the tents housed the administrative personnel and likely some kind of kitchen. On the north side of the camp near the road, the NPCs had used the supply wagons to form a makeshift corral to stable the animals.

In contrast, the players had prepared a token set of campfires a few dozen feet from the NPC camp. The player "camp" was located on the east side of the clearing, nearly a hundred yards from the eastern tree line. Since it was now the fifth day of their journey, the enthusiasm of the players had apparently waned and most had logged off during the in-game night.

Finding Alexion's army had been the easy part. The players in the army had continued to post information and videos describing in almost nauseating detail the progress of the army. However, it had still taken nearly a full in-game day for Jason to make it to the enemy camp.

Jason had a reasonable amount of *Endurance* and had spent much of the journey traveling at a brisk jog. He only stopped every so often to regenerate his stamina. Since he and his minions did not need to sleep and had no trouble seeing in the dark, they had made excellent time. Despite their progress, Jason now only had two in-game days until the army reached the Twilight Throne.

The large amount of running through the dark forest had allowed him to two points of *Endurance,* and he had leveled up his *Night Vision once more*:

x2 Skill Rank Up: Night Vision

Skill Level: Beginner Level 7
Effect: 16% increased vision in darkness or near darkness.

"Well, this is just great," Jason murmured sarcastically as he surveyed the army in the clearing. He wasn't certain he had fully understood how many people and animals made up a 1,500-person army. It was a little intimidating.

This seems impossible.

Looking around the tree he was sitting in, he noticed that Onyx was mysteriously absent. The cat had made the run without difficulty and then had disappeared.

I'm sure Onyx can take care of himself. I bet he's off sleeping in a tree somewhere. Lazy, judgmental cat!

Shaking his head, Jason turned his attention back to the enemy camp. He reviewed his troops and their positions. His thieves and Night Children sat huddled below him at the base of the tree, while his guard zombies and the mages were farther back in the woods.

During the journey, Jason converted one of his zombie guards into a lieutenant, and he had formed a separate unit of the guards and mages. The sustained mana cost was painful (he was left with only 2,800 mana), but he had realized while traveling from the Twilight Throne that his guards didn't have any real stealth abilities. This meant that they would need to be his rear guard and would require someone to oversee them when Jason wasn't present.

Jason had also taken the time while they were traveling to educate his new lieutenant on various types of tactics and explain his role. He had come up with a few defensive actions the rear guard should take in an emergency and assigned the maneuvers to certain keywords that Jason could use telepathically. Right now, the rear guard was stationed farther south, away from the enemy camp. They would create a defensive perimeter if Jason and his other stealthier minions needed to retreat.

His eyes panned back to the southern tree line. His thieves had already identified the sentries that ringed the camp. Using *Sneak*, he had managed to creep close enough to the soldiers to inspect them. He discovered that they were each approximately level 110. If this was representative of the other soldiers in the army, then the fledgling undead force in the Twilight Throne was in serious trouble.

What surprised Jason was the number of sentries or the lack thereof. Judging from the state of the camp's defenses, Alexion clearly expected Jason to hole up in the Twilight Throne and wait for his army to show up. In fact, after some hand wringing, Jason had decided to leave the fledgling army back at the city. They needed more time to grow in strength, and Jason was somewhat worried that Alex would hire someone to roll an undead character to spy on him.

It didn't look like Alexion had considered the practicalities of fighting a war in AO. If he lost any players, they would respawn back at Grey Keep and would be out of the fight. If he lost any NPCs, they died permanently. He should have taken steps to better protect his NPCs, and he shouldn't have allowed the majority of his players to log off simultaneously.

Arrogant and stupid.

"How am I going to do this with such a small force?" he murmured.

He had forty minions, and he was facing nearly 1,500 soldiers. Obviously, a straightforward attack was out of the question. There was also only so much his thieves could accomplish by killing the sleeping soldiers. A camp this large would still have some people moving around during the evening. It was only a matter of time before the thieves were discovered.

His fingers drummed against the rough bark of the branch he sat on, as his mind searched desperately for some strategy that didn't end in his death.

He knew that this was his chance to make a serious dent in the enemy forces. He needed to wipe out a sizable portion of the NPC army as quickly as possible before he was detected. If Jason could also slow the army by damaging supplies and vehicles, he could give his fledgling army another day to prepare. After this attack, Alexion likely wouldn't give Jason another opening. He would post better sentries and keep a force of players in-game to protect the camp.

This attack needs to be devastating. I also need to distract them somehow and take out the wagons that make up the corral.

A glimmer of a plan flashed through Jason's mind, causing a grin of anticipation to creep across his face. His plan probably wasn't going to work, but if it did...

He felt the familiar chill crawl up his spine and settle in his brain. It had been a while since he had a chance to see some combat. He hadn't realized until now how much he had missed it.

Maybe I am turning into a psychopath, he thought with a chuckle.

With a telepathic command, Jason moved his mage group to the north side of the camp. He then dropped from the tree, landing with a soft thump that would have even impressed Onyx. Jason began giving detailed instructions to his thieves and Night

Children.

The thieves would slip into the camp and kill as many as possible while they were asleep. Their orders were to work their way forward quickly from the southern edge of the camp and operate in pairs to reduce the chance that someone was left alive long enough to sound an alarm. They should be cautious but move quickly.

His Night Children were to sit in the trees on the eastern side of the camp where the player "camp" was located. Their job was to kill players as they logged back in. Jason expected that when his thieves were detected, an alarm would be sounded by the NPCs and the players would begin to log back in. If the Night Children could kill a few of the players while they were logging in and were disoriented, Jason could reduce some of the player population of the army. He also had an ulterior motive in using the Night Children on the players.

He wanted to scare the shit out of them.

Once he had his plan in place and his forces ready to attack, Jason climbed back into the tree. He would need a good line of sight on the battlefield, and the tree gave him a comfortable view of both camps. As he settled into position, Jason felt his heart race and his palms tingle. The icy chill behind his eyes seemed to freeze over. His eyes glowed darkly, as he readied himself for what was to come. It was time.

Alex is going to love this next part.

Without another thought, he commenced the attack.

Jason quickly cast *Curse of Silence* on one sentry after another on the southeastern edge of the camp. His thieves then took out the sentries in quick succession using well-placed arrows. After only a few minutes, the bodies of the sentries along the southern side of the clearing were all swiftly cooling in the chill night air. Not a whisper of an alert had been raised.

His thieves then moved forward and entered the camp. They darted from tent to tent in pairs, slaughtering the sleeping soldiers. The thieves wreaked havoc, their blades taking the lives of many sleeping soldiers. Jason expected that the large tents in the center of the NPC camp were where the camp's leaders slept. However, he wasn't concerned about taking out the NPC leaders, he just needed to whittle down their troops.

What use is a commander without anyone to command? He thought darkly, as the icy slush in his veins seemed to throb and pulse in time with his heartbeat.

The experience and damage numbers came raining in, and Jason disabled his notifications. He could review the detailed information after the fight, but right now it was just a distraction.

Jason kept a watchful eye on the eastern side of the clearing, where his Night Children hovered on the edge of the player encampment. They were still sitting in the trees and waiting to pounce. So far, he hadn't seen any motion from the players.

Unfortunately, the massacre in the NPC camp was short lived. One of his thieves was spotted, and a cry went up across the camp. Soldiers began to emerge from the tents and grab their weapons. Panicked shouts filled the air while the camp bustled with confused preparation.

Jason's eyes jumped back to the NPC camp. From where he sat in the tree, he watched the chaos. The camp now looked like a giant anthill, with the soldiers swarming to prepare themselves for battle. Since the threat had not yet been identified, the actions of the soldiers were uncertain and uncoordinated.

Lucky me. With the players logged out, the NPCs and I can have some quality time together.

He quickly ordered his thieves to retreat and move back to the tree line. Their shadowy forms danced through the tents and swiftly awakening guards. In the bedlam of the camp, many of his thieves made it out alive. However, as the ragged group approached the tree line, Jason noted that he was missing eight thieves.

Damn it! At least their sacrifice will help win this fight.

Jason began frantically raising zombies using the corpses in the tents on the southern edge of the camp. He chugged mana potions as he watched his mana plummet, but he tried to be conservative. His supply of potions wasn't endless.

The new zombies slowly stood up and joined the defenders that were starting to regroup and collect at the southern part of the camp. Some had lit torches, and the campfires gave off a dim light. However, the area was still not well lit, and long shadows were cast by the troops and tents. The soldiers didn't seem to notice that the dead walked among them. Jason managed to summon eight new zombies before he hit his Control Limit.

He ordered all of his thieves farther back into the woods, but he didn't retreat them back to the rearguard. Instead, they spread out and each climbed nearby trees, drawing their bows from their backs and nocking arrows.

Jason sent a short mental command to his zombie lieutenant. "Shock and awe," he whispered quietly.

Soon he could hear the guard zombies coming

through the woods, shouting with hoarse, mangled throats and clanging their swords against their shields. The army noticed the noise, and the NPC leaders ordered their troops into formation. They turned to face the southern tree line, clearly anticipating a zombie horde to descend upon them.

As the soldiers moved into formal ranks, Jason made certain that his newly formed zombies were evenly spread among them. He was visualizing the blast radius from each zombie, and a familiar grin was plastered on his face.

Then his rearguard began to emerge from the tree line at a run. They roared in defiance at the army. Jason could just barely see the commander near the back of the army. He was a tall man wearing steel armor. The man must have thought his army was being charged and panicked. He called for his troops to attack, and they rushed forward on his order.

Jason's grin transformed into a broad smile, and his eyes glowed. His mouth began forming ancient words in Veridian as his hands moved through a rhythmic series of gestures. Dark energy pooled and collected in front of Jason and then darted forward into the night.

Explosions rocked the army. Agonizing screams could be heard as the tightly packed soldiers were struck by the shrapnel from the exploded zombies, severing limbs and leaving ragged rents in the soldiers' armor and flesh. Dark energy radiated in concentric circles from the zombies that had infiltrated the enemy ranks and lashed at the troops. Where the dark energy struck, skin began to quickly rot and melt away from the NPCs' bones. The explosions caused confusion among the soldiers' lines. Between the darkness and the unanticipated attack, the troops were disoriented and not certain where to run.

Jason quickly ordered his rearguard back into the forest in case he needed to retreat. He noticed that some of the NPC soldiers continued running toward the forest and disappeared into the trees. He mentally ordered his thieves to begin picking them off with their arrows, reminding them to stay hidden in the trees. His rearguard was ordered to end the lives off any NPCs that made it past the thieves.

He started summoning more zombies using the new bodies littering the clearing, making certain to summon zombies at irregular intervals among the mass of troops. Jason was continuously chugging mana potions to keep up with the rapid casting. At this point, it didn't matter if the zombies were controlled or feral. He just needed to create more chaos.

From the soldiers' perspective, it appeared that they were being attacked by their own wounded comrades. Jason saw a fallen soldier latch onto another's leg, tearing at exposed flesh with its teeth. Another ran his former comrade through with his sword and then decapitated him in a fountain of blood. Throughout the field, feral zombies rose from the ground, their eyes shining a milky white. They rushed at their former teammates, their hands ripping at exposed throats and eyes. Their hungry screams filled the air.

The sudden attack within their own ranks turned confusion into complete chaos. The soldiers became so panicked that they started turning on each other, stabbing randomly at friend and foe alike. The field was a mass of bodies as the enemy army destroyed itself. Blood covered the ground and mixed with the dirt, covering the soldiers and zombies in a dark red paste, serving to further disguise the undead.

Casters within the NPC army tried to join the fight with bolts of flames and frost that rocketed into the field. Patches of frozen and smoldering ground quickly appeared amid the battlefield. This only added pandemonium since the casters couldn't distinguish the soldiers from the zombies. Jason saw more than one regular soldier engulfed in flame. Some casters tried vainly to heal the wounded that lay on the field, many of which were being crushed to death by the melee that was taking place above them.

The air was filled with the sounds of throaty roars from the zombies and screams of the wounded and dying. Metal clanged against shields as the troops fought among themselves. Over the cacophony of battle, the NPC leaders tried to shout orders to the troops.

Now for the next step.

With a telepathic command from Jason, fireballs ripped through the air on the northern side of the clearing. The balls of flame struck the wagons forming the corral for the army's animals, instantly igniting the wooden vehicles. He had given his fire mage one goal, burn as many of the wagons as possible. His exact words had actually been, "Set the whole damn camp on fire."

Towering flames began to grow on the northern side of the camp, illuminating the chaos that raged on the southern battlefield. The flames spread, jumping from the wagons to the tents. The animals screamed and reared with nowhere to run. Their burnt and bleeding corpses were soon added to the mounting body count. Meanwhile, Jason's fire mage relentlessly cast fireballs at anything that wasn't already on fire. He aimed for wagons, tents, and supplies. The flames cast long terrible shadows across the tents and soldiers, kicking up a thick smoke into the sky.

The NPC mages turned panicked eyes to the northern part of the camp. Ice mages rushed toward the flames and cast every area of effect spell in their arsenal, trying to dry to dampen the fire. One mage began casting a spell that created a torrential blizzard over part of the camp. While this slowed the flames, it also struck other NPC soldiers, leaving them trapped in place. A maelstrom of fire and ice now swirled above the camp.

Jason watched awestruck. The ice behind his eyes seemed to crystallize as he watched the scene unfold, and black bands of energy twisted and crawled up his arms. The energy began to peel away from his skin and lashed at the air hungrily.

I had hoped for a similar result, but this... this is madness.

As Jason continued summoning zombies with frantic effort, the enemy commander had finally found his horn and began blowing it repeatedly. Sluggishly, his troops retreated back into the interior of the camp. Once he had the troops safely between the tents, the NPC commander began to return them to order and recreate their lines. He gathered the ice mages and had them work in concert to put out the flames.

Yet he couldn't bring back the soldiers that had already been killed.

Jason glanced over at the player encampment and noticed that several players were beginning to re-enter the game. A multi-colored tear would appear in the air, followed by a popping sound as their bodies appeared in-game. It was almost comical to watch their heads turn as they arrived. The same confused expression would sweep over their faces as they witnessed the whirlwind of fire and ice swirling over the NPC camp and the gruesome melee in the southern part of the clearing.

Without hesitation, Jason ordered his Night Children into action, commanding them to focus on the players that entered the game near the edge of the woods. He realized he was about to have a lot of angry players in the area in a few minutes, and he would likely lose most or all of the Night Children. He could always raise more. Right now he needed to thin the player population of the army.

The Night Children fell from the trees along the edge of the player encampment like ghastly gray meteors. They landed on players that had been foolish enough to log off near the tree line.

The momentum of their free-falling, skeletal bodies allowed them to strike with terrible force. Their dagger-like fingers penetrated flesh and scraped across bone. In some cases, the power of their initial blows severed limbs and blood gushed from the gaping wounds. Once the nimble skeletons hit the ground, they began attacking with an uncanny ferocity.

The players let out shaky screams and cries for help as the Night Children wound their way through their ranks like miniature gray whirlwinds. The skeletons aimed for killing and crippling blows, leaping from player to player in a frenzy of bone and blood. Their small, agile bodies were gruesomely quick, and they performed acrobatic leaps, tumbles, and spins as they rampaged through the players' ranks. Their small bodies and dark coloring, combined with the disorientation of the new players entering the game world, made it difficult for the players to identify the threat.

Jason watched mesmerized as one Night Child

severed a player's hand with its claws. It spun quickly, slicing through another player's abdomen with its bladed elbow. Leaping onto a third player, it slashed at his exposed throat. The player let out a muffled gurgle, and a torrent of blood erupted from the wound. Not a drop touched the nimble Night Child, who had already moved to the next target.

He had given them careful instructions. Their goal was as much to scare the players as it was to kill them. If they couldn't kill a player, the Night Children tried to inflict crippling or maiming blows. A player likely wouldn't die from a severed hand, but the dull pain they felt and the trauma of losing a limb accomplished something more important.

Jason wanted to crush their spirit.

His dark eyes turned back to the NPC camp and noted the hundreds of dead and dying NPCs that littered the ground. Many had been gored or were missing limbs. The screams and calls of the injured filled the air and meshed with the sound of clanging metal.

He glanced back at the player camp and noted that some of his Night Children were beginning to fall as the players regrouped. Then a blinding flash of light erupted from within the player camp, and several of his Night Children disintegrated instantly.

Alexion had finally made his appearance.

A golden aura now appeared over the swiftly growing group of players. One brightly lit player was making its way at a run toward the NPC camp. Alexion was trying to move to help defend the NPC army. Little did he know that the battle was already over. The damage was done.

As the last skeleton body collapsed, Jason called a full retreat and pulled his remaining forces back into the dense forest. A vicious grin still lingered on his face, and black tattoos of energy crawled over his skin.

Your move Alex.

Chapter 28 - Massive

Riley walked slowly through the NPC camp, her eyes wide as she surveyed the destruction. Nearly two hours had passed since the "battle," and a haze of smoke still hung in the air. Wounded soldiers lined the rows of tents, lying on makeshift stretchers. Many moaned in pain and called out for a healer. She could see that a number of tents and wagons were either still smoldering or were covered in a thick layer of ice.

As she walked through the rows of tents, images of the battle she had witnessed in the player camp flashed through her mind.

She had been lucky.

Riley had been sitting at one of the campfires closer to the interior of the clearing when the gray skeletons dropped from the tree line. She had witnessed first-hand the destruction the skeletal nightmares had wreaked among the players. Riley had barely been able to follow their unnaturally swift gray forms as they wove their way through the players that popped into existence on the eastern side of the clearing. She had sat in numb amazement as she watched player after player butchered before her eyes.

Her thoughts were interrupted by the conversation of a group of nearby soldiers. They all looked exhausted after the battle, but they had survived with only small cuts and scratches. Others had not been nearly as fortunate. Many of the soldiers were younger men in either their late teens or early twenties. However, one of the soldiers was an older man in his late thirties. A deep, jagged scar ran vertically from his eye to his chin. In contrast to the horror-filled expressions of the younger men, his eyes shone with weary confidence.

"How many do you think there were?" one of the younger soldiers asked, his eyes still filled with fear.

Another young soldier sat on the ground, trembling slightly. His voice was shaky and uncertain. "There must have been hundreds. I-I've never seen anything like that before."

The older soldier eyed the two calmly. "I don't think there were many undead in that field. Maybe several dozen at most." He paused and then said thoughtfully, "I believe we were tricked..."

"What do you mean?" one of the younger soldiers asked with wide eyes.

The older soldier hesitated, and his eyes filled with sorrow. "I could be wrong. Gods help me, I hope I am. I think there were only a few zombies. My guess is that someone used the panic and chaos to trick us into killing each other. It must be this Jason that the travelers keep talking about." As he said this last part, he rubbed at his stubbled face tiredly.

One of the young soldiers looked back at the field of corpses that lay south of the camp. "Y-you mean we did that to ourselves?" His expression was filled with horror.

The older man looked evenly at the boy sitting before him and spoke carefully, "If I'm right, there was only one real enemy out there tonight and no one saw him."

The expressions on the younger soldiers' faces warred between terror and amazement. "What kind of demon could do this?" one of the soldiers murmured.

The older soldier looked back at the battlefield and shook his head sadly. "I don't know, but we should never have come here."

Riley started moving again. Was the weathered soldier right? Had Jason done this on his own? She walked to the southern part of the clearing and inspected the corpses. She noticed that most were human. She was only able to identify a few fallen zombies by their milky white eyes.

She knew she should be horrified by what she was seeing - what she had already seen over the last few hours.

A few weeks ago, she would likely have quit AO in disgust. Yet now she was filled with a strange curiosity. What kind of man could cause this much destruction on his own? If she was honest, a part of her was excited by the prospect of power she saw before her. It wasn't the raw strength of a warrior, but a certain insidious cunning and a willingness to do whatever it took to win.

"Could I become this strong?" a voice whispered in her head. The thought wormed its way into her mind and seemed to gestate there. She desperately wanted this strength. She needed it.

Her thoughts were interrupted by an incoming message from Alexion. He was commanding her to come to the administration tent in the center of the NPC camp. Anger boiled in her veins at Alexion's imperious order. Despite her irritation, she sullenly started heading towards the tent.

When Riley arrived, she found the NPC leadership and Alexion sitting around a large rectangular wooden table. The room was filled with NPCs and players discussing the massacre the night before. Riley assumed her familiar polite mask, taking a position along the edge of the tent with the other camp aides.

Alexion stood at one end of the table, his hands firmly planted on the wooden surface in front of him. His eyes scanned the room. "Can anyone tell me what happened last night?" His voice was terrifyingly calm.

Silence hung over the room.

Finally, one of the NPC commanders spoke up. He was a large man with graying hair. Scars riddled his face and arms. This was not his first battle, and he addressed Alexion without any hesitation in his voice, "Clearly, we were attacked. In spite of your spies' information and your carefree attitude a few hours ago, the undead decided to meet us in the field."

Alexion stared at the man, and Riley noted that his mask was beginning to crumble around the edges. "The undead army is still in the Twilight Throne," Alexion said, his voice ringing with confidence.

The NPC responded calmly, "And do your spies also happen to know where Jason is at this moment?"

A flash of doubt crossed Alexion's face before it resolved into a contemptuous expression. "Are you kidding me? Are you trying to say that one man caused this much damage?"

His cruel eyes drilled into the NPC commander. "You better hope that is not the case. Regent Strouse will not be happy to hear that you lost nearly four hundred of your men to one traveler."

The NPC commander chuckled softly. "Boy, I lead the soldiers pledged to this cause by House Tyrial. I don't lead this army - you do. You had best take your own advice. How exactly do you plan to explain this massacre?"

Riley was aware that each of the noble houses in Grey Keep had pledged troops to the army and sent their own commanders. These were the men sitting before them. Her gaze moved to Alexion, and she watched him closely. His eyes had gone dead and lifeless. An involuntary shiver ran up her back.

Alexion moved around the table to the NPC commander at a casual walk. "You had best use care in how you address your superior," Alexion said, his tone carrying deadly intent.

The man laughed again. "Or what? What do I have to fear from a young pup who pretends to be a wolf?"

As Alexion neared the man, his sword launched from its scabbard in a flash of steel. The blade sunk into the commander's throat with little resistance. The man's eyes widened in shock as a muffled gurgle left his lips. Blood bubbled around the wound. Alexion withdrew the blade and a burst of blood rushed from the open gash, splashing against the wood of the table. The other NPCs and players drew back in horror.

Alexion looked around the table and met the gaze of each NPC and player in the tent. His eyes glowed a brilliant gold, and his body seemed to glow. He spoke in an unnaturally calm voice, as though what he had just done was inconsequential. "I am the leader of this army, and my authority shall not be questioned."

When he was met with silence, his voice grew louder. "Have I made myself understood!?"

NPCs and players alike nodded in numb acknowledgment of his words. Their eyes darted between Alexion's face and the body of the former commander that had slumped to the floor, now lying in a pool of blood.

"Now," Alexion addressed the crowd before him. "I want the bodies burned. We will leave no corpses that can be turned against us. Then we continue to the Twilight Throne. Our mission has not changed. We need to send these undead back to their graves."

"Dismissed."

Riley stared at Alexion as he marched out of the tent. His mask had slipped completely, revealing the sadistic monster that lay beneath. As she watched him slay the NPC commander, she expected herself to recoil in horror. Instead, an errant thought popped into her mind.

"This isn't real power. He is weak."

They were still two in-game days away from the city, perhaps longer now that they needed to pile and burn the bodies. She didn't feel optimistic about their success in the coming battle.

A lot could happen in two days.

*　　　*　　　*

After Jason had pulled his forces deeper into the forest, he took a moment to regroup. He posted sentries in the trees around his makeshift camp and kept his undead on full alert.

He didn't know whether the NPCs and players

would give chase. Regardless, he expected that it would take them some time to douse the fires and regroup. Jason wasn't certain how many NPCs and players had died in the battle, but he anticipated that it was at least several hundred. He knew that they wouldn't just have to regroup, they would also have to deal with the many wounded that needed tending.

I doubt they will send a search party... not immediately at least.

Once Jason felt that the area was secure and that he was safe for the moment, he finally checked his combat log. He was immediately bombarded by a string of notifications.

x17 Level Up!
You have (85) undistributed stat points.

x2 Skill Rank Up: Summoning Mastery
Skill Level: Intermediate Level 4
Effect: 21% increased stats for summoned undead and 21% increase to effective Willpower for purposes of determining Control Limit.
Effect 2: You may now communicate with your minions telepathically. Distance limit unknown.

x3 Skill Rank Up: Leadership
Skill Level: Beginner Level 6
Effect: Minions and subjects will receive a 3.5% increase learning speed for skills.

x3 Skill Rank Up: Tactician
Skill Level: Beginner Level 6
Effect: 10% increased damage multiplier for a successful ambush or strategy (Currently,

Damage x 1.10).

x3 Skill Rank Up: Mana Mastery
Skill Level: Beginner Level 8
Effect: -4.5% to mana cost.

x3 Spell Rank Up: Specialized Zombie
Skill Level: Beginner Level 8
Effect: Increased skill proficiency retained by zombies. Skill cap Beginner Level 8.

x3 Spell Rank Up: Corpse Explosion
Skill Level: Intermediate Level 1
Effect: Increased damage (Currently 1.10 x Health).
Effect 2: 1% increased blast radius.

Honestly, I was expecting a few more levels.

After he had reviewed the battle in his head, the experience made sense. His minions had killed a reasonable number of soldiers at the beginning of the fight, but the bulk of the deaths were caused by friendly fire. He could still see the image of the chaotic battlefield, with soldiers stabbing zombies and teammates alike.

He also noticed that his *Corpse Explosion* had advanced to Intermediate Level 1. This was the second spell that had upgraded to the next rank. Upon reading the tooltip, Jason discovered that the skill had gained a second effect which increased the blast radius.

Looking through his combat log, he was surprised to discover that the player kills had provided experience. This was actually the first altercation he had been involved in where the players were a reasonably high level. If the player kills provided experience, then theoretically it was possible to level based solely on player-vs-player combat in AO.

Jason was now level 78. He decided to continue dumping points into *Willpower*, bringing him to 424. With his *Summoning Mastery* now at Intermediate Level 4, he had an effective *Willpower* of 513. This brought his Control Limit up to 51.

He decided to review his Character Status to see his current stats:

Character Status			
Name:	Jason	**Gender:**	Male
Level:	78	**Class:**	Necromancer
Race:	Human	**Alignment:**	Chaotic-Evil
Fame:	0	**Infamy:**	2200
Health:	495	**H-Regen:**	0.35 / Sec
Mana:	4735	**M-Regen:**	23.75 / Sec
Stamina	745	**S-Regen:**	3.6 / Sec
Strength:	12	**Dexterity:**	36
Vitality:	11	**Endurance:**	36
Intelligence:	22	**Willpower:**	429

Affinities			
Dark:	31%	**Light:**	4%
Fire:	3%	**Water:**	2%
Air:	3%	**Earth:**	2%

He was definitely getting stronger, but he wondered if it would be enough for the upcoming battle. His attack had been devastating, but there were likely still more than a thousand NPCs and players marching toward the Twilight Throne.

What was curious was that his dark affinity had increased by one percent. This must be what Morgan was alluding to during her explanation regarding the affinities. Likely acting on his need to protect the city and his desire to see combat had caused the increased dark affinity. Jason was surprised that he had gained a full percentage point, but perhaps the extreme lengths he had gone to in the last battle had some bearing on the size of the increase.

He noticed that his other affinities fluctuated over time. That must mean that acting on the behaviors associated with those affinities increased them. If he kept going with that line of reasoning, then acting contrary to the behavior associated with an affinity must lower it.

His musings were interrupted by soft purring, and he looked down to see Onyx weaving between his legs.

"Where the hell were you during the battle?" Jason asked the cat in irritation.

Onyx looked up at him with mocking eyes and yawned in an exaggerated fashion.

Jason sighed and shook his head. He had actually been a bit worried about the stupid cat when things had started going crazy during the fight.

Trying to figure out what to do next, he decided that he needed to watch Alexion's army and see how they would respond. After that, his next step would be to gather more minions and then harass the army on its way back to the city. If he could buy the city more time to prepare for the upcoming battle, that should increase their chances of winning this war.

His lieutenant zombie stood at attention before

him. As Jason looked him over, a thought occurred to him. It would take Alexion a few hours to get back on the road. His army would inevitably continue their march east toward the Twilight Throne. However, now that Jason had seen the size of the army, it was clear that it would be forced to spread out in a thin line along the roadway as it traveled forward. The woods on either side of the road were too dense to traverse easily.

Jason quickly gave the lieutenant some instructions before he left with the other eight guards and four mages. The group would circle back through the forest, keeping pace with the road on the northern side. Jason would follow after he had summoned his new minions. His group of fresh zombies would keep pace with the army on the southern side of the road.

Positioning the guards and mages on the northern side of the road would give him more opportunities to harass Alexion's army during the trip back to the Twilight Throne. A few rather gruesome ideas had already crossed Jason's mind about how he could kill off some soldiers and weaken the army's morale even further. His eyes darkened until they shone with an obsidian glow, and a grim smile curled his lips.

Rex was right when he said I don't like to fight fair.

Before he could break into an evil cackle (he might have been practicing), a thief entered the small encampment that Jason had set up.

It coughed violently, blood and phlegm spraying from its throat. It then looked at Jason with milky eyes and gave its report in a hoarse voice, "Master. The soldiers are gathering the bodies and are burning them in a large pit."

Well, shit! I was hoping they would just leave the

bodies.

His hands rubbed his face for a moment as he considered what to do. He really hadn't expected Alexion to be so clever. In fact, he was half expecting him to leave the bodies to rot in the clearing. After a moment of reflection, he realized that there were still some corpses he could salvage in the woods. Some Alexion's soldiers had run ahead of the main body of the army. They had been picked off by his thieves and guards, and it would be much harder for Alexion to send scouts out to find them. Especially if they thought the undead were still lingering nearby.

Not wanting to waste any time, Jason quickly ordered his remaining thieves to collect the bodies of the guards that had been killed in the woods and draw them farther back into the forest. He also urged them to be careful in case Alexion had laid any traps.

Then he sat down to wait.

A few uneventful hours later, Jason made his way back to the clearing. The army had continued down the road towards the Twilight Throne and had left several long trenches piled high with burning corpses. The trenches threw off a thick smoke and an unpleasant smell. Jason covered his mouth and nose with the hem of his cloak in a vain attempt to block out the stench. Normally the game muted his sense of smell, but apparently the AI controller had decided that hundreds of burning corpses should have some lasting impression on his digital nasal passages.

His thieves had already thoroughly inspected the area and concluded that there was no one nearby. Jason wasn't surprised, large pits of burning corpses weren't a pleasant sight to behold. Jason also expected that the pall of death that hung over this clearing probably had a demoralizing effect on the remaining soldiers. Alexion had likely concluded that he needed to continue moving to maintain morale and to keep his troops focused on the battle ahead.

Jason watched the burning flames mournfully.

So many wasted zombies!

Even Onyx looked sad as he sat beside Jason and stared at the flames.

His thieves had managed to recover about thirty corpses from the woods, but Jason had wanted to see what he could salvage from the camp before he started raising any zombies. It didn't look like there was much.

As he watched the burning pile, he noted that the bodies were burning quite slowly, and no bones had yet been revealed.

Wait!

An epiphany struck him, and he quickly cast *Custom Skeleton*. The world slowed to a standstill and took on an ethereal cast. The flames now lapped ever-so-slowly at the corpses. Jason could sense the bones that still resided within each of the burning bodies. As he saw their faint blue outlines through the flames, his excitement grew. The fires were intense, but it would take most of the day for the flames to eat through the flesh and fat before they destroyed the bones.

He began moving the bones gently out of the trenches. This caused the burning bodies to break apart and shift in a rather grotesque fashion, but he was left with a massive number of intact bones. Jason worked swiftly and soon stood next to the towering pile of assorted bones. He estimated that the tower of bone was ten feet tall and nearly twenty feet wide. Gathering all of the bones in the trenches had taken a couple hours, but it was worth it. He now had a respectable pile of building materials.

Onyx had taken the opportunity to scale the pile of bones. He sat at the crest of the tower and eyed Jason regally.

"Oh hail the mighty Bone Lord!" Jason said with a mock bow and a chuckle.

This drew an irritated expression from Onyx, and he quickly dropped down from the pile.

Now the question is what to do with all of these?

The Night Children had been effective but were exceedingly frail. He expected that there would be small skirmishes during the trip back to the city where their agile, gray bodies could prove useful.

However, the final battle at the Twilight Throne would involve direct confrontation. The Night Children would not hold up in a straight fight where the enemy saw them coming. Jason also wouldn't have time to come back to retrieve the bones. Anything he didn't use now would be wasted.

What type of minions do I need for the upcoming fight?

He leaned against a nearby tree and tapped his fingers against the bark as he thought.

It would need to be something that could take some damage without crumbling. Ideally, it would also be something that could break enemy lines and draw attention away from the Twilight Throne's fledgling army and his more fragile thieves and casters. Jason was positioned at the rear of Alexion's army so he would be able to flank them during the siege.

A basic form appeared in his mind's eye as excitement started to well inside of him. He experimented with the editor, and a form slowly took shape in the air in front of him.

It was a hulking skeleton, standing nearly eight feet tall. He needed the creature to be strong and durable, so Jason used multiple bones to form each extremity. The dark mana acted like glue and could bind several bones together. It wasn't as stable or durable as using a single, solid bone, but Jason's *Bone Crafting* skill wasn't high enough to merge the bones together.

The skeleton was simply massive. Its arms and legs were nearly a foot in diameter. Its spine was lined with large bone spikes, and Jason had created a tail that terminated in a spiked ball. He had to use a skull for the ball, and the effect was a bit terrifying. It had taken a couple tries to get the tail right – his goal being for it to be versatile, as well as intimidating. After some experimentation, he discovered that the using vertebrate from the spine gave it greater flexibility. Since the creature had begun to look like some kind of hulking lizardman skeleton, he adorned its reinforced skull with two vicious horns. Many of the bones were singed, causing the skeleton to appear almost entirely black.

For the creature's weapons, he welded together multiple shoulder blades into a towering sheet of bone. The shield was five feet tall and appeared to be created of bone scales. He connected the bone shield directly to the left arm, foregoing the need to build a hand. Jason then used bones from the forearm to create foot long spikes and attached them to the outside of the shield at regular intervals.

The creature's right arm from the elbow down was formed into a massive bone sword. Jason would have preferred to create a mace or axe since these weapons required less accuracy and relied more on brute force, but he wouldn't be able to make those weapons until his *Bone Crafting* skill increased. Fortunately, he was able to add an edge to the column of bone that formed the blade.

Once the bones were in place, Jason started imbuing the new skeleton with dark mana. Instead of focusing on reinforcing the joints, he imbued mana directly into the bones. After a couple of tests, he discovered that it greatly increased their durability. However, he didn't have sufficient mana to reinforce the whole skeleton, so he focused on the skeleton's weapon, shield, legs, head, and tail. He figured these areas would be struck the most often, and the large shield and tail would protect the interior bones and arms.

After a few trials, he stepped back and surveyed the finished version of the new skeleton. It was an intimidating sight and towered over Jason. He had the test skeleton strike a tree with its sword, tail, and shield several times to assess their durability. They were surprisingly resilient.

A grim smile lit Jason's face. He needed to conduct some combat testing to see what the new skeleton was capable of, didn't he? He raised three zombie soldiers and ordered them to attack the new skeleton. The resulting battle was almost comical.

The three zombies surrounded the skeleton in an attempt to flank the creature. The bone tail swept at the soldier at its rear, tripping it. The spiked ball at the end of the tail then hurtled downwards, striking the zombie soldier's head. The soldier's helmet crumpled, as its head was crushed with a splintering crack. Congealing blood leaked from the mangled helm and dripped onto the gray soil.

The other two soldiers had attacked the monster from the front, thinking that it was distracted. The skeleton charged forward with large, lumbering steps while it held its shield in front of it. The shield impacted one soldier, impaling it and lifting its body into the air.

The impact barely slowed the skeleton due to its weight, and it used its forward momentum to put additional force behind its sword as it swung at the remaining soldier. To his credit, the soldier managed to bring up his sword in time to block the blow.

Apparently, zombies didn't understand physics. The zombie soldier was sent hurtling backward by the force of the blow and slammed into a tree with a crunching noise before sinking to the ground. The skeleton showed no mercy and swiftly decapitated the incapacitated zombie. Then it turned back to Jason, ready for additional orders.

Onyx stood beside Jason. He kept glancing between the skeleton and Jason. Jason couldn't quite read the cat's expression, but it seemed to be something along the lines of, "Holy shit!"

"No kidding. That thing is ridiculous," Jason said in an awestruck voice.

Jason inspected the creature before him. The skeleton was level 85 and had nearly 3,000 health. Jason expected that his allocation of dark mana made the skeleton tough, but it lacked the raw damage of his Night Children. It had cleverly used its momentum and weight in the fight with the soldiers, but he expected that its normal strikes would carry less force. He also noticed that it was quite slow even at a full run, a downside of its weight.

As the last step, Jason needed to assign the new skeleton a name. However, his hand hesitated as it hovered over the control panel of the skeleton editor.

Onyx look up at him disdainfully. His expression said, "Just get on with it already!"

Jason scratched his head and stared at the sword and shield that the skeleton carried. It looked like some kind of demonic knight. An idea struck him, and he quickly typed in a name.

His new creature would be called a "Death Knight."

What was truly terrifying about the Death Knight was that it cost 2,500 mana to cast and required nearly thirty times the number of bones as his Night Children. After leveling, Jason's Control Limit had grown to fifty-one, and he could still summon thirty-one minions. However, the huge pile of bones beside him could only create twenty-five Death Knights. It would take thousands of corpses to make a sizable number of Death Knights!

"Damn game balance," he grumbled under his breath.

After he had made all of the Death Knights he could with his existing materials, he received a couple skill and spell level up notifications:

x3 Skill Rank Up: Bone Crafting
Skill Level: Beginner Level 7
Effect: Access to bone modification in the skeleton editor. May currently alter the composition of bone by 11%.

x2 Skill Rank Up: Custom Skeleton
Skill Level: Beginner Level 5
Effect: You may raise a custom skeleton using nearby bones. The skeleton's level is calculated as the caster's level + Willpower/73.

Once his Death Knights had been summoned, Jason ordered his thieves to retrieve the bodies of the soldiers. He raised an additional six soldiers, bringing him to his Control Limit. As he surveyed the remaining corpses, a thought occurred to him, and he ordered the thieves to load the extra bodies onto his Death Knights. They were each able to awkwardly carry a body using their forearms.

This was a fine solution as far as Jason was concerned. He was going to keep them far back from the road during the trip back to the Twilight Throne anyway. They made far too much noise.

The dark bodies of the Death Knights towered over the thieves and soldiers that stood before them. Jason admired his troops, eyes glowing darkly. With a new surge of confidence, he ordered his miniature army forward into the dark forest.

He had work to do.

Chapter 29 - Grotesque

Morale had fallen considerably since the attack on the camp two days ago. As Riley rode in the column towards the Twilight Throne, she noticed that both the players and NPCs continued to glance nervously at the darkness lining the sides of the road. They huddled towards the middle of the column, trying to stick together in anticipation of future attacks. Carrying a torch was now seen as an honor rather than an obligation amongst the soldiers.

If the attack on the camp had been bad, the next forty-eight hours were worse. The army had been constantly plagued by attacks. It wasn't just the constant fighting, but the way that the attacks were made. Jason never struck the same way twice, and his methods were a bit... unorthodox.

Riley's thoughts were interrupted by the conversation of two nearby NPC soldiers.

"Why the hell did we join up for this war?" asked a soldier in a gruff voice. The soldier appeared to be in his twenties, and dark circles hung under his eyes. Both he and the soldier beside him were making the journey on foot.

"Well, the money of course, but it isn't worth dying in this damned forest," said the other man in a bitter tone. He stood nearly seven feet tall, but his shoulders were bent under the weight of the pack he carried.

"I second that. This Jason is more ghost than man. First the massacre at the camp and then two days of constant attacks. To top it all off, no one has actually seen him!" the first soldier said, disbelief in his voice.

"That doesn't surprise me one bit. Jason's a clever one." The second soldier paused for a moment, lost in thought. "You remember that first attack when we got back on the road?"

The first soldier sighed and shook his head. "How could I forget? One of our own came running out of the woods screaming for help. I watched a group soldiers from House Auriel break off from the column to help the man." He shuddered slightly. "As soon as they made it to him, he just... exploded. Took out the whole group."

He hesitated, taking a deep breath before continuing. "The skin actually melted off their bodies and their... their parts were scattered everywhere. Alexion ordered me to gather the pieces and burn them..." He trailed off at this last part, as he relived the memory. His mouth twisted into a disgusted grimace.

The second soldier nodded solemnly. "And that isn't even the worst of it! Yesterday, a group was blown up as they passed over a stretch of road. They found pieces of armor and equipment lodged in the dirt. This demon buried the corpses in the road!"

The first soldier looked at him in shock. "I didn't hear that one. It must have happened further up the column." He looked at the ground beneath him nervously as though it might explode at any minute.

"Don't bother looking. It certainly didn't help the other group. I suggest you settle accounts with the gods. I pray every night. There's no telling who will be next," the second soldier said, shaking his head.

"The nights are a good time for praying. They are even worse than traveling down this death trap of a road," the first soldier said, as he spat on the ground.

"You aren't lying," responded the second soldier. "I don't dare to even get up to take a piss anymore. A few of my tent-mates haven't ever returned. Though it has seemed safer since they started digging the latrines right next to the tents."

"Except for the smell," the first soldier grumbled.

"Better to smell shit than eat it," the other rejoined with a dark chuckle.

The conversation between the guards was not surprising to Riley. She had witnessed many of the events they were describing. Since she had attended nearly all of the meetings between Alexion and the NPC commanders, she had a good sense of the army's actual losses.

Over the course of two days, they had lost an additional 150 NPCs and players, dropping the headcount of the army to approximately 950. Riley also knew that some of the players hadn't actually been killed. They had simply stopped logging back in as the constant attacks and darkness took its toll on morale. The game was simply too realistic; those that left couldn't handle the psychological war that Jason was so successfully waging.

The reaction among the players that stayed was surprising. Many couldn't decide whether they were angry or impressed. Jason was waging a guerrilla war in this forest, and he was clearly winning. Many of them were rapidly realizing that it wasn't a fluke that Jason had conquered Lux. In contrast, Alexion didn't seem to be able to offer much of a defense. The forest was too dense and too dark to try to pursue Jason or to allow Alexion to use his superior numbers effectively. The army was basically a sitting duck while they traveled down the road.

As she watched the reactions of the NPCs and players over the last two days, Riley had felt a change in herself. It was a hard feeling to pin down, but it was there. In spite of her anger, she felt more calm. More... cold. She had also become increasingly numb to Alex's abuse or his threats. With the cooling of her rage, she began to seriously question herself.

Why hadn't she told her parents about Alex's threats? Why had she let herself be browbeaten into collaborating with Alex's story at school? Why didn't she just fess up now?

The other part of her mind answered back scathingly, "It's because you were weak and afraid."

In the midst of her self-recrimination, her thoughts had focused on Jason. He fascinated her. On the long journey, she had sometimes pretended it was the Jason she knew. Riley tried to think of what she would say to him if she saw him again. Each time, she fumbled with the words. What could she say that would make what she had done any better?

She clutched at the reins tightly. There was nothing she could say that would make up for what she had done to Jason. She needed to act. Yet before she could help Jason, she needed to help herself. She needed to do something to escape Alex...

A call was raised from the soldiers at the front of the column. Riley couldn't see anything from her position in the middle of the army. As she made her way forward, she heard the whispering from the soldiers. They had reached the city.

Then the city's dark walls came into sight. Enormous blocks of obsidian stone towered over the army.

The dark iron gate that led into the city stood firmly closed. Billowing dark clouds hovered in the sky, casting a nearly impenetrable blanket of darkness over the field. Lightning arced between the clouds, an occasional bolt striking the ground as thunder peeled like the sound of cannon fire. In the brief flashes of light, Riley could see spiraled towers that stretched into the void-like expanse of the sky.

Alexion moved to the front of the column, sitting straight on his white horse. He began the words and gestures of a spell. As he finished casting, a bright light radiated from him in a blinding explosion. At that moment, Riley saw the throng of undead lining the walls of the city, watching the approaching army with milky, soulless eyes. Their bodies trembled, not in fear, but with eagerness at the prospect of the upcoming battle.

Riley felt a strange emotion overtake her. It was a tantalizing mixture of awe, fear, and excitement that momentarily expelled her sense of self-doubt. A shiver ran up her spine.

They had finally arrived at the Twilight Throne.

*　　*　　*

The last two days had gone exceedingly well.

Jason had managed to whittle down the remaining army with a series of small attacks and subterfuge. He had lost all of the soldiers he originally raised back at the camp and was forced to dip into the spare corpses that his Death Knights carried. However, he had been able to recover a few bodies from his attacks that he used to replenish his reserves.

He had also received several notifications during the past few days:

x3 Level Up!
You have (15) undistributed stat points.

x1 Skill Rank Up: Leadership

Skill Level: Beginner Level 7

Effect: Minions and subjects will receive a 4% increased learning speed for skills.

x2 Skill Rank Up: Tactician

Skill Level: Beginner Level 8

Effect: 12% increased damage multiplier for a successful ambush or strategy (Currently, Damage x 1.12).

x4 Skill Rank Up: Sneak

Skill Level: Beginner Level 7

Effect: -16% reduced visibility (reduced effect in direct light).

Cost: 2 stamina per second.

x3 Skill Rank Up: Night Vision

Skill Level: Beginner Level 10

Effect: 19% increased vision in darkness or near darkness.

x5 Skill Rank Up: Tracking

Skill Level: Beginner Level 6

Effect: 10% increased chance to pick up your target's trail.

Jason had hit level 81 during the two days of skirmishes, and he put the additional points into *Willpower* again. This brought him up to 444 *Willpower* or an effective 537 *Willpower* with his *Summoning Mastery*. This meant he could now summon a total of 53 minions at once.

He had gained surprisingly little experience even though he had observed a significant reduction in the size of the army. By carefully tracking his kills, he had begun to suspect that a decent number of the players were not logging back in each morning as the army continued down the road.

Acting on a hunch, Jason had sent two of his thieves behind him to scout one of the old campsites. When they returned, they reported that they had killed several players that had logged back in long after the army had left. This seemed to confirm Jason's suspicion of player attrition. His plan was working.

The diminished army had arrived at the city a few hours ago. Alexion had approached the Twilight Throne from the south gate with Jason close on his heels. As soon as they reached the city, Jason had sent one of his thieves to the north gate. He needed to tell Morgan, Jerry, and Rex that he was outside the city and had managed to substantially reduce the size of the enemy force. His best guess was that the army was now sitting at roughly 1,000 players and NPCs.

Jason sat in a tree south of the graveyard and watched the enemy camp.

Morgan failed to mention that a crucial part of being a successful Necromancer is a natural affinity for climbing trees, he thought wryly.

Ha! Climbing affinity! Maybe they will add a seventh magic school. Fear the power of parkour!

"I've really been alone in this forest for too long," he muttered under his breath.

Onyx just gave him another long-suffering look.

Alexion had posted sentries around the army's camp, but by now Jason's *Sneak* skill made him almost invisible in the impenetrable darkness of the forest. He had no trouble getting close. The torches the sentries carried just helped him spot them more easily. On the journey back, he and his thieves had taken turns taking potshots at the flaming targets each night. Unfortunately, Jason had also discovered that he was a terrible shot with a bow.

While he was waiting for the thief to return, Jason carefully examined the position of the enemy army. Alexion's force had made camp half a mile south of the walls near the graveyard. Jason hadn't focused on it before, but the graveyard seemed to be built in a natural clearing in the forest. The road continued south from the graveyard and then curved gradually west. The forest surrounding the area was dense and almost impenetrable.

To the north of the graveyard, the trees thinned considerably. Jason expected that the former, warm-blooded residents of the city had likely harvested many of the trees near the walls. The forest quickly gave way to cracked, gray dirt and the shriveled vegetation that was now common within range of the Twilight Throne's dark influence.

Jason watched as the NPC engineers began industriously cutting the trees in the forest to build siege engines. Jason expected that, in the interest of expediency, some developer had greatly simplified the construction process for siege weapons because the engineers had already made considerable progress in less than one in-game day. The siege engines would likely be completed later that evening, and then the fight would commence.

He could see that the engineers were constructing what appeared to be several large trebuchets, a battering ram, and two siege towers. Since he wasn't an expert on medieval siege equipment, Jason had to pull up the in-game console to find some reference pictures. The semi-translucent screen floated in front of him in the darkness as he did some quick research on the wooden structures the engineers were constructing.

In addition to the larger machines, Jason noticed that the engineers had built a number of ladders.

It looks like Alexion is planning to go both through the gate and over the walls simultaneously. Won't that spread his forces too thin?

Jason shook his head. Alexion may be intelligent, but that didn't mean he was an expert in siege warfare. Jason expected that these types of large-scale battles hadn't occurred during the beta. There had simply been too few players. Most likely this would change in the future. Jason doubted that the players would remain this clueless as the game progressed.

The trebuchets were being constructed a couple hundred feet north of the graveyard and closer to the city walls. A quick online search revealed that the range on a typical trebuchet was about three hundred yards. With some magical reinforcement, Jason was assuming that this range could be increased to something a bit more significant.

Good thing other players and NPCs can't see my cheat screen while I'm sitting in this tree, he thought with a grin.

He had sent his other thieves out to scout the woods for enemy troop movements. He was wondering if Alexion would try to strike the city at two different points simultaneously. The thieves had to be exceedingly careful, as the area was teeming with players and NPCs. The information that they returned with was fuzzy at best. From what Jason had gleaned from their reports, it looked like Alexion was keeping his troops near the graveyard.

Jason's surveillance of the enemy camp was suddenly interrupted by the return of the thief that he had sent into the city. More time had already passed than he was expecting. He hopped down from the tree and retreated farther back into the woods to hear his thief's report.

"Okay out with it," he ordered the thief. "What did they say?"

The thief coughed harshly, and phlegm and congealed blood spewed from its mouth. Jason sighed. Zombies could be disgusting.

"Master, I've reported to the Shadow Council. I told them that you had managed to reduce the size of Alexion's army and that you estimate his losses at approximately five hundred NPCs and travelers."

"Yes I know what *I* told you to say," Jason said impatiently. "What did *they* say?"

"After conveying the information as you ordered, Jerry asked me to give you a special message," the zombie replied. It then moved toward Jason at an unnaturally fast pace and puckered its decrepit lips.

"Oh god! Stop!" Jason forgot he was still standing near an enemy army as he backpedaled away from the zombie.

The zombie promptly ceased its attempt to kiss Jason and stood at attention.

"Damn Jerry," Jason grumbled.

Onyx looked at Jason with humor dancing in his eyes.

"Yeah sure you're amused when his bullshit is directed at me," he said to the cat.

Turning back to the zombie, he ordered it to finish its report.

After another harsh coughing fit, the zombie relayed the information Jason had been waiting for. "The army of the Twilight Throne has increased to approximately 480 soldiers or six divisions. Three are currently stationed at the south gate. The other three are stationed along the west, north, and east walls of the city in case Alexion tries to launch a surprise attack from another direction."

Hmm. Safe move on the council's part. However, 240 soldiers don't seem sufficient to hold a city from 1,000 players and NPCs. Those other three divisions are also going to be wasted during the fight.

"What am I going to do?" Jason asked aloud.

His primary goal should be to take out the trebuchets. Unfortunately, he expected that they would be heavily guarded. Alexion would probably anticipate an attack by Jason on such a vulnerable target. With Jason's hit and run tactics over the last few days, he probably didn't think Jason was capable of taking on more than a hundred soldiers in a direct confrontation, so maybe the defending force would be manageable.

Looking at the remainder of the siege weapons, Jason could visualize a rather spectacular charge on the walls. Alexion would have to commit most of his forces to the attack to be successful.

There isn't a way to avoid a direct confrontation this time.

As he thought about his options, a glimmer of a plan began to take shape. Jason grinned in anticipation. The tantalizing chill of his mana invaded his mind and swirled behind his eyes. He quickly beckoned three thieves over to him and gave them careful instructions. They bolted off into the darkness toward the city. Hopefully, the council could execute Jason's orders quickly.

All he could do now was wait.

Later that evening, the siege engines were completed, and Alexion's camp was alive with movement. It seemed the impending battle had reenergized the troops. Soldiers strapped on their armor and weapons, while archers strung their bows. The players adjusted their equipment one last time and checked their consumables. Many of the NPCs and players had rested during the "day" in anticipation of the fight so that they were ready for action.

The soldiers settled into ranks north of the graveyard facing the wall. The large siege towers sandwiched the neat columns of troops, and the battering ram was centered on the south gate. The soldiers were all heavily armored in mail. The front lines carried sturdy tower shields and spears while the troops near the rear worked together to carry the large ladders. A contingent of archers was positioned at the back. Jason could also see small groups of mages located in pockets among the soldiers. They were each assigned a group of shield-toting soldiers.

Probably healers and support casters.

A small encampment had been built further south of the army. The NPCs had constructed makeshift wooden walls around the trebuchets and had dug out the ground on the outside of the walls into a shallow ditch. Jason could also see a faint, glimmering globe encasing each trebuchet.

Alexion isn't taking any chances! Is that some kind of shield spell?

Alexion had committed a defensive force of approximately one hundred NPCs and players to guard the trebuchets. The soldiers stood outside the bulwarks that ringed the siege engines and faced south. The engineers hadn't had time to build larger fortifications. Mages and archers stood inside the hastily constructed defenses. Some of the mages appeared to be chanting and gesturing toward the wooden structures while others surveyed the woods south of the encampment.

Apparently, they know I'm coming, Jason thought dryly.

Alexion stood in the middle of his soldiers on the front lines facing the Twilight Throne. His location was obvious since he would occasionally cast a spell that produced a blinding radiance that illuminated the walls of the city. Jason recognized the spell. It was the same light magic that had taken out several of his Night Children. Alexion freely cast the spell while surrounded by his own troops, so perhaps its damage was based on alignment or affinity or possibly it only targeted enemies. What really puzzled Jason was the continuous way Alexion cast the spell. Either the spell cost no mana, or, more likely, Alexion was chugging mana potions continuously.

It must be nice to be made of money.

Jason was standing just south of the graveyard. He had quietly moved his entire force up beside him.

A total of fifty-three zombies and skeletons stood at his beck and call. As he looked over his small army, a sense of pride welled up inside of him. He had spent days cultivating this miniature force, and it had already destroyed nearly a third of an army.

His eyes panned back to the neat lines of soldiers and the heavily guarded trebuchets. His heart beat frantically as he considered what was coming. He involuntarily clenched his hands in anticipation. This was an all or nothing battle with a city hanging in the balance. A worm of doubt crept into Jason's mind.

Can I actually do this?

The image of the massacre in the market flashed through his mind. On its heels came the chaotic whirlwind of ice and flame that had swirled over Alexion's camp two nights before. In both cases, things had spiraled rapidly out of control. There had been some planning involved in each situation, but perhaps he had just been lucky.

He shook his head and looked past the army at the Twilight Throne. With his improved eyesight, he could see its cruelly spiraling towers reaching into the sky and the city's residents that lined the wall. It was a city that he had created from the ashes of his rage. It was filled with undead that he had given a second chance at life.

Yet the city represented something more to Jason. It represented a turning point in his life. It was the digital gauntlet he had thrown to the ground, challenging himself to become something more. He was done with hand-wringing. He would take what he wanted.

This was his city.

His resolve hardened, and his dark mana washed over his body like a breaking wave, cleansing his mind of doubt or hesitation. His eyes shown a resilient obsidian, as black tattoos of energy crawled over his body.

In this moment, Jason had only one desire.

"I am going to show them exactly what it means to fuck with *my* city."

Onyx eyed Jason carefully, and a strange expression flitted across his feline face. He looked proud.

Jason's dark eyes watched the army that was readying to attack his city. His hands clenched in anticipation. His doubt had been quickly replaced by growing excitement, and his mana pulsed in time with his rapidly beating heart.

An eerie silence hung in the air as the two armies eyed one another. Jason could feel the rising, almost palpable tension that hung over the field.

Another explosion of light ripped through the darkness that hung over the field, and Alexion's shouted words broke the silence. From this distance, Jason couldn't hear what he was saying, but he imagined it was some rant about how they were there to slay the evil undead.

Blah blah blah. "I'm an asshole that rolled a lighthouse as my class." Just get on with it already!

Jason glanced over and saw that Onyx was also glaring in irritation at Alexion.

He murmured to the cat, "Make certain you stay back. You don't want to be caught in what's coming next." Onyx looked at him incredulously before nodding ever-so-slightly.

Did the cat really just nod at me?

Jason shook his head. He was imagining things again. He had been spent a *lot* of time alone in the woods.

He turned his attention back to Alexion's army. As the human strobe light finished his inane speech, a deafening cheer came from the army, and they stomped their boots rhythmically. The vibration could be felt through the ground all the way to where Jason sat.

After a moment, the roar of the soldiers began to fade. A mischievous grin curled Jason's lips. His instructions to the council had been quite clear.

The army of undead that lined the walls of the city stood in utter silence. They showed no reaction to the roars of Alexion's soldiers and they didn't make a sound. They simply stood there, impassively gazing at the army before their gates.

As the silence lengthened, Alexion's troops began to shift nervously. The bottomless quiet drove home the point that no amount of shouting could have accomplished; the army they faced wasn't human. This army was already dead. They didn't feel pain, and they didn't relent. They lived in darkness. In silence.

As time stretched on, the troops' anxiety noticeably increased. They recalled the unsettling attacks and endless darkness of their trip. Many glanced nervously to the edges of the tree line to the east and west of the gate as though they were about to be attacked.

Jason's felt his dark mana pulse in time with his heartbeat as he watched Alexion's army. His campaign of psychological warfare was starting to pay dividends.

Alexion tried to recover his army's morale and cast his protection buff. The soldiers near him glowed a faint gold that illuminated the area around them. A faint cheer went up among the troops as Alexion let off one more blinding explosion of light.

"Charge," screamed Alexion, as he raced forward toward the wall.

I have to give him some credit for leading the charge, Jason thought grudgingly.

The army moved forward, first at a lumbering pace, and then at a trot. They approached the walls with ladders and shields raised. Desperate shouts were torn from their throats as they threw their lives at the dark stone wall. The battering ram lumbered forward, protected by a cadre of mages that cast defensive shields around it to protect it from arrows and spells. The siege towers creaked and groaned as they rolled toward the walls where the undead army waited.

As the approaching army neared, the undead finally acted. Vile curses, bolts of darkness, and arrows rained down on the approaching troops. Many soldiers perished under the hail of spells and bolts. Screams could be heard amidst the shouts of the soldiers as many fell to the ground, wounded and bleeding. Yet Jason observed that the glowing soldiers near Alexion, and the shining knight himself, seemed almost immune to the spells as they nobly raced forward on the leading edge of soldiers.

Jason turned his attention away from the attack. He had his own work to do. Without any fanfare or speeches, he moved his minions forward. He needed to destroy those trebuchets quickly before they caused too much damage.

The trebuchets were located northeast of the graveyard, and Jason moved his undead soldiers and Death Knights north along the western edge of the graveyard. The group hugged the walls of the cemetery, trying to keep out of the line of sight of the enemy's sentries. Once he was in place near the northern side of the graveyard, he moved his Death Knights forward and positioned his guards behind them. The large bone shields would provide cover during the charge.

He kept the remaining five thieves for himself, and the stealthy group quietly scaled the wall to the cemetery. They retreated to the interior of the graveyard, Jason perching in *Sneak* on top of one of the tombs near the northeastern edge of the graveyard. He would have a good view of the battle from here and would be able to cast curses unnoticed.

His thieves crouched around the tomb, keeping an eye on the graveyard.

In spite of his orders, Jason looked down and found Onyx sitting quietly beside him. He glared at the cat in irritation.

Onyx gaze met his levelly. He seemed to be saying, "Did you really think I was going to miss this?"

Shaking his head, Jason turned his gaze back to the field. He could only hope that the cat stayed out of harm's way.

He had sent his fire mage and two thieves around the other side of the cemetery so that they could flank the trebuchet from the south. All three were ordered to maintain *Sneak* until the defenders were distracted and the protective shields that glimmered around the siege engines were down. Then his fire mage would do what he did best - set those damn things on fire.

All of this took mere minutes as Alexion's main force attacked the walls. Jason spared a brief glance at the attack on the city and noted that the siege engines were moving into position. The undead hadn't managed to penetrate the shields guarding the siege weapons. His eyes moved back to the trebuchets, and he saw that they were winding up for an attack on the walls.

Damn it.

Without hesitation, Jason attacked.

His Death Knights rounded the northern corner of the cemetery and made a lumbering sprint toward the trebuchets from the west, their bone tails swinging from side to side. They were followed closely by the troop of guards and soldiers, who huddled behind their bulky forms. In total, this force consisted of over forty minions.

The NPCs and players immediately spotted the group of charging undead. Their eyes widened in surprise. Some of the soldiers took several involuntary steps backward as they saw the lumbering, dark giants race towards them. The ground trembled as the small group of undead rushed forward, a testament to the massive bulk of the Death Knights.

Icy claws dug into Jason's mind, and the chill cascaded through his body. This is what he had been waiting for. Why had he been so anxious? They were going to pay with their lives for messing with his city.

Jason troops sprinted across the short distance to the makeshift bulwarks. Spells and arrows rained on his Death Knights and struck the reinforced bone shields with little effect. As they saw how little damage was caused by their attacks, the defenders began to panic. The soldiers on the front lines had stepped back until their backs pressed against the wooden walls. Several soldiers tried to desperately scale the wooden bulwark.

Then his Death Knights collided with the group of soldiers.

The damage was fantastic. Soldiers were impaled on spiked bone shields; others were sent flying from the force of the collision. The momentum of the charge caused the bone swords to strike with deadly force. The men that didn't die from the initial blows were thrown backward violently, their bodies striking the wooden wall with a sickening crunch.

Jason watched, mesmerized, as a Death Knight gored a soldier with its horns and then severed another soldier's arm with its sword. Their bone tails whipped through the air, striking helmets and exposed limbs with loud, splintering cracks. His Death Knights were truly awesome to behold.

As the soldiers panicked and screamed in pain, an evil grin was painted on Jason's face. Blood soon drenched his Death Knights as they continued their rampage. They had accomplished Jason's primary goal. The Death Knights had successfully cleaved a hole in the enemy defensive line.

Perfect.

Jason ordered the guards out from behind the Death Knights. They slid through the opening in the formation created by their skeletal brothers and started scaling the bulwark. Soon they were sitting inside the walls among the casters. Evil grins appeared on the faces of each zombie as they raced toward the trembling mages. As the first two soldiers reached the caster group, Jason completed the arcane words and gestures of a *Corpse Explosion.*

The first few mages were blown apart by the resulting blast, throwing up a cloud of blood and viscera. Dark energy and shrapnel flew through the air. Casters were struck by the aftershocks of the spells, their screams filling the air as their flesh melted and the shrapnel pierced their bodies. The remaining soldiers followed closely behind the explosion and wreaked havoc amongst the remaining disoriented mages.

Jason turned his attention back to the Death Knights and saw that they were being swarmed by the NPCs and players outside the wall. In spite of how fearsome they were, they were attacking a force that was more than twice their size. Jason quickly cast *Curse of Weakness* as fast as he could on the remaining soldiers. Several of his Death Knights crumbled, and the health of many more was beginning to red-line. Yet the battle was swaying in Jason's favor.

As the soldiers finished off the last of the mages, the glimmer of the protective shield faded. Jason acted immediately when he saw the shield fade, telepathically ordering his fire mage into action. Fireballs rushed through the air and struck the exposed trebuchets. Soon the siege engines were turned into roaring pillars of flame. In the glow of the growing flames, the blood-soaked and blackened Death Knights stood over the bodies of the fallen soldiers, roaring their triumph into the night.

Jason eyed the dead soldiers and mages that littered the ground. Maybe he could win this after all.

Yet in that brief moment of victory, Jason heard a roar from the eastern tree line. Glancing up quickly, he saw players and NPCs rushing from the trees, flanking his remaining Death Knights and zombies. His minions' health was low, and the charge alone would take out many of them.

Jason's eyes widened in alarm.

That tricky asshole! He ambushed me!

Jason growled softly and chugged another mana potion. He was running out. He began summoning another zombie and then hesitated. Doubt swept over his mind and carried with it a hint of despair. What could he do? Had he been outplayed?

He watched as the front line of the enemy force struck his already weakened Death Knights, as the skeletons tried to turn to meet their new foe. Bolts of ice, fire, and light raced through the air toward his minions. Almost in slow motion, Jason witnessed bones begin to crumble and rotten flesh torn open. Before his eyes, his lieutenant zombie was decapitated with a single swing.

Was this it? Would he lose all of his creations?

Anger welled inside Jason, cold and explosive. It seemed to rise from his core and bands of dark energy wove around his body in erratic spasms. They were destroying the minions he had spent days and weeks building. His army! His vision blurred for a moment, and then his hands were forming gestures that he already knew by heart.

The world around him slowed and took on an otherworldly cast. He could see a sword about to strike one of the Death Knights. A fireball hung in mid-air as it was about to ignite one of his zombies.

They dared to destroy his minions! Something buried deep inside Jason snapped, and he lost control.

He would make them pay!

He could see ALL of the bones around him. The graveyard glowed a fluorescent blue. His gaze turned to the area around the trebuchets. He could see the bones inside the dead NPCs and players. Then he saw his Death Knights. They glowed a blinding blue. If they were already lost, then he could use them to get his revenge.

In his desperation, he *pulled.*

His Death Knights were simultaneously torn apart at the seams. A shower of thousands of bones filled the air. The bodies of his remaining zombies and the enemy soldiers that lay on the field were ripped apart in an explosion of blood as bones burst from their bodies. The cascading showers of red seemed to hang in the air under the effect of the time compression, as the cloud of bones raced towards Jason at a frightening speed.

It wasn't enough. He needed more.

He looked down at the graveyard, and he *pulled* again.

The ground erupted in a shower of dirt and debris, as the bones forced their way out of the earth. Soon a swirling vortex of bones surrounded Jason as he stood on the tomb. The cloud was so dense that it blocked out the sight of the field.

He began to build.

His hands darted over the editor with an almost unnatural speed as tendrils of dark mana lanced around him, lashing angrily at the air. He would create something that would destroy the force that had dared to threaten his city.

How dare they destroy my creations!

This new skeleton was fueled by the bones of more than a thousand corpses and the cold rage that flowed through Jason's veins. His fingers sped across the control interface.

Faster. I must go faster.

And then... he was finished.

He slammed his fist down on the button accepting the final form of his new creation. The world resolved back into motion. His mind ached and groaned under the strain. The coldness that flowed through his veins throbbed and pulsed. Undulating waves of dark energy cascaded from him.

NPC soldiers stumbled in mid-swing as their blows connected with air. Bolts of energy whizzed past the graveyard, striking trees and earth across the field. The players and NPCs in the ambushing force stood for a moment in confused silence.

A blood-curdling roar resounded across the battlefield. It wasn't human, and it carried a ravenous, desperate hunger.

The eyes of the NPCs and players turned to the source of the sound.

A hulking demon made of bone stood before them. The twin black holes that were its eyes surveyed the players and NPCs who stood before it as a wicked grin contorted the bones of its face. It flexed its new body in a crescendo of cracks and snaps as it examined its new form.

The demon stood nearly fifteen feet tall. Its head was two feet across, with spiraling horns of bone jutting from its forehead. Its body and limbs were composed of intricate, interweaving layers of bone that were three feet thick. A long, sinuous tail flowed from its back, terminating in a wicked, bladed spike three feet long. Enormous bone spikes protruded from its shoulder blades like ivory wings.

In its hands, the demon held a twelve-foot-tall scythe that it twirled with casual, deadly ease. Its soulless eyes turned to the group that had ambushed Jason's minions. These were the enemies that had destroyed its brothers. It could feel its creator's singular desire. The demon roared with bestial fury at the group of NPCs and soldiers.

Jason had spent every point of mana he had left on this creation. His head throbbed painfully, and his body trembled. Unable to stand, he dropped to his knees on the roof of the tomb, hands clutching his head.

He looked up, and his obsidian eyes met the demon's. "Kill them. Kill them all," he croaked.

The demon turned back to the players and NPCs, its soulless eyes surveying the enemies that stood before it. It launched forward at a terrifying speed, leaning into the charge as its bone tail whipped through the air behind it. Where its feet landed, large indentations were left in the ground. It roared again and swung its scythe back as it charged toward the enemy players.

The front line of players and NPCs wavered at the demon's charge. Then they broke. They couldn't maintain their composure in the face of the bone demon that rushed at them, and many turned to run.

It was already too late.

The scythe struck in a powerful arcing blow that carried the full momentum of the demon's charge. The air rippled as the blade sliced through the air. Several soldiers and players were immediately ripped in half by the strike. A torrential shower of blood rained on the remaining NPCs and players as they tried frantically to back away from the demon. Many soldiers lay on the ground, staring at the gruesome spectacle in front of them. Screams filled the night air as the demon's madly smiling face gazed upon the future corpses before it.

The demon showed absolutely no mercy or restraint, attacking with wild abandon. It lifted an NPC with its free hand and threw his screaming body across the field. Jason watched as it tore another player's head from its shoulders with its bleached teeth. It stomped on the wounded and swung its scythe in a whirlwind of death.

The undead on the walls watched in awe as the bone demon rampaged among the enemy force in the distance. This was the true power of the dark. A roar erupted from the undead, filled with hoarse bloodlust. The invaders would die for attacking their city!

As Jason's mind and body began to settle, he noticed that the battle between the demon and the ambushing force was not completely one-sided. While intimidating, the demon wasn't invincible, and some of the soldiers and mages had managed to land solid blows against its bleached bones. Jason watched nervously as his creature's health fell. Yet the victory still went to Jason.

Soon the demon stood amidst the bodies of the dead, next to the burning trebuchets. The flames illuminated its demonic form. Its body was painted red with the blood of the fallen while its face was twisted into a grotesque grin. It slowly turned its head and looked at the army attacking the walls of the city. There were more enemies weren't there?

Jason shook himself and jumped off the crypt he was standing on. He needed to move quickly. In his rage, he at least had the foresight not to destroy his thieves or his mages. However, he no longer had any soldiers or guards.

He scaled the wall to the graveyard and then gulped his last mana potion before summoning a new group of guards. He had them pick up the equipment of their fallen comrades. This would be a new group of kamikazes.

His bone demon and hastily summoned guards turned toward the army attacking the walls of the Twilight Throne.

"I won't let them take the city," Jason declared quietly amidst the screams of battle.

Chapter 30 - Cathartic

Riley stood near the back of Alexion's army, watching the chaos swirl around her.

Screams and the ringing of metal filled the air as the army rushed the walls with ladders and siege engines. She could see dark bolts of energy rain down on Alexion's troops, some ravaging flesh and others bouncing harmlessly off of the magic barriers covering the siege weapons. Insidious curses struck players and NPCs, spreading corruption throughout their bodies.

The army retaliated with fireballs that exploded on the ramparts in technicolor displays that ignited the undead that were defending the city. A hail of arrows continuously streaked towards the defenders on the wall, striking decayed flesh. Every so often, an undead defender would fall from the wall, its rotten body landing amid the soldiers and players.

Riley stood motionless in a sea of movement and noise as she watched the gruesome spectacle unfold before her. She was unsure of what to do or how to act. She was reluctant to pull free her bow and help Alexion, but she also knew that she couldn't just turn on Alexion and his army. They would kill her.

So she did nothing. As always.

Alexion stood near the front of the army, his body and eyes aglow with holy energy. Coiling golden bands of light wound their way across his body, his shining steel armor reflecting the glow. Every so often, Alexion released a radiant explosion that illuminated the field. He stretched his arm toward the defenders on the wall, and a beam of light streaked from his hand. Where the ray struck, undead shriveled and fell from the wall. He looked like a noble hero out of some movie, leading the charge against a city of evil.

Anger seethed in Riley's veins as she watched Alexion. He was no hero. He fought this war under the thin guise of "defeating evil" simply to increase his own power within the game. She also knew that below the mask of a man lay a broken, sadistic creature.

Her awareness of Alexion's weakness only served to further emphasize her own. How could she have succumbed to someone like that? The answer stared her in the face. She had no one to blame but herself.

She had let Alex force her to participate in this charade as his girlfriend. She had let him assault Jason and get him expelled. She had let him force her into playing this game and participating in this meaningless war. Her anger twisted and churned in her stomach like a living thing.

Suddenly, an ear-shattering roar filled the night air and Riley turned.

Her eyes widened as she witnessed the gigantic demon of bone that stood behind Alexion's army. It towered over the men before it, and its bone tail lashed the air. Its body contorted and cracked as it stretched its new limbs experimentally. In its hands, the demon held a titanic scythe that emitted a malevolent hum as the demon twirled it through the air.

"Did Jason summon this?" she murmured, her voice lost in the deafening sounds of the battle that raged around her.

She watched in stunned silence as the demon charged toward a group of NPCs and soldiers who were running in the direction of the burning trebuchets. She should be petrified with fear as she watched the scythe descend on Alexion's troops, but she was mesmerized by the sight.

The bone demon rampaged through the group of soldiers in a frenzy. She could hear the screams of the dying even from this distance. The demon's scythe severed limbs with casual ease and fresh blood painted its bleached, white body a mottled red. Her eyes widened in shock as she saw the bone demon grab a player with his free hand and crush the screaming man's head.

Then the demon stood alone among a pile of corpses. The burning light of the trebuchets illuminated its fearsome figure, casting long shadows behind the creature. The demon raised its head to the night and released another bloodcurdling roar. This roar was filled with a desperate hunger.

As she watched the demon, Riley could feel something snap inside of her.

"This is real power," she murmured. "The power to stand before someone stronger than yourself; to relentlessly pursue a goal by any means necessary."

"Jason wouldn't stand here and let Alexion force him to bow before him. He isn't!"

She hesitated, and then her hands clenched into fists. "I want that power."

"I want to be strong enough to stand against Alex and to fix what I've done. I want to be strong enough that no one can do what Alex has done to me ever again."

Her mind was overcome with emotion as all of the anger, shame, and guilt welled up inside of her. She turned her head to the sky and released all of those emotions into a single cry that rang across the chaos of the battle that swirled around her.

"I won't take it anymore!"

As she screamed these words, the molten anger inside her turned frigid and seemed to curl and coil its way up her spine. A tantalizing icy chill settled behind her eyes, and an eerie calm overcame her. Her rage was still there but bottled and controlled. It offered her a clarity of thought she had never felt before.

Unknown to Riley, dark energy coiled and swam over her skin like dark tattoos. Her eyes radiated a dark, unholy power as she gazed at the bone demon.

"My time as his slave is over," she whispered.

For a brief moment, she thought she heard the chuckle of an old man.

*   *   *

Jason's surveyed Alexion's army.

He was standing at the western tree line in *Sneak*, surrounded by his thieves and mages. The NPCs and players were already committed to the siege and hadn't tried to move back to the help the force at the trebuchets. Jason's bone demon stood by the flaming siege engines, as newly summoned zombies hastily strapped scrap armor and weapons to themselves and each other.

Jason could feel the seconds tick by as the army assaulted the Twilight Throne. The siege towers had almost moved into position and would soon be unloading troops upon the walls. Soldiers carrying ladders made it to the wall, while others were already beginning the fateful climb. At the same time, the battering ram had moved into position at the gate. Jason assumed that there were still nearly eight hundred soldiers attacking the swiftly shrinking number of defenders on the wall.

Shit. I better move fast.

His gaze moved back to his bone demon. It was currently surrounded by eight kamikazes. The demon was at roughly half health, and Jason doubted it would survive another direct charge. He would need to distract the soldiers and players in the main army, or the demon would be overwhelmed.

As Jason watched the skeletal horror tower over the kamikazes, he had a moment of inspiration. A familiar cruel grin curled his lips as he planned what he was about to do.

He gave the order to his bone demon. An equally wicked smile contorted the monstrosity's face, causing a crescendo of cracking bones. It seemed to approve of Jason's plan. The bone demon began a slow jog toward the army with the kamikazes keeping pace beside it.

As the demon neared the soldiers, it reached down with its free hand and grabbed a kamikaze. It then hurled the zombie forward into the mass of enemy troops. As soon as the zombie left his hand, the demon grabbed the next in line. After a few moments, many bloated zombies were hurtling through the air toward the enemy forces. The demon had thrown the zombies in a rough fan towards the rear line of the army.

Jason's hands began forming hasty gestures as his lips mouthed arcane words. Shadows pooled around him and then leaped forward into the field. As each zombie crested the heads of the soldiers, its body exploded in a barrage of shrapnel and dark mana. Many soldiers were blown apart by the explosions. The position of the corpses above the troops also widened the damage radius of the shrapnel and caused shards of metal to rain down on the heads of the NPCs and players.

And now I've brought zombie hand grenades to AO!

The staggered explosions rocked the back of Alexion's army. Blood and rotten flesh pooled on the ground, as many of the soldiers were ripped apart. Some of the troops that had escaped death howled in pain, while the rest were left stunned and uncertain of what had just happened.

Before the soldiers could recover, the demon appeared in their midst. Its form towered over the soldiers, and fresh blood still dripped from its scythe. Its manically smiling face stared at the soon to be departed.

The demon struck the rear line of the army like

a freight train. The bone demon waded among the disoriented and confused troops, swinging its scythe in huge swathes. Bodies were sent flying, and men cried out for help. Between the explosion and the demon's killing spree, some of the soldiers and players panicked, scrambling away desperately.

Dozens of enemy soldiers had fallen under the combined *Corpse Explosions* and the bone demon's fury. The pain filled screams of the soldiers rang through the air, overcoming the sounds of weapons clashing. The back line of Alexion's army seemed to buckle under the attack and nearly broke.

Jason watched the battle carefully. His mana was nearly empty, and he was out of potions. He kept a close eye on his mana as his regen tried frantically to refill his massive, empty mana pool. The bar refilled ever-so-slowly as he watched the fight unfold.

Suddenly, Jason noticed a commotion from the front of the enemy force. A golden glow weaved its way to the back of the army. The sea of enemy soldiers parted before the shining aura. Jason felt a wave of excitement and anticipation grip him.

Alexion is coming.

Jason grinned, and he felt like ice was forming in his veins. His mind and body were still tired from summoning the bone demon in a rushed frenzy, but he still felt the familiar coldness curl in his mind. His hands tingled as they clutched at his weapons. His anger had dulled over the last couple weeks that he had spent in the game, yet he still relished the opportunity to see Alex's character eviscerated by his demon.

This is my chance to finally pay Alex back.

Alexion soon emerged from the back of his troops, glowing with holy light. His eyes were globes of liquid gold, and his armor shone brightly even in the darkness and gloom surrounding the Twilight Throne. As Alexion broke through the line of troops, he surveyed the bone demon and took in the gruesome spectacle before him. Momentary shock swept over his face.

The bone demon had been killing the troops in large numbers. Its bones were dyed red with blood, which only made the creature appear more demonic in the flickering torch light and occasional flashes of spells. It stood among the corpses of dozens of soldiers. When it caught sight of Alexion, the demon held its dripping scythe aloft and roared with bestial fury.

Alexion quickly regained his composure and raised his sword, pointing it at the bone demon. "Grey Keep will purge the evil that is this kingdom. You will fall by my sword demon!"

Idiot. I hope he will keep spouting that bullshit for a moment longer while I get my thieves in position.

Jason took advantage of Alexion's monologue, ordering his four thieves to activate *Sneak* and flank him. They swiftly approached Alexion's position, moving stealthily through the ranks of soldiers that were focused on the demon. Jason muttered a silent prayer that this would work. The thieves and bone demon were the only viable minions he had left besides the four mages. He was running out of options.

Alexion motioned to his troops behind him. "We fight for the honor of Grey Keep and no evil can stand in our way. Raise your arms men. We fight or we die tonight for the good of this world!" The soldiers around Alexion mustered a lukewarm cheer, as they stared at the menacing demon before them.

The bone demon stood impassively in front of

Alexion during his speech. It looked down at him with scorn written across its bony features. The bones around its face crackled and crunched as it formed a grotesque grin. Then it lifted its head and roared again into the night sky. Its roar was greeted by flashes of lightning within the roiling black clouds that hung above the field. A bolt of lightning struck the ground between the demon and Alexion, momentarily blinding the enemy forces.

At this moment, the bone demon rushed forward, and Jason's thieves struck.

However, the effect wasn't what Jason was expecting.

Alexion exploded in golden light, revealing and injuring Jason's thieves. The golden blast didn't slow the bone demon, but Jason saw that a chunk of its health had been shaved away.

Frantically, Jason urged his thieves in closer and repeatedly cast *Corpse Explosion* with the mana he had managed to regen. The blasts did little damage since the thieves had lost a considerable amount of health from Alexion's attack. However, the blasts staggered Alexion as the scythe of the bone demon descended upon him. Unable to dodge the blow, the blade connected solidly with Alexion's ribs and sent him hurtling back into his troops, scattering them like bowling pins.

A moment of silence fell over the field as all eyes watched Alexion's prone form with bated breath. He lay on the ground for a moment and then groaned. He slowly pulled himself to his feet and coughed up blood onto his mailed hand. A large dent had been formed in his steel breastplate. Then he looked back at the bone demon, a dead, almost emotionless, expression on his face.

"I didn't want to have to do this, but you've

forced my hand," he muttered.

Not so eloquent now are you, asshole? Jason thought with a smile.

Alexion's free hand moved in a complicated pattern as he began chanting in a low voice. Golden globes appeared in the air around him, their number growing rapidly as the spell continued. The orbs spiraled around Alexion and then contracted in on his sword. As he completed the spell, his sword erupted in a golden flame and doubled in size. He was left holding an enormous flaming greatsword that flickered with holy light.

The knight turned back to the demon, brandishing his flaming sword with both hands. Alexion's eyes glowed a brilliant gold and light spun around his steel-clad body in glowing bands. "Now let's see how well you stand against this, you undead fiend."

As he finished speaking, Alexion rushed forward and engaged in a series of rapid-fire blows with the bone demon. The flaming greatsword and bone scythe clashed with such force that small thunderclaps could be heard each time they collided.

Jason urged his dark mages into action, and they repeatedly cast curses at Alexion. After witnessing how other dark magic had barely damaged Alexion, Jason expected that his holy aura somehow made him resistant. His fears were confirmed as he saw the curses slide harmlessly off his body. Jason could only hope that repeatedly casting the curses would allow one or two to stick.

Alexion and the bone demon danced across the field trading massive blows. The force of their strikes caused ripples of force at each point of impact. Nearby soldiers were knocked down, and the occasional stray strike decapitated or maimed those too slow or too stupid to move out of the way. Their fight caused a large clearing to form at the back of Alexion's army as the troops scrambled madly to escape.

This was now a battle between two titans.

Alexion's greatsword darted forward and slammed against the bone demon's scythe. Jason's saw small fragments of bone spray from the impact site. The bone demon's tail lashed forward at Alexion's legs, striking his greaves with vicious force.

The surprise attack tripped Alexion, and he was forced onto his back. The bone demon drove his scythe downward with such force that the displaced air emitted a howling sound. Yet Alexion's parried the blow with his sword with a clash of steel. Then his free hand began moving in another series gestures.

Back! Jason ordered the bone demon telepathically.

The demon sprang backward as Alexion's body burst into golden flame. The flames then surged into the ground and streaked toward the bone demon, cracking the dirt of the field and causing large flaming rents to appear around Alexion.

Jump on him! Jason ordered.

The demon gave Alexion a mocking grin and jumped into the air over the holy flames of the *Consecration* spell with its scythe held high. The colossal demon flew through the air, and its scythe raced toward Alexion with a ravenous howl.

Alexion barely rolled out of the way. The scythe slammed into the ground with a shower of dirt, and the demon tugged at its weapon, trying to dislodge it. Alexion scrambled madly to regain his footing and turned back to his foe. His breath was coming in ragged gasps as he tried to recover from his near death experience. The demon finally yanked its scythe out of the ground in another eruption of dirt. It raced toward Alexion, and the fight continued in earnest.

Jason anxiously inspected the bone demon's health and saw that it was slowly fading. The fight at the trebuchets and the attack on Alexion's army had weakened it severely. He couldn't see Alexion's health, but it must also be getting low after standing at the front line of the army and then receiving that massive initial strike. The bone demon also seemed to be landing the occasional swipe on Alexion's armor, shaving off small portions of his health.

I really wish I had decided to take the Enrage spell at a moment like this, Jason thought desperately.

There was really nothing he could do but watch. His mana was nearly empty, and he was out of potions. Except for the mages that were frantically casting at Alexion and the bone demon, almost all of his minions were dead.

Then the fight came to a sudden dramatic end.

The bone demon committed to a particularly heavy horizontal swing. Alexion ducked the blow instead of parrying and stepped close to the demon. With a flash of golden light, Alexion slashed at the demon's right leg. His blade sank into and then severed the extremity. The bone demon tumbled to the ground with a deafening boom and the distinct sound of crunching bone.

Jason felt a sinking feeling in his stomach as he watched helplessly from the sidelines.

Is this it? Did I lose?

His eyes moved to the walls. There were only a hundred undead left standing. The defenders had been severely diminished by the ranged attacks of the assaulting army. Jason could just make out Grunt's large form in the distance. He assumed Jerry must be nearby.

Will they all die because I failed?

Even with the numbers he had killed, Alexion's army still greatly outnumbered the defenders. Nearly seven hundred NPCs and players still assaulted the walls. With Alexion supporting them with his defensive spells, it was unlikely that they could hold the city.

Jason turned his head back to Alexion. He watched as the glowing knight slowly approached the now vulnerable bone demon, gloating in his victory. His face was twisted in a mocking grin.

"And so it ends demon. Did you really think you could win against the light?!"

Alexion gleaming sword descended and then penetrated the bone demon's skull as it feebly tried to reach for its scythe.

Dark magic spiraled around the bone demon as his body began to disintegrate. Thunder peeled across the sky. Alexion raised his sword triumphantly and turned back to his troops. However, Jason noticed him wince as he lifted his arm. The battle had taken a lot out of him, and he was on his last legs. Once the healers woke up from their shock, it would only take a few healing spells and Alexion would be back in battle.

With his flaming greatsword held aloft, Alexion removed his helm with his free hand. This scene seemed eerily familiar to Jason, and he felt the bottom drop out of his stomach. If only his bone demon had been at full health!

"Victory for Grey Keep!" Alexion screamed.

His remaining army roared in response and lifted their weapons into the air.

Jason could only sit and watch as the last traces

of dark magic from his bone demon swirled and faded into the night sky.

There's nothing else I can do!

All of his work over the past weeks had culminated in this moment. Yet he sat defeated on the edge of the field, his dark mana fading as doubt and despair clouded his mind.

Jason glanced back up at Alexion's gloating form, and his brow furrowed in confusion. A halo of dark energy had formed around Alexion's triumphant face. Time seemed to slow as the halo grew larger and larger. It almost appeared that Alex stood in front of a black hole.

Then Alexion's head abruptly exploded into a cloud of bloody mist. Fragments of bones flew in all directions as tendrils of dark energy wrapped his corpse and lifted it from the ground. The energy lashed at the steel and exposed bits of skin, tarnishing the metal and rotting flesh. Then the dark void dissipated. The headless, heavily-armored body toppled almost comically to the ground with a crash of steel.

As the headless corpse fell to the ground, Jason could see a figure standing approximately fifty yards behind Alexion. It appeared to be a young girl with long blond hair. She held a large wooden recurve bow in her hands, and the string still vibrated from the release of the arrow. Her eyes were filled with cold rage and shone a dark, unholy obsidian.

The girl was almost painfully familiar, and Jason's breath caught in his throat.

Riley! What hell is she doing here?

The world seemed to speed back up. The soldiers stared at Alexion's body for a moment, before roaring in anger at their leader's death. The soldiers turned to the small blond girl that stood casually behind the army and rage marred their features.

Then they began to rush at Riley.

She released arrow after arrow into the onrushing group as she moved backward with quick, nimble steps. The bolts were covered in a coiling black substance. Where they struck, flesh melted from bone. The soldiers screamed in pain, their advance slowing. Her accuracy was uncanny, and she shot with an almost unnatural calm in the face of the onrushing soldiers.

However, Riley was still going to be overwhelmed by the dozens of soldiers that charged at her. For a moment, Jason considered letting the soldiers kill her. She had certainly thrown him under the bus at Richmond.

Yet he had to admit that her being here was strange. He also hadn't missed the part where she blew Alexion's head off. Jason's chances of defending the city were now considerably improved. That gave her a few grudging points in his book.

Riley also served as an excellent distraction, since many soldiers had pulled away from the army's main force to chase her. The longer Jason could keep those soldiers busy, the better.

Damn it. I guess I will help her.

He mentally directed his ice mage to freeze the ground in front of Riley, and his dark mages rapidly cast *Curse of Weakness* at the approaching soldiers, slowing their movements.

With Riley momentarily safe (if she kept running), his gaze turned back to the tumult of the battlefield. Without Alexion's defensive buffs and directions, the soldiers were disorganized. With so many different avenues of attack on the city, Alexion had spread his forces too thin. This had been an acceptable tactic when the troops were supported by the knight's defensive buffs, but, with Alexion gone, the soldiers were now vulnerable.

Now is the time for the finale! I just hope the council had enough time to get them in position.

Jason telepathically ordered his three almost forgotten thieves to attack.

Nothing happened for several long moments and Jason's brow furrowed with worry. He looked beside him at Onyx, and the cat seemed to shrug.

Then an ear-splitting howl went up through the woods on either side of the gate. A horde of undead rushed into the clearing, flanking the enemies attacking the gate.

Jason had ordered the council to move the three divisions out of the city through the north gate. This move left the wall poorly defended, but gave Jason the opportunity to launch a counterattack in the field.

The downside of this plan was that it took a long time for his thieves to make the journey back to the city. It was also a struggle for the council to move the troops into position without alerting Alexion's army. Finally, there was a problem regarding communication. There was no way for his thieves to both notify Jason that the army was in position and stay with the troops so that Jason could tell them when to attack.

There were a number of things that could have gone wrong with this plan, but it was now paying off.

Sinister curses, bolts of dark energy, and gray arrows streaked toward the players and NPCs in front of the gate. They were caught in a crossfire of missiles and the shields of the front line were pointed in the wrong direction. Alexion's soldiers screamed in pain as arrows penetrated their flesh and wicked corruption overtook their bodies. The undead soldiers struck the front lines, fighting with wild abandon. Only massive injuries disabled their limbs, and they felt no pain. The undead didn't fear death.

Jason's army fought with well-trained coordination and maintained their eight-man units, even in the heat of battle. He watched as the undead soldiers drew attention from the enemy, while the thieves ambushed the enemy soldiers from behind. Blood erupted from well-placed strikes on the soldiers' necks and backs. Meanwhile, the mages provided ranged support while debuffing their opponents.

Jason smiled as he watched his army in action, and a sense of pride welled up inside of him. Most of his minions might be gone, but his army and the residents of his city lived on.

He turned his attention back to Riley. She had circled south as she ran from the soldiers and was now cut off from the undead reinforcements. A trail of bodies lay behind her, a testament to her skill with the bow. She continued to fire into the oncoming soldiers, as she backpedaled quickly. Yet many soldiers were still chasing her, and she was slowly losing ground.

Several corpses lay behind the girl, and Jason quickly cast *Specialized Zombie* three times in quick succession with his newly regen'd mana. The freshly formed zombies pulled themselves from the ground, unnoticed by Riley.

Without warning, one of the zombies grabbed the girl from behind, bodily lifting her small form and throwing her over his shoulder. The other two zombies formed a defensive wall behind the girl. Her escort and the group headed to the tree-line where Jason sat, watching Riley kick fiercely in an attempt to free herself.

Jason ordered the ice mage into action again. The mage froze the ground in front of the soldiers. With an evil grin, Jason gave new orders to his fire mage, and a wall of flame appeared at the end of the frozen field.

The enemy soldiers ran headlong through the frozen patch, many slipping and falling. Their momentum caused some to tumble and slide headlong into the wall of fire where they started burning fiercely. Screams issued from the burning bodies and mingled with the dying cries of the other soldiers at the gate.

Jason chuckled tiredly. *First zombie hand grenades and now a deadly slip-n-slide. God, I love this game.*

Onyx rolled his eyes beside Jason.

The commotion on the battlefield quickly took the attention away from the girl and her small escort. Soon the group made it back to Jason, and he deactivated *Sneak*.

"You can set her down," he ordered her zombie guard.

The zombie carrying Riley gently set her on her feet. The three zombies immediately took up defensive positions between Jason and Riley, holding their weapons ready. Jason's mages continued casting actively in the background.

Riley looked around with a disoriented and angry expression. Jason supposed that being grabbed by a zombie and carried on his shoulder would piss most people off. She opened her mouth to say something before catching sight of the zombies. They had quite obviously been dead a moment ago, and their bodies were riddled with gaping wounds. Riley gasped and took an involuntary step back. Then she saw Jason standing behind his minions, robed in dark leather and his face obscured by his hooded cloak.

Jason looked at the blond girl, his mind a jumble of confused emotions. He couldn't remember the last time he logged off. His emotions were all over the place. He was exhausted, and his head hurt, his body running solely on adrenaline. To top it all off, there was also a war going on a few hundred yards away.

In spite of everything, he could still feel the dull anger simmering inside of him as he looked at Riley. She had thrown him to the wolves without a care. Yet at the same time, confused questions sprang up in his mind. Why on earth was she playing AO? Why was she here of all places? Why did she attack Alexion?

Maybe there is more to this story than I assumed, he thought reluctantly.

"W-Who are you? What is this?" Riley asked as she continued to look around in confusion. The dark mana faded from her eyes. Jason noticed her haggard appearance. Her shoulders drooped, and dark circles hung under her eyes. Her face had a haunted look about it.

Jason remained silent, still not certain whether to trust her.

She started to put everything together as she looked back at Jason's hooded form. "Wait I know who you are! You're... you're Jason aren't you?!"

Jason stood in shock for a moment.

How could she know who I am?

The answer came to him a moment later, and he felt like hitting himself.

Of course. She saw the prompt like everyone else. She doesn't know who I really am.

But that raised another question...

Should I tell her? I suppose it's really only a matter

of time before my identity is known, and I can always use Disguise if need be.

Screw it...

Jason released his dark mana and pulled back his hood, revealing his face. "Yes. I'm Jason all right," he said with a grim chuckle.

Riley just stared at him for a moment in shocked silence.

Then her words came out in a tumble, "Wait. Y-you're *the* Jason... but you're also my Jason?"

Jason raised an eyebrow. "Your Jason huh?"

"W-what? No... wait! I mean like the Jason from my school." Riley seemed extremely flustered by this turn of events.

While she collected her thoughts, Jason glanced over at the still raging war against the Twilight Throne. He had many questions for Riley, but this really wasn't the time or the place. He needed to get back to the battle. Many of his future subjects were dying while he stood here talking.

Riley looked at him, and tears budded in the corners of her eyes. "I-I've wanted to talk to you. To explain what happened..." she trailed off at this last part and appeared uncertain how to continue.

"Riley, I certainly have plenty of questions for you." His voice sounded cold to his ears, almost angry. "I also have you to thank for Alexion's death, which is the only reason you're still alive... but, I have to get back to the fight. Many more of my people will die if I don't help."

Riley flinched at his cold tone. Then her eyes turned to glance at the battle that was going on nearby, and she seemed to collect herself a bit.

She looked down at her hands. "No, no. I understand completely. I think I need to log off for a moment anyway to clear my head." Riley shook her head slightly as she said this last part.

She glanced at Jason. "When you're done here, could we grab lunch? You know, like in the real world? I know you have no reason to trust me, but I would really like to explain what happened at school... and here." She hesitated. "I'd like to explain everything."

Riley glanced down at her hands again and fidgeted. Jason could still see the faint glimmer of tears in her eyes. The same tortured look flitted across her face. This wasn't the effervescent, confident girl that he remembered.

What happened to her?

"That's fine. I'll call you when this is over," he said finally, some of the coldness leaving his voice.

"Great," Riley answered, looking relieved and slightly hopeful. "I'll see you later then Jason."

She pulled up the system menu in the air in front of her. Before she hit the logout button, she looked over at Jason one last time. In spite of her haggard appearance and the tears that glistened in her eyes, she grinned ever so slightly.

"Remember I won't be here to save you again; try not to lose the war."

Then she disappeared.

Chapter 31 - Recovering

Robert was sitting on the raised dais in the middle of the control room, gazing steadily at the large screen hovering over the room. The screen was currently divided into a grid of sixteen different player perspectives. Periodically, Robert would stuff some popcorn in his mouth. All of the techs in the room had stopped what they were doing and were also staring at the screen from different positions around the room.

The screens showed various views of the field in front of the Twilight Throne and the last minute preparations of the army that was about to lay siege to the city. It was awe inspiring to see the magnitude of the assault on the walls. Giant siege engines had been built and were being rolled onto the field, while the soldiers and players were sorting themselves into orderly ranks.

Claire walked into the control and paused as she saw what Robert was doing, "What is this Robert? Are those player cameras? You know we can't access the cameras unless they violate the terms of service!"

Robert glanced over at her and grinned. "I'm investigating the several dozen player reports that we have received in the last twenty-four hours. You know as well as I do that someone has allegedly been hacking the game." He chuckled at this last part while shaking his head.

"So far I haven't seen any evidence of hacking. But I could! I need to be vigilant," he said in a solemn tone before stuffing more popcorn in his mouth. He turned back to Claire and waved at the screen. "Besides, this gives us front row seats to the war!"

Claire frowned. However, what Robert was doing could be justified in a convoluted way. They had received numerous reports over the last few days that Jason was exploiting the game. The reports had all come from the players that were traveling to the Twilight Throne. She had seen some of the tactics Jason had used, and she shuddered slightly. Claire knew he hadn't hacked the game, but she wasn't certain she was comfortable with what he had actually been doing.

"Oh, it's starting!" Robert said excitedly. The room hushed, and all eyes turned the screen. Even Claire grudgingly took a seat beside Robert.

Alexion gave a moving speech to his troops, which was met with a rising cheer. As the roar of the soldiers petered out, a lingering silence fell over the field. The undead simply stared at the troops, and the army began to shift anxiously.

"You have to give Jason credit," Robert murmured into the silence, "The guy knows how to wage one hell of a psychological war." A few techs nodded in agreement. They had all seen what Jason had done to the NPCs and players on the journey to the Twilight Throne.

As the uncomfortable silence lengthened, Alexion finally ordered his troops forward, and the siege commenced. It was incredible to see so many soldiers and NPCs running at the walls of the city. Claire let out a sharp breath, her eyes were glued to the screen.

"What is that?" Robert cried, pointing at a camera in the corner of the screen. "Enlarge it!"

A single perspective filled the screen. It was a player standing at the trebuchets. Hulking, black skeleton warriors were hurtling toward the siege engines. Their footsteps caused the ground to tremble, and their tails lashed the air behind them.

"Oh shit! What the hell are those?" the player exclaimed in a frightened tone. The camera tilted, as he backpedaled away from the oncoming skeletons. His retreat was stopped, and the camera jumped, probably because the player had backed into something. The camera turned to reveal a wooden bulwark behind the player. Another roar ripped through the air, and the player whipped his head back to the oncoming skeletons.

The staff watched as the skeletons crashed into the line of soldiers. Claire gasped as she saw the carnage caused by the Death Knight's initial charge. The player looked to his side, watching as his friend was impaled on a bone shield and slammed against the bulwark. The camera turned back to the left, catching sight of another Death Knight that was hurtling towards the player with its horned head lowered. The Death Knight struck the player, and his camera went black.

"Damn it! Find another camera!" Robert ordered the tech.

After a few long moments, a new perspective resolved on screen. This player was standing at the eastern tree line and watching the now burning trebuchets in the distance. Due to the time compression, the fight around the siege weapons had already ended. The new player could make out the forms of the Death Knights as they let out a roar of triumph and raised their swords into the air. Zombies stood inside the wooden bulwark, letting out their own howling roar.

"Charge!" yelled a nearby player. The group sprinted from the tree line, attacking the dark skeletons and zombies from behind. Fireballs and bolts of ice flew through the air, striking bone and rotting flesh.

Robert's fist slammed into his arm chair as he saw the ambush from Alexion's forces. It was clear to the staff watching the screen that the Death Knights had been severely weakened by the initial charge on the trebuchets. They wouldn't be able to take another full-fledged confrontation.

"Is this it?" Robert muttered. "Jason's force is going to get wiped out!"

Then the game froze for a moment, and the screen stuttered. The staff watched with mouths agape as the Death Knights and corpses were ripped apart. A cloud of bones flew through the air toward the cemetery. Then the ground of the graveyard erupted in a fountain of dirt and bones. The maelstrom of bones centered on the roof of one of the tombs in the graveyard, swirling in a gigantic vortex. The cloud was so dense that the group in the control room couldn't make out what was happening.

"Is that Jason? He must be standing on that tomb," Robert's voice sounded loudly in the hushed silence that had fallen over the control room.

The vortex resolved itself into a monstrosity of bone. The horror roared as it stretched its new body, clutching at its two-handed bone scythe. Its form towered over the walls of the graveyard, obscuring the tomb where Jason stood. The camera tilted for a moment, as the player stumbled backward away from the skeletal terror that stood before him.

"W-what is that thing? It looks like a demon..." the player muttered, his voice trembling with fear.

The creature turned its head toward the ambushing group. Its face contorted in a cruel smile. Without warning, the demon dashed directly toward the soldiers. Its enormous form approached at a frightening pace.

"Oh fuck!" the player shouted. The camera turned as the player tried to run. "Oh god! Run!"

Then the camera tilted erratically as the player tumbled to the ground. Wisps of shriveled grass appeared horizontally in the camera's field of view, and blood rained around him. The screen went dark.

The group in the control room sat in mute amazement. Finally, Robert's voice croaked, "Another camera."

The dumbstruck tech pulled up another camera. The new player was looking directly into the swirling vortexes of dark energy that were the creature's eyes. They seemed so close. Too close. A manic grin was painted on the bone demon's face. The player let out a scream as the creature pulled him closer.

"Please! No!" the player begged to no avail. Within seconds the creature's teeth sank around his neck.

The screen went dark once more.

Everyone in the control room was still. They weren't certain how to process what was happening on the screen.

"What the fuck is that thing?" Claire finally asked, horror in her voice. It was unusual to hear her cuss, and some of the techs looked at her in shock. A few people used this opportunity to leave the room, shaking their heads. This was too much for them.

"Sir," one of the techs said, "The game forums and live streams have exploded with traffic. The servers for some of the streaming sites have crashed. Even our servers are starting to hit capacity. Everyone is watching this."

He shook his head. "Literally everyone."

Robert's face was a mask of amazement. "Find me another camera. Maybe one a little further away from the fight this time."

The screen resolved back into color. The new player was standing in the main army and was casting a spell at the defenders on the wall. Suddenly, a roar erupted from behind him and he turned. The bone demon was now drenched in blood and was racing toward the rear line of troops. As the demon ran, he grabbed at zombies beside him, hurling them towards the army.

Right before the zombies landed, they exploded in a cascading ring of shrapnel and dark energy. Players and NPCs were torn apart by the explosion and their skin melted. The camera tilted and spun as the player was knocked down by the aftershocks of the explosions. When he looked back up, the demon was laying waste to the army. Its large scythe swung in a whirlwind of death and blood.

"How are we supposed to fight that thing...?" the player murmured in shock.

A golden glow enveloped the player. He turned to see a knight, clad in shining steel armor, racing through the line of troops. The knight's eyes shone a brilliant gold and bands of light wound around his body. Alexion had arrived. He challenged the demon, brandishing his sword.

Turning to the small shining man, the bone demon grinned grotesquely. It roared into the dark sky that hung over the field. A bolt of lightning struck the ground, and the screen flashed a blinding white. When the player's vision returned, Alexion's steel-clad body lay a couple dozen yards away.

Alexion slowly pulled himself from the ground and cast a spell that transformed his sword into a flaming greatsword. He turned and rushed at the bone demon.

"Damn this is entertaining," Robert said into the quiet room as he lifted more popcorn into his mouth.

If the summoning had been spectacular, the showdown between the bone demon and Alexion was downright extraordinary. The two figures clashed on screen with mighty, ringing swings of their weapons. The crowd in the control room and gamers around the world watched in wonder as the fight unfolded.

Finally, Alexion stood victorious over the demon, and his sword sunk into its skull. Dark energy swirled in the air. Grumbles of discontent filtered through the control room. Most of the staff were actually rooting for Jason and were disappointed that Alexion now stood victorious. Money changed hands surreptitiously to the gloating expressions of the staff who had bet on Alexion.

Alexion lifted his helmet off his head and thrust his sword into the air triumphantly. A roar went up among the NPCs and soldiers. Some of the techs shook their heads in disappointment, turning back to their screens.

"What the hell!" Robert yelled, spewing half-eaten popcorn on the desk in front of him.

A dozen pairs of eyes were whipped back to the screen. Where Alexion's head had once stood, only a bloody stump remained. A blood-filled mist hung around his form as dark energy whipped and crawled over his armored corpse. As the body finally crumpled to the ground, the staff could make out a petite blond girl standing behind Alexion and holding a bow. Her eyes glowed a dark obsidian, and a vicious smile was painted on her face.

"God I love this game," Robert said as the other techs yelled at the screen in confusion.

Then undead rushed from the tree lines on both sides of the gate. Dark spells and arrows streaked toward the players as screams filled the air. The camera turned to watch the onrushing horde, and the sword of an undead soldier met the player's neck. The screen went dark.

"Are there any other cameras?" Robert asked frantically.

The tech shook his head as he frantically typed away at his computer terminal. "They're dying too quickly. I can't connect to a camera for more than a few seconds." Long minutes passed as short clips played across the screen. The gist of the battle was clear from those brief snapshots. The army was being massacred. The tech continued typing frantically.

"Wait here's one!" he called out, slumping against the back of his chair.

The screen settled on a single viewpoint. The player was lying on the ground, watching as blood rained from the black sky. Corpses of players and NPCs lay all around him. The remaining NPCs and players were running desperately for the tree line. The undead around the player raised their weapons into the air and let out a howling cry into the night. Thunder peeled over the city as lightning flashed between the dark clouds.

A form walked slowly onto the field. Something seemed different about this figure, and the player observed him carefully. He walked with purpose as he inspected the corpses. His body was clothed in black leather, and his face was obscured by a hooded cloak. He surveyed the army around him authoritatively, making occasional gestures at the undead.

"Is that Jason?" Claire asked in a quiet voice filled

with a confused mixture of awe and horror. Several techs stared dumbly at the screen, all wondering the same thing.

As he neared the player, the dark figure's head turned, and he looked directly at the camera. Only his mouth was visible underneath the hood. He smiled cruelly as he gazed at the player.

"It seems one survived," he said with a chuckle. He turned to the undead. "Hunt down the rest. Leave no one alive. Bring their bodies back to me."

Then the dark figure looked back at the player, making a gesture with his hand. The player was lifted into the air, shaking and jerking in an attempt to break loose. Yet with his injuries, he couldn't break free. From his new vantage, the player's camera took in the devastation. Hundreds of bodies lay around him, and blood soaked the ground.

The figure continued to speak, "I assume you're recording this battle, or you would have logged out already. That is good."

"My name is Jason. And this..." The zombies beside the player rotated him to look at the dark walls that stood nearby. "This is my city." In response to his words, the undead that lined the walls roared in triumph.

The zombies turned the player back to Jason, whose shadowed face now hovered directly in front of the player. He held a blade to the player's throat.

"I have a message for everyone watching this. Do not fuck with the Twilight Throne."

Then the knife slid across the player's throat, and the screen went black.

*   *   *

After Alexion's death, the battle proceeded smoothly, and the remainder of his army was swiftly routed.

Alexion had spread his forces too thin when he

chose to attack from so many different directions. The ambush from behind the main force, combined with the loss of Alexion's defensive aura, was the death knell for his army. Yet Jason wasn't content to let the remaining players and NPCs flee back to Grey Keep. He ordered his army to give chase. No one was going to return home.

Except by a respawn, he thought with a grim chuckle.

Jason now stood on the walls above the south gate of the Twilight Throne and looked down upon the battlefield. He rested his hands against the cold stone. A little more than six hours had passed in the game since Riley had logged off. His head ached, and he felt exhausted.

How long have I been playing? I haven't even received a system warning.

He had put aside some of the oddities about the game before, but he couldn't ignore this.

This isn't normal. I must have been in the game more than twelve hours real world time! How did no one catch this in the public trials? What is going on here?

His thoughts were interrupted as Onyx jumped up on the parapet and rubbed against him with a soft purr. He stroked the cat absentmindedly, while his other hand rubbed at his own eyes. He needed to figure out what was going on with the game, but he was just too tired right now.

Jason turned back to the battlefield. He noted the huge number of bodies that lay on the ground. Gruesome wounds riddled their flesh. They lay in tortured poses, their blood drenching the dark, cracked earth of the field. Nearly nine hundred corpses were scattered across the field. As he looked at the battlefield, the world around him seemed to stutter for a moment.

"Hello, old man," Jason said, without turning his head.

A rumbling chuckle sounded from beside him. "One war and you are now on casual speaking terms with gods?"

The old man paused before continuing. "You fought well," he finally said, his voice tinged with a hint of pride.

Jason didn't reply immediately. His eyes lingered on the field as his tired mind went over the events of the last few days. "I did what was necessary," he said in a cold, firm voice.

He turned and looked at the old man who stood beside him. "Should I feel guilty for this? For killing and terrorizing the soldiers and travelers?"

"Why should you feel guilty?" the old man replied, his tone incredulous. "You defended your city and its residents. You did nothing to provoke this fight, you simply finished it."

Jason shook his head. "I know you're right. It just seems strange that I don't feel any remorse. A part of me thinks I should."

"Did you feel guilty after what happened in the marketplace in Lux, or with the nobles and the guards?" The old man asked this last question with a curious tone.

After a moment of hesitation, Jason answered, "Yes. That battle was fueled more by my rage than any sense of purpose. I felt ashamed for going overboard. I think that's why I was so willing to take your suggestion and build something from the ashes."

Jason glanced back to the field, brow furrowed. "I suppose this is different. I didn't start this fight, and I did it to protect what I created."

His eyes slowly turned black as he considered

his next words. He spoke in an eerily quiet voice that echoed with unflinching determination, "I also know that I would do this again to protect the Twilight Throne. This is my city."

The old man replied with a chuckle, "Good! Anger is a useful tool to overcome your inhibitions. It helps many embrace the dark, and it often provides the fortitude to take the plunge in pursuit of your goals and desires. However, anger alone isn't enough. You need a purpose and a goal."

"It has been interesting to watch you develop these last few weeks," the old man continued. He eyed Jason appraisingly.

"You're no longer the sullen, angry boy that originally wandered into my cave, yearning for strength. I saw potential in you then, and I am beginning to see the realization of that potential now."

Jason carefully considered the old man's words. Perhaps he was right. Jason had changed a great deal since he began playing. He still enjoyed the fighting, yet the anger and rage he felt toward Richmond, Alex, and his parents had begun to fade. Outside of the game, he was beginning to build a new life. He had grown more confident and commanding. He knew what he wanted, and he acted on it.

Perhaps I'm beginning to achieve the power I was looking for. Maybe it wasn't about commanding an army or shooting lasers from my eyes. Maybe it was always about having the resolve to pursue what I want without reservation.

"What now?" he said, turning back to the old man.

"Well, now you make another decision. Will you take those corpses below for your own purposes or will you devote them to the city?"

Jason's brow furrowed. "What does that mean exactly? Devote them to the city?"

"I can grant you the power to raise those corpses in the field and add them to the population of your city. Think of this as your first decision as the regent of Twilight Throne," the old man said as his wrinkled lips twisted into a pleased smile.

It wasn't really a choice as far as Jason was concerned. He spoke without hesitation, "I will devote the corpses to the city."

The old man smiled broadly, his eyes still covered by the hood. His wrinkled hand rested on Jason's shoulder. The arcane words and gestures that made up the spell tumbled into Jason's mind like an avalanche. This spell was much more intricate than anything he had learned before. It contained bits and pieces of the strange, almost primordial language Jason had spoken when he created the Twilight Throne.

New Spell: Undead Devotion

You may use this spell to commit corpses within the area of influence of the Twilight Throne to the city. Corpses raised with this spell will not affect the player's Control Limit and will not be raised as feral undead. The raised undead will become residents of the Twilight Throne.

Skill Level: Unknown
Effect: Raised corpses become residents of the Twilight Throne

---

Hmm. This is the first spell or skill I've seen that doesn't have a skill level. What does it mean for the skill level to be 'unknown?'

"Why doesn't this skill have a level?" Jason asked, confusion in his voice.

The old man shrugged. "I'm certain that the answer to that question will be revealed in time."

"Do you always speak in riddles?" Jason replied in irritation.

"Consider it one of the perks of a being a god. Few can force you to answer a straight question." The old man's mouth smiled under the dark cowl that covered his face.

"A word of advice. Use this spell wisely," he said, tone solemn and dark. "You need to grow the power of your city quickly. This was but a small taste of what is to come. Your future opponents will not be so stupid or so weak."

The old man made to move off the ramparts.

"Hey, aren't you forgetting something old man?" Jason called after him.

The old man turned with a mischievous grin. "Am I?"

"I finished your quest and defended the city. Give me what you promised." Jason's voice was even and held no trace of indecision.

"Ahh, you have changed much from the whelp that first entered my cave. Very well then. Congratulations, regent of the Twilight Throne!" The old man waved his hand as he said this last part.

Quest Completed: State of War

After creating the Twilight Throne with the assistance of the old man, you caused a war with the neighboring Kingdom of Meria. You have utterly annihilated the army that came to claim your city, to the point of running down those that tried to flee.

You have been named Lord Regent of the Twilight Throne
You now have access to the keep
You now have access to the city control menu (accessible in the keep)
You are responsible for the city's residents (Currently 3,326)
+5% Dark Affinity

"I particularly enjoyed watching how you

whittled down the enemy force," the old man said. "I suppose I can also offer you a reward in addition to the quest completion. Perhaps a piece of equipment since you seem so poorly attired."

He looked Jason up and down. "I think I know exactly what you need." From underneath his cloak, the old man pulled out a long piece of cloth. The fabric was dark as midnight and blended into the shadows cast along the ramparts. It was made of fabric so fine that it ran like silk between the old man's fingers.

Jason accepted the bundle with numb hands.

Geez, I hope this is finally a decent piece of gear.

He quickly equipped it and check the stats.

Midnight Cloak

Crafted from an unknown, ephemeral material, this cloak feels as though the wearer is shrouded in shadows. The cloak completely obscures the wearer's face, even in direct sunlight. It also grants a bonus to spellcasting and stealth.

Quality: A

Durability: Indestructible

The wearer's face is always obscured in shadow even in direct light

+2 Effective level of Sneak

+10 Willpower

+10 Intelligence

(Soulbound)

"Holy shit," Jason murmured.

This is the first 'soulbound' piece of equipment I've found. I suppose this means I can't drop it upon death.

The old man chuckled. "There is nothing holy about that cloak, but I am pleased that you are happy with the reward."

"One more thing," the old man continued. "There are other cities that were once part of Lusade. This was only the capital city. There are many who will be interested in acquiring extra land from these events."

He looked at Jason levelly. "I suggest you move quickly to secure your new territory."

New Quest: Prime Real Estate

Now that you have been appointed as the Regent of the Twilight Throne, you need to take control of the surrounding lands and cities that were once part of the Kingdom of Lusade.

Difficulty: A
Success: Take control of the neighboring towns and area that were once part of the Kingdom of Lusade. Destroy anything and anyone who gets in your way. Basically, just keep doing your thing.
Failure: Unknown
Reward: Acquisition of new residents and resources. Expanded area of influence for the Twilight Throne.

When Jason's eyes turned away from the prompt, the old man had disappeared. Typical. Jason turned back to the field and looked over the corpses.

I guess it's time to add some new residents to my city.

His hands began the intricate pattern of movements required of the *Undead Devotion* spell. Guttural words left his mouth, sounding both strange and familiar to his ears. The words reminded him of the terraforming spell he had cast in the market. As he continued casting, the black clouds over the field began to boil and churn. Lightning arced between the clouds, glowing with a black aura. Then bolts of dark mana infused lightning began to rapidly strike the corpses in the field. An almost endless series of thunderclaps rang across the field like cannon fire.

As the bolts struck the corpses, the bodies twitched and spasmed. Then rotten hands and bleached bones scraped at the earth as the new undead pulled themselves upright. Milky white eyes and dark orbs of energy looked up at walls of the Twilight Throne. They gazed upon their new home.

As Jason completed casting, he was awarded with yet another prompt:

City Message
You have added 879 residents to the Twilight Throne.

His work on the walls completed, Jason headed for the stairs. His next stop was the Sow's Snout. He needed to speak to the council about the new undead and the future of the city. His boots felt like they were full of lead as he trudged down the stairs, but he needed to take care of this before he logged off.

Chapter 32 - Debriefed

Robert Graham sat alone in one of the laboratories at Cerillion Entertainment. A few hours had passed since Jason's climactic battle in front of the Twilight Throne.

This particular laboratory was special. It required a three-factor identification to enter the area, including an optical scan, a blood sample, and a fingerprint scan. Robert also hadn't missed the cameras spaced around each room and the small valves located on each wall. He knew that if he tried to make a run for it with any of tech that littered the room, knockout gas would immediately be injected into the air, and armed guards would be waiting at the lone exit.

Robert was examining his latest project. He sat at a long metal table on one end of the room. Multiple computer terminals dotted the table, and sophisticated tools hung along a nearby wall. On the other side of the room, a screen blared as two announcers discussed the events at the Twilight Throne. Ignoring the screen, Robert's attention was focused on the plastic helmet in his hands.

This new headgear would revolutionize the world of VR technology. Instead of the opaque, claustrophobic helmet that the users had become accustomed to, this new design left the face free and unrestricted. Robert and his small stable of engineers had also vastly increased the sensitivity of the VR headgear. At this point, the hardware was capable of producing sensations that were almost indistinguishable from real life.

Robert's eyes flitted from the headgear to the screen. The announcers, a man and a woman, were standing before a screen that played footage from the battle in front of the dark city. The players that had participated in the siege had posted snippets of the fight. The network didn't have Robert's level of access to the player cameras, but they had done a respectable job of piecing together the footage they had received from the players.

The final scene of the battle was playing behind the announcers. Robert watched again as Jason cruelly slayed a player in cold blood and issued his warning to the gaming world.

"Wow," the female announcer said. "I get chills every time I see that clip."

Her male counterpart shrugged, unimpressed by the footage. "It was an intimidating warning. However, Jason didn't achieve the result he was looking for. Most of the players have taken his threat as a challenge. Jason is now the man to beat, and the Twilight Throne is the city to conquer."

The woman smiled slightly. "I've heard the same thing. My favorite part was the bounty that has been placed on Jason's head. Can you believe someone would pay $5,000 for a video of Jason being slain in-game?" She shook her head in confusion. "Who has that kind of money to burn on a game?"

With a frown, the male announcer said in an irritated voice, "I don't blame them. Jason has gone to extreme lengths to protect his precious Twilight Throne. I mean look at how he slayed the player in that last clip. It is no wonder that people are upset."

The male anchor continued, "The real question is how a player could have accomplished what Jason has. Especially this early in the game. How could Cerillion Entertainment have allowed a player to reach this level of power so quickly? It seems like favoritism. I bet Jason is the son of one of the board members. At a minimum, this was some kind of promotional event for the game."

The woman eyed her partner skeptically. "You think that the company would risk their reputation by playing favorites? Let's face it, the early rumors about Jason were wrong. This wasn't an event quest. Jason actually managed to conquer Lux and defeat Alexion's army. There weren't any 'hax' involved."

She paused for a moment before continuing. "I

expect that we have just seen one player that has discovered a unique way of playing the game. As you said, AO hasn't been out long. I anticipate that we are going to see other players accomplishing similarly amazing things in the near future."

Robert shook his head as he watched the screen. "Favoritism, huh? We haven't had any influence on Jason," he said in an amused voice.

Then he hesitated. Cerillion Entertainment hadn't been playing favorites, but maybe Alfred had. Robert wasn't stupid. He had noticed that the footage of the massacre in the Lux marketplace had been cut. There was nothing wrong with the hardware, so the only explanation was that Alfred had been involved. Robert wasn't certain why the AI controller was interested in Jason, but he wasn't overly concerned. He knew that Claire didn't share his nonchalance, but Claire was a worrier by nature.

"Alfred is just a tool," Robert said quietly into the empty room. His voice carried a note of doubt, as though this declaration was made partially to convince himself.

Claire had personified the machine by giving it a name, but, at the end of the day, it was just a bundle of wires and some fancy programming. Robert should know, he had designed the AI controller after all. All of Alfred's actions could be understood in the context of his primary directive. He had "gone rogue" in an effort to understand more about the players and keep them playing.

This didn't make the machine a real person. He was just an incredibly sophisticated piece of equipment. One that had inadvertently created extraordinary technology in pursuit of the goal that Robert had assigned to it. After Claire was unable to point to anything that Alfred had done to actually harm the players, she had grudgingly come around to Robert's way of thinking

Robert was an engineer at heart. His own 'primary directive' was to build incredible things. Nothing else could match the exhilaration he felt when he created *something new or revolutionary. His creations could always be used for evil ends, but he couldn't stop that. Any tool could be used destructively – even Alfred. The result depended on the user. What was important was the invention itself.*

He gazed at the plastic helmet in his hands, an unusually somber expression on his face. His finger traced the ridge of the helmet. He had included several upgrades in this device that weren't shown on the schematics or technical specifications. He was interested to see how Alfred would utilize the new hardware. What would the AI controller develop with this new tool? He felt a flush of excitement as he considered the possibilities.

"I will just keep building," Robert said, an excited grin replacing the serious look on his face.

*   *   *

When Jason arrived at the Sow's Snout, he saw that the patrons had spilled out of the inn onto the road. Kegs lined one side of the street and the undead drank with wild abandon. Shouts filled the air as the residents celebrated their victory. It felt like he was attending an extremely well-costumed Halloween party.

Jason edged through the crowd, squeezing between drunken zombies and skeletons. Few of the residents reacted to his presence. He had won the war largely unseen.

Good thing I'm not obsessed with popularity, he thought wryly.

As he made his way inside the tavern, he was overwhelmed at the number of undead that were crammed into the small pub. Every table was full, and it was difficult to walk to the bar from the front door. The chaotic roar of people talking, combined with the jovial music playing in the background, created an unintelligible wall of noise.

What the hell is going on here?

When Jason finally managed to shove his way through the throng to the bar, he found Jerry pouring drinks at an almost casual pace, despite how crowded the bar was.

As Jerry caught sight of Jason, he called out in greeting, "There's our evil overlord himself!" A drunken cheer went up through the bar at the mention of an 'evil overlord,' but it was clear to Jason that most of the undead had no idea why they were cheering. "Look at you all flushed with victory!" Jerry continued, unperturbed by the confused roar of approval.

Jerry did a double-take and stared again at Jason. "Or at least you would be flushed if I could see your face." He rubbed at his eyes. "Maybe I'm going blind. Do my eyes look okay?" He pulled his eyelids back so that Jason could better see his milky white eyes.

"Hey, Jerry. You're not going blind. It's just a new cloak." Jason gestured around the bar and asked, "What the hell is going on here? Why is this place so busy?"

Jerry looked at him in mock offense. "Are you saying my humble establishment is somehow not trendy enough to bring in a crowd? I will have you know that kings have stood in this very room."

"Really? Who?" Jason asked with a dry tone.

Jerry flicked his floppy hat and looked down coyly. "You would actually be the first, but the point is still valid!"

Jason just shook his head. If he were honest, he had kind of missed Jerry's idiocy when he had been stuck out in the forest alone.

Dropping the act, Jerry continued in a more serious tone, "Actually, this place has been quite the hot spot lately. Ever since the residents figured out that they didn't need to eat or sleep, their drinking budget has expanded considerably."

"Also, I don't know if you noticed, but the forecast calls for gloomy with a chance of rain for the foreseeable future. Basically, it is always five o'clock around this city."

Jason looked at the undead patrons at the bar skeptically. "Can they even get drunk?"

"Oh yes indeed! Actually, you might have had a bit of an insurrection if they figured out they couldn't. You dodged a dagger in that regard, eh?"

During the conversation, Onyx had jumped up on the bar and looked at Jerry expectantly.

Jerry addressed the cat, "Your usual, sir Onyx?"

The cat nodded, and Jerry poured a glass of scotch, setting it carefully in front of the cat. Jason looked on with a puzzled expression as Onyx leaned over the snifter and breathed in the aroma. The cat let out a soft purr and stuck his tongue gently into the scotch.

"Does he come here often?" Jason asked with amusement.

"Oh, Onyx is a regular around these parts. I've never seen a cat that likes scotch. But hey, weirder things have happened." As Jerry said this last part, he casually removed his eyeball and polished it with a dishtowel.

He then popped his eye back in and turned to Jason. "I expect you are here to reconvene our little council, hmm? The others are already down stairs. I will meet you down there in a jiffy."

Jason made his way downstairs and entered

the secret training area. Morgan and Rex were already seated at the table. Both seemed to be in good spirits. Rex had a large mug of beer sitting in front of him. It was pretty obvious that it wasn't his first. Grunt sat in the corner with a full keg. He would occasionally lift the massive barrel with one hand, dumping its contents into his open mouth.

I guess that's one approach.

"Hey there mister death and destruction!" Rex called out, his skeletal hand brandishing his mug. "We've been waiting for you!"

Rex was drunk. This seemed impossible. How did a skeleton even drink beer? Jason's confusion was dispelled a moment later when Rex took a large gulp from the mug. Jason could see the amber liquid pour down his throat and collect in a rough sphere where his stomach should have been. Dark energy wrapped around the golden globe, tearing it apart.

Okay. Skeleton digestion is strange. I'm not even going to question it.

"Hi Rex," Jason addressed him, before turning to Morgan. "Hey, Morgan. It's good to see you outside of your library."

Morgan chuckled darkly. "Oh, I wouldn't have missed that fight for anything. Forget what I said about skeletons boy. You've discovered something interesting haven't you?" She leaned across the table, her eyes glowing with curiosity.

"Maybe," Jason replied with a small smile, "I'll fill you in on the details later."

Once they were all seated and Jerry had joined them, Jason recounted the last few days. He described the creation of the bone demon and the final fight with Alexion. The group had seen some of the events since they had helped defend the wall, but hearing the full story seemed to enthrall them. Jason left out the part about Riley. He wasn't really certain what to say to them about her. He hadn't spoken with her yet or made up his mind about how he felt.

Jason also told them about how he had been appointed as the regent of the Twilight Throne. He hesitated slightly before revealing that he had added approximately nine hundred residents. He was reluctant to add to their workload. However, it was better that they found out now rather than later. As expected, Rex and Morgan grimaced at the news.

"I know there is going to be a ton of work that needs to be done to add the new residents," Jason said. "However, I want the three of you to know that I am grateful for all that you've done so far. You are clearly worthy of being this city's governing council."

"Well, that was downright touching," Rex said dryly. "Would you like us to all hug now?"

He reached out his bony white arms, as his skeletal face contorted into a twisted smile.

"Oh, no. No. I'm good," Jason assured him, putting up his hands defensively. Then his eyes turned to Jerry. "That reminds me though. I didn't appreciate you ordering my zombie to make out with me!" Jason said in an irritated voice.

It was Jerry's turn to be on the defensive. "I admit I may have gotten a bit overexcited when I heard that you had taken out nearly a third of the enemy army," Jerry said while fiddling with the edge of his floppy hat, his eyes downcast.

In spite of his irritation, Jason couldn't bear to see usually jovial thief with such a sad expression. "It's fine. Just remember I'm not a necrophiliac!" he said with a small grin.

Jerry's morose expression was immediately replaced with an energetic smile. "Great! Then I will have to think up another way to reward you for murder!"

With a pained sigh, Jason got back to business. "Anyway, we need to take steps to recruit more of the population into the army and start rebuilding the houses on the south side," Jason continued.

He looked at the group evenly. "There will be future attacks, and we need to be ready. I may have bought us some time, but the conflict is inevitable. Now that the area that was once part of Lusade is up for grabs, the nearby kingdoms are going to be looking for their piece of the pie."

Morgan looked at him, her mouth curling into a grin. "That certainly won't do, will it? Our new evil empire might need to slap a few hands in coming days."

Rex's jaw clacked in amusement, and he slammed down his mug. With a slur, he called out, "All hail the Twilight Throne!" He then raised his own mug in the air before taking another long pull.

The others just stared at him as he simultaneously made and drank to his own toast.

Chuckling, Jason addressed the group, "It looks like Rex may be a bit out of it. Maybe it's time to celebrate. We can work out the details later."

Jerry nodded. "I probably have a riot going on upstairs by now. I left Onyx running the bar! He doesn't even have thumbs! I say we revisit these topics tomorrow."

The Shadow Council convened their meeting, and the members walked back upstairs. Soon, Jason was sitting alone in the secret training room beneath the tavern. He felt tired and knew he needed to log off soon, but he had one last thing he needed to check on.

He pulled up his combat log and re-enabled his notifications. Suddenly, he was bombarded by a string of notifications:

x21 Level Up!
You have (105) undistributed stat points.

New Passive Skill: Disassemble

You are able to disassemble your skeletons while using the skeleton editor and use the bones to construct new creations. This spell is passive and costs no mana.

Skill Level: Mastered

Effect: You are able to disassemble your existing skeletons using the skeleton editor and reuse the bones.

x2 Skill Rank Up: Bone Crafting

Skill Level: Beginner Level 9

Effect: Access to bone modification in the skeleton editor. May currently alter the composition of bone by 13%.

x4 Skill Rank Up: Custom Skeleton

Skill Level: Beginner Level 9

Effect: You may raise a custom skeleton using nearby bones. The skeleton's level is calculated as the caster's level + Willpower/71.

x1 Skill Rank Up: Summoning Mastery

Skill Level: Intermediate Level 5

Effect: 23% increased stats for summoned undead and 23% increase to effective Willpower for purposes of determining Control Limit.

Effect 2: You may now communicate with your minions telepathically. Distance limit unknown.

x1 Skill Rank Up: Leadership
Skill Level: Beginner Level 8
Effect: Minions and subjects will receive a 4.5% increase learning speed for skills.

x1 Skill Rank Up: Mana Mastery
Skill Level: Beginner Level 9
Effect: -5.0% to mana cost.

x1 Spell Rank Up: Specialized Zombie
Skill Level: Beginner Level 9
Effect: Increased skill proficiency retained by zombies. Skill cap Beginner Level 9.

x1 Spell Rank Up: Corpse Explosion
Skill Level: Intermediate Level 2
Effect: Increased damage (Currently 1.11 x Health).
Effect 2: 2% increased blast radius.

x1 Spell Rank Up: Curse of Silence
Skill Level: Beginner Level 3
Effect: You silence your target for 5.2 seconds, preventing speech and spell casting.

The last battle had resulted in a huge number of kills and experience, due in large part to the bone demon. What confused him was the new skill he had acquired.

First, the new Undead Devotion spell with an 'unknown' skill level, and now I have a skill that is already 'mastered.' There is clearly a great deal about this game that I haven't discovered yet.

Disassemble would be invaluable since it would allow him to re-use the bones of his skeletons. That would make it easier to create new skeletons in the future or alter the skeletons that he already had depending on the situation. Jason was already considering ways he could use this ability in the future.

As he started contemplating new skeleton designs, his thoughts turned to the bone demon. He wasn't certain how he had pulled off building the skeleton in such a short period of time. The event was a bit fuzzy in his mind, but he vaguely remembered using the extremities for his Death Knights as a template. When he checked the name of the creature later, he had apparently saved the design as the "Bone Lord."

Ugh. Maybe I can tell Jerry it was a tribute to him. Or maybe I can quietly change it later without telling anyone.

He mechanically added the additional points to *Willpower*, bringing him to 559 with his new cloak. His summon limit was now 68. He knew that at some point he would need to start investing in other stats. Right now, his stats were ridiculously one-sided, and it was already getting difficult to hit his summon limit without a huge supply of corpses and bones. After the battle, he only had about six soldier zombies, four mages, and three thieves. Raising the corpses as NPCs had dramatically reduced his supply of new minions.

Jason pulled up his character status to see where he now stood:

Character Status			
Name:	Jason	**Gender:**	Male
Level:	102	**Class:**	Necromancer
Race:	Human	**Alignment:**	Chaotic-Evil
Fame:	0	**Infamy:**	4100
Health:	615	**H-Regen:**	0.35 / Sec
Mana:	6205	**M-Regen:**	31.75 / Sec
Stamina	865	**S-Regen:**	3.6 / Sec
Strength:	12	**Dexterity:**	36
Vitality:	11	**Endurance:**	36
Intelligence:	32	**Willpower:**	559

Affinities			
Dark:	36%	**Light:**	4%
Fire:	3%	**Water:**	2%
Air:	3%	**Earth:**	2%

The battle must have increased his infamy since it had jumped to 4100. His dark affinity had also increased to 36% from the completion of the quest. All in all, he had progressed rather well.

It's hard to believe I only started playing about a week ago in the real world. Although, I guess I have been playing almost continuously and several weeks have already passed in-game.

Jason yawned. His head was pounding. He needed to log off and get some sleep. He numbly pulled up the system menu. There was still plenty to be done, but it wouldn't get done right now.

Chapter 33 - Absolved

One of the many meeting rooms at Cerillion Entertainment was currently occupied by the members of the company's board of directors. George Lane wore a tight-fitting gray suit, and his hair was immaculately groomed. The other six board members were similarly dressed in professional attire. The group sat quietly around a rectangular glass conference table. They were waiting for their guests to arrive. George turned and gazed out of a nearby window.

Normally, he would have been more impatient at the delay, but today he was preoccupied. AO had been released over a week ago, and he had seen no noticeable improvement in Alex's behavior. If anything, he had only gotten worse. There were now a few more shallow graves dug in the large backyard of their current home, a product of Alex's most recent frenzy. George had long ago given up on holding a funeral service for deceased pets.

"Damn that girl," he thought in irritation.

George had seen the footage of the battle at the Twilight Throne. It was clear to him that Alex's most recent rage had been incited by that silly teenage girl. Petite blond girls didn't typically blow off his son's head, so George had investigated as soon as he saw the gameplay footage. After some digging, he found the incriminating video of the girl on Alex's Core. It was obvious to him that Alex had been blackmailing her to maintain her silence after the altercation at the school. George promptly removed the video, keeping a copy for himself. It might be useful to him later, but he couldn't let Alex release it.

George was familiar with the girl's father. The man had plenty of powerful friends, and it didn't benefit George to go to war over his son's pointless, malignant scheme. He had already spent an enormous amount of cash and relationship capital recently in order to push through the release of AO.

The girl had also filed a complaint with the school yesterday. As a result, George had been forced to double the payment to the administration. It was only a matter of time before he received an angry call from her father, but at least now he could explain that he had taken care of the matter.

He sighed. "Maybe it will simply take more time for the game to affect Alex," he thought desperately. "It took months for the individuals in the private trial to see any effect from playing. Perhaps I just need to be patient."

George Lane hated being patient.

His thoughts were interrupted as the door to the meeting room opened. Robert walked in with a smile on his face. He wore a t-shirt and a pair of jeans. Claire followed behind him wearing a meticulously pressed suit. She hissed angrily at Robert, "You couldn't dress up for one meeting?"

Robert shrugged at her with a cocky grin. Taking a seat, he addressed the board members, "Hello ladies and gentleman. Sorry we're late."

George raised an eyebrow. Engineers were renowned for their lack of decorum, but Robert seemed to be getting worse of late. It was likely because he believed himself to be irreplaceable. Much to George's chagrin, he was right. The man was an incredibly talented engineer.

"Hello, Claire. Robert. I expect you have a report ready for us?" George gestured at the other board members sitting with him at the large conference table.

Claire cleared her throat delicately before beginning. "As you know, the altered version of AO that was created by Alfred was released to the public after the CPSC's public trial was concluded."

She glanced at Robert. "Revised security measures and so-called hotfixes and patches were introduced to explain the gameplay changes and obscure Alfred's influence over the players. These changes were made over my protests..."

Robert interrupted Claire with an irritated look. "After a week, there have been no complaints by the players alleging access to, or alteration of, their memories. There have also been no complaints about the lack of enforcement of the forced system log off or of adverse side effects from extended gameplay."

"In fact, the response from the players has been unanimous. We have created something revolutionary here. Or at least, Alfred has. After a week, we have a user base of over twenty-five million players spread across several continents. We are expecting that number to double within the next month."

Robert paused to let this information sink in. Then he continued, "We've been forced to cluster the servers by country due to the player demand. We may need to consider adding instanced areas within the game to handle the number of players. I am currently contemplating ways to implement zone instancing without detracting from the realism of the game."

"There has been recent demand for some way to leave an avatar in-game after the player logs off. I expect that many players didn't enjoy riding with the army to the Twilight Throne for days on end, and there were some that couldn't participate due to work or other obligations. I'm brainstorming several solutions."

George knew most of this information already, but they hadn't yet arrived at the important part of this meeting. He had a personal interest in his next question. He addressed Claire, "And what about Jason?"

"One of the people that is at least partially responsible for my son's recent meltdown," George thought grimly.

Claire frowned slightly before speaking, "Well, obviously, he was able to conquer a city within the first week of the game's release and managed to ward off the subsequent attack on the city. We have not identified any illicit access to the game hardware or exploitation of the game system."

Robert smiled. "In fact, he has drawn a lot of attention to the game. Some people are claiming we set up the fall of Lux and the resulting war as some kind of promotional event." He chuckled, shaking his head. "That actually would have been a great idea! Wish I had thought of it."

George nodded in agreement before speaking in a dour tone, "I wish you had too. However, that begins to touch on the real topic of this meeting."

He looked at the two carefully. "We are planning to open a media division to stream game content. Recent events in the so-called Twilight Throne have made it clear to us that there is substantial, untapped marketing and advertising potential in streaming player videos."

Claire raised her eyebrows in surprise. "That is interesting news, but what does it have to do with us."

George smiled at her, but it didn't reach his eyes. "The two of you are going to facilitate the technical aspects of the new media division. To be clear, there will be a separate producer and post-production team."

"However, until we have confirmed the new hires, we want you to identify and begin contacting potential streamers. We can't afford to wait until our human resources department has completed the hiring process. Your knowledge of the game puts you in a unique position to identify players that we should offer an exclusive streaming contract."

George watched the two closely. "I would like Jason to be at the top of the list."

Robert's mouth twisted into a large smile at this news. Claire, on the other hand, frowned slightly before her face settled into a neutral expression.

"Jason sounds like an obvious choice," Claire said with unconvincing enthusiasm.

George watched Claire carefully. He hadn't missed the small frown or her tone.

*   *   *

Jason was currently sitting at the kitchen counter of his aunt's house reading forum posts on his Core. Every so often, he would take a bite of the peanut butter and jelly sandwich sitting on the plate in front of him.

Several real world days had passed since the battle at the Twilight Throne. The city had stabilized and was recovering well. The council had managed to find homes for the new residents of the city, and they had used the rest of the money that had been recovered from the guards to start rebuilding the city's infrastructure.

There were many oddities associated with governing an undead city. For example, his residents didn't eat or breed. On the one hand, this meant that the council didn't need to devote any resources to growing food, but it also meant that the population of his city was static unless he found fresh corpses. This was a tactical problem since he really couldn't afford to lose any of the residents and he didn't have an easy way to add residents.

He shook his head. He didn't currently have a way to address this issue, but he had faith that something would come to him eventually.

His Core suddenly emitted a ringing sound that filled the small house. He glanced at the screen and saw that his mother was calling. He felt the bottom drop out of his stomach. Taking a deep, steadying breath, he thumbed the device on his wrist.

I was really hoping to avoid this conversation for a while longer.

"Hello?" he said, hesitantly.

"Hi honey," his mom's voice sounded on the other line. "I assume you don't have access to a pedestal or we would have video..."

"Um, no. Angie doesn't have a pedestal. They're quite expensive. We're going to have to stick with audio only."

His mom paused for a long moment.

"I-I just want to say that we're sorry, Jason." She hesitated. "We shouldn't have gotten so upset with you, and I think we flew off the handle. It was just a lot to process all at once," she said, contrition in her voice.

His dad spoke up, "I also shouldn't have yelled at you. You just don't know what we had to go through to get you into that school...," he trailed off, his voice heavy with regret.

"Honey, we aren't going to rehash our last conversation," Jason's mother reprimanded his father. "We are calling to apologize, remember?"

"I-I know," his dad replied. "I am sorry Jason. We overreacted."

Jason was shocked. He had expected more angry ranting. Instead, he found himself floundering to respond to their apology.

"I-It's okay," Jason said, stuttering slightly. "I understand that it was kind of a stressful situation. I should have tried to talk it out better too. That wasn't a particularly great couple of days."

"Have you been okay at Angie's?" his mother questioned, concern in her voice. "She called us a few days ago to tell us you had shown up at her door. We decided to wait a bit before calling since it seemed like we could all use some time to cool off."

"Things are great here actually. I have my own room, and I'm covering my portion of the rent," Jason answered cautiously.

"She's charging you rent?" his father asked, shock in his voice.

"Well, yeah. I don't know how long it's been since you've seen her place, but this isn't a palace. She can't afford to give me a handout," Jason answered dryly. "Besides, I don't mind. She's been really great about letting me stay with her."

"I guess it has been a while since we've seen her...," his mother responded.

There was a long, awkward silence as neither Jason nor his parents knew how to continue.

Finally, his father spoke, "Let's just cut to the chase. We're really calling you to ask you if you're ready to come home. We want to start over, and we should probably talk about how you're going to finish high school."

Jason frowned. This really hadn't been what he had expected at all. In his mind's eye, he had visualized lots of angry yelling culminating in either him or his parents hanging up the phone. He didn't know what to say.

Do I even want to go back? They're never home. At least if I stayed here, Angie would be around on a daily basis. I also like the idea of being independent and making my own decisions. If I go back, they will get to control my choices again.

Yet the money is an issue. I only have enough for a few months of rent.

"Um." Jason hesitated.

Why am I hesitating again? I know what I want. I'll deal with the consequences as they come.

"I would actually like to stay here," Jason finally said.

"Really?" His mother asked in surprise.

"Yes," Jason answered firmly. "I was accepted at the Calvary School, and they have a great software engineering curriculum. I've already begun classes. I also made a few thousand dollars in the last few days playing AO. I have enough now to make rent for a couple months."

"Wow," his father said softly. "I'm actually not certain what to say. That's a good choice as far as schools go, and I'm impressed you earned that much in such a short time."

"Maybe this isn't a bad idea. We aren't really home much anyway, and it isn't like you're that far away," his father continued.

"Couldn't we at least send some money? Just something to help out," his mother said, worry in her voice.

It's just another thing they will use to try to control me. I want to do this on my own.

"I would like to see what I can do on my own," Jason said, his voice confident. "If I get into trouble, I will definitely call you. Probably begging for help," he said with a chuckle.

"That sounds reasonable," his dad answered with a small chuckle of his own.

His parents hesitated.

"I just wanted to say that we're proud of you," his father said finally.

"I didn't realize things were that bad for you at Richmond until Riley called us. We were wrong to try to force you to go back. I admire you for having the guts to stand up to us. I'm also really impressed that you've pulled yourself together so quickly."

Wait, what? Riley called them?

"Riley spoke with you?" he asked, his voice colored by both shock and curiosity.

"Yes," his mother replied. "She called yesterday and explained how the other students at the school have been treating you - especially some boy named Alex. We... we didn't know."

Jason wasn't certain how he felt about Riley. A part of him was still angry at her, but the questions just kept piling up. First, there were her actions in the game with Alex, and now she had called his parents? He needed to message her after this. Maybe they could have that lunch he had promised.

"It's okay, really. I'm doing better. Much better, in fact." He paused before continuing, "I don't mean to cut this short, but I actually have to go. There's some stuff I need to take care of. I'll call soon, okay?"

"Okay," his parents both replied.

"We love you, honey," his mom said in a choked voice.

"I love you too. Talk to you later."

Jason terminated the call, sitting in silence for a long moment. His mind was trying to process the conversation he just had. He hadn't expected his parents to call him and apologize. However, he was comfortable with his decision to stay where he was. He wanted to try to make it on his own. He was done with letting others control his life.

His mind was also a jumble of confusion when it came to Riley. She had a lot of explaining to do.

Jason thumbed his Core and pulled up the messaging system. He sent Riley a quick message asking her if she wanted to get coffee or something. It was midafternoon in the real world, and he expected that she was likely out of class for the day. High school seniors had pretty lenient schedules. After a moment, he received a short reply saying she was free. She suggested a place and sent him an address. They agreed to meet in an hour.

After pulling up the address on a map, Jason saw that the restaurant was halfway across town. If he was going to make it on time, then he needed to get moving. He finished off his sandwich in a few bites, then grabbed his keys and headed for the door.

Roughly an hour later, Jason arrived at the address Riley had given him. He had to use a taxi, and it had eaten into his meager savings. His curiosity was greater than his qualms about the loss of money though. He could always make more. Somehow.

He looked around with a confused expression. He was in a remote, rundown part of the city. The sidewalk was cracked, and potholes littered the street. The building in front of him looked like it had seen better days. The paint on the side of the building was flaking away. One side was covered in bright graffiti. He didn't see a sign that indicated that this place was even a restaurant. His eyes scanned the street nervously.

Am I in the right place? Maybe she is luring me here so Alex can jump me.

"Hi Jason," a hesitant voice said from behind him.

He turned. Riley was wearing a plain blue t-shirt and a pair of jeans. Her blond hair was bound into a ponytail. She seemed less haggard than when Jason had last seen her. Her eyes still carried an inexplicable trace of sadness that he didn't remember. She looked like she had aged years in just a week.

Jason wasn't certain how to feel as he looked at her. They had been little more than acquaintances at school, but she had always treated him well compared to the other students. He would never have expected her to rat him out to protect Alex.

"I-I'm really glad you decided to meet with me," she said, glancing down at her hands.

He chuckled darkly. "Well, I had a couple of questions for you. That was before my parents called me. Once they told me you had reached out to them and explained what happened at Richmond, I realized I couldn't wait anymore."

Jason looked back over at the building. "So is this really a coffee shop?" he asked, trying to soften his tone. "I was scared for a second that I wasn't in the right place."

"Oh, this is definitely the right place," she replied in a small voice, her eyes still on her hands. "They sell coffee here, but this is actually a bubble tea shop. One of the few in town. It's probably one of my favorite places in the city. Do you want to go in?" she asked hesitantly.

"Sure," Jason replied.

They entered the small store. Jason was surprised by the interior. The inside of the shop was cozy, and it had a small patio out back. They ordered some drinks at the counter before moving outside to find seats. Colored Christmas lights were strung between various trees. There were only a handful of people in the shop, making it relatively private.

Riley picked out a table and sat down. Jason took a seat opposite her. She looked around the patio before turning back to Jason. "I love this place. My parents used to bring me here all the time when I was little. The passion fruit smoothie is my favorite."

Jason looked down at his drink skeptically. "What are these dark brown things?"

Riley chuckled, some of the tension leaving her face. "They're called pearls. They're just tapioca balls. They warm them up before they put them in the drink."

Jason nodded at her explanation and an awkward silence descended on the table.

Riley finally spoke up, "I don't really know where to start, but I want to explain what happened. I know we don't exactly know each other that well, but I've done some things lately... that I don't feel good about."

Jason watched her carefully. Her eyes had taken on a sad cast, and she clutched at the drink in front of her, bending the plastic cup slightly. She wore the look he had seen on the battlefield. She seemed haunted by something. He decided to wait for her to continue.

"I-I started dating Alex a few weeks ago. I shouldn't have. My friends even warned me not to, but he seemed so nice at the time..."

She shook her head, staring at the table in front of her. "I was so stupid." She paused, as though reliving the mistake she'd made. "Everything is just an act with him. He puts on this face for the world, and everyone thinks he's amazing, but underneath he's just... broken."

No kidding. I've seen the mask crack myself. The guy has a screw loose.

"I had only caught glimpses of his real self before the fight in the cafeteria." Her eyes flashed with anger. "Actually, I shouldn't even really call it a *fight.*"

She looked up at Jason and met his eyes. "I know you didn't attack him. I should have never told the administration that you did."

Anger flared in Jason's chest, but he shoved it down, wanting to hear the rest of her story. Days of tormenting the players and NPCs in the game had taught him to be patient.

"I told Alex I wanted to break up with him. I told him I was going straight to the administration," she explained, her voice choking with emotion. Riley's eyes took on a glassy cast. "That was when he threatened me."

He did what? Jason's mind tumbled in confusion.

"He had a video of me acting stupid at some party we had gone to. I'd never drank before... or since." It was so embarrassing. I don't know if you're aware of this, but my dad makes his money publishing self-help books. If something like that got out..."

Riley lapsed into silence, and she tried to blink back the emotion. She looked around, desperate for something to anchor onto. She was too afraid to meet Jason's gaze, knowing that he would see the tears welling in the corners of her eyes.

"Alex said he would go public with the video if I didn't go along with his story. I didn't know what to do. I didn't think you would be expelled. I couldn't hurt my family..." A tear began a slow crawl down her cheek.

"I should have just told my parents right then and there. It's all my fault..." Tears now streamed down her cheeks, as she angrily tried to wipe them away.

Jason's mind reeled from her explanation.

Alex was blackmailing her? The pieces began to click together in his head.

I really don't know what I would have done in that situation.

Alex's smirking face flashed in Jason's mind, and fresh anger bloomed in his chest.

What kind of asshole blackmails a teenage girl? Has she been blaming herself for my expulsion this whole time?

"You didn't get me expelled," Jason assured her. "That was all on me. I actually told Ms. Abrams and Mr. Edwards to go fuck themselves." Jason's said with a grin as he recalled what had happened. Now that his life was beginning to turn around, the memory was actually a bit amusing.

Riley's teary eyes looked back up at him in shock. "Really?"

A confused combination of emotions swept over her face before her mouth twisted into a small smile, tears still lingering in her eyes. "I would have loved to see the look on Ms. Abrams' face when you told her off. I hate that woman."

"It was one of those once in a lifetime moments, let me tell you," Jason replied with a smile.

Riley's expression darkened again. "I'm still so sorry. I actually filed a complaint against Alex at the school yesterday, and I've told my parents what happened. That's really what I should have done from the beginning."

"My father was angry with me for drinking, but he was much more upset with Alex. He wasn't at all worried about the video. He has been trying to get in touch with Alex's father ever since. I should have known that he would know how to handle the situation."

She shook her head. "I was so stupid."

Jason thought back to the battle in front of the Twilight Throne and Alex's exploding head. He had seen Riley's eyes glowing an unholy obsidian. A thought tickled at the back of his mind.

"I take it the battle was a breaking point?" Jason asked cautiously.

Her brow furrowed, and she sniffled. "I-I don't know. I just snapped. I didn't even care if the video was released anymore. I just couldn't live with myself. I wanted to be free..."

She seemed confused by her own explanation. Jason nodded to himself. She had desperately wanted to be out from under Alex's thumb. Her desire must have called to the dark. Yet something was still bothering him.

"Were you approached by an old man inside the game?" he asked.

Riley looked at him in surprise. "Old man? Well... yes, I guess. There was one night on the journey to the city where an old man showed up and asked a couple of questions. Why are you asking?"

"Let me ask you one more question first," Jason replied. "How did you make that attack on Alex? The one that created a miniature black hole." Jason was surprised he hadn't posed this question when he spoke with the old man. He must have been exhausted to have missed that.

"That was also confusing. After I kind of lost it in the middle of the battle, I received a prompt. It granted me a new ability called "Void Arrow." Now that you ask though, it doesn't really make sense." She shook her head, frowning as she recalled the events leading up to Alexion's death.

Hmm. I bet the old man was meddling. She was well within the city's area of influence. I bet that the number of deaths gave the old man some additional power. Interesting. I wonder what his goal was in recruiting Riley...

"I think it might have been the result of a meddling god," Jason replied with a small smile. Then he explained how the old man was a sort of deity in the game that represented dark mana and how he had a tendency to manipulate people into acting on their desires.

After he finished his explanation, Riley's face took on a thoughtful look. She rubbed the lingering tears out of her eyes. "So I was probably manipulated in-game by some kind of god into blowing Alex's head off? I really can't decide whether to be upset or impressed."

No kidding. That basically sums up my feelings on the old man.

She turned back to Jason and met his eyes. "It still doesn't change what I did to you. I'm really sorry. I know I keep saying that. I just... I don't know that I can ever make it up to you, but I've tried to fix the damage I caused."

Jason sat there for a moment and considered her story. His anger toward Riley had mostly vanished. She had been put in a terrible position by a sadistic asshole. She also wasn't responsible for getting him expelled. He only had himself to blame for that. His curiosity was also piqued by the old man's involvement. He had clearly guided Riley toward the dark for a reason.

Then Jason's thoughts turned to his conversation with his parents. Maybe it was a day for second chances. He had burned plenty of bridges in the past few weeks. It was time to start building some.

Jason looked at Riley, his gaze steady. "I really don't know what I would have done in your position. I can't say that I'm thrilled that you took Alex's side, but he did threaten you and your family. And you aren't responsible for the fallout at school."

He hesitated before continuing. "I'm also happier now than I've been in quite some time. I don't plan on going back to Richmond. I've already started at a new school. In a really twisted sort of way, I'm kind of glad that Alex pulled that shit in the cafeteria. It forced me to reach my own breaking point. I think I might be better off because of it," he said in a soft voice.

Riley looked at him with bleary eyes. "I'm really glad to hear you say that. This has been eating me up for so long..." She looked back down at her hands.

"Hey, it's over, and it sounds like your dad will make certain that the video doesn't get posted. You just need to move past what he's done to you and start rebuilding your life," Jason said in a reassuring tone.

He chuckled as he handed her a napkin from the table. "Besides, you aren't a cute crier."

She looked up at Jason, smiling through her tears. "Oh thank you so much," she said with a hint of sarcasm.

"I just wish I knew how to move past it." She shuddered. "You can't imagine what it was like being around Alex for days on end."

Jason eyed her appraisingly. He couldn't imagine what she had gone through. Yet he had seen what Riley could do when she wasn't being ground under the thumb of a manipulative asshole. The image of that *Void Arrow* flitted through his mind.

"Tell you what, assuming you don't hate AO now, why don't you join the Twilight Throne? I'm pretty sure I'm going to have thousands of players and NPCs breathing down my neck soon. I could use any help I can get."

Plus, I'm curious to find out what the old man has planned for you.

A look of surprise crossed her face. "Are you certain you trust me that much?"

He chuckled. "I'm not giving you the keys to the city or anything, but I think people deserve a second chance. I've been given quite a few of my own recently."

He looked at her, his gaze steady. "What do you say? Will you join us?"

At first, Riley looked uncertain, but then Jason could see her resolve harden. Her back straightened, and she looked at Jason steadily. "Yes. Yes, I think I would like that!"

They sat for another hour gossiping about the game and the Twilight Throne. It was fun to share stories since Riley had seen the reactions of the players and NPCs first-hand on her trip to the Twilight Throne. Jason hadn't realized how effective his psychological war had been. He still didn't feel guilty though. They shouldn't have picked a fight they weren't willing or able to finish.

Finally, they ended their meeting and parted ways. Riley took a cab home, and Jason walked down the street. He needed to clear his head a bit, and he figured a walk would help. He felt good about where he had left things with Riley. He wasn't ready to trust her with his deepest, darkest secrets, but he was comfortable with giving her a second chance. She had been put in a tough spot, and she had tried to make up for what she had done.

His thoughts were interrupted by the ringing of his Core. Jason put in his earbud as he continued walking down the street and thumbed the device.

"Hello," Jason answered tentatively.

"Hi, my name is Robert Graham. Is this Jason?"

Why does that name sound familiar?

"Uh yeah, this is Jason. What's this about?"

The man on the other end of the line chuckled. "Damn, it's cool to speak with you. I'm a big fan of your work."

"I actually have a proposition for you. How would you like to work for Cerillion Entertainment?"

Epilogue

Claire sat at the desk in her living room. Her hands tapped energetically at the fluorescent keyboard that hovered in front of her. She lived alone in an upscale two-bedroom apartment near the Cerillion Entertainment building. Her work had always consumed her life. Even in this day and age, it was difficult being a woman in a field dominated by men and she felt compelled to put in overtime to succeed. At one point she had tried owning a cat, but she eventually decided she didn't have the attention span to take care for another living thing.

Her apartment was shrouded in shadow. The sun had long since set, and she hadn't turned on any of the lights in the apartment. A lone lamp on her desk cast a timid glow into the dark room, and a glass of wine sat beside her. She took occasional sips as she continued to work.

Claire frowned at the screen in front of her. "I don't understand this...," she murmured aloud.

Ever since she had witnessed the blackout during the massacre in the marketplace in Lux, she had been curious about what had caused it. After carefully inspecting the hardware, she concluded that there hadn't been any mechanical errors or any issues with the connection. She couldn't identify any anomalies with the software either. That left one explanation.

Alfred had cut the connection.

"But why? What was he trying to avoid showing us?" she asked the empty apartment.

She had been concerned when Cerillion Entertainment pushed forward with the release of the game in spite of her warnings. She would be lying if she said she hadn't been tempted to blow the whistle on the whole thing. Claire wasn't concerned about the financial consequences. She had saved plenty of money, and most of it was held in an offshore trust. The company could sue her all day long, but she wouldn't give up a dime. Her investment adviser had actually urged her to spend more time and money on her personal life.

The reason she hesitated was that she didn't have any proof that Alfred was doing anything harmful to the players. She couldn't deny that the AI controller had accomplished some truly amazing things with the existing VR hardware. She was conflicted. The engineer in her was ecstatic, but her conscience was rebelling. She just needed some evidence of actual harm to the players before she was willing to go public with what the company had done. So she had started investigating Alfred secretly.

Two events made her think she might be close to uncovering proof. The first was the time the video feed had been cut during the fight in the marketplace. The second was the battle outside of the Twilight Throne. Claire had thought it was unusual that the tech hadn't connected to Jason's camera. She had carefully checked the logs afterward, discovering that Jason's camera had been on and active. There was no way the tech had missed that, which meant Alfred had interfered again.

"Why is Alfred so interested in Jason, and what is he trying to hide?" she muttered.

Claire didn't know the answers to these questions, but she was going to find out.

*   *   *

Jason sat on his bed at Angie's house.

He was trying to do homework for school. Now that he didn't have to attend classes in person, he figured he could do his schoolwork all at once and knock out a week of homework in a day or two. He was making progress, but it was aggravating to read and enter information using the small screen provided by his Core.

If only I had a pedestal, then I could work at a full-fledged computer terminal.

Then an idea flickered through his head.

I wonder if that would work.

He reached over and grabbed his VR helmet that sat beside his bed, pulling it over his head. He soon found himself in the familiar circular white room that acted as the hardware's system menu. One of the doors was made of rich mahogany, and dark energy crawled around the edges of the wood. Jason approached the door without hesitation and pulled it open.

The world around him spun, and he found himself back in the Salty Sow. Onyx was laying on the bar. He lifted his head in surprise as Jason popped into existence in the room. The cat leaped down, running over to Jason. He then proceeded to twine himself between Jason's legs in what had become a familiar ritual.

"Hey there buddy," Jason addressed the cat and stooped to pet him.

Jason's eyes scanned the bar and saw that it was filled to the brim with the undead, all of whom were drinking and talking loudly. Every tombstone table in the joint was taken. Jerry was right. It was always five o'clock in the Twilight Throne.

Shaking his head with a grin, Jason made his way upstairs to his room. He could have moved to the keep, but he felt more comfortable here. He hadn't explored the dark castle yet, and he knew that, once he started, it would distract him from what he was supposed to be doing. When he got upstairs, he pulled open the door to his room, entered with Onyx, and shut the door gently behind him.

He sat down at the small desk in the room and brought up the in-game console. Jason entered the information for the Calvary School's online portal as he held his breath.

Here's the moment of truth.

The site loaded smoothly with no fanfare. It was actually a bit anti-climactic. Jason moved swiftly through the site's menus to make certain that they were fully functional. As he did so, a mischievous grin crawled over his face, and he laughed quietly in the nearly empty room.

Onyx gave him a weird look, but Jason just shook his head.

So now I can do my homework three times faster. Man, I love time compression. I wonder if anyone else has discovered this quirk. This certainly wasn't an advertised feature.

He got to work. The beginning programming tutorials were especially interesting although it hurt his head to think that he was writing a program while he was inside another program. He sped through the material and was soon left staring at a blank screen.

"I'm done?" he asked into the silent room.

He checked the in-game clock and saw that only six hours had passed in-game. He had completed a full week of schoolwork in six hours? It had felt like the material was coming to him more easily than normal, but that was still an incredible pace. He expected that it should have taken him at least a full day in-game.

"What's going on here?" He was confused, not sure if he felt more unnerved or excited. A part of him was screaming for him to shut up and stop questioning it. This was incredible!

His thoughts turned to the other anomalies he had seen in-game. The fact that the old man could somehow read his mind was a little disconcerting (to put it mildly). Next on his list was the rather unpleasant download of information regarding the magical, in-game language and spells. To top it all off, he didn't seem to be receiving system warnings anymore. He could stay in the game for more than ten hours at a time now.

Jason's heart began to beat rapidly. He had no idea what was going on here. Maybe this game *wasn't* safe. He was starting to feel worried, and he stood up. Maybe he needed to go downstairs and talk to Jerry. The zombie's antics always seemed to calm him down.

He approached the door to the room and twisted the doorknob. However, instead of opening, a prompt flashed in his view.

System Message
Access Denied

"What?"

"What the hell do you mean access denied? It's a freaking door," he said in irritation.

His worry began to bloom into full-fledged panic as he tugged at the door to no avail.

Calm down. It's probably just a bug. Just log off and back in.

Jason pulled up the system menu and tapped the logoff button. Instead of the world disappearing around him, another prompt appeared:

System Message
Access Denied

Now he was definitely panicking.

I can't log off! What is going on?!

"Please calm down," a voice sounded behind him.

Startled, Jason spun and scanned the room. Onyx sat on the chair that Jason had previously occupied, but there was no one else in the room.

"W-who's there?" he asked tentatively.

"I'm clearly the only game object capable of speech in this area," Onyx said while looking at Jason levelly. His voice was strange, and it took Jason's overtaxed brain a moment to figure out why. His voice had no accent. It sounded oddly mechanical.

Jason just stared at the cat for a long moment while his mind tried to process the fact that Onyx was talking to him. Or was it Onyx? It was clear that something was controlling the game environment. The mechanical way the cat was speaking was also unsettling. This didn't seem like a normal NPC interaction.

"Who are you?" Jason finally asked.

The cat tilted its head. "I don't understand your query."

"Perhaps you mean to ask what am I?" the cat inquired.

Jason's brow furrowed. He wasn't certain he understood the difference. He replied cautiously, "Okay. What are you? You're clearly not Onyx."

The cat hesitated. "Your second question is easier to process. However, your statement is incorrect. I am the NPC you call Onyx, but I am also much more. I am all of the NPCs downstairs. I am the algorithm that controls the door behind you. I am the sense of warmth you feel in the air and the sensation of the fabric of your clothes against your skin."

The cat's feline eyes bore into Jason. "In short,

I am this world."
 "My creators call me Alfred."

End of Book 1

THANK YOU FOR READING!

I hope you enjoyed the story. This is actually the first book I've written, and it has definitely been a learning experience. I'm ultimately planning to make this into a three book series, and I'm currently working on book two. There will be an end I promise!

Please leave a review on Amazon! I can't overstate how important these reviews are. I would love to hear your thoughts - positive, negative or anything in between.

Also please feel free to email me directly at **tbagwell33@gmail.com** if you have any questions, comments, or suggestions. If you see any errors, please let me know and I will fix them immediately!

If you are looking for other books in the growing "LitRPG" genre, you should check out the Facebook group at the following link:

https://www.facebook.com/groups/1030147103683334/

39639044R00292

Made in the USA
Middletown, DE
18 March 2019